M

W

Fiction Crowl.J

Crowley, John, 1942-

The translator /

c2002.

DATE DUE

	AUG 2 2 2003
APR 0 9 2002	NOV 1 4 2003
APR 3 0 2002	AUG 2 9 2004
	~~FEB 0 4 2008~~
MAY 3 1 2002	FEB 2 5 2008
	APR 2 5 2008
SEP - 3 2002	
SEP 1 9 2002	
OCT 7 - 2002	
DEC 1 1 2002	
JAN 5 - 2003	
MAR 2 1 2003	
MAR 2 9 2003	
MAY 3 0 2003	

DEMCO, INC. 38-2931

MAR 1 4 2002

THE TRANSLATOR

John Crowley

wm

WILLIAM MORROW
An Imprint of HarperCollins*Publishers*

HarperCollins books may be purchased for educational, business, or sales promotional use.
For information please write: Special Markets Department, HarperCollins Publishers Inc.,
10 East 53rd Street, New York, NY 10022.

FIRST EDITION

Designed by Debbie Glasserman

Printed on acid-free paper

Library of Congress Cataloging-in-Publication Data
Crowley, John.
The translator / by John Crowley.
p. cm.
ISBN 0-380-97862-8
1. Translating and interpreting—Fiction.   2. Cuban Missile
Crisis, 1962—Fiction.   3. Russians—United States—Fiction.
4. Translators—Fiction.   5. Exiles—Fiction.   6. Poets—Fiction.
I. Title.

PS3553.R597 T73 2002
813'.54—dc21   2001040324

02 03 04 05 06 RRD 10 9 8 7 6 5 4 3 2 1

"Poetry is power," M[andelstam] *once said to Akhmatova in Voronezh, and she bowed her head on its slender neck.*

NADEZIIDA MANDEL3TAM, *Hope Against Hope*

I

1.

The first time that Christa Malone heard the name of Innokenti Isayevich Falin, it was spoken by the President of the United States, John F. Kennedy.

In February of 1961, Christa stood in a reception line at the White House with twenty other high school seniors whose poems had been selected for inclusion in a national anthology of young people's poetry called *Wings of Song*. All but four were girls, a flock of ungainly bright birds in their suits and dresses, all with hats and white gloves too. A gravely courteous aide had arranged them in a row, instructed them how to respond and step away, and now looked at his wristwatch and toward a distant door; and Kit Malone sensed the quick beating of their hearts. The anthology had the sponsorship of a major foundation.

He was stopping to meet them on his way to a grander affair, Kit wouldn't remember later what it was, but when the far double doors opened he was wearing evening clothes; his wife beside him wore a gown of some unearthly material that gleamed like the robes of an El

Greco cardinal. The aide guided them down the line of young poets; the President took each one's hand, and so did the First Lady; the President asked each one a question or two, talking a bit longer with a tall girl from Quincy.

A little longer too with Kit: making an easy joke in his comical accent but seeming to turn her in his gaze like a jewel or object of curious interest. When she told him what state she came from he smiled.

"You have a new poet living there, I understand," he said. "Yes. Our new poet from Russia. Falin. You've heard about him?"

She hadn't, and said nothing, only smiled, her own smile compelled by his huge one.

"Falin, yes," he said. "He's been exiled. From over there. And come here."

Jackie took his arm, smiling too at Kit, and drew him toward the next poet.

There were photographs taken then, and a few words from the President about the importance of poetry, to the nation, to the spirit. He said that the poets were the unacknowledged legislators of the world; he reminded them that he had invited Robert Frost to speak at his own inauguration. The land was ours before we were the land's. His pale eyes fell momentarily again on Kit, piercing or perceiving.

That night in their hotel, in the unaccustomed city lights and noise and the girl from Quincy unquiet in the other bed, Kit dreamed of a tiger: of walking with one in the corridors of a featureless palace (his?), watching the heavy muscles slide beneath his gorgeous clothes in the way a tiger's do and talking with him about this and that: aware that she was to listen more than speak, awed and alert but not afraid.

In that month she wrote a poem, "What the Tiger Told Me," the last poem she would write for a long time. And later, years later, she wondered if the President had lingered close to her for an extra moment and studied her with that smiling voracity because he perceived a sexual aura or exudate coming from her. His senses were inordinately acute that way, and had been alerted, perhaps, by something she herself hadn't yet discovered: that she was pregnant.

In January of that year, on his way to the United States, Innokenti Isayevich Falin had begun writing a linked series of poems whose titles were dates. The first was sketched on Berlin hotel notepaper with his new German fountain pen, and was revised on the plane to New York. The original—later lost with all the others—is a sonnet, fourteen lines in Falin's own peculiar rhyme scheme. The unrhymed rough translation that Kit Malone later worked out with Falin looked like this:

1961

Tip up this year on the fulcrum of its final serif
Revolve it through the degrees from right to upright
Like a lifted flagpole without a flag
Or a flat raised upon the stage of an empty theater
Before which histories will soon be enacted.
Now drop it farther, push it entirely over
As the statue of a deposed leader is thrown
Supine, his gloved finger that pointed Onward
Driven into earth to point Endward instead.
See what you have accomplished?
This rarity comes but once in centuries:
A year that can be overthrown but not reversed,
And after all our labors seems to become itself again.
It is not so. As always, we will never be the same.

2.

It's always a surprise and a wonderment when our plane breaks through a ceiling of cloud and, as though shedding some huge entangling dress of tattered lace, comes out naked into the naked blue sky and the sun. We on earth think there are blue skies and gray skies, but in fact of course the sky is always clear.

Then the reverse too. Christa Malone's plane descended out of the clear desert air and was clothed again in clammy batting; came down through the ceiling into the house. There a light rain was falling: steely ocean, colorless heaped-up city, air of tears. Remembering what earth is like. Auden once said that it shocked him that airplane passengers, able to look down like gods on clouds and the earth, so often paid it no attention: pulled down the blind, read a thriller.

"I don't know if it's still the same now," Christa's seatmate was saying to a man across the aisle. "This was before '89. Aeroflot. You took your life in your hands. And shabby. And *mean*. These stewardesses like prison camp matrons. About fifty of us on a big jet, Moscow to

Vladivostok. They let us in the back door, and she walks up ahead of us directing us into seats, starting in the back row and filling every seat till we're all in. No changing seats. Two-thirds of the plane empty!"

"Different now," said his listener. "In the republics there aren't even reserved seats. Everybody tears across the tarmac and fights to get aboard. Devil take the hindmost."

"Democracy," said the other, and they both laughed.

In Russian, then in English, then in French, the stewardess asked them softly to prepare for landing.

When she was a child, and for a long time afterward, Kit Malone always imagined Russia as dark. It *was* dark then; a Dark Continent from which no real news came, a dark star absorbing its own light. When she thought of it she saw long roads leading into the hinterlands, cold featureless steppe without color or sound, and huddled people silent too, their backs turned to her.

It was all she had, this metaphor of her own ignorance, because she wouldn't believe or couldn't believe in any Russia then offered her. She didn't believe in the Russia the nuns taught her about in school, where priests were killed and churches despoiled and nuns were beaten by booted commissars. She didn't believe it, not because she had evidence that such things were not true but because the nuns insisted on them, insisted so much that Kit withdrew her assent. She decided they were wrong about Russia and Communism, which probably weren't so bad. Who would do dumb things like beat nuns just to be mean? Who would care that much? Kit saw, beyond politics and religion, a grown-up world where these childish exaggerated oppositions were put aside, admitted to be false: like her parents admitting at last that there was no Santa Claus.

No God either, eventually, on whose side to be. And yet the dark country persisted, unfolding inwardly under dark skies, through the years as she grew up; she never imagined traveling there, as she imagined traveling almost everywhere else.

Christa looked through the scumbled cloud still tearing past her window. The gray city, turning like a piled platter in a waiter's hand as the plane maneuvered, was called St. Petersburg, once again. Gavriil Viktorovich Semyonov's handwritten invitation was in the bag in her lap that she was clutching somewhat too tightly: she didn't like landing, though she loved taking off. *A celebration of the 75th anniversary of the birth of Innokenti Isayevich Falin, and of his life and poetry. June 1993, St. Petersburg, Russia.* Had it been gratifying to him to write the real name of his city, as though a fog had lifted from it?

It had still been Leningrad when Semyonov had first written to her, twenty years ago now. In the same exquisite tiny handwriting, learned in a prison camp it seemed, a hand for writing down poems on cigarette papers. The weird orthography so like Falin's own that for a minute she had been unable to open it, only stared at her own name on the front of the envelope and felt the hard beating of her heart.

But of course it hadn't been from Falin; it was from this man G. V. Semyonov, asking her in the most delicate terms what no other Russian apparently dared to ask: what had happened, what was the truth, and what had become of the last poems of I. I. Falin.

Semyonov had sent her that letter because of her own first book of poetry, a book newsworthy not for her own slight poems (she would write stronger ones later on) but for the fifteen poems of Falin's that it contained. "Translations without originals" she had called them: poems neither his nor hers, or both his and hers; poems written in a language that she couldn't read, and surviving only in a language he couldn't write.

Russia had been deep in the Brezhnev freeze then; nothing went in unauthorized, nothing came out; how this Semyonov had even got hold of her book she didn't know, nor how his letter had reached her. She had answered it as well as she could, but she heard nothing more. She couldn't learn if her letter had been received or not; answered or not. But ever since then she had gone on explaining to the writer of that letter what had happened: answering, trying to answer, the charge that he had not made: that she had let their poet die, and then taken his poems for her own.

Now at last he had written to her again, in a new world, and summoned her. Invited her, actually, and in the kindest and most flattering terms. But she felt it was a summons, and one she couldn't refuse.

The airport was a frenzy, with uniformed men and women everywhere whose role seemed to be to make things worse, to stand in the way, stir rage or frustration. Not for Russia the sterile cool calm of big European or American airports. It was like a vast crowded living room, with a faint homey repellent smell too. Christa waited for her bags to appear amid the expensive leather suitcases of her traveling companions, and then she joined the lines at the customs counters.

"Passport, please."

The man in a green uniform with red tabs looked once, twice, three times from her passport picture to her and blew expressively, in boredom or exhaustion. She handed over her visa, and she had the invitation to the conference ready in her bag too, and a little speech prepared; but she was waved on, and when she put her bags before the customs clerk he also wearily waved her on, and she sailed out into the crowded space where everyone was hugging and kissing, old people, children, men in suits; and there ahead was a tall and very thin, very old man, who held up a small sign, a torn piece of cardboard, with her name on it in that same odd orthography, a sign that shook slightly in his hand. His face was infinitely sad and yet his smile was kind, as though he waited to conduct her to an afterlife that was better than she deserved yet not all she might desire. He turned his eyes on her and seemed to know her immediately.

"Good morning," he said, in English and then in Russian. "I am Gavriil Viktorovich Semyonov. Welcome to my country."

Already she was uncertain she had heard correctly; she replied with a Russian greeting, and he began to speak again in Russian, turning away and pointing toward far parts of the terminal.

"I'm sorry," she said. "It's thirty years since I spoke Russian. Is it possible to speak in English, at least at first?"

"Of course," he said with great courtliness. "In English I am not fluent. I am fluent in Russian, Estonian, Polish, French. Not English however, unfortunately."

"No?" Christa said. "Oh well. You speak it better than I've ever spoken any language but my own. Americans, you know . . ."

"Yes," he said. "I know."

He insisted on carrying a bag for her, and she chose the lightest to give him; he led her down corridors and up escalators until they emerged into a vast garage where dozens of ugly black cars were waiting, their motors running. Semyonov looked a long time before locating the one he wanted and waving it forward. A ZIL sedan; Christa could read that name at least. The windows were tinted and the backseat huge; it smelled of smoke and sweat.

"Vasili Vasilievich is driver for government official," Gavriil told her. "Once he spent hours waiting for his official to be done with meetings, et cetera. Now, rule is, instead of waiting he is allowed to use this car for taking others. Like ourselves." He smiled, as though the situation were comical, which it was: the fearsome car, the thick-necked driver, the innocent moonlighting.

When he had done talking to the driver and the car began crawling from the airport with other traffic, Gavriil Viktorovich turned to her, for a long moment only regarding her with his face of tender apology, which maybe meant nothing that it seemed to mean, was just an old Russian's face.

"So," he said. "We meet."

"You know," she said, "I did answer your first letter. Long ago. I did."

He made a wonderful elaborate shrug that forgave, proclaimed ignorance, dismissed the question, invoked Fate, all at once.

"I wanted to tell you," she said. "What I knew. It wasn't much."

"Here nothing at all was known of what became of him in U.S.," Gavriil Viktorovich said. "This was our period of reaction, after fall of Khrushchev, after Cuba missiles crisis. Here we withdrew again into our castle, or we were again locked in our closet, however it is put. Very dangerous once again to talk to foreigners, or about foreigners, or about past, or the dead. Poets then who wrote about the dead were always saying only farewell to them, turning away to face future, you see." He was smiling. "The dead had just begun again to speak to us when we stopped for a long time listening."

"But now again," she said.

"Yes. Now again we listen. Some of us."

Vasili bore them through a region of identical concrete apartment and office buildings, a bad idea that seemed to have been given up on lately, idle cranes and piles of building materials that looked as though they had been standing untouched for a long time. It made her think of her father's apartment. *Oh forget it* he said when she tried to gather up years-old magazines or wash the windows.

"We have program," he said to her. "First, to restore his citizenship, which was taken from him. To put up monument perhaps, though where? We don't know where he was born; he lived in many places. And many places now gone; homes, schools he was in, places of work. Gone. As though time ate up these traces of him as it moved along." He laced together his long yellow-nailed fingers in his lap. "We would want above all to bring him home. But he was not ever found."

"No. No, he wasn't." She, she herself, had known that he wouldn't be found as soon as his great pale-green convertible had been pulled up empty from the river, spilling water from every opening. It had been shown on the news again and again. Yet even then she wouldn't say that he was dead. She hadn't known, not for certain. She thought there was a period of time, years maybe, that had to pass between a disappearance and the assumption of death; of course that period was long gone by now, gone decades ago. And yet still she couldn't say *I know he's dead.*

"Hotel," Gavriil Viktorovich said, sounding relieved. "Pribaltiyskaya. Not splendid but very near to me, and I will be guide. You will have view of water," he said.

It was vast, concrete and glass. The rainy gulf was what it looked at or glowered at.

"You will want to rest," he said. "Then perhaps come to my apartment, is not far, and we will go to dinner."

"All right. Whatever you want."

"Many people would like to meet you," Gavriil Viktorovich said. "I have invited small number to dinner. I hope you will not mind."

"No. No, of course not."

The woman behind the desk spoke to Kit, and then—seeing no sign of understanding—to Gavriil Viktorovich, in a voice imperious and petulant at once. He turned to Kit.

"Your room is it seems not ready now," he said. "One hour. Perhaps you would like tea."

"I met him at the university I went to," she told him. The tea before her in a glass: she hadn't drunk tea from a glass since then, since that fall. "He taught there. Poetry. It was the year after he came. I was nineteen years old."

"And you were a poet then?"

"Oh, well. I'd won a prize. I was supposed to have a, you know. A bent."

"And you studied there with him."

"I was supposed to begin at the university in the fall of 1961," she said. "But I couldn't; something else had happened, something . . . well, it doesn't matter, anyway I couldn't go to school that semester. By then Falin had come to teach at the university in my state; and I'd read about him, in *Look* and *Life*." She saw Gavriil Viktorovich lift his great eyebrows curiously. "The magazines. We were fascinated by people who had, you know, come over: Nureyev, running away from his bodyguards in Paris, we all knew about that. And the people trying to get over the Berlin Wall. And Falin, the poet, who couldn't bring his poems with him. I didn't hear about him when he came, but I knew he was teaching there when I went in the second semester to start."

"You planned to meet him?"

"No," she said. "No. I had sort of given up poetry."

"Yes? And for what reason?" He took her glass from her and began to pour her more.

"Falin once asked me that," she said: and she knew then that it would not be easy to be here, nor to go on with this story here. For as far in space as she had come she would also have to go in time, or in that dimension that was not either, where they had parted. "I told him I had nothing I could say. And he said that's what poetry is, the saying of nothing. The Nothing that can't be said."

"Later on, though, you did write again," Gavriil Viktorovich said. He waited, leaning forward slightly, to show that she had his full attention, or on account of his hearing.

"Yes," she said. "Later I did. Afterwards."

He still waited.

"I'll tell you it all," she said. "I'm here to tell you it all. All that I know."

3.

It was a university huge even in 1961, a city rising on a piece of high ground pressed up for some geological reason from the surrounding prairie. It was built as a land-grant college, and the original cluster of red-stone buildings in toybox Gothic style still stood under big elms and sycamores. By the time Kit went there, though, these were immured within new concrete dorms and featureless towers that stepped even beyond the little willow-bordered river whose Indian name the early scholars had resurrected and the school song celebrated.

Kit's parents brought her down in the family station wagon, its back loaded with her books and a set of Samsonite luggage, battered and marred from the many family moves it had made. Her brother's portable typewriter too, which had devolved on her, a long-term loan, when he joined the army. He had no use for it. In the service he had no use either for the black leather jacket, lined in cerulean satin, zippered at the sleeves and across the breast, that he had worn only a few times riding his motorcycle. Kit had accepted it, or taken it from him, after he reupped in November. A hostage she held, or an oblation, or just the old slipper that a lonesome dog chews in its master's absence. She wore it, way too large for her and distressingly strange and barbaric to her mother, who had plucked at the wide shoulders on Kit's slight frame and almost wept when Kit insisted on wearing it here, to her new school, not as a joke or a gesture but as a coat, to keep her warm.

"That's it. Tower 3," said her father, the University map spread out over the steering wheel. Central one of a group, almost identical, like three pyramids in a row in Egypt. *The lone and level sands stretched far away.* Kit hated and feared it immediately. Only when they had parked the wagon and hauled her stuff up the elevator and opened the door to her room did she see that, although dreadful to look at, it was wonderful to look out of. A last watchtower, facing the plain brown west and the evening; the river's little oxbow, peach-colored like the sunset sky. All of that too was fearful in its melancholy but didn't make her afraid.

"Well," her father said again.

"All yours I guess," said her mother, looking into the closets. One of Kit's fears had been of the roommate she might get, creepy doppelganger of some kind or cold and imperious. She had had enough of roommates at Our Lady, other souls too near hers.

Leaving her belongings there still packed (her mother wanted to fill the cunning built-in drawers of blond wood and hang pictures, but Kit wouldn't let her), they drove around the campus until it was too dark to see. ("'The Old Wishing Well in its grove of oaks has long been a traditional spot for marriage proposals,'" her father read from the guidebook. "Gee. Must be a long line come June." And Kit saw her mother frown and put a silencing hand on his slacks.) Then they drove down into the little town, to the one big old hotel, and had dinner. A cocktail? Ma glanced for approval at Dad and said, "I'll have a grasshopper."

Dad ordered a martini, and when it was brought he pushed it toward Kit. "Back on track," he said to her, and a big hard lump suddenly rose in Kit's throat, that only a swallow of the awful pale drink dissipated.

Late that night she awoke in her new narrow bed as though she had

heard a whisper in her ear, and when she sat up, she could see that outside the window snow was falling fast and thick.

Registration for second-semester classes was held next day, in the great
Romanesque field house, toward which students pressed, slogging
through the uncleared snow and churning it to slush. The boots to
have, Kit could tell, were those stadium boots with fur collars, white
polar bear or gray kitten: her own Capezios, and her feet, were icy wet.

Inside, banners in the University colors hung from the iron rafters,
and the tall barred windows lit the dusty air in columns. Sawdust, now
wet too, was spread over the dirt of the floor and the markings of the
running track. Rows of long folding tables had been set up, above
which signs were hung announcing what classes could be signed up
for at each station.

Like a bazaar, Kit thought. The hum of talk and activity arose into
the height of the old building, up to where calling sparrows darted amid
the rafters. As an incoming freshman, Kit was told she had first to be
photographed for her identification card. Signs and monitors guided
her into a roped-off area where a portrait camera and lights were set up.

"Card?"

What card? The proctor or assistant neatly fingered it out of Kit's
packet. We were all getting used to these oblong punch cards then,
one corner clipped, their rows of perfect rectangular holes. You were
not to fold, spindle, or mutilate them. There was a comb there, and a
mirror, for her to use. Kit stopped still for a moment, unable to move
forward, reminded for no good reason (the big camera, the harried
proctor) of Our Lady. All through the coming year in her ID photo she
would see in her eyes what she had seemed to see at that moment
when they were taking it. Hunted: or not hunted, caught.

She exited that area, permitted now to wander in the busy souk. She
thought maybe she'd toss away the list of sensible choices she had
worked out with the freshman adviser, and instead go over there, sign
up for Introduction to Music Theory, or Uralic-Altaic Studies. But she

went meekly and stood in the right lines, English Composition, the advanced French course she had tested into, a Psychology course (her required-science choice), World History I (from the Stone to the Middle Ages), Major Works of Western Literature I (Homer to Cervantes). Down the table from where she signed up for Composition, a line pressing toward a harassed young man threatened to break up into a crowd: people apparently trying to sign up for Comparative Literature 401, The Reading and Writing of Poetry. The anxious students in their duffel coats and canvas bags, white breath coming from their mouths in the unheated building, made Kit think of people in Russia lined up to buy something scarce, toilet paper or salt fish.

It was all gone, though. The graduate student was trying to explain: the class was filled.

Kit finished her list, getting from each station a punch card to be handed in the first day of class; then she and jostling numbers of others (her forehead was growing damp and her heart beat hard) were pressed through a passage where cashiers from the registrar's office awaited them. When it was Kit's turn, and she had laid down her hand of cards, her bill was totted up. At seven dollars a credit hour it came to ninety-one dollars, plus a ten-dollar lab fee for Psychology, where she would be doing what, exactly; and Kit put her hand into her crowded big pockets for her money. Her father had taken her to a bank and opened her an account, but because his check would take days to clear he had also given her an envelope of cash with which to pay her tuition.

And it wasn't there. Not in her brown handbag either. The folded plastic checkbook was there but not the heavy fat envelope. She put down on the cashier's desk her cascading class materials and handouts, syllabi, lists of recommended reading, and searched her pockets again. Oh God nope.

What was awful in that year was how every bad surprise or scare seemed to be one with all the others, all of them recurring at once within her in a flow of blinding freezing panic: caught. "Okay," she said. "Okay." Around the cashier's patient folded hands were displayed several checkbooks from various town banks, which you could use if you had forgotten to bring your own. As though hitting on the right plausible lie at the last minute, Kit pulled out her own checkbook, unclasped it and flattened it with a hand, and filled in the first virgin oblong, number 0001. "Okay," she said again, and ripped it from its fellows.

The envelope of money was back in her room, it had to be: she could see it, lying among the bedclothes or on the floor, she tried to feel in advance the relief and exasperation she would feel when she found it.

Then down to the bank and deposit it.

She couldn't find it in her room either, though. Lost somewhere between here in her room and the cashier's table. Somewhere between morning and noon, lost along the way.

She sat on the narrow bed. At Our Lady you weren't allowed to use your bed during the day. If they'd allowed it, half the girls would have done nothing but lie there.

Retrace your steps: she heard her father's voice saying it. She pulled herself erect and retraced her steps, down the hall and stairway and out into the quads amid students who had not lost all their money.

In the field house, the bazaar was over, the set being struck. Men in overalls were pushing, with brooms absurdly huge, the masses of the day's waste paper into great heaps. She thought of fairy tales, impossible tasks that magic helpers taught you how to do. The workmen's voices echoed like faint song, and there was almost nobody else in the building; someone far off in an overcoat, looking at a book. But the tables were still in place, and the signs above them. She decided to go back to each, and stand in the lines she had stood in. French. Phys Ed. Psychology. At each station she walked forward studying the remaining litter.

English Composition. This was basically stupid and hopeless. Lost money is one of the things that doesn't return: even she knew that much. It had been so much, though, more cash than she had ever held in her hand at once. Why did that give her hope? A disaster so great was just too rare, too unlikely: following on all that had happened to her. Just too sad, statistically.

Eyes on the way she walked, she only suddenly became aware that she had come up on the man standing reading in the window light: aware of his galoshes, unbuckled. Then his hound's-tooth overcoat, collar turned up. His hair, thick black and upstanding but so fine it seemed almost to move in the random airs of the place, like undersea grasses.

That long V of a face, at once gaunt and tender, merry and haunted. There are so few photographs of him, none at all of him as a youth. The one used over and over was the one taken that first day in Berlin: harsh as an interrogation, it made him seem wary and weary and maybe harmed. Smiling though: this smile Kit saw.

Kit nodded to him, smiling too in response. Near him the banner of his seminar, The Reading and Writing of Poetry, still hung, as though he waited here for latecoming customers.

"Are you," she said, and then rapidly discarded several ways of going on, are you the famous poet, the Soviet poet, Mr. Falin, Professor Falin, Comrade Falin, that guy who you know. "Are you teaching that class?"

He looked at the sign, and nodded.

"It sounds interesting," she said. "How, I mean, who all can take it?"

"Anyone who loves poetry enough." One word Kit could always remember him saying was *poetry*. In his voice the vowels seemed to run or stream over the rocks of the consonants to pour away at the end in one of those double I sounds only Slavs can make.

"How much is that?" she asked.

He laughed, as though, unexpectedly, she had got his joke. "It's small class," he said. "That's all."

She lowered her eyes momentarily, as though abashed, and saw that the toe of his black rubber boot pointed at a paper oblong half buried in the sawdust. It signaled to her as soon as her eyes fell on it, yes yes here I am, and she bent and picked it up: still fat, still full.

"Oh my God."

He watched as she slid the bills from within. "Lucky," he said, smiling.

"It's mine," she said. "I lost it here."

"Oh yes? It would have been more lucky if it was not yours. Yes?"

She laughed in relief, thinking how many had stepped on the envelope, trudging forward as the line moved.

"I'd like to take your course," she said suddenly.

He looked from her to her money, as though she meant to bribe him. "And what year are you?"

"A freshman."

"Ah well." His eyes were the kind that, in looking, seemed to have no purpose but to admit: not probers or perceivers or hunters but only portals. "Is difficult."

"I'm taking French Poetry 330," she said. What was she doing? "A poem of mine was published. I could show you."

"No need, no need," he said, and turned to go.

"I mean it," she said, but he had thrust his hands into his overcoat pockets and was walking away. Then he stopped, and turned again to her. "What poem?" he asked.

She had to think a moment what he meant. "Well it was only published in a student book."

"And?"

"It was called 'May'."

He said nothing, only regarded her, and she realized that he was waiting for her to recite it. She felt like Alice before the Caterpillar. "I don't know if I can just. Say it." The poem might be unretrievable, like a lot of things from the other side, from before.

"Ah," he said, not in reproach or dismissal—those feelings were her own—and saluted her again as he turned to go.

But why had he been there anyway, in that empty field house? She was sure he hadn't been there earlier. What was he doing there, standing by her money as though on guard, waiting to point it out to her?

"He was strange and wonderful man," Gavriil Viktorovich said. "He had ability to appear suddenly behind or beside you when you had not seen him approach. At school forming up for exercise or games, I would be sure he was late and would receive reprimand, and a moment later he would be there, just as the roll was called, alert, calm. Where he had come from?" He looked wildly around himself to show the confusion he had felt, and lifted his hands in surrender, who knows. "I asked him how he comes by this ability to appear and to disappear, and he told me it was easy, and I could do it too: I needed only to practice invisibility, as he had."

"Invisibility?"

"Now you must understand that in those years we all desired invisibility. We wanted above all not to be noticed. Or if noticed to be taken for standard model citizen. Our disguises did not always work very well, of course. But Falin. He was most undisguised man. His head always high and his face so, so provoking, frank and open. And yet he said to me *Be invisible*: and he was, and could be. I think it was because he was without fear."

"Do you think he was?"

"Those who live on the fear of others can sense it, you know, just as predator senses prey; and since he had none, their eyes just passed over him as though he were tree or telephone pole, of no interest, not there. . . . One fear only he had, I think: that they would touch him, soil him—that they would find somehow means to make him one of them."

Kit thought that if this was so then there had come a time when Falin could no longer go unseen: when he had ceased to believe, maybe, that he could. She had been with him then. And he hadn't hid, or run away. He had stood forth.

"What was the poem he asked you to say?" Gavriil Viktorovich asked her gently.

"I could have remembered it if I'd thought a minute."

"Of course."

"It was a poem about my brother," Kit said. "About my brother, come home from the army."

4

Because her family moved often when she was growing up, Kit and her brother Ben had grown up more intimate than most siblings. The girls she met in each new school always spoke of *their* older brothers in tones of profound contempt and disgust, only surpassed by how they regarded younger brothers. It was one of the small divisions that usually began opening between her and them right after the first few easy questions (*What's your name? Is that your bike?*) and then widened.

It was because of her father's job that Kit's family moved from place to place, from seacoast to desert, sunbaked towns of new square buildings to old cities of mansions and stone churches. Ben had been able to remember a time before they began to move, several staid years spent in an Eastern college town, summer and fall and Christmas, and now and then he would be caught by the smell of blackberries or the creak of porch floorboards and say how it called forth that place, still whole within him. To Kit the places they lived were vivid, but she remembered them like scenes from novels: separate and poignant and hers, but not her.

What her father did, exactly, she never quite knew. He would joke about it, putting off questions. When Kit or Ben insisted, he would turn grave and frank and explain, in terms that explained nothing. His job was connecting one place to another, he said; he was trying to connect them by connecting their big computers with phone lines, so they could call up one another and talk. It was a *network*, he said, a network of electronic brains. He talked about computers as if they were a game he played for the fun of it; he collected cartoons from *Look* and *The Saturday Evening Post* showing roomfuls of great square machines covered with lights and buttons, and puzzled men in white coats who read out the paradoxical little message that popped out of a slot. *It says it won't answer till we sacrifice a goat to it.*

Well then, who did he work *for*? The children they met wanted to know. *Their* fathers worked for Studebaker or Sunbeam or Bendix or they were policemen or barbers or sold cars or houses. Oh, he would say, I work for lots of people, there are getting to be a lot of computers, more every day. How many had he connected so far? Well, so far—and he solemnly held out a circle of thumb and finger that said Zero.

And when eight months or a year had passed they would pack and sell the house they had just bought (for some reason they always bought them, made money or lost it, the same money over and over) and in their big station wagon they sailed on. Sailed, skated: Kit felt she skated, over the truths her father knew or hid, the *network* which lay under their rapid, placid lives like the tangled duckweed and roots down in a frozen pond.

Tall house in an old downtown, a Midwestern city; bamboo-patterned wallpaper, dark polished woodwork. She was ten, her brother twelve. Before anything else, their household gods needed to be brought in, the things that had been put last into the moving van so they could be unpacked first: the percolator and its sister the toaster; their mother's mother's chest full of family photographs in crumbling albums, faces their mother progressively forgot the names for; their father's shoe bag with its pockets for his wing-tips, brogues, golf shoes white and brown, each pair with its shoe trees; the chenille clothespin bag, without clothespins, wherein Kit's eyeless and grimy stuffed white lamb always traveled, the lamb she'd had since birth, no amount of teasing would cause her to give it up; and the encyclopedia, twenty-six brown volumes to be unpacked and put in order in their own small brown bookcase: this Kit and Ben alone could do.

Maybe it began when Ben had showed her the words or letters on the back of each volume, read them aloud to her before she could read: *Annu to Baltic*; *Baltim to Brail*; *Brain to Castin*; *Castir to Cole*. See, he said: This one goes from Annu to Baltic; and she thought that they were places—that you could go from one to another—and that the heavy books detailed these journeys, the lands and peoples, delights and terrors.

The hundred iron fighter-kings of Baltim had armies that rode on iron elephants; but one of those kings had a princess daughter with six fingers on her hand, and a white cat with six toes; she had a garden, and in the garden a lake without a bottom. They would begin to travel from the plains of Annu to the mountains of Zygo and because there was an infinity in between, never arrive. *But* they would cry out, topping each other; *but* the trees can sing, and they warn you about the tigers; *but* the water is warm and the ice ship melts. He thought of dangers, and planned for them; she invented escapes, at the last moment.

Her parents seemed hardly to notice this game, or so she then thought. She was surprised years later to find that her mother had kept a lot of the writings they had done, the drawings and the models, the chronologies and the maps. Most of the work was Ben's, which was maybe why she had kept it. When Kit took it all from the cardboard box, she felt a strange vertigo: she recognized and remembered these things and at the same time saw them shrivel and shrink; what had once been big and vivid to her became small, and not only in size. He had done it all on little pieces of shoddy paper and card, in colored pencils; he had been just a child. It was like picking up the body of a bird, and being surprised to find it nearly weightless.

. . .

Between themselves she and Ben called their parents George and Marion, not Mom and Dad: they found it irresistible that their parents had the same names as the two ghosts who bedeviled Cosmo Topper on television. *George! Marion!* the dapper little Englishman would cry in exasperation or befuddlement at his mischievous, unflappable dead friends, up to their tricks again; and the Malones would laugh and look at one another. *Their* George and Marion were so much like those ghosts: untouchable, it seemed, so blithe and insubstantial.

In the summer before Kit went into high school, they moved into a new development strung along the banks of the Wabash River. Behind their split level house were young woods, and a steep gully going down to the riverbank and the little brown river. The trees hung over it and lifted their slimy knuckled toes out of it and the undergrowth was dense.

"Bugs," Ben said as they climbed down. "Bugs and more bugs."

"You don't say *bugs*," Kit said, coming down after him with the collecting stuff, the jars and the cotton soaked in carbon tet, notebook under her arm. "That's the first thing they said. *Bugs* doesn't mean anything."

He smiled that serene smile of his, the one that meant he felt no need to respond and yet remained in the right. He had the net, and with it he brushed bugs—deerflies, mosquitoes—from his head.

Kit had been enrolled in a Catholic school for the coming year, St. Hedwige's, and at registration was told that over the summer it would be her job to make an insect collection, fifty species at least, to be mounted, labeled, and brought to Biology class on the first day of school, which now was only a couple of weeks away.

She didn't hate bugs, especially. She withdrew from them: ducked beneath the flight paths of hunting wasps, stayed far from June bugs and darning needles. Going down to the river just because that's where they were, parting the layered leaves and upturning stones out of their sockets in the mud to find them, *messing* with them—she felt a deep reluctance that Ben made fun of. A girl's reluctance, he implied, and it seemed to be so, for it was like the feeling that her own girl being was just then causing in her, unable to be ducked, her own swelling slug's alien aliveness.

So she had let the days slide away, and read her small books, which were full of earth's music and the river too, of course, and the murmurous haunts of flies on summer eves, but that was different, until it was August and her few specimens (a couple of June bugs she had found already dead and a great moonstone-colored luna moth she wrote a poem about) had already decayed, improperly mounted; and Ben started taking her down to the river in the mornings and the evenings.

"Listen," he said, standing still in the green.

The noise really was ear-filling, an orchestra endlessly tuning, strings here, woodwinds there.

"Good hunting," he said, and rubbed his hands together. At first she only followed; he was fearless and soon fascinated by the job, finding amazing beings in the city of leaves that he might have seen at any time but never had, a *robber fly*, a *cicada killer* (huge slow wasp like an attack helicopter), or a *camel cricket* with glossy russet hump. He learned to step up to a hornet or a wasp as though he meant to tame it, and slip the net smoothly over it like an executioner's hood; he made Kit try it.

"He's gonna get me, I know it."

"He's not. He doesn't even know you exist."

"I got him I got him."

"Easy. Don't catch his wing, don't hurt him."

"Hurt him! We're *trying* to *kill* him."

"Give him a little shake. There, now he's dropped in. Now the cap."

In the jar she had caught, yes, quite a specimen, a beetle painted in clown colors and in fact named (they looked it up as they sat to drink the Cokes he had brought too) a *harlequin*. So there.

And this was how she learned to be unafraid of the world, at least unafraid of this modality of it: how she became a hunter and an explorer and a namer, a *taxonomist*. By summer's end she was crashing through the shallows and the reeds in pursuit of some glamorous something whose wing-hum she had heard, digging into a black crevice where a centipede, not actually an insect, was escaping, one of a kind she hadn't seen before and wanted. The more she learned the more she wanted to know, and wanting to know displaced fear. Her poem "The Split Level" would be about that: about a woman learning the names of flowers, and thus (she believes) coming closer to nature, and really coming closer too, even though by means of the one thing nature doesn't possess of itself, its names.

The day before school started she came to her mother (who was washing dishes) and told her this weird thing had happened and she was scared: her stomach hurt and there was blood on her underpants.

Well that's not something to be scared of, her mother said (Kit remembers how she went on washing her flowered plates and standing them upright in the rack like soldiers or tombstones, not alarmed or apparently unsettled at all). She began an explanation, saying *Now you know you have this hole there, not the peepee one but the other one.* Kit nodded and listened to the rest of what her mother said, and accepted the hug and pat her mother offered (*Big girl now, my baby's a big girl*) and then went back to her room; and as though she were catching a bright centipede in its damp crevice she discovered what she had in fact *not* known before, that she had a hole there: not how far it went, though, or where it led.

How can you know anything true about someone when your memories stop just as you are becoming a person yourself? She thought Ben had been beautiful and strong, that his strength and his beauty were like a horse he rode: once a pretty pony, it grew into a tall stallion, then gone, bearing him away. That's what she remembered, not knowing if it was true or false or neither.

Home from high school on a day in spring, taking off his watch at the kitchen sink to wash his hands; his thick dark hair just cut, what they called then a "Princeton cut" for some reason, just long enough to part and brush to one side. Pink button-down shirt, a Gant, only one of the brand names he was loyal to; an inch of white undershirt showing in its cleft, its sleeves turned back one graceful turn. People say *I can remember as though it were yesterday*, but you can never remember yesterdays as clearly as these moments that are not yesterday or any day, but always now. His pleated gray slacks, pegged at the ankle, revealing now and then like a mockingbird's flicked tail another inch of white: his socks between the black loafers and the breaking flannel cuff. She remembered his clothes better than she remembered her own. A slim gold belt, buckled (it was the style that season) at the side.

But what is he saying? It's easier to see than to hear. She might have been kidding him about his weekend dates. She did that a lot in that year, trying under the guise of teasing to understand his life apart from her, his feelings about girls and dates and making out. She was like a color-blind person trying to guess the names and imports of colors; she knew these rituals were of vital importance and that she would have to begin on them soon. Yet she didn't think to connect them to the huge feelings she did feel, feelings that could be started by a summer storm or a violin sonata or a thousand other things. And she feared for him: feared losing him.

"Isn't she taller than you?"

"Maybe a little taller."

"But that's ridiculous, going on a date with a girl taller than you."

"It's not a date."

"She'll have to wear flat shoes. It says so in the magazines."

"Okay, maybe she will. We're going to a riding stable, though. I think she wears boots."

"And how can you go out with somebody taller than you *whose name is Earp? Greta Earp?*"

"Geraldine. Greta is her sister."

"Geraldine!" Collapsing in laughter. "With a riding crop, smacking her big leather boots, looking down on you!"

"She's going to teach me some riding."

"Oh my God! Teach you riding! Oh no!"

In school he never played team sports, and maybe that too was because of how often they moved: he was never inducted into the male fraternity of a particular time and place, a team's forming and knitting over several summers and school years. Instead he took up sports he could play alone. He ran, preferring distance and endurance events; swam; wrestled too, strong and smart enough to win but maybe too generous or not competitive enough to win often.

Golf. The summer after he graduated from high school they lived in an odd tall house on the edge of a golf course, a house like a summer cabin, paneled in varnished plywood. He'd get up early that summer and take a stained canvas bag of six or eight clubs he'd bought at a church sale and walk out onto the course when the grass was wet and the air still; play five or six holes until the shape of the course brought him back near his own lawn again, and quit.

He took Kit with him if she got up quickly when she heard him wake and dress. She walked out with him into the checkered shade and the sounds of birds awaking, out along those mysterious shorn rides bordered with placid trees and undergrowth, the rough. He let her try to hit the ball, stood behind her to model her stance and swing, flinging her arms like a puppet's. Now and then she lofted a ball sweetly into the day. Once she watched it float (with mysterious solemn slowness, hooking badly) right between a rising goldfinch crossing one way and a monarch butterfly sailing another, as though they played in Eden.

Eden: Falin said that we are entranced with Eden because it is at once changeless and fleeting. It was on the golf course that Ben told her he was planning to join the army.

"I can't tell Mom and Dad yet," he told her. "So I'm practicing on you."

They sat on a little bench between holes. She would remember the little herm that stuck up there by them, brushed metal, a dirty white towel hung around it: the ball washer.

"I thought you were going to college. To Thomas Aquinas."

"I thought I wanted to. But. I want to do this." He grinned at her. "That's good, though, see. That's what *they're* going to say."

He was turning a drab little flower in his fingers. Six months before he had driven home on a great black motorcycle and then told his parents it was his, he had bought it with his own money, earned at the jobs he was always able to get. He found it easier to explain and account for what he had done than to tell them what he planned to do. They were lucky that what he had gone and done so often made good sense, or at least wasn't dangerous or wrong.

"A soldier," Kit said. "Mom and Dad'll kill you."

"Soldiers," he said, "don't get killed by their parents. That's not the idea."

"Oh jeez. Ben. But."

He began to explain, as much to himself as to them or to her. He had an obligation to his country, if he didn't do it now it would be hanging over him till it was done. College wasn't cheap, and if he got all the way through his army training, not only would he have completed a lot of work that would count toward a degree—language, for instance—he would be eligible for good scholarships and loans. The GI Bill. He talked carefully, building a small watertight house around himself, putting each brick in place with care. Dad had been in the army, after all, hadn't he; this was a time when everybody ought to be willing to defend this country, everybody knew the dangers. If you joined up you served longer, yes, but you got top choice of programs and locations.

Every brick he put in place shut him off further from Kit.

She almost never thought about the future, it seemed brazen or dangerous, the very thing that the gods got you for doing. Ben though: he loved planning and believed in it. So he was probably right about the army, that it would be a good deal for him, and work out well. But why didn't he see that it would leave her without him, with no future that she could envision, no way to get ready?

"They'll miss you so much. Mom will miss you so much."

"Oh," Ben said. "I think they're ready. They say I eat too much."

"You do. But they love that. They love you."

"Well," he said softly. "I love them." Kit clapped her hands over her face then so that he wouldn't see, pressed her hands into her traitorous eyeballs, but it didn't help. The one thing she knew she mustn't do, weep, the one thing that would push him away; knowing always made her weep more.

"Oh here we go," he said. "Old Goofy Glass."

That was so cruel that she began to laugh. The Goofy Glass was part of a magic set he had had once, an ordinary water glass that somehow sweated or oozed from invisible pores so that whoever held it was soon awash, or the table where it was put down, the knee it was rested on. She laughed and then went on crying, and though he had never done so before, he put an arm around her shoulders and waited, saying nothing, till she could stop, and they could go home.

The next week, after a talk with George and Marion, and another with Father Conklin at Little Flower Church, he went on his black bike to the recruiting office on Courthouse Square and did whatever he had to do (she wanted to ask him, make him tell her every detail so that it would be hers as well as his, as she had made him describe his dates and his road trips, but just to show him the depths of her desolation she hadn't).

He would (he had told her this much) stand and take a vow, his right hand raised, a vow he could not then get out of unless he turned out to have been lying to the army in some way in order to get in, about his age, or his criminal record or whether he was a member of the Communist Party or another subversive organization. And then they would tell him to take one step forward, after which he would be declared to have obeyed his first order without question, and would be a soldier.

She lay on her stomach on her bed, the blind half-drawn and the room hot and dim and smelling of varnish. She wondered (though the wonder never quite rose over the limn of hurt consciousness) how she would ever be able to do anything daring or good ever again. She would never again dare to go down to the muddy end to get what she wanted or needed, and if she did she would crush it and lose it. Everything, everything in the world; what everyone had that she didn't know how to get, or even to want.

She hadn't moved when she heard the bike come back in the late afternoon, approaching down the far highway and still only a wish, then turning onto the long drive, then loud, day-smashing, beneath her window. When he cut the engine the noise raced through the air, homeless for a moment, before dissipating.

"Why are you here?" she asked him from the top of the stairs.

"Well," he said.

"Are you in the army?"

"Yup."

"Why did they let you come home?"

He had hung up his jacket, and turned smiling to her. "You weren't listening," he said. "I didn't think you were. I explained it to the folks. If I sign up now, I get a month's leave right off the bat. I don't go in till September. Special deal."

She looked down at him looking up at her. She hadn't listened, had hid in her room for the last two days.

"I was thinking," he said. "I promised a while ago I'd teach you to drive. That would take about a month. Does that sound good?"

She would not exult or unbend or giggle or do anything stupid. Nothing he had done or offered warranted that. September was far away, but it was already coming closer, closer now by a minute than when he had made his offer. "I'm not old enough to get a permit," she said. "Not till January."

It was another of those objections that he didn't deign to hear. He only stood smiling, and waited for her to come down the stairs. And soon she did.

5.

Once again it is May and the walls of my house have grown thin
And the windows where I wait and watch are wide open.
How high it is up there where the tops of the trees are speaking sign
And the swallows are turning, white bellies, blue backs, in the sun!
Before any human eye has seen it, before even mine,
They see the jonquil-colored taxi at the court's end turning in.
Now rejoice, all you Courts and Drives and Circles bearing him on!
Now lift up your heads oh you Gateses and Flynns
And be you lifted up oh you houses of Wozniaks and Paynes!
Cast off your junipers and dismiss your stone foundations
And rise up into the heights of the new air like lost balloons!

In her room in Tower 3, she beat out the lines with two fingers on Ben's typewriter. The secret, for her alone to know, was that hidden among the many rhymes and half rhymes and slant rhymes that ended them there was one unsaid: the name they were all intended to rhyme with or against. She tried as she typed to remember May: not the last lost May but the May before that, back before. And she could not. But she remembered the poem, she only needed to string the lines like beads, or like the balls of an abacus, to make them come out right and add up.

See: they have given him back his eyes in exchange for their gun,
The one they made him carry; but his clothes are still olive and dun,
The color of wet fallen leaves, and the bag he has brought with him
Buckled and strapped and long enough to stuff a dead child within.

He hadn't actually been wearing his uniform when he came home, nor did he come home in a taxi; George had gone to the bus station to get him, and Kit had been at school and only seen him when she rushed into the house, having run home from the bus, hot in her wool skirt and sweater, dropping her books on the floor of the hall.

Once again it is May and the walls of my heart have grown thin
And the tall small windows are lifted up so my princeling may come in.

She wrote a note and put it and the poem in an envelope and carried it out into the day, now turning gray and hostile, the snow freezing again as the sun went down. In the Comparative Literature Department on the third floor of the liberal arts tower, the secretary pointed to the wall of pigeonholes where mail for professors could be left. And there it was, with a little typed paper slipped into the brass frame: *I. I. Falin*. There was nothing else in the box. She saw him, Falin, just turning to come out of the chairman's office, nodding a farewell, as she slipped out the door.

When she returned to Tower 3 she found that she had a roommate. She was sitting on the unused bed smoking a cigarette, in a wrinkled khaki raincoat, her bags around her, as though she were waiting for a train.

"Aha," she said, looking up at Kit's entrance and smiling reluctantly.

"Aha," said Kit. "I wondered."

"Yeah well," the other said, not quite an apology, but not quite in annoyance either.

The university had chosen for Kit a roommate who was also starting her freshman year in the second semester, and who was also a year older than her class: she related this to Kit with what seemed a grudging satisfaction. Her name was Fran. She was from New York City, and had come here for the music school, because, she said, it was world-class and she hadn't got into Juilliard.

"What do you play?" Kit asked.

"Viola," Fran said, with a wonderfully gloomy enunciation, as though she were answering a different question (*What are you in for?* maybe). And there by her feet was indeed a violin case, but too big. "I might do philosophy instead though," she said. She dragged deeply on the cigarette, and let the thick smoke out her mouth to be drawn up her nose—what Kit had heard called a "French inhale."

"I don't mind starting late," she said. "It means at least you're not in a *Class of*. You know, like *Class of 1965*. We're not."

"Why are you?" Kit asked. "Starting late, I mean." As soon as she said it a hard hollow opened in her breast, for it was evident that if Fran told her story, Kit would have to tell hers.

Fran shrugged. "My parents took me to Europe for six months," she said levelly. "They had decided to get a divorce, and wanted time to be with me. To, you know, be a family for me."

"Oh."

She stubbed out the smoke. "They had this whole plan they thought was secret. Of course I knew. They announced it, the divorce, at the end of the trip. In Amsterdam."

"Oh."

"We'd just been to Anne Frank's house." She shook her head in grave contempt. "It's all right. I hope they'll be happy. I never want to go back there, though."

"Europe?"

"Amsterdam. Cold and gray and the damn canals and the damn rain."

"Amster, Amster, dam dam dam."

Fran looked at her and after a moment's puzzlement laughed, seeming to surprise herself by doing so, or to be amazed at Kit for causing it. "So what about you?"

"Ah," said Kit, shrugging, know-nothing.

"What are you going to be studying?"

"Oh, I don't know. I didn't come with as much as you."

"What courses are you taking?"

"Well, French," said Kit. "Psychology. World Literature, and you know, Composition. And a course in poetry."

"Writing it or reading it?"

"I think both."

"You a poet?"

Kit shoved her hands into her pockets. Like Fran she hadn't taken off her coat.

"Oh that reminds me," Fran said. "You got a phone call. The proctor or monitor or whoever she is put a note under the door." She pointed to the pink slip on the desk Kit had claimed. A professor had called to tell Kit she was welcome in his class, but (the note read) he hadn't said what class it was.

"So," Kit said, crumpling the note and grinning with radiant glee (she knew it, but not why, not why she was doing this at all), "you going to take your coat off?"

"You first," Fran said.

Many people loved poetry enough, it seemed, to sign up or show up for Falin's class. It was held in a seminar room in the liberal arts tower, a building lacking, as yet, a name, many alums being tempted with the honor, none of them biting so far. The windows were wide and the sun on the snowy prairie dazzling. People sat at every place around the oval table and perched on the registers and stood in the back leaning against the new green blackboard. Falin appeared among them—his magician's trick of suddenly being there without having been seen to arrive—and looked at them all, amused and maybe a little alarmed.

Kit gave him the form he had to sign, granting her permission to take the course, and he took it without acknowledging her, maybe having forgotten her she thought; he puzzled over it a moment and then uncapped a fountain pen and signed it with childlike slow exactness. Kit realized that he had left behind not only his language but his alphabet, and had had to learn another.

He sat down among them, taking a place a student vacated, and placed a cheap new portfolio of imitation pigskin on the table before him; opened it, took out class cards and a record book, a pack of cigarettes and a box of wooden matches. He seemed to have no self-consciousness, no consciousness of being the object of their attention, fascination even. "I am asked to speak to you of poetry," he said. "I would have liked to talk only of poetry written in the language you know best, but that would be English, which I myself do not know so well. Also the University wished that you learn something of poetry of other languages, of Russian, which I do know well, but German and French too. Here is a packet or package of them which we will read, one for each of you, which later I will hand around. Because one reason for education is to learn more deeply about what you already know, but another reason is to learn a little about what you do not know at all; and perhaps one day, when you meet these poets again in their own lands, you will not be wholly stranger there.

"Now.

"Since we will be together long while, I thought we should come to know one another. We might begin now to introduce ourselves, in this way: I will ask you each to say a poem that has meant something to you."

He looked around at them, maybe the faintest curl of a smile to his mobile mouth, his hands laid one over the other now and unmoving:

Kit had noticed before how large they were, long strong fingers and jut-
ting wrist bones. They were all silent, maybe trying to decide if he
actually meant what he said, or if maybe he meant only that they
should name a poem, or a poet, they had liked or read; knowing he
hadn't, though, and that they would have to recite poetry, if they
could, before their fellows and this personage.

"We will perhaps start on my left," Falin said.

"Okay," said the student on his left after a moment. She was a pretty
moon-faced blue-eyed girl of a kind there seemed to Kit to be a lot of
in the world, cookie-cut, but sometimes very different inside, she
knew. "I like this one:

"I'm nobody! Who are you?
Are you nobody, too?
Then there's a pair of us—don't tell!
They'd banish us, you know."

"It's Emily Dickinson," she said. "There's more I don't remember."

Falin nodded, regarding her or what she had said in a kind of plain
wonder, then turning his gaze to the boy next to her, who passed the
glance along with a shrug to the one next to him. This one said: "All I
can think of is one by Swinburne," and he began it:

"When the hounds of spring are on winter's traces
The mother of months in meadow or plain
Fills the shadows and windy places
With lisp of leaves and ripple of rain . . ."

He was a small guy with a red crewcut growing out raggedly and a
spray of childlike greenish freckles across his nose; one button of his
button-down shirt was undone and his glasses a little askew.

"And the brown bright nightingale amorous
Is half assuaged for Itylus

For the Thracian ships and the foreign faces
The tongueless vigil, and all the pain."

Kit thought of him reading these lines so often that they had lodged in his memory, and found herself liking him. He began on another stanza before running out or growing embarrassed; seeming to shake free of a little trance.

The baton was passed, or refused mostly with shrugs or giggles, which seemed to interest Falin as much as the poems or bits of poems recited. Kit wondered if the other kids felt like what they seemed to her, prisoners summoned out of dungeons and ordered to speak, who had almost forgotten human speech. A beaked storky guy with a bobbing Adam's apple recited in a weird basso:

"The moving finger writes, and, having writ,
Moves on: nor all your piety nor wit
Shall lure it back to cancel half a line,
Nor all your tears wash out a word of it."

Many nodded when another girl began, "Two roads diverged in a yellow wood," and though she didn't seem to be one who had gone down many less-traveled roads, you couldn't know that, which was maybe what this exercise was for. Then it was Kit's turn, whose mind was empty, there were no poems in her except her own, the one she had given him: it stood in the way of all the others she knew. Falin waited.

"*Je suis comme le roi d'un pays pluvieux*," she said. "That's . . . well, it's what I remember right now. It's Baudelaire, and it means I am like the king of a rainy country." The line had appeared on her French placement exam, this glowing sentence among the ordinary requests for directions and statements of fact, opening like a casement. She'd had a hard time moving past it. "The next lines are, I think, like this: *Riche, mais impuissant; jeune, et portant très vieux.* Rich but powerless; young and yet very old." She stopped, for she found her eyes had filled with tears and her throat trembled: because of the poem, and because she had remembered it, but for more than that. She seemed to see that country, to which a long time ago she had been able to go so easily, where rain was as exquisite as sun, where pain and even boredom could have the same golden weight and worth as joy or triumph.

"Anyway," she said, ceasing, embarrassed and abashed. "Sort of like that. There's more, but."

Falin was looking at her, leaning somewhat forward over the table toward her. She would later think that he seemed often to listen by looking as much as by hearing. He said: "This is an English word, 'rainy'?"

"Sure," Kit said. "Sure. A rainy day."

He lifted his head as though remembering that yes, he knew this locution. "Rainii," he said softly.

No one else was willing to speak, and Falin spread his great hands on the table.

"Very well," he said. "In exchange for yours, here is one."

He began to speak in Russian, in a voice entirely different from the one in which he had spoken before, sounds that don't exist in English, complex fluid vowels and strange soft consonants drawn out impossibly: it was as though he sculpted the poem in the middle of the air with broad steady strokes of rhythm and rhyme. Kit didn't know whether she wanted to laugh aloud or to moan in amazement.

He finished, seeming to settle again, a hawk that had just roused and beat its wings. "This," he said in his usual—or was it his American?—voice, "is quite famous poem in Russian, poem of Pushkin, known to everyone who reads, as perhaps some poems you have repeated are known to everyone here." The students were still, and did not look at one another. "I cannot tell you what it says, not at all exactly, because meaning so much resides in Russian words; this problem we will talk much of. I will tell you though something of what it is about."

He looked within, as though marshaling again before him the lines he had spoken.

"He says—Pushkin—that the poet, until he is summoned by the god Apollo to sacrifice to him, is afraid, confused, immersed in the world and its troubles; his lyre—poet's instrument—is still muffled, his soul is wrapped in sleep. And of all the world's worthless children, he is most worthless.

"Until he sings."

He let them think about this, or anyway said no more for a long moment.

"Well, I will tell you something of myself," he said at length. "Because it may be that some of you have come chiefly to have look at me, someone who has come from so far away and from somewhere so—strange to you.

"Okay.

"My name is Innokenti Isayevich Falin. I was born and grew up in the city of Leningrad, at that time Petrograd, before that St. Petersburg. My father was an engineer, I his only child."

He picked up and put down again his cigarettes; took his fountain pen from his pocket, and put it back.

"When very young I liked poetry, nursery rhymes as you say; I was very intent on these, and I like them still today. But for a long time I showed no further interest in poetry. When I went to school I wished to be engineer like my father; but this was not possible. I became instead a drawer; not an artist but a drawer of plans, for machines . . ."

"A draftsman," somebody said.

"A draftsman," said Falin, tasting the word like a gourmet tasting an exotic morsel. "After that a soldier, trying not to die; after that a maker of furniture, that is worker in a prison camp where furniture was made; after that, draftsman again, and poet too. Then no job. Then exile. Then here."

He opened his hands: here.

"My name you may have heard, from newspapers, but probably not read any of my poems. For a long time none have been printed or published in the language I wrote them in, in the country where they were written. Those that were published long ago have mostly disappeared, though they were sometimes typed up or copied out by friends and passed around. Memorized too." He tapped his brow. "Recited, one person to another, as we have recited. For a poem to live within a reader, reader must be able to say it in his own mind and heart. And for this reason I tell you now of class requirements and final test."

He drew out and piled before him the packets of purple mimeographed poetry, and patted them. "I cannot give you grade on what poetry you write. This would be foolish, as though to grade you for your beauty or your strength. I can grade on how hard you try, and how hard you try to understand poetry of others. And so midterm, and final, test will be only that you write down in blue books the poems we read together. So you must memorize, commit to memory, learn them *by heart* is how you say it, yes?" He looked around at their faces, which were stunned or amazed or amused. "Which poems will be asked for on these tests? Any or all. Best to memorize all. Observe this motto of Soviet Young Pioneers: *Be Prepared.*"

"I think they were all astonished," Christa said to Gavriil Viktorovich in his St. Petersburg apartment. "We were all astonished. To be told that the only poems you could understand were the ones you had memorized."

"Yes."

"Like the one of my own, that he wanted me to recite. I could have remembered it if I'd thought a minute. I just never had to, I mean . . ."

"Of course not. You need not memorize poetry. You need only to open book."

"Yes," she said. "All we need to do. If we do."

He bent his head as though he would not pursue this topic, maybe shaming to his guest. His little apartment, cement-walled like a jail cell, was deep in books and papers. A small ikon amid them on a bookshelf, and by it a small framed picture, a woman with a gray bun and a flowered dress who hadn't wanted to be photographed.

"You know," he said, "we have a view of poets unlike anyone's."

"Yes. I think you do."

"We did once. Now, I do not know."

"Yes."

"Because, perhaps, they arrived so suddenly among us, with Pushkin—almost none before, Russian poets writing Russian. Then perhaps because after the Revolution they spoke truth long after others ceased or were silenced. And even when they themselves were silenced we could say truths they had said, in their voices, because we remembered their poems. Could be banned and burned but not plucked from memories."

"Yes."

"At one time we greeted one another with these poems. A line, a stanza of Akhmatova, of Mandelstam: if the other could complete the poem or the stanza, perhaps you could trust—perhaps be friends. Perhaps not." He smiled. "Once poetry seemed capable to bring the dead to life. Maybe only our dead, in that age. Because of that power poets were killed, in several ways, not always reversible."

"What do you mean, not always reversible?"

He regarded her as he had before, in that way that seemed to challenge her, gently, to seek in herself for what she surely already knew. And yet it was she who was to have brought knowledge, or at least news. She said—surprised to find that she was going to ask it, right now, though it was what she wanted to know— "Do you think it was wrong of me, to publish those translations? In a book of my own?"

He didn't answer immediately. "It began your own career, I think?"

"Yes."

"So long ago. And now you are most famous of American poets."

"Well no. No. And even if that were true, no poet in America is famous really." She looked down at the wedding band on her left hand, turned it in her fingers, a habit. "I've never known if it was right of me. If I did it for the right reasons."

He took one skinny knee in both his hands, and smiled. "Tell me," he said. "Was it perhaps because of this doubt that you never studied Russian more?"

She didn't answer.

"And that for so many years you have not talked of him? Because you thought perhaps you wronged him?"

"I don't know," she said. "It might be. I don't know."

The sun came in his window, the clouds passing away, and lit the little place for a moment, then was covered again.

"What will they say, tonight, the ones I meet?" she asked. "And at the conference? What will they say to me?"

"I believe they will say *Spasibo, chto priekhala v takuiu dal,*" he said. "They will say thank you. Thank you for coming so far."

When she left the liberal arts tower, the weather had again turned strangely tender; the sun gilded the wet pavements and roofs and turned the piles of snow translucent and black-speckled. Unwilling to go back to her dorm, Kit walked down through the old campus, past the library and the Wishing Well and out the tall gates into town. She felt, absurdly, fledged. On College Street she was invited by stores and streets but gently refused them, until she neared the central square of the town. There she turned, down Elm then Lincoln, not actually choosing these streets. In front of the Reformed EUB church there, a peculiar little car was parked, a man messing in its tiny trunk, from which smoke issued.

No, she was wrong, the smoke was from his pipe, a big curling gourd thing like Sherlock Holmes's. And it wasn't the car's trunk he was peering into in bafflement but its engine compartment. Yes: it was one of those comical German cars that were just arriving, Kit had seen a few but had never been in one, a car that looked like the one in the circus from which a huge number of clowns tumbled. A Volkswagen. VW.

"It wants to die," said the man, looking down at the absurdly tiny engine. "It just wants to die." He took the gourd pipe from his mouth and spat delicately, a fragment of tobacco. He had not spoken to Kit exactly, but when he looked up to see her, she shrugged in sympathy.

"Got gas?" she asked.

"Oh hell yes." He hunkered again and fingered a part tenderly: the carburetor? "Could I ask you a favor?"

"Um sure."

"Could you just sit in the driver's seat a minute and step on the gas while I."

"I guess."

He arose, and opened the door for her. There was the key; there was the choke; that was the clutch, that was the gas. Kit slid into the seat. With its round dials and simple switches, its little pedals and shapely wheel, it was the car, incarnate, that you drew for yourself, wanted for yourself, when you were six. A deep pleasure entered her.

"Okay," he called from behind. "Start her up." He had a slight Southern accent, unplaceable. She pulled out the choke and tried to start the car. In cartoons Volkswagens were shown with a big wind-up key in their backs.

For five minutes they worked, he calling for Kit to give it gas or turn it off, and finally a little cry of triumph. She eased off on the gas; it ran. He appeared in the window, great pipe in his teeth, and reached in to push the choke in with care.

"Well hell," he said, grinning. He was actually not old at all, a young man, very fair, thick blond nearly white hair falling over his brow that he tossed back when he straightened, narrow blue eyes and high cheekbones like an arctic explorer's. He held out a hand to her, and she took it.

"My name's Jackie," he said.

"Christa."

"Would you like a ride somewhere?"

"Sure."

"Could die again," he warned her.

She shrugged. He opened the door and she clambered over the gearshift sticking out of the floor like an old truck's, and onto the passenger's seat.

"Where'd you need to go?" Jackie asked.

"Nowhere," she said. "Where were you going?"

"Out to look at a new room to rent," he said. "Want to come?"

"Okay."

While they answered each other's inquiries—year, major, home-town—Kit tried to remember where she had seen Jackie before. There weren't as yet many places at the University she had been. It wasn't in the liberal arts tower or the dining room or at the French placement test.

He'd been around the campus on and off for a long while, it appeared; dropped out one semester, uncertain what he wanted to learn, went to work for his father (plumbing and heating) and read books. Bought this car. Turned twenty-one, which meant he could have it on campus, and live where he liked, but he still had a ways to go to get his degree.

"Philosophy," he answered in response to her own vagueness about what she would study. "Knowledge about knowledge. Seems basic to me."

She held the VW's steering wheel for him while he relit his pipe. The pipe, big as a plumbing fixture, should have seemed comic, but it didn't; he handled it with negligent expertise, stoking and sucking until the bowl glowed and threw off sparks, ropes of smoke snorting from his finely cut nose. Then she remembered where she had seen him: the field house. Not signing up for classes, or enrolling others in them, but amid the long tables set up in the corridors beyond the cashier's desks, tables which she had hurried past after finding she had lost her money: the tables where registered students could sign up for dozens of clubs, societies, and activities, the Newman Club, Hillel, the chess club, Helping Hands. She had hardly seen them, only marveled at the variety of them and their epigones. Young Americans for Free-dom, burr haircuts and striped ties. Booster Club in lettered sweatshirts and box-pleated plaid skirts. The Nietzsche Study Group, a joke maybe, two men in turtlenecks with a hand-lettered sign. One of them was holding a friendly intense discussion with a blond man in a duffel coat: Jackie, who was standing propped against the next table down the line, under a banner that said: YPSL.

"What did that mean—YPSL?"

"Young People's Socialist League." He looked over at her, and smiled at what was maybe wonderment in her face; she shut it.

"So are you a member of that?" she asked.

"Yipsle? Oh no. No no."

They were passing the gas stations and auto parts stores of the west end of town, and then the shuttered farm stands; the houses grew farther apart, and between them the corrugated fields, each black-earth furrow topped with frost, all lining up for an instant as you passed by and revealing the field's secret geometry.

"He lives down that way," Jackie said, pointing to a small road running between pied sycamores. "Your Russian poet. I think that's the road." Kit had told him about taking the course with Falin, and he had listened with interest. She looked quickly down the road as it went by; the way was blocked with evergreens; she thought she saw a gabled roof.

"How did you know that?" she asked.

"Well haven't you been paying any damn attention?" he asked in mock astonishment. "The man has appeared in every national magazine and the local rag too. A story about his vegetable garden. And that's where he lives. Right back there."

"Oh."

"Maybe we should go visit," Jackie said thoughtfully. "I can recite poetry. I can recite most of 'Little Orphant Annie' by James Whitcomb Riley."

"Sure, let's."

He made a sudden U-turn in the road, plenty wide enough for the toy car and completely empty.

"No!" Kit said.

"No? No?" He spun again, bouncing off the frozen shoulder to take them around again to face the way they had been going. "Now you see you have to make up your mind," he said with equanimity. "We can't be spinning here like a damn bumper car."

"I never meant it," she said.

"I'm happy to do whatever you like," he said. "Just give me that little advance warning." He looked at a wristwatch on a gold band. "I believe, however, that I'm now on the wrong damn road."

"You didn't leave the road you were on."

"I was on the wrong road from the start," he said. "I just now figured it out. West North Street, not East North Street. Ain't that something? North Street, named for a man called North, but then it got so long they had to name it East and West. All the way on the other side of town. It'll be too late to go visit them." He turned again in the roadway; as they went back past the poet's road, Kit could see lamplight in the windows, the short day darkening.

6.

Mondays, Wednesdays, and Fridays was Psychology, which Fran was taking too, a big lecture class followed by lab sections in which students, by feeding them or withholding food, caused white rats to press or not press bars or turn wheels. It wasn't what Kit or Fran either would have thought was meant by psychology; they had envisioned an array of explanations of themselves, convincing or not. But this university was a center of behaviorism, and in class they were taught never to speculate about what went on within the Black Box into which they fed their Stimulus and got their Response. We never say *The rat wants to get the food*, we never say *The rat is afraid of the electric shock*, we only count the number of repetitions or avoidances. Delightful small cold model of aliveness, it was hard to resist extrapolating from the twitch-nose rats to every birthday present, campaign promise, love letter, torture chamber, school prize, and any other human connection that could be thought of. They didn't resist, either, not the professor at his lectern (a beaky and high-domed Englishman who said *shed*-jewel and la-*bore*-a-tree), not his graduate assistants, not his students. Let your boyfriend undo your bra on one date, then forbid it the next two, then maybe yes again on the fourth: you are hooking him deeply through *intermittent reinforcement.* Stop answering his calls long enough, though, and you'll *extinguish the response.*

Tuesdays and Thursdays it was Falin's seminar in the same time period. *Another world* she wrote to Ben, but a world just as exact, just as precise in its accounts and descriptions, and less like a kid's game somehow, more serious—though she knew the Psychology grad students would have said the same the other way around: to them it was Poetry that was the game.

"We look now at a famous poem by English poet A. E. Housman," Falin said, turning the purple mimeo sheets to find the little thing, one of the few in the packet familiar to Kit. He looked down on it, nodded slightly as though in greeting, and then looked up. Kit wrote *famose boym* in her notebook. "What does it say and how is it made.

> *"Loveliest of trees, the cherry now*
> *Is hung with bloom along the bough,*
> *And stands about the woodland ride*
> *Wearing white for Eastertide."*

Two couplets, he pointed out, in a meter also favored by the Russian poet Pushkin and others writing in that language. Kit wrote in her notebook *D'Roshin boyt.* The stanza is very simple in form and thought, and has a figure only in the last line: the cherry trees are girls in white clothes, for church at Easter.

"Now the poet does some arithmetic," said Falin.

> *"Now, of my threescore years and ten,*
> *Twenty will not come again,*
> *And take from seventy springs a score,*
> *It only leaves me fifty more."*

"Arithmetic is hard to do in verse without clumsiness," he said. "So poets sometimes like to see if they can do this. And I have learned, though I did not know this when I first read this poem in Soviet Union, that the poet was professor of Latin, and worked for many years on a Latin poet who wrote about astrology, a poem filled with arithmetic in verse. So."

Kit wrote *Sov yetchunion*. Then she tore the page from her notebook and crumpled it, looking up to find them all regarding her, including Falin; and she lowered her eyes.

"Now see how he ends this small poem," Falin said. "He has said that he is young, but even so he knows life is short; here is what he now says:

> *"And since to look at things in bloom,*
> *Fifty springs are little room,*
> *About the woodlands I will go*
> *To see the cherry hung with snow.*

"Now do you see," he said to them with great strange tenderness, as though for them but also for Housman and the young man in the poem as well, "do you see: the only other *figure* in this poem is very last word, and it compares white blossoms to tree in winter, covered with snow. With *snow*, when all blossoms and leaves will be gone. In the very moment of his delight the poem reminds him, and us, that time will pass, blossoms will fall." He leaned forward toward all of them. "And it may well be that it was not Housman's thought but the poem itself that produced this meaning; that the poet reached next-to-last line and this rhyme arose of its own accord, with all these meanings. Yes I am sure, sure it did. A gift that came because of rhyme, came because rhyme exists. Because poetry is what it is. And because this poet was faithful."

They were all immobile in their chairs before him, stilled maybe (she was) by that word *faithful*. Kit would remember it: the word he used that day.

"And how unlikely is this, do you think?" he said. "To have this coincidence, I mean; these words and this man Housman occurring together at this time; this rhyme, this quickness to grasp it before it passed away. What are the odds of this, of exactly this poem existing in the world, coming into being in this form that we can apprehend, not failing somehow along the way or getting lost? I think odds are astronomical. Only the stars can model odds so great. That is the marvel and wonder of this enterprise of poetry: that we have *this*—and all its fellows, the real poems—among all other things that we have in this world.

"Which include, you know," he added smiling, "very many poems that are not real poems at all."

She was a good student: she had nothing else to do but her homework, and she did it, as she almost never had in high school. On a Friday after lunch she went up to her room to finish a poem of her own due for Falin's class at two, or maybe to write a letter to Ben. She didn't think that the poem she was writing was one of the real ones. It was carefully impersonal, artificial even, and she guessed that its cleverness—all it really had to go on—wouldn't be apparent to someone who knew English only uncertainly; jokes must be the last thing you begin to get. After poems themselves even. *Reverse your answer, Love: not no but on.*

The letter was the same. *In the kingdom of Rayn they used to cut your tongue out for lying—they did, Ben, didn't they?—but the sunsets were spectacular. Here it's the reverse.* Would he know she wasn't really talking to him, wasn't telling him anything because of something she couldn't tell? She hoped he knew, and she watched her hope carefully, so it wouldn't betray her to him.

That day she wrote nothing after all. She sat for a time unmoving at her tiny desk and then lay down on her bed. She closed her eyes and thought of having a machine like a tape recorder, only small, not suitcase-sized like George's, and so sensitive it could record her words as she thought them.

When she woke up, two hours had passed and half of Falin's class was over.

She lay a moment in astonished shame, feeling pinned to the bed. Except at Our Lady (sitting up in the dayroom chair, head lolling), she wasn't someone who slept in the day; it always made her feel dizzy and sad and heavy and hateful (as she did all the time at Our Lady). She felt horror too, the first class she'd missed. Oh well oh well. She went out into the silent halls (everybody else dutifully in class) and went to the bathroom to wash out her woolly mouth.

Then what? She sure wasn't going to walk into that class when it was almost over. She went back to her room and her desk and her letter to Ben. *I see Elvis got his discharge. They didn't wipe that smirk off his face though. If he can get out why can't you? I'm glad there's no war going on now Ben except for a Cold War. I really hate that term, Cold War, it almost makes me feel crazy to write it down: a war that's cold, what could be worse, that freezes instead of burning, everyone frozen in place, without passion or motion, as though it could last forever. But anyway they don't shoot at you, do they, the bad guys? And you don't shoot back. So that's all right.*

She opened her French text, and closed it again; she listened to the room and the building, lone footsteps in the corridor, tick of the heater. Weirdly, transgressively free. She put on her coat and went out walking.

Running from the University gates to the center of town, where a comical courthouse lifted a pointy dome, College Street passed by bookstores and diners and an art theater that was showing *The Cranes Are Flying*, and a coffee shop or restaurant that was a local landmark, the Castle, its front made to look like stone and little crenellations carved above the door.

Kit went into the bookstore, a crowded and cluttered one that had literary magazines and books of poetry and glossy paperbacks put out by university presses, and the *New York Times* a day late, and more commonplace things too. All her life Kit would find herself to be stingy and close about only one thing, and that was the buying of books, and she would never find out why, much as she questioned herself when she stood in a bookstore pondering the purchase of one, one she needed or wanted but couldn't bring herself to put down money for, since maybe after all she wouldn't read it: a kind of shyness or self-effacement. She looked them over now, her covetousness aroused but her hands remaining in her pockets. Among the books in Poetry was one called *Terror and the Muse: Soviet Poetry Under Stalin.*

She pulled it out. There was one poem of Falin's in it. Above it was a note by the translator, saying that it was part of a long poem called "Bez," which meant "without," or "-less" in compound words like *bez-lyubye*, "lovelessness." He said that in the long poem Falin created a choral meditation somewhat like a Russian *Spoon River Anthology*, or like Stephen Vincent Benét's celebrated *John Brown's Body*, a poem Kit had hated. She moved her finger down the lines, almost shy to look upon them; then she began to read, going back when she lost the thread, stitching it into her own thought as best she could.

After long thought I have at last decided:
I must write to denounce my neighbor.
Evidence both seen and invisible has so accumulated
That it cannot be ignored
And I know what my duty is.
I believe that nothing that has been reported can ever be erased,
And everything unreported likewise will not go unrecorded,
And everything that can be known is somewhere known,
If we are vigilant, and if we have done our duty.

I will tell how once returning home
On an evening when snow was beginning to fall
Seeing the light far off in his window
He began unaccountably to weep
And for a time could not go on.
It lasted only moments and he has forgotten it but there is no denying it.

I will denounce my neighbor for it is my duty
As smiling boys do their duty to wild birds:
Once, he cut a cabbage in half, and saw that the two halves
Were a demon's face and its reflection;
And he saw that each face also had two halves, left and right,
And he wondered if symmetry was the deepest truth about the world
Or if he only wondered at it because of his own division,
Himself a creature struck in two as by a swordcut
One half the inexact mirror of the other.

I will write if I can find paper and a pen
Though there have been sudden shortages lately of these things
Shortages that are certainly someone's fault
But around here we have done all right without these and other things.
If I can find no paper or pen, I will write in the wet sand
With one arm of a broken pliers;
I will sew letters together with hawthorns and straw,
I will write in spit on the pale undersides of leaves,
I will write with the torn hieroglyphics of moonlight on water.
It is my duty as a citizen not to keep these things hidden
But to bring them to the attention of those who need to know.

She sat down, on a box of books waiting to be unpacked, and read it again. She wondered what the duty of smiling boys to wild birds was; she wondered what words in the poem gave the sense of desolation and cold that she found in it. Something more than the "snow beginning to fall." *Bezlyubye:* lovelessness.

She slipped the book back into the space it had left.

Did it seem to be a poem by him, was it what she would have expected? She couldn't tell. She thought of him standing before their class and reading the poem by Pushkin; is that how he would read his own poems, this poem?

She went out of the bookstore and turned left the few steps to the

Castle; went to the counter and asked for coffee; sat with it before her, still seeing the page she had read. She wondered if there are some poems that are moving or touching simply because of the things to which they refer, the griefs and terrors that stand behind them. Would that be a bad kind of poem, would it be too easy to do that, to evoke those things that the reader will surely be thinking and feeling, though not because of anything you wrote, only because of the world in which you wrote? And would such a poem be different for readers who read it in another world, as she did, overhearing it maybe, something not intended for her ears at all?

She turned halfway around on her revolving stool just to feel it move, and found herself looking at Falin. He was sitting very near, in a high-backed booth, and he was looking at her. It was hard to believe she hadn't seen him when she came in. Maybe he had been summoned here by her thinking about his poem; or maybe she had been made to ponder his poem because he was himself so close by.

"Professor Falin," she said. She was about to go on, *so sorry about today*, when he raised a finger and wagged it No.

"Not professor," he said. "No. I profess nothing. I have no, no . . ." He was stuck.

"Degree. Ph.D.," she guessed. He nodded and shrugged as though that might be it.

"Well, um," she said, and he watched her search for some other form of address.

"Innokenti Isayevich," he said, smiling as though he knew this was well beyond this American girl to say, and he pointed at the booth seat opposite him. She got off her stool and slid into the seat somewhat mousily (could feel her head duck and her shoulders contract, why should they, but they did) and pressed her hands into her jacket pockets.

"Not in class today," he said. "You were sick?"

"Asleep," she said, unable not to.

"Ah well."

The counterman, before Kit could protest, placed her (cold) coffee before her. "I," she said. "I just now, just a little while ago, read your poem. It was printed in a book, an anthology . . ."

"No, no," he said, smiling again. "No, not my poem."

"The one about denunciation."

"My poem," he said, "was a poem in Russian. The poem in the book was a poem—perhaps a poem—in English. This I believe you read."

"Was it a bad translation?"

"I can't say," he said. "There were no rhymes, and my poem rhymed, and had a certain meter. The one there had no strict meter that I can perceive. It was free verse. Two poems could not be the same that differ so much."

"But I could see the poem in it, a little. What it was about."

"Ah. My poem and this one are *about* the same things. Perhaps. But even so they do not say the same things about those things."

"It was just so sad."

"I point out one small example," he said. "Where this translation said *I will denounce my neighbor* my poem said only *I will write about my neighbor.*"

"Why would they translate it that way then?"

"Because the translator was clever enough to know that in my country now, if we say someone has *written about* someone else, we mean the person has supplied to authorities information or just speculation, enough perhaps to have him investigated, even arrested. We say of someone, *I don't trust her—I think she writes.* So the poem may be read in that way, and that is why the translator chose this word *denounce.* But to write, in Russian, is still also to—to just write. Write letters, poetry."

She had never tried to translate poetry in any way except literally, as though cracking a code in which it was hidden, a chest or safe more beautiful than what was kept in it.

She said: "I don't see why it couldn't be translated more accurately."

"Perhaps it could." He moved the papers and things before him square with one another, his cigarettes and box of matches, notebook, a small book bound in pale green linen. "But it would then be differ-ent poem in English. Still not mine."

She thought this was too chaste, or too abnegating. It was too sad to think of too. She knew there were poets everybody said were impossi-ble to translate (Horace, Pushkin) and others that weren't (Shake-speare), but she didn't know why they said that, or what made the difference.

"Now in your poem of May," he said, and she felt a small sensation in her breast. "Could it, do you think, be translated so that every line would end as yours do, with a certain consonant?"

"I don't know," she said. "If I were a translator, I'd try."

He laughed in delight at this, and she thought she hadn't seen him laugh before; still his eyes went on taking her in, her and everything.

"Do you think," she said, "you'll ever write in English?"

"It would be hard choice to make," he said, as though he pondered it often.

"But why would it be a choice?" she asked. "Couldn't you write in both?"

"I don't know," he said. "It may be that languages are like lovers. You can have more than one at a time. But perhaps it is possible to love only one at a time."

She knew as little of lovers as of languages. She thought of a piece she'd read in *National Geographic* about an old Indian, the last of his tribe able to speak its language: it had never been recorded, and there was no one else left who understood it. You couldn't be more alone than that.

He had begun to gather up his things and put them in his funny case. He said: "May I ask you. In your poem. Was it, the soldier, a per-son now alive?"

"Well yes."

"It seemed when I read," he said, "perhaps not. Perhaps this poem told of a boy who every May returns. But who can come no closer."

"Oh no," she said. She saw that it could be taken so, she hadn't seen it but now she could, and always would. "No."

"Well." He stood, as though unfolding his long body. "Now. You must come to class next week."

"Oh yes, yes," she said ardently. "I mean that was just so not like me. Falling asleep."

"Since you have no doctor's excuse," he said, "you can now not get perfect grade. So you must come always."

He smiled at her, shrugging on his great enveloping coat; his smile, this amazing open secret. She didn't know whether to laugh because what he said was a joke, or look grave because it wasn't. She had understood all that he had said, with no way of knowing what he meant. It was as though he himself existed here in this town in this state in translation, ambiguous, slightly wrong, too highly colored or wrongly nuanced. Within him was the original, which no one could read.

He looked back, at the door, and she waved a small farewell.

She pushed away her cup, feeling both privileged and besmirched: anyway as she had not felt ever before. On the table was the box of matches he had toyed with, left behind. She touched it, pressed her thumb against the little paper drawer. Then closed her hand over it and pocketed it.

When she got back to her room, Fran was practicing, but stopped and put down her viola as soon as Kit entered.

"I like it," Kit said. "Go ahead."

"Eh," Fran said, a dismissive New York sound that by the semester's end Kit would have acquired from her.

"No really." Kit had avoided all her mother's efforts to give her music lessons, and the sight and sound of someone actually playing an instrument, in the flesh, an otherwise ordinary person like herself, thrilled and fascinated her, a magical act, or at least a magic act.

"Somebody called for you," Fran said, falling back on her bed with her Kierkegaard. "A sort of redneck-sounding guy? Named Jackie Norden?"

"Really?"

"Really," Fran said wearily.

"Well," said Kit. That sense of doors opening if you dared press on them, if you could find their knobs and jambs in the apparently seamless world around you. This one being the one she had long avoided or chosen not to see, the one she had skirted so artfully through school.

Except that she hadn't skirted it, not in the end. She had not skirted it at all.

"Well," she said again, alarmed and elated. "Well I'll be."

7.

The Christmas when Kit was a senior in high school, Ben came home on the last leave of his enlistment. He had been lucky to be posted in the States, he told her, he could have been one of the CIs they watched on TV, getting turkey dinners on desert islands or arctic airstrips, unwrapping presents from home.

That winter Kit had begun baby-sitting, and learned to write blank verse. She had little interest in babies and no natural ability with them, except in the telling of stories; yet she preferred infants and toddlers, who could be put to sleep early with any luck, releasing her to explore the still house in a close approximation of solitude, close enough to make her giddily gleeful. A sip or two out of the dusty liqueur bottles. Once she came upon the family supply of condoms in a blond dresser, though at first she didn't know what they were.

Blank verse was just a matter of nerve. At the library she'd come upon the old Mermaid series of Elizabethan poets, beautiful books that just fit into her new Mark Cross bag; and she started reading

Marlowe and Massinger and Webster and counting the beats on her fingers, da-dum da-dum da-dum da-dum da-*dum*. As soon as she found the courage to do it too, it began immediately knitting lines up as though by itself, long swatches growing longer, like the scarves Marion knitted while watching TV, holding them up at the night's end startled by their sudden length.

> *This Park is green. I will not see him here.*
> *So fall, you leaves, and change your seasons, trees;*
> *Turn, moons, from full to dark to full again*
> *Until earth bows her head before the sun*
> *And winter comes, and snow; and so does he.*

"Who's this 'he'?" Ben asked.

"Nobody," she said.

"Oh come on."

She meant it though. She thought her "he" was like that "she" who appeared in the poems of male poets so continually, who also appeared in their biographies sometimes, sometimes not. The Eternal Feminine, George had said, as though he knew this, as though everybody did. Female poets didn't seem to have an Eternal Masculine; the "you" or the "he" in their poems seemed to be more often actual people, being chided or pleaded with or charmed. *How do I love thee? Let me count the ways.* Kit loved nobody, but she thought she had a right to this faceless he anyway, and set herself problems in verse to solve, all about him. One or two she had put, anonymously typed, in Burke Eggert's locker or bookbag at school, knowing he'd never guess.

Burke was a football player and senior-class officer a year ahead of her, lean and tall (a quarterback), with Ben's dark short hair, but thick glasses too, designed probably to correct a still-detectable crossed eye: Kit cherished that weakness. She couldn't think of any way to attract him, and didn't try. In her diary and inwardly she assembled the parts of her crush like the elements of a hard poem, oddly assorted things to be connected in such a way that they made an anfractuous figure, a tetrahedron maybe, solid and gleaming and worthy of the feelings that had evoked it, that it evoked.

She hadn't written to Ben about Burke. She found she couldn't write down his silly name on letter paper. For one thing.

"Well it's swell," Ben said, and gave her back the sheet of onionskin.

He had changed while he was away. She watched him, they all did when he wasn't noticing; they could watch him because he didn't notice. Watched how he looked out the windows at the brown lawns and bare trees, trying to remember them maybe, or maybe not seeing them at all, his attention on something else: as though during his absence he had grown a private self, and was no longer whole, all of a piece, the way he had been. Kit babbled at him and teased him, afraid and cold inside.

Christmas Eve after George and Marion went to bed, Kit and Ben sat up; Kit insisted they watch an inane Christmas movie they'd seen together as kids. The only lights were the TV and the gray-green tree; already it looked a little tawdry and leftover, on the way out. On the sofa's broad arm were the two books Kit had given Ben, printed by the Peter Pauper Press: *The Flowers of Evil* by Baudelaire and Pascal's *Pensées*.

"A matched pair," she said. "Small, so you can carry them."

"Uh-huh," he said, nodding earnestly, maybe too earnestly. The Baudelaire had harsh, black woodcuts, dark women, demon lovers. It was for him, but even more it was from her: something of her, a part of her life for him to carry. The Pascal, though, was just for him, for his faith and his clear-eyed austerity: it scared Kit, but she thought Ben would respond. "So nicely wrapped too."

Kit had got a Christmas-season job at a department store downtown; they'd taught her to wrap, tie bows, skills she'd never lose.

"So Merry Christmas," she said; and because it was allowed, on this night of this year surely, she hugged him, laid her cheek against his rough one and held him a long time: feeling a hot dreamlike relief in his touch, a completeness, even as she felt him shrink and begin to extricate himself. *Merry Christmas* they said on the screen, the bishop's wife, the suave angel who had come from heaven to help them, the happy people. *Merry Christmas*, while the big flakes of snow fell on the black-and-white town and the overcoats and fedoras and pheasant-feather hats.

"So tell me," he said. "What's the plan? What are you going to do next year?"

"I don't know yet." She spread her skirt flat with her hands, far from him again; shy to be questioned, her imaginary futures brought forth. "I've sent away for some college catalogs. I could get a scholarship maybe. Mom wants me to apply to Vassar."

"Good school."

"Oh my God," Kit said. "All girls? I don't think so. I don't really like girls that much."

"No?"

"No. You know that."

"Just boys?"

"Well no, I mean . . . Oh you. You know. Ben: you know."

He wouldn't talk about his own plans for when he got out, whether he'd use the GI Bill to go to school or if he'd get a job or what; he deflected his family's inquiries with jokes, maybe he'd be a cop, the army was good training for police work, a lot of guys he knew. Or janitorial work too. Then Christmas night, as they sat in the kitchen eating cold turkey and pie, he told them what he had decided: he was going to reenlist when his hitch was done. *Re-up* he said: he'd learned a new language, and used it shyly but willfully, as though abandoning his old one in its favor.

"What?" Kit whispered in horror, before her parents could speak. "What?"

"I've been offered Special Forces," he said. "It's a program. Languages, and politics, and counterinsurgency." He spoke to Kit, until her face made him look away. "How to help ordinary people: what they call nation-building. You serve in lots of places."

"But for how long?" Kit asked, hearing the rising edge in her voice. "For how long this time?"

"Same again," Ben said smiling. "Just the training takes a year."

"But you've done what you were supposed to do," Kit said. She could feel her parents looking not at him but at her, at her weird intensity of feeling, her fear if that's what it was, the thing come to life in her stomach. "Your part or whatever. Why do you have to do more?"

"I don't have to. I mean it's not a law. I feel like I have to."

"You don't."

"I do. And I did. I mean I've accepted. I'm telling you now. I've re-upped."

She had stood now, napkin gripped in her hand. "Well why did you do that?" she said. She hated it that George and Marion could see her ask it, see her come out of herself to ask it in a voice full of tears. "Why did you go and do that? I thought you were coming home."

"Special Forces," George said. "They have the different uniforms, is that right? The green berets."

"That's right," Ben said. "Green Berets is what they're called. A special uniform."

"A special uniform!" Kit cried. "A special uniform, that is so great! Well gee no wonder!"

"Kit," Ben said.

"You said you'd come home," she said. Marion put her hand on Kit's arm but Kit shook it off as though not recognizing what it was. "You told me."

He shook his head, looking down at his folded hands and smiling. It was a look she knew. And Kit turned away, threw down the napkin, and went out.

Ben found her in the garage, wrapped in her winter dress coat, smoking a cigarette.

"When'd you start that?" he asked her.

"A while ago."

"What about . . ."

"They don't know."

"Well you ought to cut it out."

"All right," she said. She tossed the butt to the oily concrete and

ground it out. In the corner of the garage into which she stared was his
bike, covered in a tarp. "I hate you," she said.

"Kit." He sat beside her. "What did you think. What did you want
from me."

As soon as he spoke she saw clearly what she had thought, that he
would come home and that everything would be as it had been, which
was impossible. Nothing is ever as it was, it is always as it *is*, and then as
it will be.

"It happens," he said. "People grow up and move on. They have
things they want to do. Have to do."

"What," she said. "You mean your war."

"Not mine."

She waited, not looking at him still but poised to counter whatever
he might say. For a while he didn't speak further, as though what he
thought was gathered within him but hadn't ever been wholly said,
and needed a moment to turn into words; and when he spoke it was as
carefully as if the words might be the wrong ones, or words the wrong
medium. "I do think there's a war on," he said. "I do think I have to
fight it. I think everybody has to. I think Dad is fighting it in his way.
Maybe you'll find your way. This is my way." He clasped his hands
between his knees and studied them. "I haven't shot anybody and I
probably never will. The whole idea is to do what it takes so that you
don't have to shoot. But it's still a war, and you can be on God's side or
not: there's no other way to say it."

She still wouldn't look at him, but she could see the light of the bare
bulb overhead caught in the red stone of his high school ring.

"You know," he said. "When I was wondering what I should do,
what I could personally do, and they pitched this program to me—I
thought: Okay, I can do this; or I can join the priesthood."

Now she looked at him, and he smiled at her amazement. "The
priesthood, yeah. Yup. I've thought about it. A lot. I decided I can't do
it, though. I'd have a problem with the vows."

"You would? You?"

"Well. Not with poverty, or obedience."

She laughed, feeling a sudden awful vertigo, a doom opening beneath her that she had known about all along and hadn't wanted to see: why she was losing him. It wasn't war or Cold War or the army, he would go away from her no matter what, into whatever life he could flee to. He had asked her *what did you want from me* in that way, meaning that what she wanted was impossible, and it was, and she knew why. She shook her head, hands pressed to her eyes as though to keep from looking down so far: laughing, laughing and then crying, crying at last.

"Sis," he said. "Sis."

What she had *thought*, what she had *wanted*. He had stepped back from the edge of an abyss, that's what he had done; and she was the abyss. He put his arm over her shaking shoulders and in heedless defiance she turned into his embrace and wrapped her arms around him and pressed her wet cheek and mouth against his cheek.

"No look," he said. "Look, you've got to get over this," not trying to tear himself from her now or slip from her but speaking to her tenderly and insistently. "You've got to grow up, Kit. You've got to. Everybody, everybody."

"You won't come back," she said.

"I'll come back," he said. "I'll always come back." But she knew what this meant now, what it meant for him to say this: it meant that he wouldn't come back, could not ever come back, that no one ever can; to say that he would was to admit that he couldn't, to admit that there was no way back at all.

She didn't behave well the next days, the last of Ben's leave, she knew it but couldn't stop, would every day hit upon the wrong thing to do and then with grim elation do it. Mostly she stayed in her room, waiting for his knock on her door, once slamming it in his face when he did come and then said the wrong insouciant impertinent thing. Sat folded up in her little velveteen armchair or under her quilt feeling herself seethe and boil uncontrollably, trying to think who she could be if she could no longer be herself, which she could not. Then she emerged suddenly, hectic smile pasted on, willing to let him take her for walks around the courts and drives and circles; she'd talk and talk, romping and frisking by his side like a bad puppy. *Okay okay* he'd say at last and she'd shut up and turn to go back, walking far ahead of him, hands in her pockets and shoulders hunched.

The morning he left he put his leather jacket around her shoulders. Keep it till I get back. Don't lose it. Don't give it away. She put it on over her nightgown and said nothing and did nothing until he had gone out the door with George and she heard the car start and turn out onto the street; then she tore open the door and broke away from Marion and ran in her slippers over the snow crying his name, knowing they wouldn't hear or turn back.

Her job downtown changed after Christmas: now she stood at the window where people brought back the ravished packages she had made up the month before, dissatisfied, annoyed, exasperated, apologetic. Kit took the unwanted things and looked at them while their owners gave their reasons for rejection. Harmless hopeless unwanted things. After a dinner break she didn't go back to the window where she had stood; went out of the store to the bus stop blocks away. A bus stopped but she didn't get on; let it roll away.

Sometimes looking back Kit can see herself—by that trick of memory or imagination whereby we see our past selves from the outside, like people in a movie—on that street corner in the evening as she must have looked when Burke Eggert saw her, skinny in her flat shoes and straight skirt, hugging herself in Ben's jacket, trying to warm herself with a cigarette. Why he chose to pull over and talk she couldn't know, but surely it was something like his pulling over that she was trying to cause by her standing there.

"Hey."

"Hey, Burke." She hadn't seen Burke since he had graduated in June. She felt a profound and exhilarating indifference. If nothing mattered then it didn't matter what she said, or what she had once felt or not felt or written or done. "Hey, how's it going. How's tricks."

He grinned at her, maybe a little baffled, leaning out the open window. The car was a Studebaker, a Hawk. Burke's father had a dealership.

"Whatcha doing?" she asked. "Big graduate."

"Oh. Not much."

"*Not much?* What, not much?"

"Well." He laughed at her vehemence. "I don't know. Working for my dad."

"Hey! Your dad!"

"Thinking of going to pharmacy school."

"Pharmacy school!"

"Well. It's only two years. Not like college."

"Well sure."

"I always got pretty good grades in chemistry. Hey, are you cold?"

"I'm freezing."

"You want a ride somewhere?"

"Um sure." She went around the Hawk's sloping snarling nose and into the warm insides. "Nice car." She knew that the girl she was imitating here would say this, so she did. She even stroked the dash appreciatively.

"Well, it's not mine. I mean it's the dealership's."

"I've none of my own, said the Hatter, I only keep them to sell," said Kit. "Right?"

"Um right."

"So how's it going?" she asked again. "You married or engaged or anything?"

"Jeez no." He grinned. "Give me a while."

"What about what's-her-name. Mary Anne."

"Mary Jo." He shrugged one shoulder, eyes on the street. "She's at school. State."

"Oh." Mary Jo had worn Burke's great ring around her neck on a chain, too wide for her finger. How about through her nose, Kit had asked of no one, like a bull's, or a cannibal's bone. "You want to know something? I used to have an awful crush on you."

He grinned sideways at her, pleased and surprised but not exactly astonished; his walleye gave him an expression of devilish interest Kit was pretty sure he didn't intend.

"Oh yes," she said. "Of course you never gave a look my way." *As far as I could tell* she thought of adding, and laughed.

"Well," he said. "Hey. You were so, I don't know. Standoffish. Like you thought we were all beneath you."

"*Beneath* me?" she said. "Really?"

"Like you were better than us."

" 'Us'?"

"Well, everybody."

"No," she said. "I never thought that." She had, though; and realized in amazement that what she had felt she had shown. "I even," she said, "gave you a poem I wrote. A couple."

"That was you? You? And you *wrote* those?"

"Yup." She shrugged, she'd done it, couldn't help it.

"I thought somebody copied those out of a book. Like for homework. God."

"Nope. Me."

He shook his head and let a little sound escape his throat, a little cough of disbelief. "Damn," he said.

"I had it bad," she said.

"You were just kidding," he said. "Come on."

She didn't answer. For some minutes she had been filling with some clear astringent fluid, a fuel that raced effervescent in her veins and skin, and she didn't know what she would do or say next.

"So how come you're not in school?" he asked. "You didn't quit, did you?"

"Christmas vacation!" she said, and slapped his wrist lightly, you silly.

"Oh right," he said. "Yeah. Two weeks."

"Not for you, huh."

"No. Day or two at Christmas." He hooked an arm over the seat between them and looked ahead as though seeing more than the street. "School was easy," he said, and Kit seemed to see a devolution in Burke Eggert's life, a decline in status that might go on a long way; and felt a delicious pity. "So how are you spending all the free time?" he asked.

"I got a job at Robertson's. Actually I just quit."

"Huh."

"And I baby-sit. You know." Her heart suddenly filled with that hot clear blood and she said, "Actually I'm baby-sitting tonight. Right near here."

"Really."

"A Dr. Thorne. Pippi. Pippi Thorne."

"No."

"Yep. Hey, maybe you could come over later. They've got a big house. Big TV."

He smiled at her in a way that she would come to recognize, after she'd seen it in enough men: a look of glee and uncertainty mixed, as though they've pulled off a trick but wonder if maybe they're the butt of one too: even in this first instance of it she sensed what it meant, and that she had caused it. "We can catch up," she said. "The old alma mater."

"Sure."

"I'll show you where his place is. It's on the way to my house."

They both fell silent then, and watched the road till she pointed out the Tudor pile of Dr. Thorne's house. "Pippi's good," she said. "She'll be asleep by eight."

"Hey. Good."

"Okay," she said. "So. My place is down that way. Take Elderberry Drive."

He let her off—didn't get out to open her door as she momentarily waited for him to do—and she went in and up the half-flight of stairs to her room.

"Kit?" her mother called. "You home?"

"Yes."

"It's early."

She didn't answer. On the back of her closet door was a mirror, a full-length one; by swinging open the door fast and wide she was able to take from the closet what she wanted without seeing herself in it, and close the door again before it caught her. She thought for a mad moment of calling down to her mother, asking her how it actually happened, this that was going to happen to her, for she knew it was going to happen, all of it or some part of it.

You've got to grow up, he'd said, everybody does.

"Do you want an egg?" Her mother called. "It's what I'm having. I didn't expect you."

"No, Mom, it's okay."

She took from her drawer a panty girdle; she had two, worn so far only once each, a Little Godiva by Warners and a Magic Lady by Exquisite Form. When she had got into the one she chose and felt its grip around her, she picked a cashmere skirt to go over it, soft over strong. She thought: This isn't so hard.

She drew on pale stockings. Once in a poem she had compared her mother's peeled-off nylons to rags of sunburned skin. The skin of her own legs was weirdly cold, her knee a cold stone, her toes nearly numb. The stockings went clipped to the stretchy clips that dangled from the girdle. The poem was called "Skin." Ben's leather jacket was in it too. It would be one of the poems that eventually Kit lost, that was lost for good, burned up and lost.

8

The house on East North Street where Jackie had found a room was a bleak frame place of dirty white clapboard, as square and plain as an old farm wife; but there was a tangled grape arbor that would be green in summer, and tall elms along the road whose graceful lyre shaped arms would be full of languid leaves (only they wouldn't; the blight of those years would reach them that spring, and they'd begin to die). Jackie took Kit up the back steps to the kitchen door, called a greeting into the summer kitchen (where boots and coats and unreturned bottles were piled) to let his housemates know he was there, and led her in.

"Howdy, Max."

Max looked around the book he held up before him propped in the fingers of one big hand, and nodded to Kit.

"Don't get up," Jackie said. "Don't feel you have to."

"I had no plans to," Max said. His soft accent was country, like Jackie's, but some other country, farther west or north.

"This here is my friend Christa Malone."

"Hi, Christa Malone."

"Kit," she said.

"You'll like Max," Jackie said, pulling off his long scarf. "Max, Kit's a writer. A real writer. A poet."

"Well say," Max said with sweet careless awe.

"Do you write?" Kit asked.

"Just letters," Max said, and laughed. All this while he had held the book up before him (it was called *To the Finland Station*) and now he let it down. "What poets do you like?"

"Oh gee," said Kit. "Oh lots."

"She reads Bode Lare," said Jackie. "In French."

"Well I should hope," said Max. "You've heard about this guy Falin?"

"She's taking his course, for Christ's sake. A freshman."

"Huh."

"She's kind of in love with him too. Am I right? Anyways I hear a lot about him."

She wouldn't answer that, shook her hair and lifted her chin as her mother did when something was said in her presence that she chose not to hear.

"Well. So. Welcome to our house, Kit," Max said. *"Bienvenue."* And he raised his book again.

Jackie took her around. The house was comically grim in some ways, the window frames black with years of fingerprints, the furniture and walls covered with materials that someone must have chosen long ago, but which were so resolutely ugly that you couldn't imagine how or why, indecipherable squiggles of brown on brown or lurid false flowers and fruit. The rooms were piled with the gear of four men in amazingly thorough disarray, books stuffed into shelves made of concrete blocks and boards and piled-up orange crates, records in a stack beside the record player and soda bottles clustered on the refrigerator's top: she thought it was the happiest place she'd ever been in. Jackie's room held a walnut double bed clad in a ratty quilt and a dresser and mirror that matched it, like the furniture a ship's captain might own, and a huge plush armchair.

"All mine," he said. "Twelve bucks a week."

It smelled of his tobacco and his woolens and his maleness. She thought of having her own room, in a house like this; a chair like that one, a lace curtain, a whispering radiator. Girls couldn't: not unless they were married. "Nice," she said.

That spring she and Jackie went to the movies, and to restaurants to eat what he called pizza pie; they sat in student lounges together and she listened to him talk; they went to lectures and readings and they studied together at the library. Everybody did those things and she thought it was strange and remarkable that she was doing them too, that these things had been waiting here for her to do, who so far in her life had done so little that everybody else did. But the house on East North Street wasn't like the places everybody went, and it had been waiting for her too.

Max was the one renting the house, to whom the others paid rent— Jackie; and Rodger, a fastidious Negro; and the new housemate they'd just acquired, a graduate student who was not taking any classes just then: his name was Saul Greenleaf, and with his round steel-rimmed glasses and his tight shabby overcoat and almost shaven head he looked like he had emigrated from a Dostoevsky novel, or had decided to seem so. The place was too far out of town to live in without a car, and that meant no undergraduates under twenty-one: they each had one, except Rodger, who got back and forth on a comical Vespa, perched on its little seat, his porkpie hat and earmuffs on his head.

"But are they really Communists?" she asked Jackie in the Beetle, going back to campus on a Thursday night, trying to beat the clock.

"Now how am I supposed to answer that?" he said. "I mean right now at this moment. You know I'd be accusing them of being members of a criminal conspiracy?"

"It's what you said," she said. "My Commie cell."

"Oh, hell, girl. Oh my lord." And he wiped the little windshield with the back of his gloved hand in apparent exasperation.

Kit had only ever half-believed in the existence of Communists in America; they were like fairy-tale bears or the burglars that crept into Dagwood's house in the midnight. At twelve she watched the robotic conspirators of *I Led Three Lives* on TV and wondered why they spoke without their Russian accents. If they were Communists, why did they sound American? George had taken the family through Washington, D.C., on their way from one city to another, and there they toured the FBI headquarters and the government buildings; and, because the committee was in recess, they could look into the room where Senator McCarthy held his hearings: far smaller-seeming than the blackish crowded pit they watched on television where the draconic senator talked and talked and never listened. He's an ugly son of a bitch, George would say, but he's *our* ugly son of a bitch. And Marion begged him not to swear.

But Max said: "Last summer I spent working these peace booths at state fairs. We'd go around in this bigole pickup with this knocked-down booth in the back and boxes of literature. People'd come up to me and hear me talking about colonialism or the bomb or who was responsible for the Cold War, and they'd start railing on Communists. Communists, these damn Communists. And I'd say hey, hold on now, *you're talkin' about my mother.* They'd look at me like I'd turned into a Russky before their very eyes. It certainly shut 'em up." He smiled to remember, delighted. "They were good people. Country people. Didn't want to say anything bad about a fellow's mom."

Saul was a city kid from Chicago, but he and Max were both red-diaper babies, they said; their parents had been involved all their lives in what they called progressive politics. Saul Greenleaf's earliest memory was being wheeled in the May Day parade in Chicago. Kit listened, thinking of the May Day processions she had walked in, to crown the Virgin Mary Queen of the May.

"Oh yeah," her roommate, Fran, said dismissively when Kit tried to taxonomize these specimens unknown to her. They weren't unknown to Fran, who'd gone to the Little Red Schoolhouse in the Village ("the 'little pink schoolhouse,' everybody called it") and had known the type well at her Manhattan high school, which she called the High School of Music and Ott. "Oh sure. Solidarity. The peace-loving peoples of the world. Ban the bomb. Oh all the time."

So they were real after all, and there were lots of them, and there were others who took what they said seriously or with the easy contempt that comes with familiarity, but who still themselves held what seemed to Kit to be children's opinions: they said things that no grown-up she had known, her relatives and teachers and parents, the priest and the principal, ever said plainly, that war was criminally stupid and bombs were insane, that fairness was better than cruelty, and that people were all basically the same, at least in their claims on the means of life: convictions that she had unconsciously supposed you had to give up or at least keep quiet about in order to grow up yourself.

Jackie laughed and shook his head at her naiveté, delighted to lecture her about the jealousies and hatreds that in fact divided these people, the deep and narrow gulfs fixed between CP and Trotskyists, between the Young People's Socialist League and the Young Socialist Alliance, the War Resisters League and the Student Peace Union, and which were the fronts of which others, who took orders from whom and who didn't: an encyclopedic knowledge that seemed at odds with his general approbation of people like Max and Saul, *people who think* and *sharp minds*.

"So which one do you belong to?" she asked him.

He regarded her as though, a child, she had made a coarse *faux pas* she couldn't have understood. "Oh," he said. "I ain't a joiner."

It was evident to Kit that the FBI had nothing to fear anyway from these people. They had the cheerful contempt for Russian Communists that a smart young pony might have for an old gelded cart horse. They acknowledged the Russians' primacy, and allowed only one another to slight them or make fun of them; in any face-off with the United States they were quick to point out where their own country was in the wrong. But their heroes were different ones: Trotsky, fallen eagle, murdered in Mexico; Mao in Yenan, writing poetry; Joe Hill, the bosses couldn't kill him; above all Fidel and Che and their young bearded men, stripped to the waist cutting cane alongside the people, teaching kids to read. They talked of how when Fidel came to New York to speak at the United Nations, instead of the Waldorf-Astoria he went up to Harlem to stay at the Hotel Teresa; how he joked in English with the students at Johns Hopkins. The young men at East North Street seemed to feel about Fidel and the Cubans the way so many she knew felt about Kennedy: whatever else they were or might become, they weren't old and sick and stuck.

The group formed a Fair Play for Cuba Committee chapter and held meetings in the living room at North Street. Delegates came from some of the alphabet-named groups on campus, and some refused to send one, but it was Max and Saul who ran the meetings, read from the literature sent out by the national committee, answered the questions.

Was it true that the Soviets were sending military help to Cuba?

"Sure," Saul said. "And isn't that reasonable? I mean the U.S. invaded the country. But the U.S. line is that anybody who thinks our intentions are anything but sterling is either falling for Communist propaganda or is paranoid. Right. Sure. Look at Arbenz, for Christ's sake. Look at Lumumba."

Did he think that the United States would actually invade Cuba again? The cigarette smoke was thick in the room. Kit didn't know the persons who were asking.

"Yes. Absolutely. They'll invade as soon as they think they can get away with it. But as long as they still care about world opinion, they might hold off. That's why we're here. That's why we're doing this."

And so then will the United States be able to overthrow the Castro government? Or not?

"That depends," Saul said, and lifted his head.

"Depends on what?" Kit said.

"It depends on whether, right now, History needs a martyr, or needs a hero," he said. The shine on his glasses hid his eyes, and Kit couldn't tell if he was wholly serious; but a kind of premonitory black triumph arose in her own breast that amazed her. Martyr or hero.

The delegates agreed on an open letter about the U.S. threat to the existence of Cuba as an independent nation, to be sent to whoever might print it and signed by as many important people on campus as they could persuade. And they went on talking, talking. At last Kit tugged Jackie's sleeve: she had to get back to her dorm.

"You ought to take that open letter to your friend Falin," Jackie said. "He's the kind of name it needs."

"Oh sure," she said. "I'm supposed to ask him that?"

"Why? You think he wouldn't agree? Wouldn't want to sign? What makes you think that?"

"I don't know."

"Just because you got a crush on him," Jackie said. "Don't mean you know him." At that she decided to take offense, and said nothing more the rest of the way home.

"Anyway," Jackie said, letting her out at her dorm. "You keep it with you. That letter. Keep your eyes open and wait for a good time to ask him. Learn a little about him meanwhile. You owe it to yourself."

A crush, an obsession with a magnetic teacher: she couldn't believe that it was actually a category of feeling, a very common one around here, Jackie said. She did think about Falin a lot, but it was because she knew nothing of him, of his self and his past; only of his future, which she knew just to the extent that it was hers too, American. What she didn't and probably couldn't know about him gripped her, it was a fascination that seemed to her pure, almost impersonal, like a scientist's obsession with the source of a river or the unseen side of the moon.

She watched for him. She did do that. There was always the possibility that he might appear near her or in her view on campus or at lectures or elsewhere and some tiny thing more would be revealed. When she did see him she could often not keep from following him, unseen, *shadowing* him, which was easier to get away with than she would have thought; all it took was alertness and a heart quiet enough to make the right smooth movements so that the other's *peripheral vision* was not alerted. She had measured Fran's peripheral vision in Psychology, where she had learned the term; one day it would become the title of a book of her poems. She kept the open letter in her bag, a sort of so-there to Jackie, she was only doing her part as Jackie had said she should: but she didn't tell Jackie or anyone.

She came upon him on a March night taking his long strides across the old campus, and she followed not far behind, ready to turn away and be no one that he knew if he turned toward her, if he felt her glance on his back and his high head, which he wouldn't, because it was so light, so nonexistent. She lost him, though, from being too care-fully inattentive, and she slowed uncertainly; she could see down all the lighted paths, he couldn't have gone far.

He was gone, gone entirely, vanished.

She walked on toward the library, feeling an Alice feeling of having been put in the wrong by a being who didn't follow the laws of physics. Then she found she was walking right toward him: he stood before the library, and he was talking to a slim dark woman, or rather listening to her talk, she seemed distraught or upset somehow, she talked and shook her head and almost seemed to tremble: and then as Kit came close, almost too close, unable not to, the woman pressed her cheek against his coat.

Kit couldn't walk on or she'd pass right by them, but if she stopped or turned abruptly away she'd catch their eye, she knew it. She fell in behind two students going up the steps into the library, and went in too, nothing else she could do, feeling the scene she had witnessed go on behind her, precious and lost.

Now what. She moped in the atrium for a time, peeked out the doors when they were thrown open, but there was nothing to see. She couldn't go back out, for fear he and the woman would be still there, having decided to sit on one of the benches there by the library. She had no chores to do here. She walked in the reading room; she climbed the stairs; she went to the sepulchral toilet on the second floor that no one ever used.

She walked back through the periodicals room and saw him sitting at a table and reading. His coat over the back of the chair and the green-shaded light on his book as though he had been there for hours.

She moved closer to where he sat, going carefully up between the open periodical shelves filled with bound journals, till she found a gap wide enough to see through, see the room and him.

One elbow on the table and the L of his finger and thumb supporting his chin. Slowly and infrequently his other hand turned a page, but the rest of him was very still. What was it he read? She could sense his eyes moving over the big pages, absorbing what he looked at. She stood on her toes to see.

It was an ad, a double-page spread: a huge purple Nash Ambassador of 1955 or '56, passing diagonally through the white space, gleeful dad at the wheel with hat and pipe. She knew what car it was because Ben had taught her all the cars of those years, all the distinctive grilles and taillights.

He was reading a bound periodical, *Life* or *Look* or *Colliers*. He turned another page: a story of sea rescue; a mom and her new refrigerator; a bottle of Scotch. *Don't spill a drop, that's Old Smuggler.* Was he practicing his colloquial English, learning to be an American?

She walked back down the stacks and came out behind the row of tables where he sat, careful to stay just barely in motion, and not stare, so that no student in his line of sight would puzzle at her, and awaken his notice. He turned the page again.

Kit had sometimes thought heaven would be like the reading of an endless, or eternal, big slick magazine. Always interesting and undemanding, a new page to be turned whenever boredom threatened, to reveal something welcomed and unexpected: new things to desire, but not seriously; new beautiful movie stars or homes you might be or live in; moving stories of children far away, of dangers or bad weather, but not where you were; always more silly or witty ads and clear-eyed people looking right at you and brief cute anecdotes, no end to it ever. Happiness.

It was as though he were feeling or thinking just that: feeling what she felt, looking at the same magazine she had looked at five years ago, the cars and dresses by now already replaced by different ones. Maybe it was she he was trying to understand.

She actually laughed to think this stupid thought, and he looked up and saw her.

"Hi," she said or whispered, still laughing a little.

"Miss . . . Malone," he said.

"Kit."

"Kyt." He folded his hands in his lap. She had to lean close to him so that their talk wouldn't disturb others. "I do not need to ask why you are here. To read books. Poetry."

"No," she said. "Actually."

"Not I either," he said. He folded shut the huge book, big as a Gutenberg Bible, with a smack that caused heads around the great room to lift and look. "Enough," he said. "Time for tea, and a smoke. Yes?"

It seemed like an invitation. He took his overcoat from the back of the chair, and his case, and went out and down the stairs, she following his long stride.

"So why were you looking at them, those old magazines?" she asked. "Why do they interest you?"

He shrugged, which didn't seem to suggest he didn't know. "To live in any world—in any country—you must know the dreams."

"Not everybody dreams of a new refrigerator."

"I think in this way," he said. "Here as in Soviet Union you are promised a better future. Have always been promised. A bright future. After a time this future grows old, and has no power to come about. Yet promise is not forgotten. Stalin famously said long ago: *Life is getting better, more cheerful.* Then came purges, then fear, then war."

The library was closing. They went out under the rotunda with the last stragglers and into the night, which seemed warmer than it ought to be, a sudden warmth, a promise.

"So promises are not fulfilled," he said. "But they remain, they can

be found. And there remains caught in them the happiness they promised. This precious thing."

Happiness. She was silent beside him, her feet falling alongside his,
knowing she hadn't understood.

"So," he said, as though he had made himself clear. He had stopped
beneath a tall lamp by the path, and drew out a cigarette and lit it with
a wooden match. She caught a whiff of its odor, mingled with March
night air. He had not bade her good night, so she walked beside him
when he set off again.

"Tea," he said. "Now I think this place just down there, where once
we talked, has just closed for the night. We have been long at our studies. We will go to All-Night Cafeteria, I think its name is. Down and
left and further down."

She skipped to keep up with his long stride. She thought how easily
she could take his arm to keep up; or she could put her hand in his,
though her little spidery one wouldn't fill his. She could· she could
change the world just by deciding to do that. Like a general deciding
to throw all his forces at a single point, knowing it would change everything, for the better or not for the better at all, and no going back. Take
his hand and stop his walking and make him turn to her; and put her
face against his coat's lapel. She would never dare. Just to think the
thought made her burn.

"In June," he said. "Last year. At graduation ceremonies. Though I
had been here but few months, I was asked to sit on the platform,
the . . ."

"Dais," she said.

"Yes, where sat all teachers and professors. And there listened to
speech by the president of university. He said to students that they
must be true to their dreams. He said it was not so important what
dream or goal or hope they had; most important was that they had a
dream. That they held on to this dream, through, through . . ."

"Through thick and thin?"

"Just what he said, thick or thin. And I thought that perhaps after ceremony I might take him aside and tell him that after all one dream is not like another. Some dreams we do *not* wish that people stick to: we hope they are weak, and do not cling to these dreams, that they fail to hold on. A dream that one day this world will be free of Jews. That Soviet Union will be destroyed. That all enemies of the state will be crushed. That only one God prevail everywhere."

"Well he wasn't talking about that kind of dream."

"No. Certainly not. I understand. I think how wonderful it is, what wonderful country, that you may speak to young people and tell them to *believe always in their dreams,* and not be afraid of what those dreams may be.

"Now. Here."

It was called the 24-Hour Grill, in fact, a funny little streamlined submarine powered by the great fan in its backside, lifting the periscope of a tin chimney. She wondered how he had first found this place, whether there was some memory of home for him in it. The heat inside steamed the windows opaque, and the coffee urns and the griddle steamed and smoked too; the place smelled pleasantly of grease and coffee and burnt toast and people's damp wool. The jukebox was loud:

> *Be my be my baby*
> *My one and only baby*

"Draw one," called the elderly waitress to the cook after hearing their order. "Drop one."

"Coffee and tea," he said confidentially to her. "The coffee is *drawn* from the urn; the tea is in the bag, *dropped* in cup."

His coat hung on the brass hook by the booth's end, and she noticed that in its pocket peeping out was a book, the same hay-green volume he'd had when she met him before, by chance that time. He saw her look, and took the book out, turned it so that she could see the title on the spine: *A Shropshire Lad* by A. E. Housman.

"Was this the book where you found the poem you talked about in class?" Kit asked. "The cherry trees?"

"No no," Falin said. "No, I read that poem in a volume of English poems with Russian translations, made perhaps 1920. New English poems; new then. I read it in prison. Many times."

"You were in prison?"

"I was not only in one."

"What for? I mean . . ."

"Do you know," he said, "this was first question, often, that our interrogators asked. *Do you know why you have been arrested?* And many, many people did their best to tell them why. If they did not know, to make guess. Even if there was no reason."

She must have gaped, trying to work this out, for he lifted a hand as though to forestall what she might be thinking. "Well, well. They were overworked, you know; they used what means they could. Policemen everywhere do it, perhaps. As though to say to you: *I know, but you tell me.*"

"And the poems? They let you have them?"

"They gave them to me. Among other books. This was in transit camp. After arrest. Before sentence. We read part of every day."

"Really? Well. I wouldn't have thought."

For a moment he regarded her as though he were thinking how much he should say to her as though he measured her. "It was a former institute," he said. "In 1947 were many, many prisoners. Camps very crowded. Many buildings taken over. In mine we were seven men in room like . . . like my office here, you know? Every day certain things happened. Take out latrine bucket. Eat, twice, same thing, soup. Inspection. And distribution of books. It must be there was still large library in this place; many odd books given us. Some even explained us to ourselves. Books of history. Poetry in several languages."

"How did they choose them?"

"Oh they didn't. Guards could not read such things, mostly. They only took from shelves." He laughed, as anyone might at a funny memory. "There is no doubt this was a mistake. But giving us books kept us quiet. You see, totalitarian state—even if they wanted it to be so, there were many holes. Holes everywhere, large and small."

"So you read."

"Sat and read. As far from my fellows as I am from you. Two hours, until light was too weak."

"Then?"

"Sit. Talk. Argue. Go out for interrogation. No sleeping though. Not allowed in day."

She felt a strange grip in her insides, a shiver across her breast. "No," she said.

"You learned to sleep eyes open."

"Yes." She looked down into the muddy brown round of her coffee. When she looked up again she found he had not ceased regarding her. He had not said what he had been arrested for; for nothing, for poetry. She wouldn't ask. She opened the book; it fell open to a page he had bent it to, she thought. He saw what page it was and began to speak, looking at her, saying the lines as though he were discovering or inventing them, and for her.

> *"From afar, from eve and morning*
> *And yon twelve-winded sky,*
> *The stuff of life to knit me*
> *Blew hither: here am I.*
>
> *Now—for a breath I tarry*
> *Nor yet disperse apart—*
> *Take my hand quick and tell me*
> *What have you in your heart.*
>
> *Speak now, and I will answer;*
> *How shall I help you, say;*
> *Ere to the wind's twelve quarters*
> *I take my endless way."*

He sat back. Their submarine moved through the deep. As he spoke, the place had grown strangely silent, attentive; or it seemed to

Kit that it had. Now the music and the talk and the clatter of dishes poured apologetically back in, around her and him. It seemed a long time too before he spoke again, or as though no time passed.

"Now perhaps you will tell me," he said, taking the book gently back from her. "Why you have such interest in me."

"Oh," she said.

"Such interest that you would enjoy to follow me all this evening."

She froze. Once when she was twelve she had been caught shoplifting: something, nothing, a candy bar, a lipstick. The saleslady's hand on her wrist, a sudden roar in her ears. His face, though, showed nothing but simple interest, his eyes alight, as they always were.

"I didn't actually," she said. "I mean I wasn't really . . ."

"Was there," he asked, "something you want to know?"

She shook her head.

"Nothing? Well if you say so I will not ask further."

After what seemed to her a long moment she spoke, almost too softly to be heard: "Where did you learn English? Did you just teach yourself, or . . ."

"Oh no. In school," he said. "English was popular subject. I was prize student. Many Russians who write earn living in translation."

"I thought you studied drafting."

"Language too. A gift."

She tucked these things away. "When you came here," she said. "Did they make you come alone? Were they not going to let any of your family leave with you?"

"I had no family left. I'm sure that if I had, then no, they would not have let them come."

"You have no family now?"

"My parents are dead. I was their only child."

"No wife or kids," she said with a sense of trespass.

"I had for short time a wife," he said. "With her I had one child."

Kit nodded, alert, afraid now of how far she had gone, what door she had knocked on.

"Girl," he said. "She contracted disease—the name I know only in

Russian. Bone disease, of which she died. I do not know what year. I was then in prison."

"And her mother was . . ."

"Dead by then too. Died, 1942."

"In the war."

"In Leningrad, in the siege. While I was in army. She starved to death."

Kit, without willing it, made a moan of pity and horror, and covered her mouth.

"So in answer to your question," he said. "Same question asked by U.S. embassy in Berlin. No I have no family. Parents dead. Wife, dead I am told. I had child, and she died."

He was so still. Kit almost spoke. She almost said: *I had a child too.* She was certain that he waited for her to speak, and she felt every reason not to speak give way within her. *I had a child too, and he died.*

"I," she said, and the world bent toward breaking. But then she said nothing more.

9.

In May every year the nuns of Our Lady of Charity of the Good Shepherd changed from black to white, appearing at daily Mass one morning all changed, or almost all. It was comically encouraging, as though they had turned overnight into fat brides or friendly ghosts, choosing to discard their harsher aspects even as the girls of Kit's "class" got bigger. It wasn't so. Some of them were harsh in black, even cruel, and stayed that way in white. Some were harsh toward the sins the girls had committed, but kind too because of their own charity, kind especially toward the girls they thought were innocent. Most of the girls claimed to be innocent: wronged or fooled. Some of the nuns believed some of them.

Kit's mother wrote her twice a week (calls weren't allowed except in emergencies), brief bright letters in her blue-black hand. Often she stuck in little encouraging things she clipped out of magazines or the newspaper, poems or strip cartoons, not related directly to Kit's situation but to Troubles in general and how to bear them, things that brought acrid tears sometimes to Kit's eyes, not for the thin sentiments themselves but at the thought of her mother cutting them out, thinking of her, seeking some consolation for her.

She forwarded Ben's letters to Kit also. Sis, he called her in his little penciled missives, guarded and cool. Saigon was a beautiful city, sort of French and tropical at the same time; the people were small and amazingly beautiful, all of them. There was a cult here that she could join, that was all for freedom and independence and worshiped Victor Hugo as a messiah. He was kept busy by his duties; he was learning to build bridges and dig wells and lay water pipe. He had been out to the Delta, and was going up into the mountains where there were tribes as different from the Annamese as Indians were from white settlers.

She looked up *Vietnam* in the encyclopedia in Our Lady's classroom (*Vas-Zygo*) and studied the pale photographs of columned buildings under palms, men in white European suits, delicate country people in comical triangular hats, rickshaws, rice paddies. Long ago, long before.

She answered Ben's letters, wrote long ones for his short ones; she wrote him letter after letter, and when she was through writing them she tore them each in slow pieces, the small cry of ripped paper.

> Ben — You can see the sea from the windows of this place, and the girls look out the windows like the princesses of Sorc, but they can't leave or go down to the water or the shore; they can't be seen. Soon a long battleship with black sails and a hundred oars is going to come in sight, and there will be a face painted on its prow with hot vengeful eyes, and it will beat into this harbor on a summer stormwind cold as snow, no it won't, not for me. But God damn it's hot in here.

> Ikhnaton — It's going to be a girl, and she'll marry a little puppy of a boy, who will die even younger than we do, my brother; and he'll be buried with all his golden toys, and be dug up one day; and afterwards everyone who dug him up and took his stuff will die in awful and complicated ways; which is why you should not believe in One God and marry your sister.
>
> — Nefertiti

Ben, you know there's a group of girls here who are called the
Virgin Mothers because they are the ones who won't tell who Did
It to them. The nuns don't call them the Virgin Mothers, but
that's what the girls call them. I am one of them. I think maybe
one or two of the Virgin Mothers don't even really know they Did
It or what It is that got them here. I am one of them. You know
what, they give us all (not just the Virgin Mothers) these long
shapeless flannel nighties and make us wear them, I brought my
terry-cloth bathrobe (yours actually) and they won't let me wear
it, and you know why? *Because it has a belt.* Think about it.
There was a girl here once who hanged herself with the belt of
her robe, and they've been scared ever since. They worry too
much. *It* won't let you kill yourself, *It* wants to live and won't let
you kill yourself. I wish I could have my terry-cloth bathrobe.

She never told George and Marion who it had been; she couldn't
really understand why they even wanted to know, why it preyed on
them not to know, made her mother weep and her father rage, as
though the need to know arose from some deep-down biological part
of them that lay below where they thought or even felt. What could it
matter who it was if she wanted nothing further to do with him? If they
just thought for a second they'd see that. She made them swear not to
tell Ben about it at all, which of course they weren't going to do. They
weren't going to tell anyone anything, they stayed up late night after
night (Kit in guilty anguish imagined them) thinking of what to tell
people that would betray nothing. And from now on forever Kit would
have this not to tell, to those people and to Ben and to the people of
her future, in which she didn't believe.

Marion stopped weeping, though, when Kit refused to be put into
the hands of nuns. Her eyes got fierce and her voice low and for the
first time in her life Kit was afraid of her. *Well just what did you think
you're going to do? Do you think you're going to have it here in your bedroom? Do you think there are a lot of other things you might like to do
about this, a lot of choices you have to make?* A terrifying piece of
female wisdom was being passed to her, she knew: prematurely, and in
a rage, a knowledge as unforeseen and as inescapable as the biology

but worse. *Who did you think was going to take you in? What kind of life did you think you're going to make from now on?* George made her hush and they went out of Kit's room together, again, leaving Kit to lie alone unmoving and listening to her heart. (A long time afterwards, after Marion was dead, George told Kit that he had suggested going down to Puerto Rico and getting it over with, and Marion had refused to think about that. Just would not think about it, George said. He and Kit were eating oysters at an oyster bar in D.C. then, wet little formless things the bartender freed from their shells with a short sharp knife.)

She never once thought of telling Burke, though there seemed to be an injustice in that, in leaving him unknowing. It was as though she saw a winning move for him on the board they both sat at, and wouldn't tell him, and let him miss it. Only it wasn't winning; just knowing.

The nuns of Our Lady of Charity of the Good Shepherd, their pamphlets said, devoted their lives "to reclaiming those whom society defiles, and then rejects with scorn." They had expanded into a maternity hospital for the daughters of middle-class Catholics and some worthy poor girls, mostly not defiled or rejected, just in deep trouble. Some never wept, some never stopped. The stony-eyed ones scared Kit, but she envied them and tried to empty her heart too as theirs seemed empty.

One of them was a long-boned black girl, a Virgin Mother who crossed herself with her big slow hand but never prayed aloud. Maybe because Kit was quiet too, this girl chose her to talk to, Kit nodding when she couldn't understand. One night she told Kit who the father of the child she carried was: her brother, the same who had just come to visit her. Slim long arms and legs like hers and yellow watchful eyes half-lidded. He had brought her gum and comic books and left after a silent hour for a nine-hour bus ride home.

"He took off me what he want, that's all," she told Kit. "Ain't nobody ever going to do that to me again. I'll cut their throat." And she opened the pack of Juicy Fruit he'd brought her, and gave Kit one.

She stopped writing to Ben, stopped reading and writing altogether.

She sat huge and indolent in the dayroom and talked with the others about what it was going to be like when the great eggs they all carried began to crack. Sister said it hurt, yes, but that afterwards they wouldn't remember; it's a blessing, she said; maybe if we remembered all the anguish we wouldn't be able to face ever doing it again; God's kind enough to blot out all that part from our memories, and leave only the joy.

That was the worst horror Kit could think of, the final cruelty, that she wouldn't remember. What was suffering if you couldn't remember it? She was determined she would. He wouldn't cheat her out of that who had taken so much from her: she wouldn't forget.

But they were all so young: their first child in every instance, and they developed complications, or struggled through hours and hours of labor, prolonged by drugs that lessened pain and contractions both; they cursed and pressed down and sweated and prayed and called for their mothers as shot soldiers do. So much to remember, and she would remember too, but only by saving it in words, which dried up and grew light over time like leaves. And the pain passed from her anyway, just as Sister said it would.

Finally they gave up on her and cut her open to get out the child. It was a boy, and he had a grievous hole in his heart and an incomplete intestine. He was baptized, and lived only a few hours.

She didn't think of it as grieving. She knew that in some places women tore their garments or cast ashes on their heads in grief, but she wasn't thinking of them when she cut her hair off with shears taken from the sewing closet. She cut and cut, looking at herself in the bathroom mirror above the line of stained sinks. She had started thinking incessantly about sharp things, about broken glass and scalpels and the blades of the big kitchen disposal, into which now and then on kitchen duty they would toss a broken drinking glass and then duck down for fear of flying shards and listen to it be eaten, crunched and then ground and then whirred away to nothing. That was all she thought of while she cut.

She could still walk only with difficulty. The nuns had told her how to care for her wound and how she should do no lifting and she stared at them not even nodding yes. She wanted to say *I wish it was you who died and not him.* She made them call her parents and have them come to get her immediately. *Stay and rest, rest* they said but she couldn't rest, couldn't sleep, and if she did sleep couldn't wake. Hours before George and Marion were to arrive she went out into the hall with her Samsonite bag and sat on a bench there, as far from the delivery rooms and operating rooms as possible.

"Pixie," her mother said, touching her ruined head. "You remind me of somebody, with your hair like that. I can't think who."

That was all. They took a plane and then drove home from the city airport across the farmlands. It was October and smelled of fruit and the first days of school. At first they kept her between them in the front seat, but at a gas stop she said she was tired and got in the back alone. Her mother tried to tell her stories of home, activities, relatives she'd heard from. Nothing more. They arrived home. "Here we are," said Marion.

It ought to have been not only possible but easy to say, to tell them that she was so hurt inside, that she had almost died there, that she felt entirely alone and unbearably crowded at the same time, that she was sorry and afraid. But she couldn't speak, and was somehow not even aware that she couldn't. What was the name of the thing that kept her, poor ghost, from speaking? The words were the words and there was no prohibition on saying them. She has looked backward sometimes on herself sitting in her room in that house, on her bed, knees drawn up to her chin, and wanted to say to herself *Just go tell them what's in your heart; speak, and they'll answer.*

Grief laid too deep for speech might have been written down in poems; she'd used to believe that was how poems came to be. But she had lost or surrendered that, not even thinking about it, a traveler who's forgotten a bag on a bench in a city he won't return to, unable to remember even what it contained. For a time she went on reading poems, and would sometimes write down a bit of someone else's. *But*

such a tide as moving seems asleep Too full for sound or foam When that
which drew from out the boundless deep Turns again home.

Wasn't it they, though, George and Marion, who should have spoken? Shouldn't they have found some way to ask? Sitting on either side
of her at the kitchen table or in front of the TV, in rooms too warm for
Kit, they seemed to be clothed in impenetrable wrappings or wadding
of kindness and goodwill, but unable to feel or be touched through the
thicknesses. No: no, it wasn't their fault either. After a month's silence
they made an appointment for her with a psychologist, Dr. Biencouli,
in a stuffy office downtown whose waiting room was decorated with
things from the sea: a big aquarium, and a fisherman's net, in which
balls of colored glass were caught.

All those girls of her generation, sent to do penance with these peculiar men, talking away or refusing to talk as the doctors too of course
refused, calm and unresponsive as idols or twitchy and weird. Dr.
Biencouli kept opening his desk drawer, fiddling with whatever it contained and shutting it again, only to open it again a few minutes later.
Falin said the interrogators of the KGB asked their prisoners *Do you*
know why you're here? Dr. Biencouli asked her *Do you know why you're*
here? because like them he didn't know. And you gave them nothing,
or gave them nothing in the guise of giving them everything.

Would it have been different if he had been different, if the practice
of his art or craft had been different, as it would in time become different? Maybe if someone could just have spoken to her soul in kindness
she would not have borne all the rest of her life those faint hatchings or
hash marks on her wrists: badges of that doctor's failure, or her own, or
no one's.

It was a Sunday morning, and she'd refused to go to church, which
Marion decided was because her tummy still hurt. And maybe it was
just the sudden silence of the house and the November day: she felt
solid and foreign to herself, as though she had no insides except a
watching eye. She wandered in rooms and then into the bathroom and
looked at herself in the mirrored door of the medicine cabinet with
repulsion and fascination mixed; then she opened the door.

Always the little surprise (she'd felt it first long before as a child) to find, behind her face, not the contents of herself but only this stuff. Bactine and Band-Aids and aspirin and medicines once prescribed and not all taken, little brown bottles, maybe one with a genie in it. Take two as needed for sleep; but how many to sleep for good? Brylcreem and Barbasol on the masculine side, and a safety razor, and the Blue Blades too, a night-blue box written on in black. Each blade inside the box was wrapped again in greasy paper; she had watched how carefully her father had put it in and screwed up the razor's little trapdoors, and after, how he took the old blade and slid it through the little slot at the cabinet's back.

Once, walking to school in some city, she had passed a house being dismantled, the roof off and the walls coming down. The bathroom was open for all to see, the tub askew and the dusty toilet; and in the wall behind the sink—piled up behind the bared slats between the studs—were all the Blue Blades ever dropped into that slot. A treasure, revolting and amazing.

Blue, it really was blue; slick, fresh as a peeled fruit.

In dreams we do things and then awaken in the awful relief of finding we haven't done them after all. She had dreamed recently that, preparing to mow the lawn herself now that Ben was gone, she had lifted the can of oil and gas mixed and instead of pouring it into the machine had drunk it. It seemed in the dream a dumb but natural error. But she could get no one to help her, not her mother at work ironing vast white sheets, nor her father, distracted and dim, who kidded her and put her off.

She thought *This is dumb* even as she struck the blade hard and swift across her left wrist. Immediately the blood scrambled out all along the slit she'd made as though eager to be free. It didn't hurt, but it had run all over her hand, which was now too slippery to hold the blade to do the other wrist. She saw in horror that she had cut her fingers with the opposite edge of the blade, and at that almost stopped, but she gripped hard and made a weak slash and then another, crying out a little growl, with teeth bared.

Not so hard. Watching the blood flow from her fingertips and the webs of her fingers into the sink she thought that after all she couldn't die standing up. She turned from the sink holding her wrists aloft so the blood wouldn't fall, but more did fall, spattering rapidly on the floor and on the pink rug. Her hands were numb. She thought of going to the tub and kneeling there and holding her hands under the faucet, but then she knew she couldn't manage all that. She sat on the pink-clothed toilet seat and tried to reach the faucets on the sink. There was still not much pain except a weird dull ache in her upper arms. She felt as she had always supposed she would feel, that she was departing, dissipating, afraid and sorry but growing less so: lighter, lighter, lighter.

Her mother, coming back for her missal and her cigarettes, heard Kit fall in the bathroom upstairs, heard the tooth glass smash in the sink; when she pushed open the door her first thought was that her daughter's wound had opened again, and that her hands were red with trying to stanch it.

10.

They were thin white lines, not noticeable really, almost indistinguish-
able from the creases of her wrists: some days she thought so, anyway.
Other days she knew that everyone knew what they meant, and she
tugged down the sleeves of her blouse, and folded her arms.

"If I ever try it again I'll know better how," she said to Jackie. "I got
it down now."

"Oh yes? Well I hope you won't ever."

"First thing," she said. "You have to use a single-edge blade. They
make them for tools and for art."

"Okay."

"The double-edge kind cut up your fingers. That was actually the
most horrible part. You wouldn't think so. But cutting my fingers was
just . . . It said *hey, you have a cut, stop, stop*—and I almost did."

"Uh-huh." The day was bitter cold, a change in the weather. They
sat in the lounge of her dorm, where men were admitted at certain
hours, though it was empty now, gray dinnertime.

"And you don't cut *across*," she said. "Somehow you don't think of this, but it's like, of course." She held her wrist. "It's all bones and tendons, like a chicken leg. Probably all there just so it *can't* be cut. So you have to cut *down*." She showed him, a quick slash as though she struck a match there. But her hands shook a little.

"Down," he said.

"And you have to have hot water, flowing water. You have to do all this in a bath, so you can keep your hands in the water even after you pass out."

He said nothing. She could see he was appalled. She was appalled herself at the certainty of her knowledge. "Guess what else," she said.

"Why don't you just go ahead and say."

"Rat poison," she said. "A little rat poison makes you not clot. Which is why it kills rats. They bleed inside. But you take just a little."

"I hope," he said, "you're planning to give me a long lead time on this. Let me know when the thought's preying on your mind."

She pressed her hands together to stop their trembling.

"I ain't going to be much good at talking you out of anything you want to do," he said. "But I want the chance to try."

"What are you going to say?" she asked.

"Well sometimes, when in the past I've had these conversations, which isn't so often . . . Once, anyway, I talked about breakfast."

"Breakfast, huh."

"Well when I get real depressed that's what I think about," he said. "Tomorrow's another day, and you're going to wake up and smell that coffee and there's eggs and buttered toast. And you won't want to miss that. And you just go on from there." He laughed, and she was laughing already. "Really, really, that's what I said."

She hadn't told him why she'd done it. They'd started talking about how many girls did. Boys too, she claimed, only you didn't notice, or couldn't tell: in a car, in a blind rage. And she'd shown him her wrists, the undersides, maps where the blue rivers ran.

. . .

"So here's what I want to do," she said. "I want to get drunk."

"You do." He'd asked her what she wanted to do that night, it was "late hours night" and they could be out together till midnight.

"I want to try it out."

"What, you never did?"

"No," she said. "Never did. I think it's time."

"Well, bad on me if I was to get you drunk," he said. "A man's not to do that, it's not right."

"I thought I'd get myself drunk," she said. "You could just be there."

"Sober as a judge."

"That's up to you."

He shook his head in wonder. "Well. I suppose if you want to, you ought to get to. Got to be a first time."

"Sure."

She pulled on her leather jacket and he wound his long scarf around his neck and patted his blue navy watch cap in place. His Volkswagen was in the parking lot, ticketed. "There's company I wouldn't recommend you try this with," he said, pocketing the ticket and pulling his door closed. "But probably out t'my house you'd be as safe as anywhere."

"That's right. That's what I thought too."

"You're pretty damn sure," he said. "What makes you so sure?"

"Well, why'd you say it?"

They drove down into town. The VW's little blades flailed against the icy rain. "First thing," he said. "You got to decide what you're going to get drunk on. That's the big decision. Can't be beer, you can't get all that far on beer. Wine, you'll fall asleep first."

She pondered the question, or pretended to, having no criteria at all to go by. "Gin," she said.

"Gin!"

Clearer than water, good medicine, with the branches of juniper pictured on the label, the dusky blue berries. How did they drown that blue in this transparency? Girls didn't take Chemistry. In the car, she uncapped the bottle he bought her and inhaled it tentatively.

"Hey. Don't you know it's against the law in this state to carry an open bottle in a vee-hicle?"

"No, I didn't," she said. "So there." The gin smelled gloriously harmful, weird, what would the word be, *intoxicating*.

At the house, Max and Rodger were reading the previous Sunday's *New York Times*, acres of fine print, rattling the pages in disgust or glee.

"Gin?" Max asked in mild amazement.

"Gin," Jackie said. "Now what have we got to mix it with?" He opened the little gray refrigerator and then the cupboards. Kit stroked the glass-ringed wooden kitchen table, liking this idea of living with other people's old things, their mismatched chairs and swayback walnut beds and brass lamps with floral shades. It was like living in the woods, she thought, at once homey and strange, yours and not yours.

"You can't drink gin without a mixer," Max said. "You might not survive."

"Well I'm not going all the way back to town to get something," Jackie said. " 'Sides I got no money left. This has become a rather expensive date, no offense. Oh here." He pulled from the back of a cupboard a little envelope, and shook it. "Lemon Kool-Aid."

Rodger's mouth fell open and his tongue protruded, though he said nothing. In a plastic pitcher Jackie mixed the Kool Aid. Kit sat with arms crossed, intent on her adventure. "We don't have a lot of ice, either," Jackie said. He pulled two metal trays from the icebox's frozen heart. He found glasses, painted with daffodils and tulips, and filled them.

For many years after that night, Kit couldn't drink gin again, though in time she learned to; Kool-Aid, never.

Other people arrived and went again as she sat there engaged in her experiment, filling up gradually like an alchemist's retort. Jackie explained to them what she was up to and they nodded or kidded her gently and took a drink or didn't. There was a silent auto mechanic, a friend of Max's, who brought beer; his hands were stronger and his fingernails more atrociously broken and stained than any she had ever seen. There were Fred and Joanne, he a graduate student in Poli-Sci and she his wife, a graduate student too but in Sociology.

"Saul, you dirty Semite," Fred said, taking Saul's arm in a sudden grip. "My report to the district office is thin, very thin. They will want more. Where are the plans?"

Saul almost laughed, though he didn't seem amused, and it had to be explained to Kit that Fred was the FBI guy, or was pretending to be.

"In any meeting of any group on the Attorney General's list, one of them is going to be an agent," Fred said. "A mathematical certainty."

"In any meeting over a certain size," Saul said.

"Where two or three are gathered together in my name," Fred said solemnly.

Kit had only a slight idea what the Attorney General's list was and couldn't be certain when Fred was joking or if his joking bothered Saul or Max. He disputed coolly with them as Jackie puffed on his pipe and looked from one to another in admiration or amusement. Fred had been a member (one of only four or five) of the already defunct Nietzsche Study Group, and when the hour grew late he led them in singing the group's marching song:

> "*Nietzsche loves me, this I know*
> *Zarathustra told me so*
> *Little ones to US belong*
> *They are weak but WE ARE STRONG.*"

"I slept on their couch last summer when I couldn't find a room," Jackie told her when they'd left. "They'd just got hitched. Not a big apartment, let me tell you, but I guess they needed that little bit of money I gave them. Fine, except that night-long—*night-long*—they'd lie in their room on this bigole bed and rock and carry on, the bed squeaking and them singing out—well you know."

"Jeez," Kit said. "Oh my God." She didn't exactly know.

"Tough," said Max. "For a single man such as yourself."

"Very tough," Jackie said. "I'd lie there with sweat on my brow and just gnaw my wrist, just gnaw my wrist."

Kit shook with laughter, not altogether understanding his discomfort. Everyone watched her laugh and laugh, nodding at one another as though confirming that she was passing through the expected phases of her journey in the right order. She pushed the daffodil glass toward the pitcher and bottle standing before Jackie.

"Got to pace yourself now," Jackie said, which Kit thought was funny too; but soon a new wave of feeling rolled over her, swallowed in with the sticky sweetness (all the ice was gone) and replacing her. This one felt lofty, or deep, or both; she felt lofted out of her own deeps, which she saw beneath, or tasted, in dread and wonder. "Deeps," she said. "Lofted."

"Uh-oh," Jackie said.

She wanted to talk about poetry; about Falin, about Baudelaire in Paris and Keats in Rome. "For long," she said, "I have been half in love with caseful death. Called him sweet names in many a honeyed rhyme, to take into the air my quiet breath." She drank. "My quiet breath."

"Now now," Jackie said softly.

"Eternity's hostage," she said. "Captive in time."

"Yes?"

"That's what a poet is. Falin told us that. It's in a poem by Patsernak," she said. "I mean Piasternak. Pasternak."

" 'Eternity's hostage,' " Jackie said thoughtfully. "I like that."

"Captive in time," Kit said. "Captive in goddamn time."

"What makes you wonder about Falin," Rodger said, "is why they did that in the first place. Kicked him out. You know? What was in it for them? The comrades. What was the threat to them, the big danger? One poet."

"The unacknowledged legislators of the world," Kit said. "Of the *world*."

"Anyway, why not just shoot him?"

"Listen," Saul Greenleaf said. "If they could shoot poets, they would have shot Pasternak. They can shoot anybody *but* poets. You know this young guy, what's his name, Vosnesensky, they filled this sports stadium to hear him read. Fifteen thousand people. For poetry. Try that at Wrigley Field."

"Then tell me what they're doing throwing this one out," Rodger asked. "If they love poets so much."

"I didn't say they love them. I said they can't shoot them. The *people* love them. The bosses are afraid of them."

"Here," Jackie said, "they can say anything they want. Look at Ginsberg. Nobody's talking about exiling Ginsberg. And for a good reason. Nobody's heard of him."

Saul lifted his chin, and rose to his feet. The lamplight gilded his glasses. "I saw the best minds of my generation destroyed by madness," he spoke. "Starving hysterical naked, dragging themselves through the negro streets at dawn looking for an angry fix . . ."

"Down, down, down into the darkness of the grave," Kit said hollowly. "Gently they go, the beautiful, the tender, the kind."

"Angelheaded hipsters," Saul kept on, "burning for the ancient heavenly connection to the starry dynamo in the machinery of night."

"Quietly they go, the intelligent the witty the brave," Kit said. She too tried to rise to speak, slipped and fell heavily, still reciting: "I know. But I do not approve. And I am not resigned." Max and Rodger helped her to her feet. She looked around her at their faces, which resembled the mild interested faces of cows who watch you pass by their meadow. "Edna St. Vincent Millay," she said. "I feel quite weird."

"You're hittin' a plateau," Jackie said. "You'll rise on past that."

"Oh," she said. "Okay." She sat again, with care. The trick was to go slow, and think. She lifted the glass before her, she toasted the room, the clatter of sleet on the window, the world, the unseen. And solemnly drank.

Rodger departed to study. Max got out his guitar, sensing maybe to what point the evening had come; they sought for songs they all knew, or that any of them knew all the way through. Kit had learned "Sloop John B" from the Kingston Trio, Max had learned it from Pete Seeger at a camp for workers' children; he sang in a high true tenor and she in an earnest cry, eyes closed. He sang other Weavers songs, and Leadbelly, songs of a kind she didn't know existed:

"Me un' Marthy, we was standin' upstairs
I heard a white man say, "I don't want no colored up there,"
Lawd, he's a bourgeois man
Hee, it's a bourgeois town
I got the bourgeois blues, gonna spread the news
all around."

He taught them a song he said Pete Seeger had learned from activists in Carolina who were organizing sit-ins in Southern cities. It was an old hymn tune maybe, he thought, to which Seeger had added some words of his own:

"Oh, deep in my heart
I do believe
We shall overcome someday."

Saul Greenleaf wouldn't sing, saying he had sung enough camp songs in camp, and heard enough Pete Seeger too. Max smiled benignly on him and sang on:

"We'll walk hand in hand,
We'll walk hand in hand,
We'll walk hand in hand someday."

Kit, riven somehow by that cruel-kind word *someday*, thought of sitting with Falin in the All Night Cafeteria. *Take my hand quick and tell me: what have you in your heart.* She thought—she knew, suddenly, for sure—that he had been saying it to her. He'd meant her to answer it, though she didn't know why he did. And with a visceral suddenness she sobbed, and went on sobbing.

How could you say what was deep in your heart, how? What was in your heart could never be said, because it was what you were inside of, you yourself.

"Why would he ask, why would he," she said to them gathered around her offering comfort or a hankie. "Why."

That was about the last thing she remembered, those tears, and the sense of a rolling wave carrying her will-lessly elsewhere. She had turned into a robot or zombie, a rogue beast who went on saying and doing things even though she, Kit, had fled or been voided. Said some pretty funny stuff too, according to Jackie. Anyway before she got sick.

"You remember getting sick?" he asked her.

"No." She was in his bed; he sat at the end of it, wearing a college sweatsuit and a boy's Indian-patterned robe. Light that must be dawn was in his window below the shade.

"Oh yeah," he said, smiling. "Hugging the old toilet. Yes." He pointed out a japanned wastebasket at the bed's end: he'd put it there for her when everything that she could puke had been puked and she was still heaving. And looking at it she had a memory or recurrence, and a deep revulsion swept her.

"Oh God."

"Went on quite a time."

He seemed pretty pleased with her, or with himself. Suddenly she shuddered, and yanked aside the covers, as though suspecting something was in the bed with her.

"Don't worry," he said. "No need."

She was still fully clothed, except for her shoes and sweater. He pointed at her jeans.

"I think I could have got them off you," he said. "But I don't think I could have got them back on you again. So you can see, you're safe."

"Oh jeez."

"I shared the bed with you," he said. "Didn't think you'd mind that, seeing as how it's my bed, and the only one."

"No," she said. "No, jeez, Jackie." She hugged his pillow, laying herself carefully down, a jug of ill humors she wanted not to spill. "I guess that wasn't quite the date you were expecting."

"Well, I have to admit . . ."

"I thought maybe too. I really did," she said. He had been so far always polite and patient with her about that, or impatient in a comic and harmless way. He seemed to think of her as skittish and virginal, which maybe she was. Anyway she let him regard her that way, unable to tell him of the cold dread or repugnance that gripped her when he smiled and caressed her, and what the reason might be. "You know I'm not sure I can ever, I mean . . ."

"Well," he said. "So long as you're not sure." He smoked a cigarette and watched her. "Now we got another thing to think about," he said, "and that's getting you back into your dorm."

He must have seen a dreadful understanding dawn in her eyes then, because he nodded solemnly at her: yes it's true.

"Oh God, I never got back into the dorm."

"No, you didn't. Not exactly in any shape to."

"They'll know. They check. They tell your parents."

"You had a good excuse. The weather was real bad. Ice on the roads. Dangerous."

"No! I've got to get back in, I've got to now. Maybe they didn't check after all, maybe just this once. Oh God." She tried to leap from the bed but the contents of her self seemed to slide or slop hideously when she tried. She had to sit again and hold still till her seas stopped heaving. "Oh help me."

Now he began to laugh, as he had not done so far. "Well you got the whole experience, you really did. Including the part where you do something dumb, and the part where you only figure it out the next day."

"Oh stop, stop."

"And the part where you want to die."

She had got up and begun to make her way to the bathroom in a crippled crouch, holding the backs of chairs and the edge of the bureau, that made him laugh more. "You help, just help," she murmured. "You find my shoes."

She would have made it out of the house, determined to move and keep moving, except that she had to pass through the kitchen, the ashtrays filled with twisted butts and the sink with dishes and the table where, shockingly, the empty gin bottle still held court, its prissy lying label the last straw. She spent more time in the toilet, Jackie speaking soothingly and encouragingly to her through the door, though she wouldn't let him in.

"The proctor has left you a couple of notes," Fran told her. "She seemed pretty concerned."

"Oh God."

"You look bad. Very bad."

"Don't say anything, don't let her know I'm here till I wash. Please don't."

"Hey," Fran said, by which she seemed to mean reassurance, and solidarity, and sweet reason, and goes-without-saying, all in a tiny non-word. Kit went to stand under the feeble shower, wishing she could wash inside as well as out. Then when she was freshly dressed she went to the proctor's door, thinking hard about how to put her hopeless case.

The proctor's face stilled her: stricken and tender at once. "Your parents called," she said. "They've been calling. They want you to call right back. I didn't know where you were." She wore a terry-cloth robe cinched with a belt. She was only a couple of years older than Kit. "Here," she said. "Use the phone here." And she pushed a chair up to the phone on its table, and touched Kit's shoulder to make her sit there before it.

11.

It had been an accident with some ammunition, some shells being transported: that's what the letter said that had been sent to George and Marion. Ben had been stationed in the Philippines, and on a routine training mission this thing had happened. They didn't describe it in any way that could be pictured. They said he had died instantaneously. Two members of his outfit were accompanying his body home and would have more to tell them.

She tried not to cry out, tried with her strength, somehow thinking that if she could keep from crying out she would keep it from being true. But she did, she cried out, and it was as though the cry would break her in pieces, shake her to the ground like a bombed building.

"I'll come get you," George called to her over the phone, so far away. "I'm leaving in a few minutes. It's still raining, Kit, and it might take me a while, but I'll come."

. . .

The rain went on through the day, never quite turning back to snow, but coating the trees and telephone lines with ice, the new green tips of branches too, how could they survive that, they always did. George driving her north on the highway held the wheel in both hands; when some invisible frontier was crossed and the wet road turned to ice, the cars before him in the twilight began to stop or try to and he had to brake, and the great station wagon spun slowly around and onto the shoulder before coming to a stop. He opened the door and was halfway out when he stopped and sat again and began to sob. The falling rain darkened the felt of the hat on his bent head. They both wept there. A police cruiser stopped beside them, lights going, to ask if they were all right.

That night she lay in her bed, so near her father's and mother's that she could hear them stir and talk; could hear even the click of the lamp coming on, then going off again. Her mother's tears. She lay and looked up into the darkness of the ceiling and listened. *Just please let her sleep*, she thought or prayed. *Just let her sleep. You bastard.*

This stormlike grief. It wasn't the hollowed, blank grief that she had felt after Our Lady, like being scraped out to the rind. This grief was something and not nothing, it rose continually to sweep over you, making you sob or cry out unexpectedly, to lose your footing even, like a riptide. Marion coming out of the church behind his aluminum casket must have felt it come over her, for she moaned and stumbled and George could hardly hold her upright.

Eternal rest grant unto him, O Lord, the priest said, and let perpetual light shine upon him. Then it was Kit who was shaken with sudden disabling tears, wishing it were so and at the same time knowing that if they asked God to shine a light upon him in his box in the earth, it could only be their own light that was meant—hers and her father's and mother's—because there wasn't any other, and that light wasn't perpetual and it wasn't eternal. Marion had grown calmer by then, maybe the capsule she'd taken working at last (she'd given Kit one too), and she held her head high and didn't cry when the young soldiers, one white and one black, placed the folded flag in her lap like his baby soul wrapped up.

. . .

She lay facedown on her bed a long time, as she had the day when he went to join the army. Downstairs Marion and George gave cake and coffee to the soldiers and to the priest and the few relatives who had been able to come so far. An awakened winter fly buzzed and buzzed between the sash and the storm window. Kit knew with certainty that it was she who had caused Ben's death, by the intensity of her attention to him, by clawing at him to keep him with her on the roads from Libi to Mary and Rayn to Sorc where nothing changed and everything was possible. Until at last he broke free, broke her hold. *Broke free, broke her hold:* that was the ninth wave again arising, and she felt anew what had happened, inconceivably, irreversibly, and wept again.

Her child too: by conceiving it in her anger at Ben, by offering it a promise of life that she couldn't keep, she had done harm that could never be made right. If there really was a light to shine upon us, she would never see it now. She was going to see Ben in dreams and he was going to ask her why she had done those things, why she hadn't known how to not want them, why she hadn't just let him alone.

She pressed her head into the pillow, her teeth clenched shut on her sobs. She knew now why people can't leave the graves where those they love are buried, why they want to lie down there and grip the grass, hug the stone: it wasn't out of any stupid extravagance of grief but just a need to stop this hemorrhaging, to press something into you to stanch the wound. If she could she would go lie down there like an abandoned dog till she died.

Well she *could* die. She was smarter than she had been; she knew now how tough her body was and how it would fight back. But it wasn't all she knew.

After a time the pill she had taken, cycling through her brain and soul, ran out or let go; for a while she slept and didn't dream. When she woke the world was vacant. She left her room, but at the top of the stairs she sat down, dizzy or unable to continue. Marion, come from the kitchen in her apron, saw her there.

"Your father has taken those two boys to the bus station."

Kit nodded.

"I wonder if you could help me."

"Sure. What."

But her mother said nothing further, only looked up at her, and Kit got up and made her way to the bottom of the half-flight of stairs. Her mother's smile was more terrible than her grief. She took Kit's shoulders in her hands, to reassure her, or to steady herself.

"I am just so glad," she said, "that I found you that day. That I came back and found you that day in the bathroom. I am just so glad."

In her mother's embrace Kit felt all the tears that were to come, drawn from a reservoir deeper than she could have imagined. Oh Ben. She couldn't die: she had no right to. She had been a bad daughter and she supposed (in the odor of her mother's perfume and the sound of her weeping) that she would probably never really be a good one. But she couldn't die. Not dying was the only thing she could do for her mother, and she would have to do it.

She didn't need to go right back, George told her that. Surely they'd understand at school if she wanted to stay for a day or two, or even longer. Marion could use the help. But she went back when Monday came, refusing George's offer of a ride and taking the big smelly bus that stopped at every cornfield crossroads. The weather had changed utterly, and along the rivers the willows were yellow-green. Swollen buds made the trees seem cloudy or vague in the sunlight, as though they were in the process of vanishing, or appearing newly, which they were. Daffodils were even coming out; this part of the state was proud of its daffodils, which were featured on travel posters and city medallions; all along the road there would appear sudden glowing fields of them, nodding together like orchestras, trumpeting silently. It was a long trip.

In the house on East North Street, Jackie wrapped her in his quilt to stop her shivering, gave her boiled coffee and jelly doughnuts, and listened. Max too, in the doorway, and Saul.

"He was stationed in the Philippines, it turns out," she said, clutching her drawn-up knees. "I don't remember him saying he was there. But anyway this thing happened with the ammunition, this accident . . ."

"I don't think so," Saul said.

"What?"

"Didn't you say he spent time in Vietnam?"

"Well a while ago. I mean I guess he got moved around." She knew suddenly that she had better not talk about it anymore. She sipped her bitter brew.

"Well, because," Saul said, uncomfortable but unwilling to stop, "what we're hearing is that American Special Forces are engaging with the Viet Cong, that's the South Vietnamese insurgents, and even with the North Vietnamese army."

"What do you mean, engaging with?" Max asked.

"I mean fighting them. Having, well, not battles, but. And some Americans are getting killed." He looked at Kit and not at Max. "Then they ship the bodies back to the Philippines and tell everybody it was an accident."

Kit stared at him. "How can you say that?" she whispered, amazed. "How can you say a thing like that?"

"Well that's what we're hearing. And this fits. And if it's so, I think people should know."

"My God," Kit said. "You're saying my brother was killed in a *battle*."

"No no," Saul said, seeming at last to perceive his roommates' looks and Kit's horror for what they were. "Not necessarily. I'm just saying, well, it fits." He lowered his eyes. "You might be able to find out. You might ask some questions."

Kit struggled free of the quilt, kicking it aside, getting to her feet, wanting out with furious urgency.

"It's important," Saul said behind her. "It is."

No place to go. She sat down on the edge of the couch and embraced herself. Something unbearably sharp hurt her heart: *How could they, how could they*, she thought, not knowing what she meant by it, whether she meant Saul's cruelty to say that to her, or Ben's lie to her, that he wouldn't shoot anybody, or those soldiers who came with his body, who were his friends, who knew.

"Kit," Jackie said, and sat beside her.

Ben hadn't slipped into death, as anyone could, no he had fought his way there, into that blackness and nonexistence; pressed on in, armed. Oh please let it not be so. Let him not have lied to her, the very last thing. If they had lied, if he had, they took even her grief from her, and left her nothing.

Two days of classes had gone by, and Kit was required to bring absence excuses, signed by her proctor, to each teacher whose class she had missed. Instead she stuffed them in her purse and forgot them. One she did think she had to hand in, but rather than to class she brought it to the liberal arts tower, thinking she would put it in his mailbox as she had her poem at the beginning of the semester. When she passed by his office, though, he was standing in the doorway, apparently just leaving. Seeing her, he opened the door wider for her and showed her in.

"I wasn't in class last week," she said.

"Yes," he said. "Again asleep?"

"No. Not asleep." She pulled from her pocket the green form and gave it to him. He unfolded and read it, sitting down at his desk. The room could have been anyone's: there was no sign that he alone occupied it.

"A family member?" he said.

"My brother." He looked up from the form. "An accident. Far away." She hoped he wouldn't say he was sorry. He didn't speak.

"I think I might have to drop your class, though," she said. "I'm sorry."

He refolded the green form. "Why do you say this?"

"Oh," she said. "I guess I found out I don't love poetry enough. Anymore."

He got up then from his desk and pulled a chair close to his and indicated it with a hand. She sat reluctantly.

"Six weeks now left in this semester," he said. "Too late to drop. You can only fail."

She crossed her arms and hid her hands in her armpits. "Can I ask you something?" she said.

He nodded, unsurprised.

"When your daughter died," Kit said, bargaining hard within herself not to cry, her throat not to tremble, "well how did you . . . how did you stand knowing that. Knowing what had happened."

"I was far away."

"Still. When you learned. When you thought about it."

He thought, or was quiet. Then he said: "Where was he, your brother, far away?"

"The Philippines," she said. "In the army. There was an accident, they said. Something—some shells or something—blew up." The dark wave made itself known within her, but didn't rise. "That's what they say. They brought him home."

Falin rested his chin in the L of his index finger and thumb, as she had seen him do in the library. He went on looking attentively at her, and in that time of silence the air in the little room seemed to be withdrawn and replaced, a little cleaner or clearer.

"Did you," Kit said then, "ever write about her? Your daughter."

"There are children in my poems who die," he said. "Who are hungry, who are lost, who are hurt. But of these I knew many."

"Many?"

He seemed to consider how he might say more. "You know," he said. "We lived, in that country, in times of terrible things. Not for a short time, but for long years. There was hardly a person to whom these things did not happen; even to those who sold everything—their souls, their loved ones—so that the terrible things would not happen to them. There was no safety."

"So if things like that were so common, then you . . ."

"No, no," he said, as though he knew what she thought. "No, you did not get used to it. Only you ceased to be surprised. And you did not have the pain to yourself: you did not look around yourself and say *Why should they be happy and I have this; how can they walk in the sun and smile and not know what I know.*"

She gripped the hankie that, just in case, she had taken out.

"All those I was with in camps, they had children, wives. No: I am wrong, not all. Many had lost all even before they came."

He moved a paper minutely on the desk.

"I was, myself, a lost child," he said, and lifted his eyes to her again. "A homeless boy. I do not remember my mother or my father. And as I lost them, so too did they lose me."

"I thought you said your father was an engineer."

"Yes. I said so. I believe this to be so." He regarded her puzzlement for a moment. "I do not remember my father," he said. "But from my first memory, I could say this sentence: *My father is an engineer.* A name the others sometimes called me was Engineer."

"The others?"

"The lost children. *Besprizornye.* There were many of us. Tens of thousands. No, more: a million. Millions." He smiled, maybe at her wonderment. "Another name I had among the lost children was Monashka, the Nun."

"Nun?"

"Perhaps I was delicate child. Innocent." His smile was teasing for a moment, then gone. "I don't really know why they called me that. I have forgot much. I do not know for sure where I was lost, and I do not know why."

"But you also said you grew up in Leningrad with your parents. That your parents were dead. That you were an only child."

"Yes. I lied when I said that."

Kit, shocked, couldn't respond. He was telling her he had lied. No adult had ever told her such a thing. They had lied, many of them had—telling her about the world or God or other things—and sometimes she had guessed and sometimes not. But never had one admitted it.

"I first appeared on earth in a train station in a northern city," he said. "It was beginning to be cold, winter. I perhaps was seven or eight or six years old. I was abandoned there, or by chance separated from whoever was to take care of me. It was very common."

"You first appeared?"

"I mean I remember nothing before that. I mean that there I begin to remember something that may be told."

"No father or mother?"

He shook his head.

"Well . . . what happened? I mean . . ."

"You would like to hear?"

"Yes."

"I wonder why."

She said nothing.

"I must say: it is not always easy for me. Not easy to remember, not easy to tell."

"Okay," she said. "Well."

"You will know more about me than I have revealed in this country before," he said. "You're not afraid?"

"Why should I be afraid?"

He didn't answer. He took from his pocket his cigarettes—they were Herbert Tarcytons, with the jaunty little man in antique formal dress on the pack—and put them on the desk; he opened his coat and tipped back the office chair, stretching out his long legs "Very well," he said. "And in exchange for my story, if you think it worth it, I will ask of you one thing. All right?"

"All right," she said, and she wasn't afraid, though her throat was tight and painful. "What is it?"

"I ask that you not drop my class," he said. "That you stay till end. That you not fail."

She shrugged, and looked away. "No, it's okay," she said. "I can make it up someplace else. The credit. It's okay."

He said nothing, as though she had said nothing: and she looked up at him.

"It's only a course," she said. "It doesn't matter."

"To me, yes," he said. "That you are not there. That I do not see you there. Yes. It matters very much."

"It does?"

"It does."

It was as though she stepped off an unseen edge and fell, only not down but up. He had been thinking about her. He had been thinking about her when she wasn't there, just as she had thought about him, who he was, what he was. He had been thinking about her, and maybe for the same reasons too, reasons she had no name for.

"All right," she said. "I'll do that. I'll stay. Till the end."

12

Wherever it was, in whatever city, it was a vast and crowded station. Through its high windows the sun made great solid bars of light in the dusty air that were vertiginous to look up at: he remembered that. Before that day or moment, nothing: a sensation of warmth and light, a golden orange, a white lace curtain, that might have been earlier, and might have been home.

Who it was that took him to that station; how he lost her, or him, or them; whether he was separated by chance from parents or uncles or schoolmates—nothing of that persisted. He didn't know if he was an only child, or just the only one who was lost. Had he been set down on a bench there and told to wait, by a parent or a sibling who was then swept away in the crowds, pushed aboard a train still calling his name (*that* he remembered, his name and patronymic, of these he was sure). Or did someone just leave him there, hoping for the best, someone headed elsewhere (*stay here Innokenti and don't move and I'll come back*), to the Polish border or the Crimea or Central Asia, anyway far away and unwilling or unable to carry him? How had he lived, not knowing?

He didn't remember coming to understand that something was wrong and whoever had brought him there was gone. Maybe he had come to that conclusion at last, and got up from his bench and started searching, thereby maybe losing himself certainly and finally, no matter if he or she or they who had told him to wait there had come back at last to collect him. All that was supposition. The first person he clearly remembered knowing—the earliest he could find by searching backwards—wasn't a parent or any other kin, it was Teapot.

Probably he had started to cry, amid the endless people passing the place where he sat. Not many would have turned to listen, or pay much attention, there were just too many children like him, some crying as he was, some begging, some not moving, having stopped trying. If someone did stop for a moment, because this boy was clean and in good clothes and still seeming to think he had a claim on their kindness, they could still do nothing but ask him where his mother was, who was caring for him: and he didn't remember any of those encounters if they happened. He remembered seeing the lean boy in a coat of no color and a shapeless cap, a teapot in his hand: how he slipped in and out among the travelers, apparently one of them and on his way somewhere (travelers everywhere then carried pots like that, to make their tea rather than buying it). But someone sitting long enough there, seeing him come and go, would come to understand he was not on his way anywhere.

He saw this boy steal a cloth bag that a mother put down, just for a moment so she could wipe the face of her crying child. It was under his coat and he was gone instantly, and then a while later he reappeared without it, with only his teapot, stopping strangers and telling them a story, a story most of them didn't want to hear. Now and then one gave him a small coin, at which he immediately stopped talking and looked elsewhere.

Through the day he saw Innokenti too, and studied him. He came at last and sat next to him, and took from his pocket a scrap of newspa-

per and a pinch of loose tobacco. Night must have grown late, because
the station was emptying, the last trains having left or never arrived.
Teapot rolled his cigarette and then leapt up to pester the last passersby
for a match. When his smoke was alight he sat again (Innokenti watching the perilous thing smolder and fume) and looked the little one
over. What was he waiting for? Was he lost?

Innokenti couldn't answer; he knew where he was, where he had
been placed; how could he be lost?

Was he hungry? Yes, he was hungry.

Any money? Innokenti searched in his pockets, took out three
kopeks and a lucky gold coin. Teapot took them and put them in his
own pocket. He told Innokenti that in a while the stationmaster and
the soldiers would go through the station and put out everybody who
had no ticket. Did he have a ticket? He didn't. He wasn't to worry,
though; Teapot would get him away in time.

They never get me, he said; he said he would go on a train to
where he wanted to go, and he would go when he chose, and stay
here till then.

Innokenti asked Teapot if he had a ticket. Sure he did, ten of them:
and he held up his dirty hands. Innokenti later understood this joke, a
common one among the kids: ten tickets, ten fingers to hold on to the
rods or the ladders or somewhere else, and ride for free.

At the sound of a great door closing, Teapot leapt up, and grabbed
the younger boy by his collar, and ran. They could hear the tramp of
the soldiers, the shouting, and the homeless people who had hoped to
sleep on the benches in the warmth pleading or cursing. Teapot led
him away along the closed buffet and down a lightless passage and further downward to a locked door. A dim bulb far off showed that there
was no farther they could go. Teapot put down his pot, took hold of
Innokenti's coat, and pulled it open; he felt within the younger boy's
clothes, though Innokenti tried feebly to pull his hands away, reaching
into pockets and even touching his skin. He pulled a cross on a chain
from his throat, and a pen from his pocket; two marbles, and a pepper-
mint wrapped in paper. After he had pocketed these things he knelt

before the locked door and somehow pushed out one of its lower panels. He bent Innokenti's head toward the hole, and shoved him through into the utter darkness on the other side.

For a moment he thought he would be left there. He couldn't cry out, couldn't move. Then he felt a push from behind: Teapot cursed him, *move along,* and came in after him. When he was in, he turned and put the panel of the door back in place.

Now, he said. See?

He was close enough for Innokenti to smell him. It was hot in the lightless passage. Teapot lit a match—he had matches of his own, after all—and by its light found a stub of candle hidden in the rough wall, and lit it. The darkness lightened. And Teapot pulled him along the passage.

Innokenti would later come to learn the way down, and remember it ever after: it was dangerous not to know it, maybe fatal. How he was able to do it the first time he didn't know; only because Teapot wouldn't let him stop, or rest, or weep, but pushed him along and smacked his head when he stopped in fear or in the paralysis of total loss. Teapot had a trick of attaching the candle stub to his hat so that he could use both hands to climb downward on narrow iron ladders, warm to the touch, into airless darkness. Had Innokenti believed in hell, or even heard of it? Only a grown-up would think that a child might think of such a thing, that he was descending into those fires. But he heard noises too: a kind of sudden release of dragon breath, once there, again over there; and then an eerie long human whistle. Teapot stopped at the whistle, listened, and whistled back. They reached an iron floor slick with damp. Light came from a string of bulbs in iron cages overhead, dim as candles, many broken. They walked crabwise along the passage, inches from steam pipes whose heat they could feel on their faces, that now and then at valves released that sigh or sob, and steam hot enough to scorch flesh. Duck down here; don't touch that; now stop and listen.

More whistles to answer. Then they wiggled through a hole in the thick rubble wall, and it was a little less stifling; Innokenti began to see other candles, and Teapot laughed and banged the lid of his *chainik*, and out from holes in the passage and from under piles of rags and from packing crates came white faces, girls and boys, old and young.

Got a new one, Teapot said.

Any money? said a voice, deeper, Innokenti couldn't see whose it was. There were many children, more and more gathering, some looking at him, some uncaring. Dozens.

Nah, Teapot said. He's just a *psy*.

And Teapot, who'd taken all his money and everything else he had, put his arm around Innokenti's neck and hugged and grinned at him.

She had never heard of it, and no one she asked about it then had heard of it, this world that had been hidden within the Soviet world, down deep within it, this Dickensian world with no Dickens to make things right, to tie up all the ends. It was real, though; in Russian novels of that time she would later find them mentioned, "ragamuffins" or "urchins" in the background of scenes, you knew who they were if you had been taught to look for them, they were the *besprizornye*. And she found them in the writings of others who went there in the 1920s to visit and see the Revolution for themselves; Langston Hughes saw *besprizornye* and recorded them, and so did Averell Harriman, and Theodore Dreiser, who watched a little dirty girl trying to get on a Black Sea steamer, watched her carried off screaming by the huge genial sailors who deposited her on the docks, and carried her off again when she snuck on again, and again. Stevedores taking up hay, crates of geese, boxes of canned goods. Her bare legs kicking and the Red Army soldiers guarding the dock laughing.

Millions. The children of fathers dead in the Great War, whose mothers couldn't keep them, or who were separated from their families when their villages were overrun by advancing or retreating troops as the fighting moved eastward. Children evacuated by train from the front, carried far to the east, losing their families at stations or cross-ings: the trains stopped for hours, for days, parents got off and went to look for food, and the trains were ordered to depart while they were away, and the parents never saw their child again, who might fetch up as far east as the Urals, holding a smudged and illegible form. Chil-dren left behind when their parents died of typhus, which spread rap-idly among refugees pressed into unheated barracks or shipped back and forth by train. Children orphaned in the Revolution and the civil war that followed, their parents killed by the Reds or the Whites, shot for hiding grain or concealing livestock or aiding the enemy; children lost when families again fled before one army or the other. Children sent out by the authorities from starving northern cities, Petrograd, Moscow, to the Ukraine and the Crimea, where there might be food and warmth at least: eight thousand were remanded by the Bolsheviks to Poltava, and then when the White forces took the city and the Reds retreated, the White army was left with the children.

It never stopped. After the civil war there was famine, and millions died. "Millions died": one by one, though, each in his own way, in his house or church or by the roadside to somewhere; children sitting with their dead parents, unable to go farther, their bellies swollen from eating grass. The multitudes driven from their land by collectivization, sent to the east to make new farmlands or die; many lingered or hid, tried to return to their old homes, failed along the way, their children having become practiced beggars and thieves, and so able to live. And always there were the children of those condemned by the state, arrested, taken away: their children were shunned, sometimes given up by parents or grandparents, maybe in the hope that without the taint of their father's crimes they could survive. *My father was an engineer*: there was a purge of engineers, "bourgeois specialists," accused of "wrecking," many tried and shot: Falin might have been eight or nine then.

"We all knew of them then, *besprizornye*," Gavriil Viktorovich told her. "They were a constant threat, a grief, a fear. Papers talked much of them. Other children were afraid of them, yes, and mothers frightened their children with them—don't lag behind and be lost with *besprizornye*."

Gavriil Viktorovich lifted his eyes, looking backwards; his full soft mouth and the red-rimmed liquid eyes made it seem he wept.

"I went in 1927 with my parents and many other families from Moscow to Crimea on vacation," he said. "There is a place on that railroad line where one can begin to smell the sea, and often tracks become covered with windblown sand, and train must stop so that they can be cleared. I and my little fellows, you know, all in our holiday clothes, climb down from train to collect shells that were always in the sand. Then we rushed away frightened. Under the carriages we had been riding in were these other children, dark figures, hardly human they seemed, five, ten, a dozen, more. We children ran. *Besprizornye! Besprizornye!* We were afraid and thrilled."

"Maybe one of them . . ."

"Among so many thousands." He shook his head.

"It means *without* something," Kit said. "*Besprizornyi*. He told me. More than homeless. Without . . ."

"Without guardian, unsheltered, not cared for."

"Yes."

"There was talk, back then, that perhaps to be *besprizornyi* was good training for socialism: that such children would be toughened by life, by having to rely on others; that to have all bourgeois social conventions overturned or taken away meant they would make new, cooperative ways of living. Maybe *besprizornye* would make good Communists."

He smiled in a way that made Kit feel far from home. "Did you think so?"

"Oh, I had no thoughts of such things; I was so young. But a man who thought so was Felix Dzerzhinski."

"The secret police chief."

"Yes, he. Whose statue in Moscow was not long ago pulled down. The hugest of them all, the one we all saw."

"Yes. I saw it too." Like Falin's poem: The finger that pointed Onward driven into earth to point Endward instead.

" 'Iron Felix' he was called. There is more than one person in Falin's poems named Felix, always people of great power and, and— moral ambiguity, you would say. Of course his name means Happy, or Happy One. Yes, Dzerzhinski took great interest in *besprizornye*. There had been then established for them many *detskie doma*, children's homes; *detdoma* we always called them. Most were very poor places, no staff or materials or even beds."

"He told me. He said he nearly starved in one, and ran away."

"But Cheka—that was first secret police organization of Dzerzhinski—set up its own *detdoma*. Camps and schools too. Well funded. Often children who escaped from other homes, who refused help, were selected for these."

"Like reform school."

"Well. What was said was that Cheka recruited from these schools: chose the most *toughened* and strongest and most willing children to become Chekists. Children who had already on the streets learned lessons that they must learn. That we all were to learn."

He went to the burdened shelves and without searching or pondering drew out from the clutter a handful of magazines and papers tied in red-and-white string. He picked at the knot with trembling fingers; Kit wanted to help, but knew she mustn't.

"We were all *besprizornye*," he said. "The whole society. We were all torn away from all common bonds that we had been born into. All had to rely on others, on those we found around us, yet never trust them; had to make our lives without what we had been born with, families, institutions, protectors. But it did not make us New Man, entirely social. We pretended. But we became instead nation of individuals, of atoms; only thing left to us, instinct for self-preservation. All against all."

"He said that," Kit said. "Falin."

Gavriil Viktorovich had undone the bundle, and laid it before her: thick *periodika*, and gray sheets with typewritten lines almost invisible, and a small pamphlet on cheap paper.

"He said so," Gavriil Viktorovich said. "He said long ago, in his poems. These, *The Gray Gods.*"

It was so small. Falin's body, shrunk in death or in time. She thought of her mother lifting from a cardboard box the drawings and stories and maps that Ben had made, that she had helped to make, their land.

"Our hope is to publish all, as it was—I think—meant to be; one tale, or novel in verse maybe you would say, though consists of many fragments. I have tried to transcribe, to edit."

He put them before her and she touched the pages. The paper was dry, unresponsive.

"Has never been entirely translated," he said. "Perhaps someday you might . . ."

"No," she said, and drew her hand away, and clasped it with the other. "No. Not now, when all of you can have them. No."

He tended the little pile, straightening and smoothing. "Nothing is like it in Russian poetry in this century," he said. "There was Russian writer who called himself Grin, who would not write realistic social stories, who conceived imaginary land, Grinland, where marvelous things could happen; he died young. But Falin's country in these poems was not another country, no, but one inside or alongside this one. Inhabitants of his land seem to know of this one but do not think about it very much, as though it was unimportant to them. Example. They have city, some stories are set there, called Manitograd, and it is apparently located in or on side of Stalingrad, and the name Stalingrad is mentioned, but only as name for unknown or imaginary place."

"Maybe it was slang they used," she said. "He said they had their own words, their own language."

He was nodding. "*Manit* is beckon," he said, and with his hand made the gesture, waving her gently toward him. "To lure, perhaps."

Beckonville. The Russians had just changed the name of Stalingrad back to what it was before, another grad or gorod, what was it.

"In early poems of *Gray Gods*," Gavriil Viktorovich said, "this world of Falin is spoken of as small. Perhaps, yes, like world of child-gangs to our big society, with its own rules and laws and language, secret names for things. But as poems go on, world of Falin expands. Speakers in poems now can take long journeys in this other world, which has its own transportation system, they travel to other cities, they petition officials who have offices and powers not like ours but little bit like, they try to be heard in government buildings, which are big, very big, go on forever.

"Then, at last, this world opens further, to greater realm, beyond-human realm of powers, powers maybe reflections of earthly ones, maybe not; maybe they are *originals* of earthly ones, who only reflect them. In their own great shut offices, you see. Endless. These are perhaps those Gray Gods for whom all the poems are named.

"And yet, and yet. No matter how far out it reaches, world of Gray Gods, it can suddenly become ordinary once more. As camera might change its focus, we see that we are nowhere but in dump or ashpit in Soviet city, to which *besprizornye* have come from trains or however they have come; where they have made shelters, to keep warm by fires of ash dump; and watchmen come to drive them away, and winter coming on. Then this moment passes, like hallucination. And great epic story of gods and journeys continues."

When winter was deep, Innokenti went out from the station's underground with the others to the yards to get aboard trains bound for the south, for Georgia, the Crimea. Some would go as far as Baku and Samarkand. How did they know which ones to board? Surely Innokenti didn't know. How could they take such a small child with them, how did he endure it, how did he learn not to fear, and how long did learning take him?

The smaller you were, the more places there were to hide on a train. The smallest could ride in the dog boxes or storage compartments underneath the cars, curled up out of sight; sometimes though the conductors shut and locked the boxes, not knowing there were children inside who would be trapped unable to move for hours or days, or sometimes knowing very well. If you were strong enough to hold on you could ride farther under, on the rails, just above the tracks, the endless wooden crossties flicking hypnotically by just below your feet or your face; if you slept you could lose your perch and fall under the cars. One boy that Innokenti knew had fallen into the roadbed and lay facedown still and bleeding while the cars passed over him, one, one, one, one, a hundred: he was blind in one eye afterward and his cheek always drooped, but he could tell this story. It was easy to get into coal boxes but the air was suffocating, thick with greasy coal dust, and you carried a nail or a spike to bore a hole to breathe. There were even places inside the engines, crannies and spaces inches away from the pistons and thundering wheels, hotter even than the steam pipes of the station basement. When the train stopped the firemen would cry out to see children crawling from the engines all black and skinny as devils: *Chort!*

Maybe it was then he learned invisibility, riding the trains.

In the south somewhere he lost Teapot, or was lost by him, anyway he never saw him again. In his poems a person like Teapot disappears forever only to appear again, always returning in new guises and with new employments, but those are poems. He was taken in by another gang, older boys and girls of practiced cruelty. He begged for them, having still the trick of weeping whenever he needed to and having grown as yet not much larger, his nice clothes tattered and irremediably soiled and his shoes stolen and replaced with two mismatched ones much too large, but still the good little boy could be seen beneath, and he did well.

In another colder city they lived in an ash dump that ran along a railroad spur line; there were fires burning always, and a derelict freight car collapsed on a siding where the older children made a home. The younger dug caves in the clinkers or slept in heaps under salvaged boxes or broke into sheds, or sat out and cried. During the day they went out into the city, to the markets and the streets, to beg; at night the older children went out to steal or to sell stolen things or themselves. Sometimes they returned with vodka or candy or cocaine, to be distributed according to rules they made up: one older boy Falin remembered named Chinarik or Cigarette Butt, with a withered arm like Stalin's, particularly liked this game.

Once they brought back with them a child, a *psy* or greenhorn, and talked about how they might get money for him, ransom money. After a while the boy began to cry and struggle and tried to get away, and said he would tell; they tried to make him shut up but he wouldn't stop, and they killed him. Innokenti was one of them.

"I was set guard," he said. "To watch for *mil'ton* or yard police. What I was told."

"Did you see? What they did?"

"I saw."

They held him down and hit him, and to make him stop crying they stuffed his mouth with ashes. They held him until he stopped writhing. Then they took all he had, his shoes, handkerchief, coat.

"They did that?"

"We did that. We." He tapped the gray ash from his cigarette against the ashtray, which had the college's seal on the bottom of it. "You see," he said. "I have had child, born with illness, and before she grew I was taken away to camps, and never saw her more. I think of her every day. But I have this one too, this boy, and of him too I think every day. They are both my dead children, and they will not go."

Not long after that, maybe because of that (and now he began to remember such things, causalities, the order of events, at least a little), the ash dump was swept by the authorities and the children rounded up and processed: Innokenti Isayevich entered the system. He was fed hot soup and given new boots not much better than his old ones, and then put aboard a special train, a *sanpoezda*, "sanitary" train; he had his hair cut off and was dunked in disinfectant as the train rolled, picking up as it went other *besprizornye*. He had a ticket sewn to his coat with his surname and the city he had come from, it wasn't his name but a name someone thought she heard him say, and he would have it ever after. Many of them didn't know their names; some of them refused to say them. They were given new names, common names or the names of film stars or heroes of the Revolution, Mikhail Kalinin, Len or Ninel or Vladilen, Ulyanova or Tsetkina or Elektrifikatsiya. At stations they would be off-loaded into the care of the local officials, who put them in *detskie doma*. If there was no one to meet them, or *detdoma* was already full, or there was no *detdoma*, they would go on, or be left in the station or the street.

"Sometimes *detdoma* was not so good as street," he said to her. "Hundreds try to get in; as many try to get out soon. Stay till food is gone, run away. I ran away. Not once only."

"And after that?"

"Go to market. Beg. Ride on trains. I found other friends, as we did then. I knew then the rules of how to live, how to make—what— alliances, and make myself valuable to others. I could beg, though I was perhaps not so pitiful as once. I lived. At last, arrested again, for theft. Sent to prison. Then released to new *detdoma*. This time to stay."

He put out his cigarette: she watched the strong square wrist; did his hand tremble? How much we can stand, she thought: how much, after all.

"That was first place in all my life I knew where was," he said. "Ah no: I don't make myself clear. I mean I learned only there that world is round, where on it I am; where I stand."

"They had teachers?"

"Here, yes. Khar'kov. A labor commune; we worked and learned. There were books. Not like the others."

"Was that what happened to the others, the kids you knew?"

"No. Most not. There were so many, you know: most not. Streets, markets, trains. In the end many, many were sent to camps. You see, aim of reform, rehabilitation, was soon given up; they were by then only young criminals, hooligans, human waste. They were sent to mine gold or coal, make roads, dig canals."

"Prison camps."

"*Lageria*, yes. Camps of slave labor, men and women building new land, new world. *Novy mir*."

"But not you."

"Not then."

"Well how did you, how . . ."

He had stood, restless; he went to open his office window to the spring, and Kit felt the stale air of the room pushed aside, the cool sweetness on her cheek. "Many of us who were lost," he said. "They knew only to fight, or to run away. They could not learn to eat with fork and knife, some of them; they could not listen to any command, could not sit still, not remember what happened yesterday or guess what might happen next. This had become of them. And then further things were done to them, which they could not run from, which they could not fight."

What he was saying now was hard for him to say: Kit could see.

"*I* knew," he said. "I knew. Not to run; to listen. To be not seen when looked at; to be seen when I chose; to speak, to agree, to seem. I did not *learn* these things; if I would have to learn, I would not have been able. If I had not been able, I would not now be here, telling this to you, Kyt Malone. I would not be here."

13.

"I thought about it, what he told me," Kit said to Gavriil Viktorovich. "I thought about it all the time. I guess I needed something to think about, just then, and he . . ."

"Yes."

"He offered that. He must have thought it would help me. And it did help." She looked down at her hands; she turned the ring on her ring finger. "I wanted to write about it, what he told me, when I published the book, my book, the first one, with his poems in it. But by then I didn't know if what I remembered was so."

"It is already more than I knew," Gavriil Viktorovich said. "I knew that his name was not his own. He told me that."

"He said he thought that his father was an engineer. He said it was all he knew of him."

"Yes?"

"He never told you that?"

"No. We were not then in habit of asking after families. It was not done to look into family trees, do you say this in English, family trees? You did not know who might be found peeping out from leaves, you see? A priest, perhaps, or former noble person, Tsarist policeman. No. You were New Man, no forebears; if they could not even be discovered, well, all to the good."

"So you knew he didn't remember his parents."

"No. Not that either. I thought he had family. There was story, I forget now; parents separated by war, or maybe gone pioneers to north. I cannot remember. I remember he received letters. He said so."

She turned the ring on her finger, thinking. "If he went to that camp," she said, "the one that was run by the secret police, could he have known boys there, boys who maybe later on . . . Well, I guess I don't know what I'm asking."

"That such persons would later help him; see that he got better treatment? Perhaps even intervene at the end, when he was sent away?"

"Well maybe."

"Or that perhaps he himself . . ."

"Oh my God."

Gavriil Viktorovich piled up his small collection of Falin poems, got up, and with painful care put it all away again. "In all places and times we humans have believed in luck," he said. "So perhaps this was all. Luck and his courage. But we ceased to believe in many things in time of Gray Gods, and luck was smallest thing among them."

He turned to face her, and he was smiling. "Well. Now these days at last we can look, in KGB records; they have been opened, some at least, like—like tombs. And so far there is nothing of him there."

Nothing. Kit didn't know if she felt relieved or defeated. "Do you know why he was sent to the labor camp, after the war? I mean what his supposed crime was? Is that something that can be found out?"

"He never told you?"

"No."

Gavriil Viktorovich shook his head slowly. "Perhaps in future we can know. Not now. Not today. Wherever his name appears in records, it seems only to make more mystery; and such records are few. They are very few."

He tugged down his jacket, and dusted his hands. "Now you will excuse me," he said. "I will dress for our dinner." He made her a small bow, and went behind a flowered curtain that divided his apartment in two.

Kit thought: Maybe I didn't know anything at all about him. Maybe he was simply one of those lifelong wanderers who are compelled never to tell the truth about themselves, or to admit that they don't really know the truth, and instead continually invent new pasts and new histories, not necessarily more creditable or glamorous, sometimes just parallel to the actual lives they lived, reversed or inverted for no clear reason. And she thought that some of them committed suicide: there were the survivors of camps; there was Arshile Gorky, the painter, and Kozinsky the writer; having run through all their possibilities, maybe.

Had Falin committed suicide? Is that what had happened, after all?

The things that threatened him in America, which all seemed to be shadows of what had happened to him here, reaching out for him; the plot that seemed to surround him, which he couldn't or wouldn't explain: maybe none of it was so. Maybe it was that he could not bear the sorrows that he had accumulated, or the deeds he'd done, whatever they'd been; too great a weight even for stories to lift or deflect any longer. And on that October night, when he went out in his car, when he said that the time had come, when he said he had to go on a journey and didn't know when he could come back, he was merely slipping from beneath it all, canceling all his stories like debts.

She'd watched him drive away. It was from her he had parted; she was the one to whom he'd said those things. And there was no one else now to ask, no one who knew.

Gavriil Viktorovich returned from behind the curtain unchanged, though now with a tie on, one so anonymous and dim as to be remarkable. "So," he said.

"I brought something for you," Kit said to him. "From America, I mean. Something . . . well. This."

She had brought it in a stiff brown envelope, hoping to keep it from harm, or at least to keep it, a thing so old and evanescent.

"It's the only one I have," she said. "He mailed it to me once, after the summer we worked together, when I was at home. That's why it wasn't lost with the others."

He took it from her, a single sheet of yellow copy paper darkening at the edges, the lines of typed Russian words on it uneven and faded. He looked at it in wonder, and then at her. He sat. The paper shook lightly in the tremor of his hands.

"He wrote me that I should try and understand it," she said. "But I never really did. And then with what happened . . . I always kept it. I looked at it, sometimes, and studied it. But I never tried to make a translation. I don't know why I didn't."

She watched him read. It wasn't true that she didn't know why; she only didn't know how to say why, what delicacy or fear it was that had kept her from opening the sheet on its worn tender folds and getting help somewhere from someone who knew this language as she never would.

"Can you tell what it says?" she asked. "I mean, what sense it makes?"

"Yes," he said. "I can. Harder to say, what means, in language different from, from." He removed his glasses with a sudden gesture and pressed his eyes with his fingers for a moment. He shook his head then and pulled from his pocket a handkerchief, and held it to his face. The folded sheet lay in his lap.

"What," Kit whispered.

"No no," he said. "No no." He took a great breath, composed himself. "Only, I thank you. For this. I knew him so long ago, so long ago."

He looked down again at the poem. Kit waited. She knew how hard it was to draw out even a little of the sense of a poem from its carapace; for its carapace was the thing itself.

"Isn't it about angels?" she asked. "The angels of the nations."

"Yes," he said. "It says that there is angel who watches over the affairs of every nation; and that each such angel has an opposite."

"A little angel," she said. "A lesser angel."

He put the poem between them; he found on his table a pad of rough paper, and from his jacket took out a pencil. He put the pad before her, and held out the pencil; and the moment parted, and it wasn't Gavriil Viktorovich before her, or this place or time; then it healed, and she was here.

"See," he said. "Look."

In an hour, with his help and a dictionary he fetched, she had written out on the little pad the fourteen lines. The title was a date: *1963.*

> *Child, never forget that this too is true:*
> *So that justice in our cosmos may be preserved,*
> *The angels that watch over our nations each has an opposite,*
> *A left hand whose works the strong right hands don't know.*
> *If a nation's angel is proud, then the other is shy*
> *Brilliant if the nation's angel is dull*
> *Full of pity if the angel shows none*
> *Laughing if it always weeps, weeping if it cannot weep.*
>
> *But so that order may also be preserved*
> *(Which has always concerned the great ones more)*
> *The nation's angel is the greater, older and more terrible,*
> *And from his sight the lesser always hides.*
> *Lost, pale and bare, he shivers and sings*
> *And there is no reproach so stinging as his smile.*

Gavriil Viktorovich smiled and shrugged, unable to tell her finally if what she wrote was like or unlike what Falin had written. He thought there were other people, at the dinner tonight, who would know better, if she would show her translation to them. She shook her head, however; she ripped the sheet from the pad and put it in her purse, and returned Falin's poem to Gavriil Viktorovich.

"It was for you," she said. "Because it was all I had."

He folded it up along its old folds with care, and replaced it in the envelope Kit had brought. He asked her again the date that Falin had sent it to her, and only then did he notice that the title Falin had given it was a year beyond the year in which he had written and sent it: a year beyond the end of his own life, as well.

"Berdyayev also speaks of this concept, angels of the nations," Gavriil Viktorovich said to her as they went toward the subway, which didn't seem to Kit to be very close. The evening was alight, more dreamlike than before, and he led her through a kind of dream wilderness of abandoned or forgotten construction materials, a path that seemed to have been made long ago over heaps of gravel or sand, past heavy equipment covered in tarpaulins. "Berdyayev, Russian religious philosopher, expelled from Soviet Union 1922, perhaps you know? Well in any case." She almost wished he wouldn't talk so much, waste his strength; she felt an impulse to take his arm, help him along.

"What Berdyayev asks," he said. "Angels of nations are each different, as nations are. And do nations take their special characters from their angels, or is it opposite?"

"I don't understand," Kit said.

"Well, may it be that even such great guardians are altered by long association with nations they protect? If that is so, what has become of ours?"

They reached the subway, and he guided her downwards, gave her the fifteen kopeks for the entry, and showed her where it was to be inserted. The patch of red light turned green and she was through.

"I think the angel of our nation must have long ago become discouraged by us, and no wonder," he said to her. "Degraded, depressed, sorrowful. Perhaps corrupted even; brutal, uncaring. I hope not. I fear so."

"Then what would happen to the lesser angel?"

"Ah. Well. Of that being, we know only what Falin tells us. Yes? Even of his existence we did not know before." He smiled at her. The crowd pressed toward the escalators. She had always loved and feared subways, always rode them in whatever city she traveled to, collecting new ones as other tourists collected famous views. Why was it so crowded at this hour? It was a tremendously long way down, longer than the way down in any New York subway, and seemed to issue in darkness far below.

"I suppose," he said, "worst thing such a corrupted great angel could do would be to send away into exile the lesser angel who is paired with him. Even destroy. Just as Stalin could not bear to have around him anyone who reminded him of what he had done, no he must kill or get rid of all of them."

Like the hotel she had been put in, at once so bleak and so dowdy, the cavernous station seemed to her not very much like anywhere she had ever been. It was ostentatiously industrial but somehow not modern, as unmodern and un-Western as a gilded ikon.

"Did you know that Stalin feared poets?" Gavriil Viktorovich said. "Oh yes. Example: Pasternak. When Stalin's wife died—by suicide, though no one knew—then poets wrote condolences for newspaper. 1932. Pasternak wrote too. He wrote that *that very night* of her death he had thought hard about Stalin, thought *as poet* about him for first time; and when next day he heard news, he was so shocked, as though he had been there beside Stalin when it happened." The train slid into the station almost silently. "Stalin never harmed Pasternak. Never dared, it may be. What other powers might he have?"

It was so strange to be having this conversation, here, that Kit laughed a little; she felt like Alice, talking to the Gryphon.

"Oh is true, is true," Gavriil Viktorovich said. "Later when Mandelstam wrote his poem denouncing Stalin, famous poem, Pasternak asked Bukharin to intercede with Stalin, not to have him arrested. And Stalin agreed, and he *called Pasternak on telephone* and told him Mandelstam would not be touched. And Pasternak, such brave man, asked Stalin if perhaps they might meet and talk. About what? Stalin asked. Life and death, said Pasternak. And Stalin hanged up the phone. Pasternak grieved ever after: could not get Stalin back on phone, could not talk to him, tell him truths. One chance. Here is our stop."

As long a way up as down, their own ascension falling in a gap in the flow of people, they two alone.

"Then could it be," Kit said, "that they put him out—Falin—because they were afraid of him? That somebody was?"

Gavriil Viktorovich said nothing, and at first Kit thought he hadn't heard; then she was sure he had, and had no answer.

In the time after Falin was lost or went away, she had used to think that if ever she could come here, to this country, and could look far enough or deep enough, she would find him eventually, alive and smiling as always: here again where he should be. No matter what he had said. The certainty came back to her as they arose toward the street and the evening: she knew for sure, as she had once known for sure, that he hadn't killed himself, nor had he been killed. It wasn't possible. It was easier to believe that he was here now in this city; that because the world was no longer what it had been, because she had come here at last, he might be waiting at the top of the stairs, might appear beside her from somewhere or nowhere as he so often had: not dead, not even changed.

But they came out into golden light and the crowds along a brilliant river, nothing she had foreseen, street lights lit and shop windows full of goods, men and women in summer clothes walking arm in arm. Leaving the subway exit she felt the strangest sensation: her hand suddenly taken. She cried out in surprise. It was a child, a small boy, dirty or dark-skinned, smiling up at her and holding a single rose wrapped in cellophane.

"Nyet!" Gavriil Viktorovich beside her said, prying the child not untenderly from Kit's side and pushing him away; and now Kit could see several children working the stream of people, each with a single rose, shamelessly taking people's hands and insisting; one small boy, no more than five, pleading with and actually wrapped around the leg of a well-dressed woman, who was ordering him off, laughing in exasperation.

Gavriil took Kit's arm. "You see," he said. "Once again, *besprizornye*. It is not only the poets who now return to us." Kit looked back;

the boy who had taken her hand—his T-shirt as big on him as a smock, advertising something American—still looked after her for a moment, smiling, before he turned to pester someone else.

The restaurant, off the Nevsky Prospekt, was on a floor above the street, the steps leading upward crowded with eager people, mostly young and talking and smoking with passion. Inside it was all white and gold and draped with blue drapes, the tables covered with long cloths: Kit couldn't decide what sort of place it was, how it had come to be, if it had evolved by chance or had been created last week to look this way. It was loud and messy and the waiters in white aprons seemed not pleased to be there.

A crowd at a great round table signaled to Gavriil Viktorovich, and he guided Kit to it.

"Our committee," he said.

Most of them were old, and some were very old; they seemed to have survived more than years, they seemed like aged trees that had been harmed but not killed by long droughts and terrible winters, limbs lopped and misshapen, thick bark scarred and cut. They displayed the history they had lived through in the ropy veins of their hands, their teeth, their bent bodies.

Kit was introduced to each of them, and each of them claimed to speak no English, or only a little English, and Kit said the lines she had worked out, about her own Russian, and they laughed and some of them left their places to come and hug her. As though they had been waiting for years to meet her, she thought, as though she had been away on a long and hard journey and had come back to them at last.

A red-faced man with Brezhnev's Tartar eyes and hawk's-wing eyebrows rose at the table's end and made a toast to Gavriil Viktorovich, which everyone joined. Gavriil Viktorovich made one in return: to Innokenti Isayevich Falin. When they had drunk that, he would not let them sit; he made them drink again, to Christa Malone. And they lifted their glasses and drank.

"When conference was first proposed," the man on her left said. "When Gavriil Viktorovich first began to speak of it. Was a certain

..nent in our history, in our . . . catastrophe. For the first time exiled and forbidden writers could be spoken of openly. In *periodika*, literary journals you know, were published so many things . . ."

"Zamyatin," said another man, from across the table, who hadn't seemed to be following. "Nabokov. Kafka. *1984.*"

"We had of course read many of them already in *samizdat* or in smuggled copies, but here they were at news kiosks. Everyone read like hungry man. But as well were appearing work of those who had been sent abroad or who had escaped to other side, and of whom we had heard nothing for so long. Now books of theirs came into country, and were not confiscated; we read Brodsky, Aksyonov. Many others. Riches."

"Yes," Kit said. She'd heard about them, the people reading on the trains and crowded streetcars, swapping books and journals, reading two at a time.

"Conferences too," Gavriil Viktorovich said. "Writers discussed whose names had for so long not been spoken in public. It is true. Falin too. Now we could ask: what happened, what became of them."

Kit found they had all turned to her.

"You know," she said, "that he was never found."

They waited, neither assenting nor dissenting.

"Supposedly it was just an accident," she said. "A car accident."

"No accidents," said a tiny woman whose freckled breastbone barely rose above the table's edge. "There are no such."

"I'll tell you what I know," she said, not for the first or the last time in that week. "Everything I can tell."

"First eat," Gavriil Viktorovich said to her in Russian, and filled her glass. " 'Eat bread and salt and speak the truth.' What we always say."

The restaurant had begun to fill with parties, waiters pushing tables together and people taking pictures and rising to make toasts that made others laugh or cheer. At one round corner table a group that were surely Americans sat with several Russians in black leather or Italian suits, some with their hair pulled back in ponytails. Their table was crowded with bottles, champagne, Stolichnaya, Chivas. Gavriil Viktorovich saw her look.

"*Biznesmeny*," he said to her. "*Konsultantye*. Our new Gray Gods."

The meal went on and on without ever seeming to have begun, plate after plate of salty and piquant *zakuski*, appetizers: smoked salmon, herring, blini with caviar red and black, *griby v smetane* which she guessed were Mushrooms in Confusion but no, that would be *smyatennye*, these were only in sour cream. They poured vodka for her and leaned over to her to take her hand or to touch her and speak: *dusha-dushe*. Kit remembered her teacher Nadezhda Fyodorovna saying it, striking her breast so that her bangles sounded: *dusha-dushe*, soul to soul.

The woman next to her turned great smiling dark eyes on her. "I have read many poems of yours," she said. "Read with great interest, yes."

"You have?" There's nothing, no proposal of delight or compliment or vatic prophecy, that will enter a poet's heart as such a statement does. And here of all places.

"Contemporary American poetry is my speciality," the woman said, pronouncing it with an extra syllable, like a Briton. "I have read often your poem that begins *If you return O my dead, and you will, from your ashes and earth*. This is very fine."

It was "Ghost Comedy." Kit felt her throat tighten with strange wonder to hear the line in this heavy grave accent.

"This was written 1982?"

"No. It was finished then. It was . . . It took a long time."

"It is elegiac meter, no?"

"Well almost," Kit said. "I didn't mean it to be." The woman looked at her in puzzlement, or disbelief, still smiling. She was, still was, darkly beautiful. "I mean I didn't know it was when I wrote it. I found out later, when it was done."

Return if you can as the ghosts in ghost comedies do. She would see him in a moment at the end of this table, his drowned-man's hair afloat, his smile that knew everything and nothing. Breaking a real piece of dark bread like Jesus at Emmaus. But his feet bare that couldn't be seen: she alone would know.

il Viktorovich lifted his knife, and rising he gently tapped his
get their attention. It took some time, and even when he began
to speak not everyone turned to him or fell silent. Kit tried to follow
what he said, and understood only when he drew out the envelope that
she had given him, the poem Falin had sent to her at the summer's
end. Then they were hushed, and still. Gavriil Viktorovich began to
read, the thin old paper trembling in his hand but his voice strong and
sweet. When he reached the end and sat, there was no applause or
sound or even movement for a moment, as they all seemed to gather
again one by one from where the poem had taken them.

"You were lovers, then, in that summer? You and he?"

It took her a moment, a moment out of time, to realize that the
woman beside her had spoken to her in Russian, and that she had
understood. *Lyubovniki:* lovers. She had asked Falin then what the
word meant, if it meant what it means in English. *And what in English
does it mean?* he said; and she had tried to tell him.

"No, no," she said. "Not then. But yes a little later. Or maybe not. I
mean . . ."

The woman waited for more, an answer. The great violet lids closed
over the globes of her eyes and rose, and then again.

"*Lyubovniki,*" Kit said. "It means you, well you slept together, isn't
that right?"

"Right. Yes."

"Well I don't know," Kit said smiling. "I'm not sure. I know it
sounds crazy, that you could be not sure."

"Like a dream?" the woman asked. "Or—how do you say this—a
spell."

"A spell," Kit said, still smiling helplessly. But it didn't seem to her
that what happened on that last long October night was a spell he cast
over her. It was one he lifted: a spell she had been under for a long
time, that he broke to let her out.

At the corner table a disagreement had arisen; voices were getting
loud. People were turning to look. Kit thought that among the Americans were one or two who had been on the plane with her, though

probably they were only like those men. Were they afraid? The Russian *biznesmeny* arose suddenly in a group and filed out, glancing around themselves as if they might be challenged, or applauded. They passed where Kit sat; she thought she could smell cologne.

"You see," Gavriil Viktorovich said. "We go from country where nothing could change, to country now where every day everything is different. Interest in writing now is not what it was, even one year ago. Even *writers* are not so interested. Other things to think of. Everything becomes important, or nothing."

"*Monye* now is everything," the tiny old woman opposite Kit said.

"Like those lesser angels, as Falin writes," he said to Kit. "In her dark time Russia was kept alive by the poets, the true poets. Perhaps now in the new time they will pass. They will cease to be souls, or persons, and become only books."

He slowly tucked back into the inner pocket of his shapeless coat the envelope that contained Falin's poem. "It may be we will lose him again," he said. "And it may be that this time he will go where truly no one can find him."

The restaurant was quieter, chastened or abashed. The Americans left at the corner table looked into their glasses or at one another.

But it couldn't be, Kit thought: it couldn't be that a nation's lesser angel could be driven out, banished, for good There could be no justice and no order on the earth if that were so; no power, however great, could do that.

Child, never forget that this too is so. Had that child been she, had he spoken to her and her alone, to warn or to explain? And did he know she wouldn't discover it till she came here—here, bearing with her his fourteen lines—so long after that year in which they might have been lovers, the year the world didn't end?

II

1

When her first semester at the University was over in May, Kit collected her grades (they were sent home too, on little slips printed for the first time by a computer): a B+ in Psychology, A's in the rest except for her A– in Falin's class: the highest grade he gave anyone, she learned.

Fran wanted her to come to New York with her for a while, stay at her mother's apartment on Riverside Drive, go hear some music, sit in dark coffeehouses in the Village. But Kit had to say no (Fran nodding solemnly as though she expected nothing more); had to go home for a while, spend time with George and Marion, if her plan, her new plan, was to come off.

"You *are* crazy about him," Jackie said when she told him about the plan. "Maybe just crazy altogether." He wished he could be around the University in the summer, instead of working; taking some courses, getting some credits maybe toward his second major (economics) or maybe just some education courses, something to fall back on.

"Like a sword," Kit said.

She packed her paperbacks and her papers and Ben's letters, Ben's typewriter too, hers forever now (it would be in her attic thirty years later, in its case), and the clothes she'd brought, which seemed now to belong mostly to somebody else: she had lived the semester in three sweaters, her straight skirts and Capezios, and the black ballet leotards and tights that Fran had got her mother to send out from New York. The rest filled her laundry case, amazing contraption of beaverboard and canvas straps. Marion had carried this case with her to Vassar, and the ghosts of old postage were still perceptible on it. Back then you filled such a case with your laundry and belted it up, then turned over the little address card in its windowed holder, and back it went for Mom to empty and fill again with washed and ironed clothes smelling of home.

Home. Kit sat in the lounge, waiting again for her father to come and carry her and her bags home.

Her parents were moving again. This time back East, outside Washington, D.C., where they had lived years ago, and where George would (he said) be designing bomb shelters for computers—"*electronic bomb shelters*," he said, smiling at a joke that only he could get. Marion looked out at her June garden, and the pretty mosaic table she had made especially for it, in grief and exasperation. Kit was exasperated too: why did her mother always think they were going to stay where they went, when they never did? And only that night, in her own old bed and in the suffocating warmth and familiarity of being home again, did she see that it wasn't the garden or the house that Marion was torn to leave behind. Her son's grave was here, in this city, in the raw new part of the old Catholic cemetery, and always would be.

They treated Kit like visiting royalty, taking her out to dinners and movies and even on trips to points of historic interest, as though unwilling to stay in the house. When they were home George made them play Scrabble or casino; or he put LPs on his new stereo system, an engineer's dream all in separate parts—a glowing amplifier, four speakers, the massy turntable on its weighted base. George slipped the

records from their paper jackets as though they were delicacies, turning them skillfully by their edges with his long white fingers. And got
his wife up out of her chair to dance.

Kit and Ben had always found this music their father loved hilari-
ous, Louis Armstrong, Bix Beiderbecke, Bunny Berrigan; it seemed to
be played by cartoon animals, the singers to be kidding. But it had that
jingle-jangle sweetness that made George take his wife's hand and pull
her to her feet.

"See, you don't have to go to college to be rich and have a big life,"
George said, squiring Marion around the room. "Look at these guys.
Most of them didn't finish high school. Hell, grade school." Each of his
phrases was marked by a turn. Marion's eyes were closed, her neat little
feet seeming to be propelled by his. Kit wondered what that felt like, to
be certain and swift and surefooted because your man was. She could
almost hear their hearts beat together, like it said in these songs: to beat
as one. They'd always been like that, she thought, George and Marion;
opposites matching, fitting together the way only opposites can, like
the two magnetic Scotties that click together, the black one and the
white one. The best of friends. How much could that make up for?
They couldn't get over Ben, no more than she could: but maybe if they
could always have these moments, these moments when they couldn't
tell one from the other, then maybe they wouldn't need her so badly.

Meanwhile her letter had come from the Language Institute; Marion handed it to her incuriously along with other mail from the Uni
versity. Kit made sure the offer was what she hoped it would be, and as
they waited for dinner at George's favorite long low steakhouse on the
highway she told them what she was going to do.

"Russian?" her mother said, as though it were basket weaving, or
sexology. "Why on *earth*."

She told them about the Institute's summer program, the scholarship money she'd been awarded, the intensive study. She'd be able to
catch up, she said; with these hours and some more hard work she'd be
able to graduate with her class, her true class, the Class of 1965. Still
they looked at her, fingers on the stems of their drinks.

"It's a government program," George said.

"No. It's just the University."

"Believe me," said George. "It's DoD money, honey. Just like mine."

It was the first time Kit had ever heard him say what his money was. She worked out what DoD must mean. "Okay," she said. "So?"

"Well what would you do with it?" Marion asked. "I mean."

"Okay," Kit said. "I talked to this person, she's taking this same course. She said that the National Security Administration . . ."

"Agency," said George. "The National Security *Agency*."

"Agency. They need people with Russian. And the CIA. Lots of government places. Government bodies."

"Well," said Marion.

"You know I've always been good at languages," said Kit. A silence fell again. Kit decided not to say that on her own application she too had expressed interest in the CIA; it had seemed the right response, to win their favor. Marion's brows were knitted (it was this face of Marion's that would always illustrate that funny phrase for Kit), and George studied her acceptance letter as though for hidden watermarks. It must have been (Kit only thought this later on) like a Catholic family who've been told their daughter has decided to be a nun: hard to find grounds for objection. And maybe because they thought that what she was doing was somehow a tribute to Ben, to his impulse to service, or to George, they couldn't fight her for long. For once, like Ben, she had thought of everything. It was the first time she'd ever made and executed such a plan, and it would be a very long time till she did so again.

Marion asked her to clean out her room before she went back, and to throw out all she could; in the apartment where they would be living there would be no attic, no basement where the archives of years could be stored. So she went through her things, judging quickly and harshly, pulling out her high school notebooks, prizes, pictures of girls she would never see again with rash and unfelt protestations of eternal friendship written over them, and throwing them toward the wastebasket in a kind of rage: knowing already where this was leading.

Three black folders in the left-hand drawer; a composition book with marbled cover; some loose sheets of blue-lined school paper and pages torn from spiral notebooks. Her handwriting changing as she grew older, her preferred ink color too. Drafts with more crossed out than left alone; final copies typed on onionskin. She could hold it all in one hand easily. Almost none of it had ever been seen, except by her.

There would be times, when she was much older, that she would wish she could go back to that evening and take it all out of her hands, the hands of that child, and make it safe, whatever it contained, however unworthy to be saved: times in which it seemed to her that she had nothing, nothing but her self to care for. But she couldn't go back, and it was all carried to the wire incinerator near the garage, and thrown in to be burned up with waste and old newspapers, with *Time* and *Life*.

She came back through the kitchen, where Marion was wrapping and packing glassware with the grim efficiency of long practice, and sat at the end of the plaid couch where George was watching TV. She didn't feel cleansed, or shriven; not naked, or unburdened, or as though she had suffered a wound self-inflicted; not anything. She felt nothing. But for a long time she watched the gray figures come and go on the screen without actually perceiving them.

"Here's your pal," George said.

President Kennedy was speaking. *To recognize the possibilities of nuclear war in the missile age without our citizens knowing what they should do and where they should go if the bombs begin to fall would be a failure of responsibility.*

There were scenes of people passing city doorways that were stamped with a special hex sign; in the basements down below were piles of dry food, containers of water, medicines. It looked hopeless and sad.

"Look at this guy," George said. A man stood in a tubular space like a sewer pipe or a submarine, his private shelter; it had cost him fifteen hundred dollars to build, and he had stocked it with bottled beer, a rifle, and a 1939 *Encyclopaedia Britannica*. Nuclear war would set the world back a generation, he said, and these books would tell him how to live, back then.

They were there, she could see their brown backs in their case behind him.

She could do that too. All she needed.

"So you think they're going to drop it?" George asked her.

"No," Kit said. "It would be too stupid. Just too stupid."

"Uh-huh." He crossed his arms, grinning as though her answer was the one he expected. "Well, I hope to God you're right."

"You don't think I am."

"I think it's about fifty-fifty."

"No," she said. "I don't think that."

Kit had once had bomb dreams: she knew no one who grew up in those days who didn't have them, dreams of mysterious and total desolation, or the oncoming of disaster like a huge wind or wave rising without warning, at which you woke. Rarely the event itself, which maybe even dreams could not imagine: only just after, or just before.

There was a time when she had refused to sleep, afraid that in the anti-world it would come again, that huge hollow that opened in the world, or in her heart. To comfort her, Ben had told her about the DEW Line: far in the north, ringing the continent, there were radar stations watching day and night, and no bomber from Russia would ever come that they wouldn't see; and so we'd be warned, and we could hide.

He was right that it was the inexplicable suddenness that was the fearful part. She would lie in her bed, eyes on her night-light, thinking of the dew line, which she thought of as somewhere so far north that no dew fell: like the timberline, above which no trees grew. Hoping they were awake and listening.

She didn't believe it would fall, not anymore. She didn't think about it falling: at least not awake. But she also knew that it didn't matter what she thought or believed; and maybe her inability to imagine a future for herself, to imagine what her life might someday contain (a husband, children, work), was because of its falling, in the future: the shock wave of it so final that it not only blanked out everything that followed but reached backwards too, to the moment of her sitting here, empty and still.

When she went back to the University she brought the square mahogany Webcor record player that had been a joint Christmas gift for her and for Ben, and all the records she had bought for herself and for him since then. The bitter machine smell, unique to it, that arose when the lid was lifted was home, and winter. A little haiku-like poem of that year was about it:

> Black ivy by the window
> Beaten by cold rain.
> Inside, Brahms.

She brought her bike too. It was a long walk from the barrackslike dorms of the Language Institute to the center of campus and the town, she told George, helping him tie it to the car's roof; she'd need it. It was her first and only bike. Ben had made her learn to ride, saying he'd just leave her behind when he went to the park or the natatorium if she couldn't keep up, and she had made George answer an ad for a bike in the Lost & Found/Swap & Shop column of the paper. Fifteen dollars was all it cost, a bike like no other in the world, which made it (she felt) fit for her alone. It was a Schwinn English—styled like the ones you saw in European movies, only made (it seemed) of iron pipe; it was heavy as hell, Ben laughed aloud when he tried to take it from the back of the station wagon when they brought it home. The handbrakes had been at some time swapped for a standard back-pedal, and the whole thing had been repainted bright blue with what appeared to be house paint. But the seat was narrow, smooth black leather, and the tires were slim and delicate like a thoroughbred's withers, and Kit loved it like a pony from the first.

"Do other students use bikes these days?" George asked doubtfully, untying it now in the cracked parking lot of the Institute dorm compound. The summer heat was already intense.

"I don't know," Kit said. "No, not many. I don't care." She'd bought a lock for it, which George thought was funny, and which in the end she never used.

"Like summer camp," George said, looking around. Long gray one-story buildings, lettered A, B, C on their faces, the parking lot, and some sycamores that had grown tall since the buildings had been thrown up, just after the war, for returning soldiers crowding into the University. It was like the army, not camp. They both thought it, but neither said it.

Her room. Now and then through her life there would be places like this for her, places that looked like confinement and poverty or at least austerity but which filled Kit with a rich sense of possibility, welcomed her and made her heart's doors open as though to the same room's original, inside. The varnished wooden floors and window frames, crooked window propped open with a stick; and the black fan with three silver blades and a twisted cord of black and white; and the iron bed and thin mattress, the Celotex walls where the amber rectangles of old Scotch tape remained; and the wooden desk, and the gooseneck lamp.

"Christ," said George. "And how much is this costing, again?"

"Scholarship, Dad."

"No air-conditioning? God, I remember . . ." But what he remembered, army stories, he didn't say.

Down the hall were the showers, smelling of damp zinc and mildew, private stalls at least for the girls, who had only one-third of one of the three buildings, and only one girl to a room. Kit sat on her bed. She had a wicked impulse to apologize to George for her strange choice, for herself as girl, as young person, as strange spirit, just to make sure he understood it thoroughly. Instead she said, "It's okay. Really. It's what I wanted. Thanks."

"Well," George said. There were dark circles under the arms of his Dacron shirt, and his bald forehead gleamed. "If we can't have what *we* want, I'm glad that at least you do."

She got up and hugged him.

"Now you have to come to us when the program's over," he said, holding her tight. "Before fall semester."

"I will."

"You have to come home."

"Yes," she said. "I promise. I will."

2

First there was the alphabet, which even when she had memorized it and listened to the teacher and the tapes over and over still seemed to Kit when she looked at it to be mute. She could hear a sentence in English or even French just by looking at it on the page, but these she never could: at best she heard a dim mumble, as though the sentences were spoken by someone with a mouthful of cotton. Not so when Nadezhda Fyodorovna spoke them aloud: then they became a kind of vocal acrobatics, her red-painted mouth moving in ways that Kit was sure hers never could as she produced the long, long sounds of the language, at once ludicrous and beautiful.

> Today the weather is cold.
> Saturday the weather was cold.
> Tomorrow the weather will be cold.
> It has been cold for a long time.

Nadezhda Fyodorovna was small and solid, her too-black hair in a tight bun, her hands red and marked with psoriasis; as she listened to her students she stroked one hand with the other, secretly tending to them, the fingers searching and scratching. Kit followed their motions, sometimes losing the thread of the lesson. Nadezhda Fyodorovna lifted her hand in a magician's gesture and let her gold bracelets clash together; she plucked gently at the rattling beads around her neck. How had this woman come here? Why was she here, doing this, looking at them all with this look of hope and anger?

Her fellow students were mostly air force enlisted men, on a special course. They didn't know why they had been assigned to learn Russian, but it didn't seem to bother them at all; they said they'd be told eventually, and meanwhile seemed pleased with light duty. They were like Burke Eggert, like Ben, confident men who took their work as seriously as though it were play, at which they actually worked hard, playing one-hoop basketball on the cracked concrete with a kind of furious gaiety till the green evening began to fade from the sky and the ball grew invisible. They were big eaters who drank milk at breakfast and made themselves peanut butter and jelly sandwiches after they'd consumed their hot lunch, stuck their hands in their pant tops and belched gratefully. They wore no uniforms; knit shirts and madras button-downs, pressed khakis, white socks and loafers or desert boots. But beneath their shirts, like the Miraculous Medal on a beaded chain that Kit had worn for a while as a child, were their stamped steel tags. Ben's had been returned to George and Marion.

After supper on the Saturday night of her first week of classes, Kit pushed her bike out to the street that led away from the Language Institute housing. It was slightly downhill from the crest on which the University was built to the center of town, and she coasted much of the way, aloft in the still-sunny evening, late June, the checkered shade. At the center of town she turned on North Street as she had with Jackie in the first week of the winter semester.

This was what the bike had been for all along. Though she didn't build futures for herself, sometimes she could see one, a vivid moment that was to happen to her, and sometimes it really would happen; and this moment on her bike on North Street going west out of town was one.

The road looked different burdened with roadside brush and over-arched by heavy-leaved trees, but this had certainly been it. Her legs prickled with sweat. Blackberries were ripening in the fearsome tangled briars along the road, canes springing higher than her head. And that was the house, more modest and much more weatherbeaten than the house she had glimpsed in the winter but the only candidate; she turned into the dusty driveway, where a new car was parked, a big convertible in two nameless shades of green. Kit dismounted and dropped the bike. The silence was deep, the cicadas warning her; she walked around the front of the house, where the blinds were drawn, through a stand of lilacs, to a broad backyard.

He was working in the garden, feet bare, cuffs of his blue serge pants rolled up and a sleeveless undershirt dark with sweat. He waved a greeting, smiling, making Kit think of Soviet farmers in photographs. *The Family of Man*. Dusting his hands on his pants, he came to her.

She greeted him in Russian, feeling suddenly foolish; and he returned it to her, graciously. He offered her his hand, seeming to be unsurprised somehow but delighted: her own hand felt crushed within the heat and strength of his. She smelled him.

"Kyt," he said.

"I came out to see you," she said, not having meant to say that, having meant to say that she was out and about and just happened to be passing. He nodded and spread his hands as though to offer her what lay around them: his part of the house, with its jalousie or screened porch; a picnic table of gray wood; the brown yard and brick path. The garden.

"What are you growing?" she asked.

"I am not growing," he said. "Ah. What have I planted, you are asking. Yes. Well." He took her hand, and led her to the neat rows, where green things were coming up, rows of this kind, rows of that. "I have tomatoes, cabbage," he said. "Here. And carrots. Potatoes."

"Potatoes?" She knew of no home gardeners who grew potatoes, but how many had she known? She thought of Marion, bent over her cucumbers and radishes, one eye closed against the rising smoke of her Pall Mall.

"Yes, potatoes," he said. "For soup in winter. They are also easy, you know. Put potatoes in ground; cover a little; soon more potatoes. Like magic. Why they conquered the world."

She noticed how many of his crops were root ones, that wouldn't be ripe till late.

"Ah but they last. Any Russian knows. I knew high official in Leningrad. In autumn he must have his potatoes. Hundred pounds. In basement. Then, good winter, no matter what."

"He couldn't get potatoes in winter?"

"Oh yes. Even when others could not. But old habit. You know."

She laughed, thinking of officials in American cities with potatoes stored in the basements of their apartments, safe till spring at least. Maybe someday.

He gathered his tools, apparently done for this day, and put them in a wooden wheelbarrow. "I am very glad to see you," he said. "But why are you here and not far away at home?"

"Summer school," she said. "You know I started late. I'm trying to catch up."

He nodded, regarding her. "And studying what?"

"Russian," she said.

At first he only looked at her in mild puzzlement; then a kind of illumination filled his features, which vanished into a laugh, of delight or triumph or something else she couldn't name. "Russian," he said.

"It's an intensive course," she said. "All day every day."

"To speak or to read?" he asked.

"Well both."

"And you do this for what reason?"

She shrugged. "Oh," she said. "I don't know. I like languages. Maybe I'll be a spy."

"Aha." He gestured toward his house, inviting her to it, still regarding her, still smiling. "Come in. Have tea. Lemonade. Tell me what poems you have written."

"I told you," she said. "I've given up writing poetry."

"You would not be first to have tried that and yet not succeeded," he said. "Certain people give up poetry but poetry does not give them up."

She said nothing in reply, and that was a reply, which he seemed to accept. He pulled open the squeaking screen door.

The porch was dark after the still-bright day, paneled with pine, and there was a davenport or glider upholstered in plaid canvas; pictures on the walls with no reason for being there or anywhere, dim views of unreal places, sad clowns. He took a flannel shirt from a hall tree, seemed to consider it, thought better of it. He was larger indoors, his white skin shadowed with black hair and his dusty feet.

"Your fellow students," he said. "Also spies? Is this why they study?"

"I don't know. They say *they* don't know. They're soldiers."

"Perhaps only to read Pushkin."

"Or Falin."

He bent to the kitchen sink to wash: she watched him rapidly and efficiently scrub his hands and face, splash water on his head and neck and arms, and she knew he had done so for years in places without baths or showers; like an American of another era, a farmer or settler or miner, making do. For no reason she knew, a hot pity arose in her.

He toweled himself with a ragged and colorless thing that hung by the sink, and pulled open the refrigerator. "Lemonade," he said. "Or tea with ice, American invention, very nice."

"Either," she said. "You pick." She walked into the living room, divided from the kitchen by a half-wall; she peeked into a little bedroom, where a lumpy bed was spread with chenille. There were shelves meant for display of knickknacks that instead held small piles of books, all library books as far as she could see, and a folding card table that was a desk. Otherwise there seemed to be nothing of him here at all; if he left tomorrow no one would know he'd been here.

She sat on the couch. He brought her a glass of lemonade. "Now," he said. "You must say truly why you come to this university, this hot place, in summer, to study such hard language."

"I needed something to do," she said. "Something hard to do. Something that was all the time."

He waited.

"I wanted not to be at home. There's no one at home. My parents are moving. I like it here."

She sipped the drink. It was violently sweet, as though concocted for bees, or hummingbirds. "Also," she said. "You."

"Me?"

"You said to me once," she said, "that your poems could only be read, that I could only really read them, if I learned Russian . . ." His head was shaking No and he had raised a finger to correct her, but she went on: "And so I'm going to, so I can."

"I said that in translation they are different poems. Good or bad. Not that in other languages they did not exist."

"I wanted to read them as you wrote them," she said, and lowered her eyes. "That's all."

"Well," he said. "Maybe someday. In six weeks, no."

"No, of course." She had begun to feel stupid, having brought a gift that wasn't wanted, wasn't even a gift.

"In any case you have given up poetry, you say. So."

"I've only given up writing it. Not reading it. Not . . ." She almost said *not needing it.*

"A language," he said. "It is a world. My poems are written for the people of a world I have lost. To read them I think you must have lived in my world—my language—since childhood, and grown up in it."

"How will your poems get to them now, though? Your new poems, I mean. Who will bring them back there?"

He only went on looking at her frankly, holding his glass in an oddly un-American elbow-cocked way; and for the first time she saw the harm they had done him, that they had meant to do him, by putting him out. In almost every way that could be enumerated it was better to be here than there, she knew that; and when she thought of him she imagined an angel fled from a comical terrible hell, a sulfurous wonderland of cruel illogic from which he had escaped untouched and unharmed. But they had known what they were doing, what a vengeance they were taking.

"Would you," he said, "enjoy to read a poem of mine, with me?"

"Yes," she said, and her heart filled. "I would."

For a long moment he still stood, as though his question and her answer had not been said. Then he went to the card-table desk and picked up some sheets of yellow paper, written, she saw, on both sides, in pencil and in ink, much of it crossed out. With these he came and sat beside her on the brown couch.

"The poem is called '1937,' " he said. "It is a year."

She nodded, as still as though she watched a brave but wary animal come close. He began to read. Though his eyes were lowered to the paper he seemed to speak from memory, and sometimes his eyes closed as he spoke. It wasn't the big strange voice with which he had read Pushkin; it wasn't Nadezhda Fyodorovna's incantatory exactness; but it was more than plain speech too, the rhythms more clear and hard-struck than they would be in a poem read in English, iambs stepping gravely forward. She could hear them. She even recognized a few common words, night, bed, star. She bent her soul toward his voice as though she might be able to translate what he said by will alone, or by desire.

He lifted his head. She smiled at him and lifted her hands helplessly. "Nothing," she said. "Not the vaguest idea."

He nodded. "It tells of a young man who says he has—how do you say this—has come of age; and so now he will pack a small bag, suitcase, to put under his bed, as his father before him also did."

"Okay," she said cautiously.

"This was such common thing, you see, everyone understands. You expect that perhaps secret police will come, can come at any time; you will not be given much time, and will perhaps be not in condition to think clearly, what to take, what you will need." He nodded, smiling, it's true. "So the wise ones, they packed small bag, small enough to carry a long way; in it, warm socks, felt boots, tobacco, a book. A photograph. And this bag placed ready under the bed."

"Oh."

"In the poem the man thinks of his father and mother, who slept in their big bed near his for decades; every night beneath them the small bag waiting. While they slept, while they . . ."

"Yes."

He read the lines in Russian. "So now the son has grown up, the new generation, and the wisdom of the father descends to him, you see, and he has packed bag of his own. And what shall he put in it? What shall he try to carry if he must go?" He read again, and she seemed to hear a list, a catalog. "The innocent *yat*, among those who perished the most discreet. Some smoke of north, or northland, which is well known to him and to his father. Their city, caught in snow-puddle or snowmelt, never to fall or, or." He stared earnestly at the lines, his lips moving; then he shook his head and laughed. "No it is meaningless. Or I cannot. Cannot find equivalents."

He put the paper down on the couch between them and showed her. "You see here. The innocent *yat: yat* is that small letter, there. It was a useless, a *redundant* letter in Russian alphabet; after the Revolution, language was reformed, and that letter was got rid of." He tapped it. "Terminated. Liquidated. And it was discreet, said nothing, of course."

He was laughing again, in some kind of paroxysm of frustration, as though he were being tickled. "Look, look. *Some smoke of the northland, known to him and to me.* This is easy, everyone knows. Northland is name of popular type of cigarette. It seems both father and son smoke this kind. But also smoke of chimneys of far northern camps, prison camps, everyone knows."

She thought she understood then, that he had shown her these things so that she would know he was right: she could never understand his poems, they couldn't be changed like money. "Okay," she said. "I guess I see."

"It's very hard."

"Yes. Well. It's interesting." She got up, went to set her glass by the sink. "I'd better be going back. I have a, you know. Curfew. And lots of homework."

He got to his feet. "You must go?"

"Yeah. I guess." She shrugged, and turned away suddenly from his look; outside, beyond the darkening porch and the garden, the evening was changing from gold to blue. He opened the screen door for her, and together they walked around the house to where Kit had left her bike.

"May I ask you something?" he said.

"Yes sure."

"Will you come back?"

A soft seawave lifted her. He had spoken as though what he asked might be hard to grant him: as though he knew he might be refused.

"Yes," she said. "Yes, I will. Yes."

"We might read again."

"If you want to."

"Perhaps you will go for a ride with me," he said. "In my car."

They had come around to where it was parked, the two-tone convertible gleaming as though wet, its heavy chrome turned pink with sunset.

"That car is *yours*?"

"Yes. It is new."

"I can see."

"You like it."

"Well." She regarded it; it seemed, like all its kind, to be preening, smirking, inviting. "It's kind of large."

He went to lean against the door, as though posing for a picture. Kit, remembering Jackie's Beetle, wondered if like the wizards who once hid their souls in gems or in trees, men now hid their souls in cars, which then were like them. Or which disguised them: as this one surely did.

"When would you like to come again?" he said.

"When," she said. "Well."

"Tomorrow," he said. "Can you come tomorrow?"

"Yes," she said.

"And will you?"

"Yes," she said, laughing. "I *can* and I *will.*"

He said he would come and get her, but she didn't know how that would look, and told him no, she liked to bike. She changed after her dinner, putting on a shirtwaist dress of dotted swiss; thought of wearing her linen shoes with the little heels too, but that meant stockings, and suddenly feeling foolish she put on smudged white sneakers over her bare feet. She wished her legs were tanned; what was wrong with her that she looked always like she'd just climbed out of a cave or a rain barrel. And a red sore right in the middle of her shin, where had that come from, didn't she even notice when she banged herself bloody. She licked a finger and rubbed at the scab.

He was waiting outside his house, in the front yard by his car; he wore sunglasses though the sun was low.

"Ride I promised you," he said.

"If you want," she said.

"Good." He pulled open the heavy door for her and when she was in he slammed it shut; went around the back of the car, long trip, and to the driver's side.

"So did you get a license?" she asked.

"Of course."

"You've driven cars before?"

"Trucks. In war. Easy."

He drove his car as though it were a truck, carefully putting it in gear, backing around and out, turning with caution onto the road. He held the ivory steering wheel with both hands, constantly working it, as an old person does. They crept along.

"Which way?" he asked her at the highway.

"West," she said. "Away."

"In Russia," he said, "*east* is away."

The corn was tall and green on either side of the road, but far in the middle of the fields they could see where an acre of ground had been raised above the rest, and on it a small stand of trees left to grow, whose name she didn't know when he asked. A dusty road went out that way, drawn right along the section line, but then bending around and up to the knoll's top.

They got out there. Because for so far in all directions the land was flat and mostly uninhabited, they seemed to be very high. Not any nearer the tremendous clouds piling in the west, though, which were dizzying to look up at, like skyscrapers. There was a lick of breeze, lifting her skirt, then no more.

"Silos," he said, pointing to far twin towers, midnight blue for some reason and not red. "This word I learned from your poem of last year."

"Oh?" She felt a sudden small self-consciousness, as though he had brushed against her.

"Yes. I looked up the word." He shaded his eyes. "And those are silos too, the others, the ones we cannot see, far off."

"Not so far," she said.

That poem, "Silos," had been deliberately forged to meet an assignment he had given in class. The missile silos ringing the air force base to the west were something Jackie and Max and Rodger had told her about; there was talk of a protest to be staged out there, like the protests against the Polaris in Britain. Coolly made, the poem was intended to seem like a rush of hot, indignant rhetoric.

"Silos where nothing but the grapes of wrath are stored," he said. "I found this image striking: the grapes of wrath. But I think is title of famous American book. In Soviet Union we all read."

She laughed aloud, then covered her mouth. He looked at her:

What? And she shook her head. "It's in an old song," she said. "'Mine eyes have seen the glory of the coming of the Lord; he is trampling out the vintage where the grapes of wrath are stored.'"

Now he laughed, chagrined. "Like Italians making wine," he said. "The Lord."

"Purple up to his knees."

"With blood."

"I guess."

"I prefer not knowing this," he said. "I thought those grapes were John Steinbeck's. And yours."

"Well. They are mine, now."

That made him smile. He looked to the west again. "When they fly," he said, "those missiles, then there will not even be blood. They do not spill blood; they vaporize it."

"My brother Ben told me," she said—and she realized she hadn't said Ben's name aloud since spring, and stopped a moment. "He told me," she went on, "that all over the country now they have missiles on train cars, on special tracks, that go back and forth all the time, so the Russians can't hit them."

He nodded, as though he knew this.

"Or on trucks," she said. "They only drive at night, so people won't see them and be afraid. But they're all linked by radiophones and they can all go off in a second."

"And will they?" he asked. Just as her father had. As though the combined guesses of people who had no idea and no power might be able to fire them, or keep them here.

"I used to dream they would," she said. "So often that I was afraid to sleep. Afraid of Russians."

"So strange," he said. "You people, with daring to conceive that bomb, and knowledge to build it. Then most awful of all the courage or—what name can you give, *heedlessness* or—to use it. And then to lie awake in fear, and to have such dreams."

"Well," she said. "*I* didn't use it." It was true, though: Americans were the only ones to have dropped one, and all you ever heard was how likely the Russians were to drop them on us: as though they were capable of what we never could be, so much destruction, such madness.

"We'll go back," he said. "Possibility of rain."

"Just put your top up."

"Yes," he said. "I was shown how this is done. But I have not succeeded in doing it myself."

"Oh. Oh, okay. But," she said. "If you're going to drive this thing, you know, really, you have to learn to drive like an American."

"Ah?"

"Yes. You've got to have the attitude. For this car."

"Will you show?"

"Um sure. Look, like this." She got in the driver's seat. "See you have to relax. I mean the car does everything. You just rest." She turned the key, and felt the soft explosion of its ignition, like the downbeat of a somber symphony, and smiled at him in delight. Then she turned on the radio and pressed the wonder bar. "Next you find some nice tunes." Something vague and lilting came from the speaker. She reached across and with a queenly gesture pressed the Reverse button on the push-button transmission; she hooked one finger over the steering wheel's crossbar and turned the car around and faced the way they had come. She felt his eyes on her and a bubble of exhilarated laughter arose in her breast.

"See?" she said. "Now with this car you never need more than one hand to drive. Like this." She laid a hand lightly on the wheel as though on the reins of a well-trained horse. "The other arm you got to hold the roof on with"—she showed him how on an imaginary roof— "or you just let it lay." She hung her forearm limply out. "Don't stick your elbow out too far," she sang out. "It might go home in another car. Burma-Shave."

She turned the car at speed off the farm road and onto the highway, and he lurched against the door. The blacktop receded into distance before them like a demonstration in geometry. "I'm as corny as Kansas in August," she sang over the radio music. "I'm as high as an elephant's eye." She picked up speed, letting her hand fall down along the car's side as though she trailed it in the water from a gliding canoe. "See, with the automatic transmission you can even cross your legs if you want." She showed him, crossing her white-shod feet in the deep well and pressing the accelerator with her left.

"Brake," he said, pointing.

"Oh you almost never need it," she said. "And you got time. The main thing is to take it easy. Everything's okay."

Along a side road at right angles to theirs a truck was approaching; you could see it far off, could calculate its rate of approach.

"Careful," he said.

"He'll stop," she said. "This is the highway. There's a sign there."

"You who trust no one," he said. "You will trust him to stop."

"People aren't nuts," she said. "You couldn't drive if they were." Why did he think she trusted no one? How had she made him think that?

Did she trust no one? It wouldn't be strange if she didn't. Was that the name of the thing gone from within her?

She uncrossed her feet, and touched her left foot to the brake. The truck, dragging its long plume of dust behind, slowed at the stop sign just as their convertible approached and passed.

"Can I ask you something?" she said. She had taken off her shoes and sat on his brown couch with her legs drawn up.

"You may ask."

"I never knew why they put you out of, of your country. I never understood. I mean, what did you do, or . . ."

"Ah." He sat by her. "This was new special idea of Nikita Sergeyevitch. New plan."

"You mean Khrushchev."

"Hrushchov, yes," he said. "You see poems I had written had been taken abroad, and published by Russian presses in Europe, in France and in Netherlands."

"Yes. I know. I knew that."

"And I was not that poet; I was former *zek*, prison-camp inmate; former soldier; worker now. I was not in writers' union. No one knew I and poet named Falin were one man. Falin the poet was gone, no one knew where."

That dark huge land. She hadn't known though that you could be lost in it: she thought everyone was numbered, accounted for.

"After Nikita Sergeyevich revealed deeds of Stalin, and those in camps of Gulag began to be freed, I wrote a letter to him. But for all to read, you know, public, or . . ."

"An open letter."

"Always was done, you know, to write letters to the Tsar. Remind him of his sacred fatherhood; tell him of people's suffering." He was smiling now. "I wrote in thanks," he said. "I wrote in hope too. I said to him that I too must acknowledge past error. My error was to hide: to write under no name: to destroy or keep secret what was not mine to conceal, these poems. And now no more."

"And that's all?"

He shrugged his big shrug, so full of unnamable meanings. "In times of Tsars was common, of course: writers into exile. Perhaps Nikita Sergeyevich was remembering this."

She saw in his face that he had no more answer than that for her, and she said no more.

"And I have question," he said then. "For you."

She waited.

"Will you tell me," he said, "why you chose to write no more poetry?"

Poytrii. Precious stuff different altogether from whatever she had made. She wanted to ask him to say it again. "I just didn't have anything I could say. There was nothing." She looked at her fingertips, the blunt nails her mother deplored. " 'Whereof we cannot speak, thereof we must be silent.' Wittgenstein. My psychology teacher said that. A lot."

"But is this not what poetry must do? To say the nothing that cannot be said?"

For a long time she didn't answer further. It was something she had learned over the last year, how to say nothing in answer to questions, not pretend to answer or say *Well* or *Gee now* or shrug or do anything at all.

"You do not know," he said, "or will not say?"

She shook her head, but only to shake her hair away from her face, and she didn't look at him.

"I ask this for a reason," he said. "A selfish reason it might be. I have been wanting to have asked you question. To help me to translate my poems."

It seemed to her that this was one of the strange wrong turns his uncertain English introduced into conversations, little dead ends that had to be backed out of to return to the main road, and for a moment she waited. But he only folded his hands before him and regarded her.

"Into English," he said. "For publication."

"I can't do that," she said. "I don't know this language at all. You said so yourself."

"But you can hear it. You can hear the meanings, which are part of the music. And you have English music."

"You don't really mean it," she said. "I mean why not ask somebody else, ask a real poet?" She named two at the University, major figures. "They'd be so happy to be asked, I bet."

"Ah well," he said. "They are proud men. They would want to write poems of their own. I would not ask."

The thunder muttered toward the west. She said, "Do you actually mean it?"

He went to the table, to the papers there. "Kit," he said. "I have lost much. You know this. My name. Much more, you know how much. My readers. Dead, some of them—dead, Kit!—because they had my poems. Now no readers, except those few who have come here as I did, put out or escaped or run away. And a poem without readers, does it exist?"

He let the sheets he had picked up fall from his hand, and sat down in the one wooden kitchen chair, with strange care plucking at the knees of his trousers.

"There's so little time," he said. "I don't wish to press you."

"Why is there so little time?"

"Will you help me, Christa Malone? I ask for your help."

There was only one answer, there was and always would be only one answer, and she gave it.

He seemed to rest then, or give way, though the essential tension that made him the way he was didn't lessen. He scrubbed his head vigorously with his knuckles; stared at his shoes, and laughed; looked at her and lifted his hands in triumph, and let them fall.

"Very well," he said, nodding. "Very well, it is very well, it is very well." He slapped his knees and rose. "We will celebrate. Our partnership."

She thought she had never seen him grin, but that's what he was doing. He clasped his hands as though in prayer and went to his refrigerator; he took from the little freezer a flat clear bottle.

"Vodka," he said. He put the bottle on his table, where it immediately grew a bloom of frost, and from a shelf took two tiny glasses. With a big wave he summoned her, and filled his glasses.

"Now," he said, giving her one.

"I know," she said. "I've seen the movies. You just throw it back." Monocled archdukes and grim commissars both did it, instructing innocents, offering another and another.

"We can always quit if it doesn't work," she said. "Right?"

He only lifted his glass to her, and they drank in a gulp. It was so cold it was thick and almost silky, and though she swallowed it a huge shudder took over her and she made a sound of horror or wonder. It seemed not like the gin she had drunk with Jackie but somehow the antidote to it, a sharp smack on the cheek to bring her around. But when he reached for her glass to fill it again she refused.

"So you really," she said. "You do."

"I do." He filled his own glass, and drank again.

"I feel stupid already," she said. "Like I already tried and failed. What if you hate me."

He shook his head. "No, you cannot," he said. "Failure in this has no definition. Great success may be worst failure."

"Well I bet I actually can fail pretty good. And would you know if I did?"

"No. Perhaps not."

Lightning coruscated along the horizon far away; they could see it out the windows of the porch. "Heat lightning," she said. "That's what it's called." As though something huge and afire, an army or a navy, approached over the earth's edge. "I'd better go back."

"Ah, you remind me," he said. "I must put car in garage. It will fill with storm water."

"Yes. Well. Okay, you do that."

She sat and put her shoes on as he watched, then stood again to face him. It was a new night, one that had started like other nights but now was unlike any other night. The air was hot with the storm's electricity that made her skin alert, or was that the vodka's fire, which had now passed from her stomach to her toes and fingertips. His wide accepting eyes that had always made her shrink a little. She couldn't do that any longer, couldn't shrink, couldn't wilt or shrivel, and she didn't, she stood before him as though bared, and her heart beat hard enough that she thought it might be heard or seen. "Okay," she said.

"Okay," he said. "Tomorrow."

"Tomorrow."

He put his huge hand out to her and this time she took it and squeezed as hard as she could, and then quickly turned away and went out the screen door, which a rising wind snatched from her hand and flung against the house, so that she had to turn back and push it shut; then she ran to where her bike was and mounted it. She didn't look back. The night washed over her as she rode, the lightning flinging the fields and houses at her and then the dark instantly snatching them back, she still seeing them for a moment though, persistence of vision. She pedaled hard and fast, growing wildly afraid of the storm catching her. It almost did too, the first big raindrops pummeling her as she crossed campus. She was wet and panting with effort when she came into the little compound; the first great ripping shriek and fall of real thunder came just as she pulled open her door, and she yelled out loud with it in triumph and terror.

3

So every day that summer she rose early and studied his language; she walked to the dining hall to speak it with her soldiers through lunch, went with them to the labs where, each within his own cubicle, they listened and repeated the surreal little poems they heard. *Everywhere in Yalta you can smell the sea. Everywhere I look I see dry land. There is nowhere I can go.* And after dinner she mounted her bike and rode out to the house at the end of the street where the fields began.

He had gotten a typewriter from the Slavic Languages Department, an ancient un-American-looking thing whose name in enameled letters on its brow she worked out as he watched:

"Oondervud," she said.

"Lenin had same," he said. "Can be seen still in his office, now shrine. Undervud."

"Oh," she said, and laughed. "Oh."

He had typed on this machine all his poems, those he had written since leaving the Soviet Union, and those he had carried out with him, *here* he said, tapping his breast with the blessing fingers of his right hand. Beside his he laid the English versions she brought, typed on Ben's machine.

She felt at first, and never entirely ceased feeling, like a slow pupil, a fumbling apprentice without even the skills to know how to begin, as though he had to teach her English as well as Russian; as though her only role was to nod, and puzzle, and shake her head and laugh in bafflement, while he worked calmly (calmly, mostly) through the agonies of metamorphosis. His meanings struggling to get out, like chicks from their hard shells. But he said it wasn't like that: there wasn't a poem trying to get out of one language and into another; the shell and the chick were one.

"When I was a little kid," she said, "I mean a really little kid, I used to wonder if poems in other languages rhymed in the languages they were written in, or only rhymed when you translated them into English." She wiped the sweat from her upper lip with a forefinger; the papers between them were dotted with drops from their foreheads, hard labor for sure.

"Yes," he said, not listening.

"I guess I thought English words were the real names of things, and other languages were just like masks; games those people played. For fun."

"You see here," he said, holding a limp sheet.

"I mean how could things have two real names?"

"Let us look," he said. He put his finger on the words she had typed.

> *In some worlds my torturer is but a man as I am*
> *And his bosses are men, as well*
> *And their bosses men like me*
> *And the leader a man, a man I myself could be.*
>
> *Weep, weep, children; mothers, run and hide;*
> *Go, day; sink, sun, don't look upon us.*

"Is not instruction, you see," he said. "You *instruct* stars to turn, day to go; my lines say only that they will."

She shrugged one shoulder slightly.

"Rhythm, though, is right." He looked down at it doubtfully. "Yes, right."

> *In some worlds my torturer is a being not like me*
> *And his father is a fallen angel*
> *whose father is a heedless god*
> *whose father is the abyss to whom the leader bows.*
>
> *See not, children; mothers, blind their eyes;*
> *Gather, clouds; fall, night, and cover us.*
>
> *In some worlds he is the tongue in my own mouth*
> *In some worlds he is the child of my body*
> *He dies of shame in some and lies unburied*
> *In some he never dies, outlives the sun.*

"Can the lines not be four beats, as mine are? Ba-*dum* ba-*dum* ba-*dum* ba-*dum*."

His Russian rhythms were always stronger than her English ones; when she tried to duplicate them they sounded like drum-thumps.

> *And every world and every sun's so near*
> *To every other one! So near*
> *The subtlest blade could not be passed between them*
> *And dreamers cannot know from which to which they wake.*
>
> *And I: I lift my eyes from your letter in my hands*

" 'Look up from' is better," Kit said. "Use 'look up from.' "

" 'Look up from,' " he said. He changed it with a yellow pencil.

And I: I look up from your letter in my hands
Because I have heard a sound in every world:
In some it is a chink of spurs upon the stair
In some a raven's shriek that tears the night.

"Should be, yes, comma after 'in some'? 'In some, a little clink of spurs . . . '?"

" 'Chink.' " He looked doubtful again. He'd wanted "tinkle" at first, and she'd had to talk him out of it. "I don't understand that line," she said. "That and the next. By the way."

"Ah. You see. Everyone knows. Those spurs come from last stanzas of *Evgeny Onegin*, novel in verse of Pushkin. *Spór nezapnïy zvón*. After Onegin has read his beloved's letter of rejection. As he stands in her drawing room he hears her husband, the sound of the spurs on his boots, approaching. It is the last of Onegin we see."

He opened his hands: simple.

"And the raven?"

"Yes. This was common name, usual name, for police vans. Ravens. Because both are black. Ravens arrive for arrest. Not now, long ago. Now, simply an ordinary car." He pointed at the stanza. "So, different outcomes of a secret letter, in different worlds. In some only disappointment, trouble, an embarrassment; perhaps nothing at all. But in other worlds . . . other consequences."

"Oh," she said. "Well, people don't know that. I mean Americans." He looked at her, so hurt and baffled that for a moment she almost laughed. "There's an English word for a police wagon, the old kind; it was called a paddy wagon. But that's comical. Like silent movie comedies."

"No. Not comical."

"There's another name, a woman's name, what is it." He waited while she searched within for the term. "Black Maria!" she cried. "That's it. How about that? Black Maria's cry destroys the night."

Now it was his turn to shrug, unable to know what effect this might have. "Not a bird," he said.

"No."

"You see."

"Well," she said. "You could have a footnote."

"No! No no. You will not march all over my poems with muddy footnotes." He pondered, lit a cigarette. "And these cars are black?"

"I guess."

"Strange," he said. "A bird and woman, both black."

It had grown dark, indoors at least; the lamp he had turned on over the table where they worked no longer illuminated the whole of his little place. But in the windows the midsummer night was still alight. He stood, and then, seeming still to be absorbed in thought, he lay down full-length on the linoleum.

"Cooler," he said.

She watched him for a while, and maybe because he smiled at her she came too, and stretched out beside him. It all looked different.

"In some worlds a black bird," he said. "In some a black woman."

"Are there really different worlds?" she asked. "Do you think that? Is that why you wrote that?" It seemed to diminish it as a poem if he did, and yet to make him himself huger.

He seemed to ponder. "No," he said then. "No. There is but one world, only there are many worlds within it, for it exists in more than one way at once; and these different ways cannot be translated into one another."

"Like poems."

"Like poems. You cannot translate. You can only make other poems."

The smoke of his cigarette was like a small being, a jinn folding its arms and salaaming, turning and dissipating, appearing again. "Then what's the original?"

"I don't know. Perhaps there is not one. Perhaps there are many translations but no original."

"Or the original's lost," she said.

"Perhaps even more like poems," he said. "Events in the world can perhaps be like rhyming words in poems: they can only, what would you say, pay off in one world, one translation, not in others. In one world people are cheering and weeping with joy, for best conclusion has been reached, secret is revealed, heroes have come home safe. In another world, say this world, same events are events of no significance; a pact has been made that will be broken just as many others have been. A man and a woman have misunderstood when they were to meet at train station and train is already gone, but there will be another."

"Couldn't sometimes they rhyme in both worlds?"

"Oh yes. Sometimes, not often, a rhyme can be found both in this world and in another. We call this coincidence."

She felt the cool linoleum through her thin shirt, and she saw the undersides of the card table and the chairs, and yet she felt aloft too, rising. "How would you learn, though. That there are other worlds."

"By same means as you perceive what poems say, the nothing that they speak of: by metaphor. By seeing that two things, all uncon-nected, are connected."

"Like snow."

"Like . . ."

"Snow. The last word in that Housman poem."

"Yes," he said, and smiled again, glad for her it seemed. "Yes. Just so. A-plus for you."

She laughed, and without thinking or seemingly without thinking she turned her body so that she could place her head on his stomach. They lay looking at the ceiling or at the window where the light remained, and thought; and the worlds turned and multiplied as they thought, each within all the others, all linked yet different.

> *Wake, children, wake; mothers, lift your faces;*
> *Turn away, stars; rise, sun, and dry our tears.*

Each pale night she would ride back beside the empty road, listening to the insects, her bare legs brushed by the roadside grasses, only infre-quently a car coming up behind her and passing with a rush of air and odor. Then in her room at her own desk and lamp she studied her Russian lessons until her eyes began to close and the words to turn back into the nonsense from which they had arisen; still she couldn't sleep long, and awoke with the solstice sun thinking of what she and he had done with his lines, reshaping them, making them English, coming up sometimes with plain or commonplace English equivalents for what seemed at first mysteriously and wholly other, as though in the dark she picked up a common object and felt it come slowly or suddenly clear to her what it was. A poem called "1941" told of the Red Army troops sold to Death like grain, grain that was *na kornyu:* "in rooted condition," Falin said, gesturing, acting out the inexpressible as in a game of charades. "Growing tall, not, not sprouts, you see, you see . . ." But she hadn't, not till she sat in her room and it was delivered to her: *standing* was all it meant, troops in their ranks sold like standing grain, and it had the same fearful connotation too, for standing grain is ready for harvest. He had pulled her into his Russian and she had to make her way back alone.

She'd get up then, and type and retype the line, trying to fit her new line into the meter of his, and also keep the meaning of each successive line contained in the same boxcar out of which it had come, and almost always failing. He'd forbidden her to use rhyme unless her English rhyme words fell exactly where his Russian ones did, which almost never happened, though sometimes it did, or almost did. *Corona* and *vorona*, he wrote, crown and crow. Coincidence.

She thought, long after, that she had not then ever explored a lover's body, learned its folds and articulations, muscle under skin, bone under muscle, but that this was really most like that: this slow probing and working in his language, taking it in or taking hold of it; his words, his life, in her heart, in her mouth too. Daylong she listened to her teachers and the air force boys and the mechanical voices in the language lab use the same language and she would feel the secret knowledge of what she did with him, with it, in the nights: she alone.

· · ·

The library in the middle of the campus was as cool as a cave and nearly empty in July. It was in places like this—solemn and welcoming, high and dim and paneled in dark wood and going on in many directions—that Kit's dreams often took place. The dreams didn't have this smell, though, the sleeping breath of uncounted paper pages, old glue, what else. Because you can inhale in dreams but not smell, just as you can bleed but not be hurt.

She had asked Falin to meet her here and not come to the little language school compound for her, and he smiled and agreed without a word, and she felt a hot shame, that she was protecting him and herself too from being caught at something, something they weren't doing, the protecting being all there was to catch. Still it was better to be here, to walk over here beneath the huge old campus oaks, to drift through the stacks and open Russian books almost as foreign to her as ever, or just linger in the great reading room where no one was, walking as in a forest glade along the tall rows of books no one ever removed.

Her hand, passing idly over their backs, came to a bright red one, bright once, called *Folk-Tales and Fables of Old Russia*. She took it out, guessed at the date (old but not very old), and looked at the title page. It has been printed in 1942, and all the profits were to go to a fund for children made homeless by the German invasion.

Besprizornye.

She looked at the list of editors and translators, American and Russian, and the cheerful flat red-and-black illustrations like Easter eggs. She wondered if she had actually once read it or looked at it. She turned the pages, and there was a card at one place, a computer punch card like the ones she had been given for her classes, that day in the field house where she had first seen Falin. What was that doing here? Had someone looked at this book, so recently? The card said nothing, told nothing. She put the book down on a long table beneath a lamp, open at the place where the card had been put or left, and sat to read.

Once, God and the Devil contended for Rus, and the Devil won.

Going happily to collect his prize, the Devil found the way barred. God had decided that after all the Devil could not have the souls of the people. All else he could take from them, but not their souls.

The Devil complained that it wasn't fair, and God admitted that (thank God) things aren't always fair.

So the Devil set himself up in state, and demanded that the people of Rus come before him, and each deliver up to him the thing he loved best. In his rage at having been cheated he was most exacting, and Death sat at his side and kept the books.

The Devil took from the miser his money, from the Tsar his triple crown, from the Patriarch his staff, from the mother the love of her child. One by one they came before him and went away weeping and sorrowing.

At length one young lad came before him who appeared to have little to yield up. The Devil demanded of him what he loved best, whatever it was. The boy pleaded to be spared; he offered to give the Devil anything else, even the sum of all that he had. Take his clothes and his hat; take his felt boots, and he will walk barefoot in winter; take the sight of his eyes.

No, the Devil wanted none of that; he would be put off with no substitutes. He wanted what the boy loved best. And what was it?

At last the boy told the Devil what it was.

A song? the Devil asked.

It's my own, the boy said weeping. My very own song I have made.

Well, the Devil said, let's have it.

Begging and weeping were no use, and so at last the boy lifted his voice and sang. For a time everyone ceased bewailing to listen. The Devil listened, his clawed hand cupped behind his ear. Even Death held still to hear.

Mine, said the Devil when the song was done. Mine forever and ever. Next!

The boy hung his head in grief and went away.

But not so long afterward, among the poor people of Rus from whom so much had been taken, that song began again to be heard. The boy had fooled the Devil, and had still kept what it

was he had given away: for that's the way it is with a song, as everyone but the Devil knows. The boy sang the song in the deserted
roadways and in the villages from which every beloved cow had
been taken. And by and by, in the woods where no flower grew
and in the empty churches and even in the desolate courts of the
Tsar, the little song could be heard, a song about nothing that
filled the eyes with tears and the throat with joy to hear.

So the people of Rus had a song at least to comfort them in
those days. But still life was very hard, since the Devil had taken
every other thing that anyone loved away. And in the end, of
course, one way and another, he got a good number of their souls
as well.

She looked up. Falin stood nearby, his hands in the pockets of his
pleated slacks. She hadn't heard him come in. Without any warning,
her eyes filled with tears, and the light glittered and swam.

"You must hate them so much," she said. "For . . . for what they
took, for all that they took."

"No," he said, "no no," as though he knew why she had said this,
knew just what she meant. "Some I despised. But when you hate, you
touch. I wanted not to touch. You know in my poem 'Bez' are ones
who hate. Ones who can never take their fingers from those throats.
Now come."

She took his hand, cool and dry, and stood.

Once, he had written out from memory a part of his poem "Bez," to
show Kit how it worked. The lines made her think of his wife, how she
had starved to death in the siege of Leningrad. Had she been one of
those who couldn't help hating? Would Kit have been one of those,
who died of hate, whom the Devil got in the end?

I will do without bread: they think I cannot but I can.
I will do without, and raise my hunger like a child;
And from it I will breed a little cat.
From my empty mouth and bowel I will produce it
A cat who feeds on hunger as on bread

And by doing without, that cat will grow greater than any tiger
Its teeth of steel spoons and knives a-clatter, and its black breath of
    hunger
And it will consume all those who thought I could not do without.
So she said: but the cat when it had grown
Ate her and her abnegation up
And so was satisfied, and so died.

4.

When his apartment on the edge of the prairie grew too hot, too much a *kuznitsa* he said, a smithy where they labored together at the forge, they would go outside, walk to the end of the road under the sycamores, whose leaves seemed a burden too great almost to bear; or they sat on the wide rough steps of his apartment in the cool shadow of the house and watched the sky turn turquoise with slow solemnity, or welter uneasily and ponder what it would do next.

"Tornado weather," she said. Along the gray fence of posts and wire that separated his yard and garden from the fields beyond, the gray cat crept as though in fear, its fur upstanding and its eyes wide.

"Tornado. This is storm we in my country do not have."

"Really?"

"Not tornadoes. They are American storms. We have *groza*, *burya*, we have such round storms, how do you say, yes. Not tornadoes."

"Not American though really," she said, "only Western. I mean I think sometimes they happen in other parts of the country, but mostly they're here. Tornado Alley they call this area. Look."

From the black-sheep clouds hung a few small woolly twists: tornadoes being born. She thought she could smell them; she hugged herself and shivered in the heat. Why did fear feel so exhilarating when it blew coldly in you like stormwind? Her father had always been afraid of tornadoes, hated summers in Tornado Alley; maybe because his mother had used to gather all her children up during storms and crowd them into a closet to pray the rosary with her and wail at every thundercrash. Once Kit dreamed of a tremendous box, a sky-high cabinet divided like a shadow box, in whose divisions young tornadoes could be safely kept, as in pens. A gift for her father.

"They are terribly destructive," he said.

"Oh yes."

"There is a French dish," he said. "I have read of it. Tournedos. A dish of beef."

"This would be a different dish," she said. "Scrambled eggs. Or maybe hash." The wind was rising a little, teasing. "There are whole towns that get blown away. Russiaville, a tiny town near where I lived." He looked at her and she shrugged, yes really it's true. "Russiaville; they said it *Roosha-veeo*. No more Russiaville. All gone."

Just as she said this a white shatterline of lightning crossed from sky to earth in the west toward which they looked. They both counted their heartbeats till the thunder growled, awakened, and rolled away as though muttering to itself.

"Oz," Kit said softly, as though rhyming with it. Then that name too had to be explained to him. The child blown away by a tornado from her farm in drab gray Kansas to a wonderful new land of magic and possibility. And all she wants is to go home again.

"Oz," he said.

It was dark as night now, and the wind rose. There might be hail. "Let's go inside."

The gray cat flitted between his legs when he opened the door, and ran ahead of them to leap up on the couch, its yellow eyes alight. The cats around the place, a black one, maybe two, and a tiger, weren't his but his landlady's, and yet they seemed to prefer him or his rooms. My lovers, he called them. *Lyubovnitsy.* The gray allowed Kit to take it in her lap.

"I suppose you have lovers," she said. She thought of the woman she had seen him with, the one who wept and spoke to him as though in prayer or confession, and pressed her cheek to his coat. "Real ones."

"You do suppose?" he said.

She looked only at the cat in her lap. "Ones that talk."

"Ah, these have that advantage, that they do not talk. They need not talk that way that lovers must."

"What way?"

"The way all lovers talk. You know."

She shook her head. "I don't know," she said. "I only know before. Before people are lovers, I mean."

"After, the same." He propped his head on his fist and looked down at her. "What do they talk of. They say each other's names. They describe each other, too. To each other, you know?"

"No."

"They never tire of it. The hair, the eyes. Never tire. They ask each other questions, endlessly, to know more. What do you love, what do you need, what is favorite poem, favorite color."

Kit drew a cigarette from his pack and held it between her fingers. "My favorite color," she said. "Is the color in a bottle of Coke when you lift it to the light and the light falls through it. That dark bright red brown."

He laughed.

"Really. Sorry."

"The color of your hair," he said. He put his hand on her hair, his fingers in the curls. "The color exactly."

She shut her eyes, to feel his hand so strangely light on her. "What do you love," she said. "What are you afraid of, what do you need." She lay still, seeming to have become something other than flesh, electricity maybe or pale silk, and wondered what she would do, what would become of her, if he were to answer.

"I need you, Kit," he said.

When she opened her eyes he was not smiling. She didn't doubt what he said, not then or ever after; but after a moment she said, "Why?"

"To save my soul," he said. "Or perhaps only my life."

Another flicker of fire around the world, and then a pause, and then nearer thunder.

"Why did you say that?" Kit whispered. "What did you mean?"

He was sweating, big drops standing at his brow line and along his lip.

"I'm doing all I can," she said. "It's just such a hard language . . ."

He shook his head quickly, no no. He said nothing more, though she went on listening. She knew that he didn't answer her because he couldn't, because for the first time—she thought it was the first time—he didn't know or didn't have the words, not yet.

He laid his arm along the couch's back, which made a hollow for her at his side, and cautiously she entered it, turning into him as though within him or within the circle of his arm were a big far country, whose border only she had so far crossed: she was coming to know how big it was, and that she probably never would go very far within it.

"Rain," he said.

The storms that rolled over the land unhindered in that month didn't cool it; it would seem to Kit later on that nowhere she had ever been, rain forest or desert or Asian city, was ever as hot as that Midwest plain could be on a July night when the sun bloodied the west and the temperature did not fall and wouldn't fall till the dark of the morning. On such nights they drove his convertible into town, to eat at the nearly empty restaurants and go to air-conditioned movies. She took him to see Cocteau's *Orfée* at the art theater. They were almost alone there. Beautiful Orpheus in his nice suit received messages from his Muse

over the car radio; Falin laughed lightly and crossed his legs impa-
tiently. Only when the Angel of Death took Orpheus to the Underworld, passing through the mirror (a lovely obvious silly trick), did she
feel him quiet and attentive beside her.

"Alice," Kit whispered.

"Who is Alice?"

"She went through a mirror. Shh."

Chic Mme. Death, like a *Vogue* model in her black sedan, escorted
by two black motorcyclists: and Orpheus looked back at Eurydice in
the rearview mirror. Kit heard Falin make a small noise, of apprecia-
tion or maybe not.

"I do not much like such grandiosity," he said afterward. "Eurydice
is to me better image of poyt. She who must stay, who cannot return."

"But nobody can."

"Yes."

What he liked better was big expensive Hollywood soap operas,
where people lived in houses slung over California ravines or on rocks
by the turbulent sea, who were architects or surgeons or best-selling
authors, whose wives suffered from too much love or too little, wept
and brooded, hardly noticed the glamour of their surroundings or their
glossy sports cars or their living rooms larger than churches. For these
Falin sat still, his mouth open a little and the portals of his eyes wide;
she thought of him as feeding on the rich otherworldly colors, the
emerald grasses and pastel coordinated furniture and huge bowls of
delphiniums and roses. Like the people she read of who had been hungry in childhood and then ever after hoarded food and had to have
more than they could ever eat. But then she thought of him in the
library turning the pages of *The Saturday Evening Post* with the same
attention, and what he had said. Happiness.

"Happiness," she said. She took his arm as they went back to his car,
as she often did now, unafraid to, certain it was hers to do, a gesture
without force compared to what they had already done together and
would do.

"Now you must return to dormitory," he said.

"No," she said. "Not tonight. I signed out."

"What is signed out?"

"It means I told them I wouldn't be in tonight. I told them where I'd be, and gave them the phone number. You have to do that."

Her curfew at the Language Institute was the same as the dormitory's, ten o'clock on weekdays, an hour later on weekends, but supervision was lax; the one older woman in the program who had agreed to proctor the others seemed to enjoy letting her few charges slip in late, get away with infractions, greeting Kit at the door in pajamas and curlers, an eyebrow raised, tapping her foot but smiling too like someone in a movie where nothing really mattered.

"And where," he said, "did you say you would be?"

"It's okay," she said. "They won't call." He hadn't started the car. "I just don't want to go back," she said. "Not for a long time."

"Where then instead of back?"

"Far," she said. "Far forward." She said it without actually choosing to say it. She'd said the other things in the same way: she'd actually left no number at all with the proctor, that had simply exited her mouth when she opened it and winged toward him. "Go," she said.

He drove her no farther than their grove of trees above the fields. The weather had changed; the sky was so clear that the stars within it seemed to stand at varied distances from earth, some near, some very far. Kit climbed to the broad hood of the car and stood, feeling the heat of the engine rise beneath her skirt and the breeze move it.

"You can see farther over the earth from up here," she said.

"How far?" he said. He rested against the car door, lifting a starlike glowing cigarette now and then to his lips.

"Very far."

"Forever? To the ends?"

"No," she said. "Because of the earth's curve. The earth is curved, but vision is straight."

"Easy to bend vision," he said. "Easy as tossing a ball, or shooting an arrow. Just let it drop." He showed with a hand.

"You can?"

"Yes. Oh, yes."

"What do you see, then? How far?"

"Well. Looking eastward. I see . . . What are those flames, that orange flare?"

She closed her own eyes. "That must be Gary, or East Chicago," she said. "The mills, the refineries, burning off gases. They do it all night, high in the air. What else?"

He turned. "Northwestward. Is a city on the plain," he said. "Many crossing streets, marked with lights, like drops of dew on spider's web."

"That's, um. That's got to be St. Paul," she said. "Those lights. Or Duluth."

"Southwestward too. Another."

"Des Moines," she said. "Tulsa."

"Beautiful," he said, in his Falin voice, another word of his she would hear ever after. "Beautiful."

"O Beautiful for spacious skies," she said. "For amber waves of grain, For purple mountain majesties, Above the fruited plain."

"Is this verse of your own? Or once again common song?"

"O Beautiful," she said, "for patriot dream, That sees beyond the years, Thine alabaster cities gleam, Undimmed by human tears." She was never able to say or sing those lines, those hopes, without her own eyes sparkling. *Undimmed by human tears:* reminding you of tears, human tears, even while denying them. It was unbearably sad. She looked down to where he stood below her; she lifted her arms, and he opened his, and she leapt into them. He caught her, held her a moment suspended between the hot earth and the cool sky; and when her feet were on the ground he didn't take his hands from her waist. She lifted her face to him, sure she had guessed right, so certain of it that the little tight hand that had seemed to grip her heart all day let go of it at last, and it beat hard and wildly.

It was a long blind kiss, but then he ended it, with a breath like a sob, and laid his cheek, his rough cheek, against hers. She tried to turn him toward her, nuzzling, her hands on his shoulders. He drew away and looked down at her. How could his face be so alight in nothing but starlight, she could read it as though it were day: great-eyed and plain like an archaic Greek head.

"I'm staying with you tonight," she said.

"Kit," he said.

"You don't have to be afraid," she said. "It's not like I'm a virgin."

"But I am afraid," he said. "You make me so."

"Well you just . . . You need to get over that."

"Kit," he said again, and seemed to ponder—not what to say but whether he would say it. "I do not think it is . . . what I am for."

"Oh jeez," she said. "Not what you're for. Well, what." She swallowed, or tried to; her throat was tightening with the onset of a deep embarrassment or shame. She turned from him, crossed her arms.

"Is not what you want," he said.

"You don't know what I want."

"Perhaps what you do *not* want. Perhaps I know this."

"How?"

He didn't answer, and she wouldn't turn to look at him.

"You would like to go back?" he said.

Without speaking she went to the door he opened for her, and got in, her arms still crossed protectively, and looked at the night. The eastern sky had paled, and now an amber moon, comically huge and full, rolled up as if with a soft exhalation that could be heard. Big moon, big car, summer night, green corn. How could she have been fooled?

"So I guess, what," she said. "You think of me as a daughter? Is that right?"

She said it as sarcastically, as fiercely, as she could, turning to face him. As soon as it was said, she heard it herself as he would, as he must; and she clapped her hand to her mouth, too late. "Oh my God," she said. "Oh I'm so sorry."

"No," he said. "Not daughter, no. I would not think so of you."

"How could I say that, how. I'm such a . . ."

"No, no," he said. "No."

His hand covered hers where it lay on the car seat, his hand large and real and cool.

"Just don't take me back to campus," she said. "Let me stay."

"Yes," he said. "No reason to go there. She is fast asleep now, your guardian there."

"Oh no," Kit said, shaking her head. "I bet not."

"Oh yes. And in her hand her beads, what do you call these . . ."

"Rosary."

"Rosary: of green jade. She has not slept without this since day she took First Communion. Believes she could not sleep, if it were lost."

"Will it be?"

"Yes. Of course."

He drove them back to his little house and let them in with a key; she hadn't known him to lock his door before. In the lamplight lay the work they had done that day. She sat on the couch and he made sweet tea. They hadn't spoken further.

"Now Kit. Here is tea."

She let the steaming glass sit before her on the low table. She never in her life drank hot tea except when she was sick; tea was to her the drink of solitude and recuperation and a house of blankets, an inner watch kept on a bad tummy or a migraine. Marion gave her tea and aspirin when her periods hurt or devastated her as they did sometimes.

She felt that now: on watch over her body. Because of the tea but not just because of the tea.

And maybe he was right. Maybe it was closed, and wouldn't have opened. But you couldn't know, and she had been ready at least to knock: to open to his knock, or try.

With his glass of tea he sat beside her on the couch. She didn't look at him.

"Do you know," he said. "It is not easy to say what I have said to you."

"I don't know what's easy for you. Everything seems easy." She covered her mouth again, stupid again. "I don't mean that."

"Anyway not easy to say no to your invitation. So frank too. That I should be one of your lovers."

She laughed at that. "Oh sure," she said. "My lovers. There's only been one. Not even one. I mean, technically, but." She stopped, and looked into her glass.

"Was it," he said, "this blond boy you go with?"

She shook her head minutely, not wondering how he knew about Jackie; she had got used to him knowing things he shouldn't.

"Someone else you loved."

She shook her head no again.

"Is it perhaps," he asked, "one of these things about which you think you can say nothing?"

She nodded, so slightly it might not have been seen in the lamplight; but he saw.

"He was then . . ."

"He was just somebody," she said. "Not anybody. He was hardly even there. It was just, like, a minute."

"Perhaps to himself, though, he was there. A somebody."

"I spose." She thought how in the mess and blood and the dawning cold of its being over, of its having really been done, Burke had leaned close to her and said to her *I love you:* as though it were a precious thing, a jewel from inside him that he was obliged to yield up and was yielding up. Hearing it had been even stranger than the touch of his.

What on earth had he thought? What did he think now? What is it, the mystery of it, once inside it did you ever get back to the outside again?

Nothing to say, nothing she could say. She was surprised to feel wetness on her cheeks. Old Goofy Glass. She wiped them rapidly with her hands.

The nameless cat leapt up suddenly from the floor, she hadn't seen it come near and here it was. She put her hands on it and so did he and it looked with its demon eyes from her to him; and then folded itself up.

Kit told Falin about Burke.

She told him about her brother, and how he had joined the army; she told how he had come home at Christmas, and what had happened then. She told him about what happened after Burke. She told him about her child, and about the Blue Blades, and he took her wrists in his hands as though he had known all along. She told him of Ben's death and his burial and the lie they had perhaps been told. Sometimes she stopped for a time and slipped again into silence and the gray cat's fur and its purring. He waited and said nothing till she went on. Telling it she saw that she believed it was all one story, a web knotted at every point, and that at the center of the story was her own blind stupid willful wanting, black spider that had caused it all. And she saw too (she learned it here on this night, in this telling) that one day she would know better. She would know that it wasn't one story but many, many many, not all of them hers.

"You must one day speak of these things," he said.

"I did. I just did."

"In poems," he said.

But she didn't reply or assent.

Past midnight he brought her a thin coverlet and a pillow to put beneath her head on the couch.

"I'm still angry with you," she said. "Really."

"Yes."

"You spoiled everything. My whole plan."

"Yes. Now sleep."

"Will we ever?" she asked him.

"I do not know what you mean."

"I mean be lovers."

"We are. We will be now always."

She didn't say more. He kissed her brow: touched her brow with his lips for a long time, which seemed like an answer, an answer that wasn't yes or no. He covered her.

"Don't you go," she said. "Stay right here."

"I will not go."

"Just don't."

"No. Kit. I will not."

He didn't: he stayed with her as she slept; she knew, because it was late in the night, near dawn almost, when his leaving her side awoke her. She opened her eyes and turned to see the door of his bedroom open, and the tall shape of him, like a being not in a body, against the gray light of the far window.

5

The house that Falin lived in was owned by an old woman, Anna Petroski, who had lived in the main house all her life with her brother till
he died and now lived there alone. She had a condition of some kind,
Kit never learned the name, that kept her from walking or grasping
things except with great effort. Her brother had cared for her, and
though he was gone she managed to go on; she was tall and stooped
and broad-shouldered, with long arms that looked strong though they
weren't. In her house she moved around in an old wheeled office
chair, pulling herself across the floor by handholds worn paintless by
her progress. Old women from her church came to help, and Falin
shopped for her sometimes. He once brought Kit into her part of the
house when he paid his weekly rent, and she watched the old woman
move around her kitchen in her huge slippers and flowered housecoat;
she kept rags in various places to help strap a pot handle or a knife to
her hand. Falin counted out bills, licking his thumb in a way Kit had
never seen anyone else do and making jokes or remarks in Polish that

made Miss Petroski smile; she watched Kit sharply though, with a small glittering inquiring eye.

The cats around the place had been her brother's, and she seemed to disdain them. They had found or made their way under the eaves and out above Falin's ceiling, where they hunted mice or the little flying squirrels that nested there, and down through another gap into his kitchen, dropping to the top of the refrigerator and to the counter and the floor, where Falin fed them.

"I will be gone a day and a night," he said to Kit as he filled the cats' cracked saucers. He was going to the state capital, where the offices of the Case Columbia Foundation were, a couple of hours' drive away, where he would stay the night; she was to come to feed the cats, and after sundown water the garden. "It won't be too much trouble?" he asked. "You have too much work?"

"It won't be any trouble."

He seemed harried or distracted, as though embarking on a long journey unprepared. The Case Columbia Foundation, according to Jackie, had been responsible for getting him the job he now held; had paid him a salary while he awaited an appointment, and helped him in other ways maybe too. He avoided Kit's questions about why he was driving so far to talk to them.

He was already gone when next day she came to his house after her classes. His house was empty, and almost all that had made it his was gone with him—including the poems and manuscripts that had accumulated on the card table.

Empty. Kit sat on the couch; her couch. His absence was rich around her. She took her spiral notebook and a pencil from her bag. Since morning she had been thinking of a poem, or some verses anyway; for the first time in months, toying with lines and trying to perfect them. The idea arose as she studied her Russian, practicing her pronouns, her familiar and respectful forms, lost for so long to English. In our language, we have no thou.

She shed her shoes and tucked her feet beneath her. The blinds were drawn, the house dim and hot.

In our tongue now
We have no Thou
And must make do
With only You.

What people didn't realize about their old *thou* and *thee* was that those were actually the familiar forms, the intimate ones; now they had that air of long-ago politeness and formality, but it was really the other way around.

Thou wert my son
My childhood chum
This cat; that bum;
Wert my loved one.

She liked the way this all hovered between a sort of language lesson and a sort of declaration of something to somebody. As though she hovered too. *Thou wert my son.*

Yet Thou wert God
Incarnate Word
Immortal Bird
Death never trod.

She'd maybe have to explain that to Falin; Keats's nightingale. *Thou wast not born for death, immortal Bird! No hungry generations tread thee down.* Wasn't "tread" the word for what roosters did to hens, what male birds did to female? She saw she'd changed the rhyme scheme, and went back and altered the first stanza to match it, and liked it better:

In our tongue now
We must make do
With only You:
We have no Thou.

She lifted her head from her page: a car might have come into the drive in front. Not him though: she could tell. One of Miss Petroski's church friends maybe.

Who is it wipes
My muddied brow?
Is it Thou?
Is it You?

Was it okay that the first line of this quatrain rhymed with nothing? She hadn't known whom these lines spoke to—to no one, she had thought—and now a thickness came into her throat to read what she had written.

Art Thou so low
Or art so high?
I am but I

And then there must be a last line, ending in O; it seemed to exist already—the words of it surely existed, and they were gathering, self-selected, waiting for her to notice them; what she wanted to say to him, but not to him alone. She felt at her tongue's root the sounds the last line must make; she felt the small solemn pause the reader's eye or voice ought to take as it crossed the words, and where it would fall; but she couldn't hear the words themselves.

Well it was just a joke, really, a trick, it was nothing at all. She looked up. There was a man in the garden.

She stood, the notebook slipping from her lap. It was a big man, more fat than tall, and he wore a narrow-brimmed straw fedora and a pale suit; his arms didn't quite hang at his sides, like some big men he seemed to be holding a suitcase or something in each hand as he walked. He looked around at the growing plants, the wheelbarrow, kicked at something lying in the dirt; then he stepped up to the door and came in without knocking. He was all the way through the windowed porch before he saw Kit.

"Hi there," he said.

He had a deep plummy voice, a nice smile, and bright small eyes. Kit nodded and waited for explanation.

"Didn't think anyone was here," he said.

"Then why did you come in?"

He took a few more steps within, looking around himself. "You're a friend of Mr. Falin's?"

"Um yes."

"Hi." He put out a plump hand to her and without wanting to she came to take it. "My name's Bluhdorn. Milton Bluhdorn. I knocked on the front door, and I think someone's inside, but no one answered."

"Yes. That's Miss Petroski."

"Anna Petroski," he said, looking at her with intense interest, as he had been doing since he came in.

"Yes. She's . . . she can't move very much and sometimes she just doesn't answer. I could go get her."

"And Mr. Falin's not in." He said it the way most people did who didn't know him: *fallen.*

"No."

"And you are . . ."

"I'm—feeding the cats. He's gone for the whole day. Till tomorrow."

"You a student?"

"Yes."

His smile hadn't altered, but seemed to have become less a smile and more an instrument, a tool of inquiry, like a lockpick.

"You're a student of his? He isn't teaching this summer."

"I was a student of his last semester. This summer I'm studying Russian."

"What, he's giving you some tutoring?"

"Not really."

"Is that allowed? It would be quite a privilege. You interested in poetry? What Russian are you taking?" As he asked this he went around the room, looking at the anonymous furniture, the library books, the Russian typewriter. "Conversation? You doing conversational Russian?"

Kit had decided to stop answering. The blood beat steadily and painfully against her throat. Milton Bluhdorn seemed to take no notice of her silence. The gray cat had come down its path from the ceiling and appeared beside him, rubbing against the leg of his suit.

"He's a remarkable man," he said to the cat. "If you were interested in poetry and he took a liking to you, well." He put his hands in his pockets. "Took, you know, a shine to you." The lap of his pants was disgustingly wrinkled, the way fat men's pants in summer get. She wouldn't forget that. "I like poetry," he said. "I liked it in college. 'We are the hollow men, we are the stuffed men, leaning together, head-piece full of straw.' " His smile broadened, and he shook his head, as though marveling at himself or the world long ago. "Listen," he said. "You need a ride back to town? I can give you a ride."

"I have a bike."

"Toss it in the trunk."

Again she said nothing, yielding nothing, not knowing what her face said. At last he pushed his hat up on his head and nodded. He was still smiling. He turned away and lifted his hand in farewell; then he turned back.

"What did you say your name was?"

Could she refuse to say? Why did she feel that she ought to? "Kit," she said, and when he leaned his head closer to her, cocked his ear at her and raised his brows to ask or listen for more, the whole name, she shut down.

"Well tell me something, Kit," he said. "What do you actually know about this guy?" He opened his hands to include the room they stood in, where Falin was not. "Do you know anything about him?"

Kit thought that she knew more about him than anyone in America; he himself had said so, almost, to her; and at the same time she thought that Milton Bluhdorn knew something she didn't know, or he couldn't have asked what he asked. She shrugged, one shoulder, just a little.

"He is," said Milton Bluhdorn. "He is one of a kind. You know that. That his situation is. Ah. Unprecedented."

Nothing.

"I mean they didn't kick Pasternak out."

He studied her for a while as though to see if he'd roused her; he hadn't stopped smiling. Then all in a moment he seemed to give up on her again. "Okay, goodbye sweetheart," he said, already turning away, this time to walk out the door and go.

She didn't move, listening for the slam of his car door, the starting of his engine. And she realized that she had not even asked what he wanted, who he was, and now she could not tell Falin.

"Milton," she said to him. A light rain fell, the first soft rain in weeks, she had ridden out to the house sheathed in a billowing poncho to find he hadn't yet returned. She'd waited on Miss Petroski's porch for his car, unwilling to go in the house again without him. "Milton Bluhdorn."

"*Mil'ton*," he said, and smiled. He stood bareheaded in the rain. He had got his car's top up at least, it was darkened with wet like the shoulders of his suit. "When I grew up with the lost children this was one of the words we had. *Mil'ton* was policeman. As you might say cop, or copper." He took her hand and raised her from the porch step, led her around the house. "And he seemed to think no one would be in the house?"

"Miss Petroski. He knew about her."

"But not in back. Not here." He let them in.

"He said he didn't think there was. That he didn't expect anyone to be here."

Falin's eyes moved around the dark little apartment, maybe looking for something that should be there and was not, or something that might be there that shouldn't be. Or maybe they weren't searching or seeing at all, only moving while he thought. "Well," he said. "If he expected that I was not to be here, he must have known where I went."

"What does that mean?"

"It means," he said, and then nothing for a time; he seemed to gather himself from a scattering or diffusion, slowly, a piece at a time, to reform himself into the person she knew. "It means that we should do our work for today. Means nothing more. Perhaps he will come again, Mil'ton the policeman. And we can ask him."

He put down his black case of imitation leather, unzipped it, and took from it with care the folders of his poems and her drafts, and arranged them on the table.

"I can't," she said.

He turned to her, and Kit saw something she hadn't seen before in him. She had hardly ever seen him even surprised, and now for just an instant he seemed shocked, bereft. She felt it like a stab: that she could hurt him, and had.

"I'm sorry," she said. "I have finals to study for. My course. These are the last days."

"Ah," he said. "Yes. Certainly. You will do well."

"I hope."

"But still much summer is left."

"I have to go home. I promised my parents. Anyway I'd have no place to stay."

He looked down at the poems, hers and his.

"My parents," she said. "They're in a new city. Without . . . well, without their family." *Bez*: without.

"Yes. Yes surely."

From the bag she carried, her leather purse she had slung around her body like a tiny postman's bag as she rode, she took two small books. "I brought these for you," she said, just as she might to anyone, though her throat already trembled when she spoke and she wouldn't try to still it.

He took them from her. One, new, with a bright cover, was *The Wizard of Oz*. The other was *Through the Looking-Glass, and What Alice Found There*, her own copy from childhood. She'd carried it with her to school in the winter, and she had come to believe she would carry it everywhere she went from here, from now on: because she knew now she would go on, and would need things to carry that would stay the same. But she had brought it for him.

"The girl who goes through the mirror," he said.

"Yes," she said. "You have to read it. You'll see."

He held them, one in each hand, regarding her as though she were a puzzle, or an unknown. She thought of Ben at Christmas, holding his two books, Pascal, Baudelaire. *Je suis comme le roi d'un pays plu-vieux.* "Can you tell me something?" she said.

"Perhaps," he said. He looked older, the stubble dark in the deep furrows by his mouth.

"Are you," she asked then, just a whisper, "are you in some kind of danger?"

"No," he said. "No new danger, no."

"Because," she said. "If you are in danger. I know there's nothing at all I could do. But I'd do anything I could."

"My dear," he said, "my dear love. You have done already. More than I can say. I cannot ask you more. I will not."

"You can. Anything."

He said nothing, only went on hearing and seeing the world, and her; she could almost feel it all as he did, see herself as he did: almost but not quite.

Not at all maybe.

She picked up her crumpled poncho. "I have to go," she said.

He lifted a hand to stop her. Then from the small pile of papers before him he withdrew, one after another, her translations, the first drafts in pencil and the typed versions, themselves marked over. He squared them up and held them out to her.

"They're yours," she said, shocked. "They were for you." But he only went on holding them until she came and took them.

"I want you to keep them," he said. "Will be safer with you."

She took them, and he opened his hands to her like a question; and unthinking, still holding the poncho in one hand and the sheaf of papers in the other, she embraced him. He held her a long time, kissed her cheek and her cool brow, her mouth, her tears. She knew—she knew by now—that there really can be a person, one at least, that you can embrace as easily and wholly as though the two of you were one thing, a thing that once upon a time was broken into pieces and is now put back together. And how could she know this unless he knew it too? It was part of the wholeness, that he must: and that too she knew. With her he was for a moment whole, they were whole: as whole as an egg, and as fragile.

6.

"Mad," said George.

There was a toylike breakfast nook in the new apartment, where George and Kit sat; George buttered toast, for himself and for her too, as he had done when she was little. "M-a-d, mad. It's the new concept. Mutual Assured Destruction. MAD."

As usual Kit was uncertain how to understand what he said, whether he was teasing her or letting her in on a secret she'd better listen to. She only stared, and shook her head a little in incomprehension.

"Simple," George said. "It means that if either side initiates an attack, the other side guarantees it will respond in kind and *in toto*. You make it certain that the response will come even if your command and control centers are knocked out and your leaders are dead and even most of your people are dead. You make it a standing order that can't be countermanded: if they let fly, we let fly, automatically."

"So if they . . . so if we bomb them, they *have* to bomb us back, even though that means the end of everything and there's no winning?"

"That's the concept," George said. "I mean you can see the logic."

"So that's why we can't protect ourselves?" That was where the talk had begun, why with computers or something we couldn't know about attacks and prevent them.

"Right. It upsets the balance, queers the deal. If we, or they, started to build defenses against ICBM attacks, which is theoretically possible, and the other side got wind of it, they might feel they had to attack; because once your defense system is in place you can send off your missiles and destroy their country—you've got the capacity—without them being able to destroy you back."

"Oh my God."

He nodded, pleased, and held out his hands as though between them he held the perfect and irrefutable logic of it. "It's like two guys standing up to their knees in kerosene, aiming flare guns at each other. No matter who fires first, they both go."

"But they're just people. We're just people. What if somebody gets angry, or goes insane, or . . ."

George's eyebrows rose and he nodded as though in sympathy with humankind in its dilemma. "Have to be careful," he said. "Any little thing."

"Is this now? They have this plan now?"

"Well," George said. "If I know about it, probably it is now. Yes."

"So it *would* be the end. They've made it so they can't even help it."

"I don't know. Maybe. Maybe not."

MAD. It was like the game of chess in *Alice*: a game of unbreakable rules played by people who were all crazy.

"Dad," she said. She looked down at the little yellow napkin she held, folded it, crushed it, smoothed it. "Do you think. I mean would it be possible. That what we were told about Ben isn't true?"

"Isn't true, hon?"

"I heard," Kit said, and her throat was tight, "I heard that some Americans are fighting in Vietnam, or well Indochina in places, against the Communists. And we don't want anybody to know. So, if a soldier there, you know, if he . . ." She moved her hand in the air to represent what she couldn't say, and George nodded. "Then what they do is carry him someplace else, and pretend it was an accident."

He didn't answer, and didn't look astonished; he only knit his fingers together as though he were going to crack his knuckles, and looked at her, and waited.

"And well do you think, I mean did you ever hear of this, or . . ."

"Where did you hear this?"

"Oh," she said. "People on campus."

"Not, say, in the *New York Times*."

"No."

He folded his hands now as though in prayer, and touched them to his lips, and looked away, or within. Kit felt helpless shame; shame for hurting him, helpless because she had to ask.

"Well," he said. "Suppose it was so. That there was fighting going on, that those governments over there were getting our help. I hear the rumors too. The other side's saying it. So. Naturally we would want to deny it. Like we just said, Kit. Any little thing."

"Could you find out? I mean about Ben?"

"Well what would it matter? In a way. He'd still, it would still be the same."

"But what if it's so."

He shook his head slowly. "They wouldn't tell me. They've got their reasons. Anyway surely it's not so. Surely. I mean people imagine a lot of things now, because there is so much that can't be told. People get paranoid."

She said nothing, folded the little rag of yellow again.

"What good would it do you, Kit? To know?"

"Because," she said. "Then I'd know what world I live in."

The door to the apartment opened then, and Marion came in; George ducked his head with a glance at Kit that she understood.

She was in a bathing suit with a flouncy skirt and mules, a flowered robe over her shoulders. "That pool is the best part," she said. "Mm." She had the mail in her hand, and distributed it. "Who's this from?" she said, handing Kit one.

It was a long envelope addressed with care in pale ink, the name and address lines set out in steps down the envelope as she too had been taught to do and never did any more. A funny sweet warmth filled her that she hadn't felt before but recognized immediately: a letter from my love. It felt as heavy as gold.

"One of my teachers," she said, blushing or glowing for sure, she could feel it. "From last year."

"Hm," said Marion wisely, though without meaning anything by it; Kit knew the look. There were two sheets in the envelope. One had a few lines of verse, typed on the Undervud; the other was a sheet of typing paper written on in his strange hand, edge to edge, waste nothing.

> My dearest Kit, I will send with this letter a piece for you to have and to study. Perhaps [But this word was crossed out.] I have read with great interest the books you have given me, about lost girls who find their way back. With especial interest the one of Alice in behind-the-mirror world, with dictionary also, and much pondering of many remarks. It is frightening, is it not. The poem of the walrus and carpenter is surely among the most terrible in all your language. How is this book given to children? Did it not make you have anxious dreams? When I read I believed I discovered a flaw in it: would it not be impossible for Alice to pass through the mirror? She would I thought only kiss herself there: face to face, hand to hand, breast to breast. How to pass through? Then I saw, no, this is supreme genius of the book: that if Alice passes through her mirror, then Alice from the other side must also pass through; and while we read interesting adventures of Alice in her mirror, at the same time there is another story not told, the adventures of mirror-Alice here, where she does not belong, strange world where clocks run only one way and you cannot always tell red kings from white. A poem could perhaps be written of her adventure?
>
> Well we have kissed at that frontier, my love, haven't we? We ourselves. I have come into a world where West is away, where freedom does not rhyme with fate, and where alone you can be found. So it is enough, and must be; for unlike Alice I know no way back.

She read it again, and then again in her little room (anonymous, usable for "guests" when Kit wasn't there, not hers at all in fact except insofar as she was a guest or ghost here). Freedom was *volya* and fate was *dolya*, not a word they taught in her classes but one in a poem of his, a comic poem. She thought that Alice didn't know a way back either, not until her author gave her one.

For a time she studied the lines on the other, typewritten sheet, sounding out the words and recognizing some but unable to untangle their cases and moods and tenses; without a dictionary she soon had to give up. It was apparently about angels: if *angel* was the same in both languages. Were angels in his world what they were in hers? She couldn't guess. She thought she could smell him in the paper, the smoke of his cigarettes, the musty room, the card table; she pressed the sheet to her face and breathed it in.

On Sunday they took her to church. Something in her mother's face when she listed for Kit the times of Sunday Masses made it impossible to refuse or to fight. She went through her clothes to find something to wear and borrowed a hat from Marion, a navy straw that was at least not flowered or fruited. They parked in a big parking lot and went in and took blond pews in their brand-new church, an austerely modern one, raw concrete walls deformed out of any ordinary geometry and pierced irregularly by windows of abstract stained glass. It smelled of nothing, like a waiting room. Her own inward church, she knew, didn't smell of nothing. Above the altar was suspended a vast bare cross of rusted steel, cruel enough for a sacrifice surely, crueler-seeming to Kit than any painted wooden corpus writhen and bleeding.

They were very early. Clusters of people knelt or sat with heads bowed in the low pews or looked upward as though trying to comprehend the space around them. Marion leaned close to her and nodded toward the side aisle: confessions were being heard. Kit chose to show no comprehension, and having looked that way, she looked away again.

"Hasn't it been a long time?" Marion whispered to her. "We'd like you to go to Communion with us." She touched Kit's arm and, smiling, gently pressed her, go on.

Okay. All right. If she was going to do this.

She went to the pew nearest the minatory little box, blond wood too but unmistakable for anything else, and knelt to Examine her Conscience; and when it was her turn she went in through the purple drape as onto a tiny theater stage, actor with an audience of one.

"Forgive me, Father, for I have sinned," she said. "It has been six months since my last confession. These are my sins." She heard these formulae as though for the first time, odd as a child's made-up game. The priest beyond the veil breathed with difficulty, asthmatic or a smoker. She listened for a moment; so did he.

"Actually there's only one sin I'm aware of," she said then, reluctantly or as though reluctantly. "I've. Well. I'm having an affair with a professor. At my college."

Breath, altering. "How old are you, child."

"I'm twenty years old, father."

"And is this professor a married man?"

She thought. "He's a widower."

"And for how long has this affair gone on?"

"For a few months."

"And has this affair included sexual intercourse? Do you know what's meant by that?"

"Yes, Father. It did. It does."

"Did he force himself on you, child? Against your will? Did he threaten you?"

"No, Father."

"Did you lead him on?"

"Well. I was, you know, there."

He breathed. She wondered if he would pry for details, and what her mood would lead her to say if he did. He said: "He has done you a great wrong."

She said nothing.

"He was placed in a position of authority over you and has abused it. He should have nurtured and not done you harm."

"Yes, Father."

"He is very much at fault here."

"Yes, Father. That's what I think too."

"And you are very much at fault for having allowed it."

"Yes, Father."

"Do you know that if this were to come out, he would be disgraced, maybe fired?"

"It won't," she said.

Breath. "You must," he said, "break off this relationship."

"Well I don't think I can."

"Are you afraid?"

"Yes. But not of him. I love him."

"Then of what?"

"I'm afraid the world is going to end."

He breathed so long and painfully that Kit wondered if he was afraid of it too. He said: "I cannot give you absolution for this sin until you feel repentance. You can repent in fear of God's anger and judgment, or in sorrow at having offended Him. But you have to repent."

A low bell sounded; people called to pray. Holy hush of ancient sacrifice.

"Okay," she said. "Well."

"Pray to the Virgin, child, for help. She can't refuse."

"Okay," Kit said, with a shrug, moved by her own imaginary dilemma, no way out.

"Now," the priest said. "For any other sins you may have committed. Make a good act of contrition."

She did, saying the words with care and attention as she had been taught to do; through my fault, through my fault, through my most grievous fault. She left the booth, admitting the next sinner, a bent old man with his hat in his hand. She went to kneel again beside her mother, who had taken out her beads and held them loosely, the trembling stones catching the light of the windows; her face was calm, absorbed, alight even, and her eyes moist. It was four months since Ben had been brought home: exactly four, Kit thought, and realized why she had been taken here. The Mass began. She listened to the prayers and to the responses, changeless as nothing else ever would be, the ones Ben used to make, the bottoms of his sneakers showing as he knelt: *Quare me repulisti, et quare tristis incedo, dum affligit me inimicus?* Why do you push me from you, why do I go on so sorrowfully? When it came time she went up to the rail with her father and mother, and in a tremor of shame and delight and wonder, cloven forever into inside and outside but not alone, not just now, she took the nearly nonexistent bit of food on her tongue, where it melted like snow.

As they went out after the Mass, Marion took her arm and leaned close to her, her face a scowl of disapproval.

"Listen," she said. "Before you can go back to school. We have *got* to take you clothes shopping."

7

In Kit's mailbox at the dormitory when she returned to the University there was a small envelope that had been waiting there for her return, stamped in gold with the address of the dean of students. It contained a small folded note.

> Dear Miss Malone:
> Welcome back! I hope you had a wonderful summer.
> A matter of importance has come to our attention and I would like to talk with you about it. Will you please come to my office on this Thursday afternoon at 1 o'clock.

A kind of dread descended on Kit like a cold breastplate from her shoulders to her thighs. It seemed to her that every instrument of news, every sign of sudden revelation, could make her feel this now, and she wondered how long it would go on. Around her the students came and went and greeted and called out to one another. The day was Thursday; by the big clock above the mailboxes it was almost noon.

The office was in an older building in the campus center, high-ceilinged corridors and floors of worn stone. *Dean of Students. Office of Student Affairs.* The tall door was dark, and opened to a secretary's office cluttered and cheerful.

"Oh yes," the secretary said brightly. "Oh yes." She pressed a button on her intercom with one hand while she pointed to a farther door with the other; but it was opened before Kit reached it, and the dean, smiling, stood aside to admit her.

"Thanks so much for coming!" she said, the same alarming brightness. She was Kit's mother's age, and carefully made up too as her mother always was. *A face to meet the faces that I meet,* Marion used to say. "You've met Mr. Bluhdorn, I think."

He was there, in a broad side chair. She hadn't seen him at first, the light of the windows making deep shadows in the room's corners. He lifted himself to his feet with a sort of effortful wiggle, smiling his smile. Kit hadn't moved from the carpet's edge where she had come to a stop seeing him.

"Christa Malone," he said. "Known as Kit. That's right, isn't it? Kit." He tapped his temple with a forefinger, smart guy.

The dean took Kit's arm and brought her within the room. Kit understood now that this story, whatever it was, had taken her up and was going to keep on till it was done. Her heart beat so hard she could hear its little cries in her ears.

"Sit, sit," said the dean. "Would you like something, a cup of coffee?"

Kit shook her head.

"You know, I'm very glad to have the chance to meet you. You came here with some very impressive achievements. And you've taken a couple of advanced courses and done very well. Very very well."

Milton Bluhdorn smiled more broadly, beamed even, as though he too were proud, or as though some credit were due him. Then he sat again and joined his hands across his belt.

"Now," said the dean. "I don't know how much Mr. Bluhdorn has told you about himself." She still stood, leaning back against her wide glossy desk. "I think I can say that he's here now as the representative of a joint committee of several government agencies concerned with our national security. I think . . ." She glanced at Milton Bluhdorn, and saw something in his smile or his face that made her stop. "Well. Mr. Bluhdorn asked me to invite you here to talk about a certain matter of importance, to you and to us and to our country, and I'd like you to listen carefully."

Milton Bluhdorn opened his hands in an oh-gosh sort of gesture, waved them a little as though to dissipate the gravity of the dean's remarks; he even chortled, deep in his throat. "No no," he said. "Listen. Kit. First of all thanks for coming, and thanks for the help you gave the last time we met. You know. Now. What I'm doing here is just sort of a follow-up. Say, I see you aced that Russian course. That's the stuff."

She was to respond to that, she knew, and the dean was nodding at her, but before she could nod back or smile or speak she realized that he must have been allowed to see her grades, and what else had he learned about her?

"So," he went on. "Follow-up. You have probably figured out that this all might have something to do with our friend Mr. Falin, and you're right, it does." He crossed his oddly small feet at the ankles; his socks were argyle ones in many colors. "You probably don't realize it, Kit, but your country went to a great deal of trouble, a lot of real risk too in a lot of places, for Mr. Falin. Making it possible for him to come out and into the free world. And in some ways that job isn't done, and it isn't ever going to be done. Because this is a very dangerous world we live in, a world where it's very hard to know who to trust. And Kit that's why we've asked you here, to see if you can help us."

Kit looked from him to the dean; the dean's smile was gone, her eyes lidded, a weary old huntress.

"Your father was in the war, is that right?" Milton Bluhdorn asked. "And your brother was in the armed forces as well?"

She nodded.

"Well there is a world war going on right now too, though it might not seem like it. It's being fought all the time, all over the world, and maybe we see only the tip of the iceberg; when we do learn about incidents in this war we don't always recognize them for what they are." He leaned forward as though to come closer to her. "In this world you have to make choices," he said. "The President said so. If you're not pushing you're pulling. And everybody can push."

If she thought of Ben now, if she let him into her thought, they would get him, she would lose him again and forever. She didn't move.

"I see that you're interested in the security or intelligence services of this country as a career," Milton Bluhdorn said. "Maybe the CIA?"

She shrugged, or shrank: lifted her shoulders for a moment.

"Well that's good, that's commendable," he said. "Now. Here's what we'd like to ask you, and really it is not anything at all. We would like you to go about your business and your schoolwork and your friendships just as before. Only for the next little while, the next few months or so, we'd like you to keep a little mental record for us of what you see, I mean in relation to Mr. Falin. What you see and hear."

A case clock ticking in the corner of the office now whirred as though awaking, and struck: One. Two.

"Okay," Kit said.

"Well don't just say 'okay,' " he said, grinning. "Let's think this through. I mean I'm sure you're a stand-up girl, a real smart girl. But let's think what we're asking. We're not asking that you do anything you wouldn't otherwise do. We're not asking that you, you know, *spy* on anybody or take any measures at all. Mr. Falin is an acquaintance of yours, a mentor perhaps in some sort of way, and all we're asking is that now and then you just let us know what's been happening there with him at his place, the kinds of things that come up in conversations, whether he's had *visitors*, whether he's gone out of *town*, that kind of thing."

"Okay."

"Because it's so much easier for you than say for me. Less intrusive." He smiled the little scimitar smile. "What I'm saying Kit is this. We do need a commitment. We would like to know just how much of a friend to this country this guy is. I guess that's how you might put it." When she said nothing more for a long time, he stood. She stood too, looking only at him, and folded her arms before her. "Okay. Now as to the details of this, we'll be getting in touch with you from time to time. I mean not often. You're not to worry about it. Okay?"

She nodded.

"You might be interested to know that you aren't the only person on campus who's helping out in this way. Helping the dean here and the school. Not the only student."

She said nothing.

"Okay," he said, and looked to the dean. Her smile had returned. Kit had to take Milton Bluhdorn's hand, it came toward her, a little fat white animal that she could not avoid. Then the dean showed Kit to the door, but before she opened it she put her hand on Kit's arm.

"Your thing with the Fair Play for Cuba Committee," she said. "Going to that meeting. I understand that was nothing. Just curiosity. We understand it was nothing."

Then she let Kit go, and shut the door behind her.

Kit went out past the secretary and out the big door into the corridor, and then she thought she could go no farther. There was a women's room a few steps away and she caught the doorknob and held herself up; she opened the door and went in. It was empty. She clapped her hands to her face and cried aloud, small barks of fear and horror that she had never heard her throat make before, but that she couldn't help making. They ceased, but her chest went on heaving.

The door opened and Kit recognized the sleeve of the dean's red wool jacket, and she turned quickly away to the frosted window. The top panel was canted open, showing green leaves moving in a breeze and a blue sky. The window was barred.

"Beautiful day," the dean said. "Beautiful."

Kit slipped out past her smiling, her eyes on the floor.

She went out into the afternoon. The sun was hot and the whole sky so intense a blue it could hardly be looked at; still the morning mist seemed to cling lightly to things, to the trees thinking of turning, the rosy brick buildings, the clock tower. Students in groups or couples walked the paths, the girls holding their books to their breasts and laughing with the boys.

Kit with her secret inside her could hardly walk among them. What had been done to her had been done to none of them. The beautiful world was theirs and they didn't even know it and would never need to know it. She had felt this way—that she carried something black within her that no one could see but that cut her away from everything and everybody else—only once before, and it was when she first knew she was pregnant.

She made herself walk far enough that she was out of sight of the building where the dean's office was. She sat on the steps of the music building, where students went in and out with instrument cases; a piano poured notes out of an open window, the same huge clusters over and over.

"Hi."

Jackie Norden had come up beside her, she hadn't seen him till he spoke, and she got to her feet and in tears of relief or need hugged him hard and pressed her cheek against his smooth one, oblivious of those passing.

"Oh God," she said into his ear, "oh God, oh Jackie."

He laughed, amazed, trying to get a look at her face, interpret her. "Hey. It ain't been *that* long."

"I called the house," she said. "I called and called. They said the phone's disconnected."

"Aw," he said. "Damn Communists. They hate to pay their bills, they just *hate* it. Not like they don't have the money."

"Jackie," she said. "Something's happened."

She sat down again, and held her head. Jackie took from his pocket a great handkerchief, snapped it and spread it on the step, and sat beside her. He said nothing more, only waited for her to begin: and when she could, she told him all that had happened, what she had been told, what she had been asked of her.

"And what did you say?"

"I said I would. I said okay I would."

"You *did*?"

"Well what could I say? What if I said no and they did something, something . . . I just couldn't tell them I wouldn't."

He took his pipe from his pocket and began to stuff its great mouth with shaggy tobacco. "And do you plan to tell Falin about this?" he asked. "I mean about them and what they said?"

"Of course. Of course I will. What do you *think*."

He marveled at her. "God damn," he said. "A double agent."

"What do they want?" she said. "Why did they say those things? They said they want to be sure about him. But what does that mean? What do they think?"

"Well," Jackie said. "Look at it from their angle. Here's a guy who wrote some kind of allegorical poems some time ago, poems nobody seemed to take a lot of notice of, but nobody objected to very much either, and then got some other poems published in other countries, for which you can go to prison or worse. Then he writes a letter, an *open* letter, to Khrushchev and admits all that stuff, and calls Khrushchev on stuff. Right?"

"I guess."

"Well, then what? Nothing. They call him in to question him, but he always comes out again. Then suddenly it's in the papers that there's been a trial and he's been stripped of his citizenship and is being sent out of the country. Not what usually happens over there. So it makes you think."

"Makes you think *what*? What?"

"Well what if a deal got made. What if they told him, okay, we'll make it look like we got mad and threw you out, if you'll agree to act as an agent for us over there. It's that or. You know." He made a gun with his hand and shot himself in the temple.

"He's not a spy," Kit said. "He's not."

"Well," Jackie said. "How about this, though. Maybe he was an *American* agent, all along. And he was in danger of being exposed. And we planned it all, the open letter and all, because we had this way of getting him out, by having him kicked out for his provocative act, because we have guys high enough up in their system to do that."

"We do?"

"Maybe we do."

She thought of Milton Bluhdorn: *Your country went to a lot of trouble for Mr. Falin.* "Well then why," she said, "do they want to spy on him? Why would they want me to?"

"An agent can always be turned one more time," Jackie said. "If the Russians sussed out the Americans' plan, they could be pretending to be fooled by it. And Falin might still really be their guy. The only way to be sure a spy ain't changed sides is to end his career."

She covered her face in her hands.

"And you're planning to tell Falin what they wanted you to do," Jackie said.

She nodded. "Of course."

"Acourse you will. And acourse they must have thought of that."

She studied his face, trying to guess where his thought was headed. "If they thought that," she said, "then what good would it do them, to, to."

"Maybe all they care for him to hear," Jackie said, "is that they asked about him. That they can get to people he knows and ask them. Just to let him know they're thinking about him."

She only looked at him, until he seemed to see in her face the dread and disbelief she felt; he took her hands and lifted her to her feet. "Aw hell with 'em," he said, and put his arm around her shoulders. "They're just being paranoid, no doubt. Knowing they don't know everything, but not knowing what it is they don't know, which is probably nothing anyway." He held her tight. "Surely's nothing, in fact. Surely."

They walked.

"She asked me, the dean did," Kit said, "about the Fair Play for Cuba Committee."

Jackie said nothing.

"She said she thought it didn't mean anything that I was at that meeting, that it was just curiosity."

"Well that's all it was."

"Yes. But how did she know about it?"

Jackie shook his head, in wonderment or ignorance or disgust. "Man," he said. "Oh man."

"Do you still have your car?" she asked him.

"Oh sure."

"Would you take me out there? To his house?"

"Well," Jackie said, and stopped to light his pipe. "Yes. I'd be happy to. But you know you got to get used to this game. Maybe you wouldn't want to race right over there soon as you can. Looks . . . Well you think how it looks."

"Just take me," she said. "Please."

She made him stop as soon as they came near the house and she could see in the driveway the green convertible, its top still down, so that she knew Falin must be home; and she told Jackie she'd walk from there. He sat with the VW's engine running, looking at her as though trying to see her insides, what she knew or thought she knew that was causing her to act as she did; then he shook his head and threw up his hands, not up to me; and she kissed his cheek and got out.

"I'll wait," he said to her out the window.

"No don't," she said.

"It's a long walk back to town."

"It's okay. Don't wait."

The grasses were yellow and the trees browning and riddled by bugs, whose noise filled up the still day. The house too looked more aged, used, battered than it had. She went around past the lilacs, which had grown nearly together to block the path. When she saw that he sat at the gray picnic table in his undershirt her heart swelled and then shrank painfully. Everything now different, hurt, endangered, that had been so strong and full before.

"Hi."

He turned, and his face filled with pleasure but not surprise to see that it was she. He had a blackened bone-handled kitchen knife with which he was cutting tomatoes on a flowered plate. He rose as though he meant to come and embrace her, but she stopped before she came close to him, and so he paused too, still smiling.

"Tomatoes," she said. Her hands behind her back. "Nice."

"Yes. They are now ripe. So huge and red, so generous. Not potatoes yet."

"Something's happened," she said.

"Yes," he said. "Yes."

"You know?" she said.

"I know that something has happened. While we wrote poems and tomatoes grew." He sat slowly again, and showed her with a hand that she should sit opposite him. But she still stood.

"What?" she said. "What happened?"

"Kyt," he said. "I am very glad to see you. I am so very glad."

She sat then by him, uncertain, feeling that she was already betraying him, that if he touched her she would poison or taint him; but when he put his hand on her shoulder it calmed her. He didn't say anything, only waited, and she told him what had happened, the dean and Milton Bluhdorn and the questions asked her. As she spoke he withdrew his hand from her.

"And he asked these things of you to learn—to learn what?" he asked. "What is suspected?"

"That you might be connected to, to. Your old country and the leaders there. That you might be still on their side really."

"You mean what is called *asset* of theirs." He cut a wedge of the big beefsteak and salted it from a glass shaker.

"Called what?"

"In capitalist countries, so called. *Assets* are friendly or helpful ones, people or institutions willing to do secret work. They ask if I am Soviet asset. Not American asset." He said it lightly, dangerously. "Assets of course can become *liabilities*, move to other column of books. If they are exposed or become for any reason useless."

"What then?"

"Well. You must remove liabilities. Profit and loss. KGB also knows this well, though not by capitalist accounting."

"You aren't, are you? Some kind of . . . agent."

"Ah. But not all agents are secret. And not all secret agents are spies."

"But you aren't," she said. "You aren't any of those."

"Kyt, you know what I am." He closed his hands together and spoke in Russian: "*Vechnosti zalozhnik u vremeni v plenu,*" he said, and now she knew enough that she could recognize it, the poem of Pasternak's that he had long ago recited in his class. "Poet, take care, watch well," he said. "Do not sleep, for you are Eternity's hostage, kept captive by Time."

She shook her head, helpless, helpless before his resistance to what had happened, as though he thought it was a game: not a dangerous one like Jackie talked about, played for keeps, but one you could win just by talking, by words.

"Who *is* he?" she asked. "Why did he come here?" She asked because she could not ask another question: *Who are you? Why did you come here?*

"Perhaps he is not one thing," Falin said. "It may be he is one thing here, another thing elsewhere." He didn't smile now. "Perhaps they do not know entirely what their *mil'ton* is. The great right hand cannot always know what the little left hand is up to."

This meant nothing to her. "I had to touch him," she said. "I had to shake his hand, he made me."

"Ah," Falin said. "A good sign. In my country a good sign. The agents of the state never touch the hands of those they intend to destroy. Never."

He got up, and went to where his garden began, the big blowzy potato plants brown-edged and hairy-limbed. He'd said once that in Russia he'd known someone who kept supplies of potatoes in his cellar: a high official, he said, a party leader. She remembered that, and in horror she thought that now she would record all that he said and did, without willing it, helplessly. And as though he overheard her think this he turned to her, rubbing his bare arms, seemingly cold even in the sun.

"Kyt," he said. "I must say this now. Not easy to say. It has become dangerous that you should be nearby me. You must from now on stay away."

It was, somehow, what she had known he would have to say no matter what he felt. She didn't hear what he said so much as drink it, a terrible caustic liquid that burned her as it entered, burned her out. She wanted to beg him, beg him to forgive her or to withdraw what he had said, and because his eyes hadn't changed, were still as open and full of calm pity as always, she thought he would surely see it, or hear her thought. But she said nothing to him.

"I will drive you back to campus." He came to the table and picked up a shirt that lay there.

"No," she said, "no," and she got up and backed away from him as though he meant her harm in coming toward her. "No it's okay. It's not so far."

"I'm sorry," he said.

"No," she said. "No." She turned away from him, thinking that if now she went out of his yard, she didn't know how she would reach town and the university again, or why. She didn't turn back, though; she went out and to the road again, and down to where it met the main road.

She had let him say those things, she had let him put her out and had said nothing.

Down the road toward town in the stillness and sun she could see Jackie's Volkswagen pulled over on the shoulder in a tall tree's shadow.

8

It had fallen, it had been dropped, but the effect was nothing like any-body ever said it would be. There had been the sudden universal energy-flash covering the earth, and the great cloud-ball too (in hiding she had seen or known this) but silent: and when she came out she saw that it had changed everything and yet destroyed nothing. Everything that she remembered was gone, all the buildings and the houses and roads and the high-tension wires and telephone poles, the plowed fields and the farms and the people; instead there were only green-blue forests and a living wind that moved their leaves and showed the silver undersides. Still silent. Even the ground had been altered, into low hills and valleys, where before it had been plains.

She went down in wonder into the glens, and the way was easy, though there was no path. *I'll kill you if you tell me there's a reason for this*, she said to Ben, who followed behind her, just out of sight. *I'll kill you if you say you know.* Then, as she thought of what she had said, and wanted to unsay it, she saw that in the grass there was an animal, like a

cat but not a cat, and it seemed to be having some kind of fit: its muscles tensed and writhing, its wide eyes piteous. When she came closer,
though, she saw it was made not of flesh and fur but of grease or clay,
and the life in it was caught in this matter, and the eyes were blind.
And as she bent to study it in repulsion, she saw Ben beside her turn
away from her and go away; and though he still smiled she saw that his
flesh was white and wasted, his neck thin as rope, his legs hardly able
to support him, and she knew she had been wrong about everything.

Fran was shaking her awake.

"You okay?" Fran asked her. "You okay? You were making this
moaning." Her eyes were piggy without her glasses on and her hair was
tangled seaweed. "It was awful."

For a time Kit only looked up at her. Then she said: "I had a bomb
dream."

"Oh God," Fran said.

Kit lifted herself to her elbows. The world was real, solid, but also
somehow tentative, able to go either way. "What time is it?"

Fran read the time from her big wristwatch, which she wore sleeping, something Kit couldn't do. It was late. They both had early classes;
they had stayed up late talking, passing back and forth their stories; Kit
had told about what had become of her that summer, not all of it
though. Still filled with the dream-feelings she had felt, of wonder and
relief and then awful understanding, she struggled to rise and dress and
get ready.

They went out past the dining hall that smelled repellently of eggs
and soured milk, and into the bright still day.

"So you never told me," Fran said. "Are you going to keep on working with him? Falin. Like you were doing."

"No."

Fran stopped to light a Camel. "Did you have sex with him?"

"No," Kit said, after a moment.

"Did you want to?"

"Yes."

"Did he know you did?"

"Yes. I think." There was so much now she couldn't say, would maybe never be able to say, that this hardly seemed a secret at all. "He said it was hard not to. But he said it's not what he's for."

"Not what he's *for*?" Fran asked.

Kit shrugged. "It's what he said."

"And did he say," Fran asked, "what he *is* for?"

"And how 'bout you?" Kit asked. "Did you?"

"Did I what."

"Have sex. This summer."

Fran flicked the end of her cigarette with a thumbnail. "Depends on what you mean," she said. Kit saw that though she looked only at the way ahead, following her big nose, she smiled a little.

They went up the steps of the student union and waited in line for coffee. Fran bought the *New York Times* and opened it by her cup. "I heard a viola joke," she said.

"Oh yes?"

"If a guy comes into a bank with a violin case, everybody gets nervous, because they think maybe he's got a tommy gun in there, and he's going to take it out and use it." She studied Kit solemnly as she spoke. "If a guy comes into a bank with a viola case, everybody gets nervous; they think he's probably got a viola in there, and he might take it out and use it." And on her face, after a long moment, another small smile dawned. Kit laughed as much to see that as at the joke. Fran shook the pages of the paper, lifted her cup by the body and not the handle, and drank thirstily.

"Oh God," she said. "Speaking of the bomb." She folded over the page and scanned it. "Here's Ken Keating saying the Russians are putting missiles in Cuba."

"Who's Ken Keating?"

"He's our senator. I mean New York's. He says they may have MRBMs in Cuba. These names, how can they call them BMs, it's so bad."

"What are they?"

"Medium-range ballistic missiles."

"With bombs?"

"He doesn't say that. He says they could have. And they could reach as far as Washington and Indianapolis. He says."

She lifted her eyes to Kit. "We'd lose Indianapolis," she said.

Kit gathered her books. "I've got to go. So do you."

"This is such shit," Fran said with sudden vehemence, folding up the paper furiously, and Kit couldn't tell what the words were directed at.

When she went to the Castle later she found them reading the same paper, Max and Saul and Rodger, drinking coffee too except for Saul, who drank only water.

"And how does Keating come to know this?" Saul asked, one of those questions he asked because he already had the answer. "Someone is feeding him this stuff, because the public has to know it. We have to know that those pesky Cubans have Soviet missiles pointed at us. So when the strike against Cuba comes we won't be shocked."

"But do they have the missiles?" Max asked. "That's the sixty-four-dollar question."

"It doesn't matter," Saul said. "Kennedy doesn't know. He's making a case. That's all."

"It matters," Rodger said. "It matters if they stomp on Cuba and missiles get fired. That's the end."

"How can they find out if they have them?" Kit asked. "They hide them, don't they?"

"Spy planes," Saul said. "U-2s."

"Cratology," said Max, and everyone looked at him. "Hey, their word," he said. "It means being able to tell what's coming out of the hold of a ship by the shape and size of the crate. Cratology."

"Okay," Saul said. "Here's what Dorticos said yesterday at the UN." He looked at Kit: "He's President of Cuba." He read: "If we are attacked, we will defend ourselves. I repeat, we have sufficient means with which to defend ourselves; we have, indeed, our inevitable weapons, the weapons we would have preferred not to acquire and which we do not wish to employ."

"Man," Max said. "That sounds like a warning."

"That sounds like a *threat*," Rodger said.

"What does that mean?" Kit said. "*Inevitable* weapons?"

"Inescapable, unavoidable," said Max.

"Maybe a mistranslation," Saul said. "Maybe he meant something else."

"Ultimate," said Rodger. "The end."

All the reconnaissance flights over the island of Cuba had in fact shown nothing so far, and had been given up out of fear that a plane might be shot down, causing a diplomatic incident. It was agents on the ground who reported the long trailer trucks bearing tarpaulin-covered cargoes moving through the town of San Cristóbal in the west: trailers so long that they couldn't negotiate the streets of the little town, and knocked down telegraph poles and chipped the walls of tabernas as they ground around corners. Something was going on, the agents said: from San Cristóbal to Palacios and up to Consolación del Norte there was activity, Soviet military movements, something big. The CIA dismissed these reports, but the Secretary of Defense pondered them, and brought them to President Kennedy; and the President ordered U-2 surveillance to begin.

The weather over the Midwest was preternaturally clear, but it was the season of autumn storms in the Caribbean. Not until October 13 was the sky cloudless enough for a successful overflight of the San Cristóbal triangle; the resulting photographs showed a Gods'-eye view of the newly stripped earth of San Cristóbal, and there, the photo intelligence officer said, were the trailers and their cargoes. *How do you know this is a medium-range ballistic missile?* the President asked. (He had recently had the office he sat in equipped with recording devices; the switches were in the kneehole of his desk, and he had turned them on; years later we would listen to him thinking.)

The length, sir, the intelligence officer answered.

The what? The length?

The length of it. Yes.

Is this ready to be fired?

No, sir.

How long have we got? We can't tell, I take it.

No one could say. They said that it could be ready within weeks, or sooner, or might be ready to be armed now. There was also no way yet to know if there were nuclear warheads already present on the island. The President told his advisers they should be prepared to take out the San Cristóbal site at any time; the missiles couldn't be permitted and he saw no other options.

Within days it was learned that there were several sites on the island, and on some of them intermediate-range missiles capable of reaching the missile silos of the Midwest were detected. The President's military advisers now said that only a full-scale strike and an invasion of the island would remove the threat.

The first shipment of Soviet nuclear armaments had in fact already arrived and been unloaded at Mariel, one-megaton warheads for the R-12 medium-range missiles, twelve-kiloton bombs for the Il-28 bombers, and smaller warheads for the cruise missiles. And at that moment the Soviet ship *Aleksandrovsk* was nearing Cuba, carrying nuclear warheads for the IRBMS.

The world was so beautiful that autumn in the north; it had never seemed so beautiful. Kit had learned the term *pathetic fallacy* in her Romantic Poetry class—the projection of the poet's feelings on to insensible nature, the weather or the scenery; nature in poetry express-ing human feeling. This weather was the opposite, it was profoundly, wholly indifferent, unconscious, asleep past sleep in its own perfec-tions: as though this time it would last forever, as it never had before.

Kit stayed outdoors as much as she could, not wanting to learn that Milton Bluhdorn had tried to reach her; she sat on the sun-warmed benches of the old college, and the air smelled of fruits that weren't there, apples and pears and grapes, and she felt the feeling soul drawn out of her into it. It was painful and terribly sad and at the same time she felt an unrefusable delight. She wasn't eating very much in those days, unable to go into the roar and the smell of the dining room or touch the bland and nameless foods they heaped on her plate, but she couldn't afford to buy much more than candies and saltines and coffee, and wouldn't let Jackie buy dinners for her. It didn't matter. Not eating made the sweetness more intense, the pain and sadness too: made them sweet in her mouth like her own sweet spit.

On the 22nd of October she saw in the campus paper that Falin would be speaking in the auditorium of the Slavic Languages Department about Pushkin, and her heart shrank inside her.

"Acourse you can go," Jackie said. "What do you think, they're going to give you the third degree over some public event?"

"I'm afraid," Kit said.

"They've forgotten all that," he said. "I know it."

"Will you come?"

"Sure. I like Pushkin. Didn't he write *Crime and Punishment?*"

There were fewer people in the auditorium than Kit would have thought. She had hoped to slip in a little late into a masking crowd, but there were plenty of empty seats in the tall lecture theater and they were more than a little late. Falin looked up from his papers when they bent down their squeaking seats, and his eyes were wise to them; his smile was for her.

He spoke about Pushkin as she had heard him speak, in her classes and in the nights of last summer; he read the lines he chose in his honey-thick singing Russian voice, and she thought her heart would split. The poems he read from were the ones he had quoted for her: *Count Nulin* and *Feast in Time of Plague* and *Evgeny Onegin*.

"Perhaps because so many ikons, so many churches, were smashed and burned," he said, "that we made of Pushkin an ikon and a church. He must express our spirit, must stand for us and speak for us. Indeed he has been made even a hero of the Revolution, with mausoleum of his own, though in this no one has believed, not even schoolchildren, not anyway those who can read."

The gray hadn't been in his hair before and it was now; it was the same gray as the shiny bland gray suit he wore, what was that stuff, was it sharkskin? Why would he wear that? A soft knit shirt beneath it, but-toned to the neck. *Something has happened* he had said to her, not sur-prised or afraid, but changed.

"So hard to make Pushkin hero. You know what our great critic Belinsky said of *Evgeny Onegin*, that it was encyclopedia of Russian life. We all were taught to say this. Encyclopedia of Russian life. But he is like encyclopedia only in his even-handedness. All things are alike to him; he does not choose one thing over another; the alphabet of his eyes and his ears alone bring things together, this next to that. He is trivial; even his earliest defenders said this, so exasperated with him. Everything interests him, everything delights him. He becomes the Tsar's soldier and also the Cossack that the soldier kills; he delights in death's energy and meat pies at a feast, little too salty, then some slim-waisted wineglasses too that remind him of his old love, whom he then must address. He is like his heroine Natalya Pavlovna in *Count Nulin . . .*"

He read, and Kit thought she remembered the lines, when he had tried to make her see what Pushkin saw:

> *Natalya Pavlovna tried to give*
> *The letter all her attention*
> *But soon she was distracted*
> *By an old goat and a mutt*
> *In a fight beneath her window,*
> *And she attended calmly to that;*
> *And three ducks were splashing in a puddle,*
> *And an old woman was crossing the yard*
> *To hang her laundry on the fence.*
> *It looked like it might soon rain . . .*

"This is why Pushkin is our poet," he said. "Not because he expresses our spirit, d'Roshin spirit: but because he exactly does not. He is everything that Russia, in his age and now in ours, is not: he cares for everything and yet for nothing in particular, everything gladdens him, he approves and does not judge. He was dark man, you know: Negro, in fact. He lived short life that ended in disaster. But he shines brightly; the smile of Pushkin is a white light in our darkness, always."

In the Castle the television was on over the counter, and when Kit and Jackie came in they could tell that almost everyone there was watching it. The East North Street men were all there, all watching. She slipped in beside Saul, and turned to see the President above them, speaking.

"What is it?" Kit asked.

"Cuba," Saul said.

The transformation of Cuber into an important strategic base, by the presence of these large, long-range and clearly offensive weapons of sudden mass destruction, constitutes a threat to the peace and security of all the Americas. He had that air he always seemed to Kit to have, that he was somehow only pretending, no matter how earnestly he spoke; as though he knew better, knew how it would all come out. *This sudden, clandestine decision to station strategic weapons for the first time outside Soviet soil is a deliberately provocative and unjustified change in the status quo which cannot be accepted by this country.*

"Not like our missiles in Turkey, huh," Saul said. "Or Italy. What the hell does he think."

Kit looked over all the upturned faces, the students and the others, the two Greek brothers who ran the place, all looking and listening.

We will not prematurely or unnecessarily risk the costs of worldwide nuclear war in which even the fruits of victory would be ashes in our mouth—but neither will we shrink from that risk at any time it must be faced. He said that he was ordering a strict naval quarantine around the island of Cuba, and ships would be stopped and shipments of offensive weapons turned back; he said that there would be continued surveillance of the island, and that if work was found to be going forward on the missile sites, then *further actions would be necessary,* and that he had ordered the armed forces to be prepared for all eventualities. The United States, he said, would regard a nuclear missile launched from

Cuba as an attack by the Soviet Union on the United States, *requiring a full retaliatory response upon the Soviet Union*. And then for a moment he turned his pages and gazed out: gazed at us, though of course he couldn't see us.

The path we have chosen is full of hazards, he said. *Many months of sacrifice and self-discipline lie ahead—months in which our patience and our will will be tested.* He called upon Khrushchev to withdraw the missiles immediately. He said our goal was not peace at the expense of freedom, but peace *and* freedom. God willing, he said, that goal would be achieved.

He said *Thank you and good night*. And after a moment he was gone.

There was a soft swell of voices then in the place. From somewhere came a spectral wail or moan of grief or terror, and people turned in their chairs or on their stools to see who had made it. We had all been so afraid of this, for so long; we had been so sure it would happen, so sure it couldn't.

"Bastards," said Max softly. "Sonsa bitches." Rodger put his hand over Max's where it lay on the table.

"Gotta remember," Jackie said. "They've been firing off those bombs for twenty years. So far the world's still here. I mean this might mean war. But it don't mean we'll necessarily get hit."

"Of course we will," Saul said. "In the first exchange. Those missile silos to the west. That's exactly where their missiles are aimed. The firestorm will reach at least as far as this. Easily," he said. His small thick fingers circling his glass were still. "Easily."

"So it's the end," Rodger said. "It is, after all."

"It's not the end, *necessarily*," Jackie said; and he glanced at Kit, as though she should not hear these things, too young or vulnerable.

"Well if it ain't the end," Rodger said, "it'll do till the real end comes along."

"I have to go," Kit whispered to Jackie, and she slid from the booth and went to the back and into the little toilet and the wooden stall with the scarred walls varnished a hundred times. *Jim + Jean 4 Ever. Bobby I Love U.* Jackie had told her how the scratchings in boys' toilets were all about sex; these were always about love, eager hopeless love. She had thought of writing *John Keats ½ + Easeful Death*. In a heart cartouche, struck through by an arrow.

Death.

What she knew, all of a sudden and for sure, was that she wouldn't hide. No matter what, she wouldn't go down into the shelters they had made to put people in. The shame of that would be worse than the death they were going to inflict, it was like the shame she felt hiding under her desk in grade school, hands clasped over the tender back of her head, her butt in the air with all the others, while Sister watched. No never. She would stay up on the earth's surface and wait.

She knew something else. She had wondered if, when death came near her, she would in her fear want a priest, if she would ask for forgiveness. And now death *was* near and she knew she wouldn't: Death couldn't change her back to what she had been, or the world either. *I am myself alone*. If she were sent down then into his hell, well fine: better to be there than to grovel, to beg or praise. Praise for this? No not for this.

She found herself weeping, though; she pulled off a length of rough paper from the roll and pressed it to her eyes and blew her nose. She didn't want to die; she wanted the world not to die, or be so wounded it could never recover. She wanted to live.

That night, twenty-two American interceptor aircraft went aloft in case the Cuban government reacted to the President's speech with an attack on Guantanamo or the arming of missiles or the liftoff of the Il-28 bombers. The Soviet ships in the Atlantic received orders from Moscow to ignore the blockade and continue on course to Cuban ports. Polaris nuclear submarines in port went out to sea. The President signed an order, National Security Memorandum 199, authorizing the loading of multistage nuclear weapons on aircraft under the command of the Supreme Allied Commander, Europe. United States forces went from the worldwide state of alert that was code-named DEFCON III up to DEFCON II. DEFCON I meant war.

. . .

The next day on East North Street, the Fair Play for Cuba Committee held what Saul called an emergency executive meeting to decide how to respond to the blockade of the island. The President had called it a quarantine, but it was a blockade, Saul said, and a blockade is an act of war, plain and simple, and it was obviously not going to be the last one either. The committee members spent the day calling other campus groups and trying to get a united front together to go into the streets in a mass public demonstration against the blockade. They couldn't get a campus meeting place for a rally, not being a registered student group, but at last got an offer from a Unitarian church to hold their meeting there on the following evening. They got the Young People's Socialist League to run off announcements on their mimeo machine and Jackie and the others went around in Jackie's car tacking and taping them to lampposts and walls; they were mostly torn down as soon as they went up.

On television they showed people emptying the shelves of super-markets, buying canned food and bottled water, and guns and ammo too. *Eighty-four percent of those polled said they supported the President's action. One in five said they believed it meant the beginning of World War Three.* But mostly people went on doing what they had been doing; they got up and went to work and went to class and in class went on talking about Shakespeare and quadratic equations and the rise of the middle class. Kit wrote notes into her notebooks and walked across campus listening to the carillon at noon and went to the library. And always she felt the depth of the sky above her, maybe being sev-ered right now by the missiles coming. There was no poetry or knowl-edge or wisdom that could master or face or even survive it, it was *hopeless:* Pushkin's smile as useless against it as any other weapon, any at all.

The Unitarian church was bleak and homey at once, like a school cafeteria or a basement game room. There was no cross and no colored glass and the pews were square-backed and had worn velvet cushions to sit on. It was the first church that wasn't a Catholic church Kit had ever been in; a little shadow of trespass was only one of the new feelings she felt sitting there. She watched the people come in and the minister in a blue button-down shirt and no tie set up a microphone and folding chairs for speakers in front of the altar.

Saul and Max and the YPSL guys registered the people who came in, got signatures from those who were willing to sign. There were people from ADA in ties or in dresses; there were two women from SANE who each wore the black button with a white figure on it that Jackie told her was the semaphore letters for N and D laid one over the other, and they stood for Nuclear Disarmament. Kit wondered how anyone would know this.

"So are you guys representing the Student Peace Union?" Max asked two boyish blonds, almost twins, in argyle sweaters.

"We're not representing it," one said. "We are it."

In the end the church filled and the speakers one by one got up and tapped the mike and spoke. "Don't say it's too terrible to be used," the SANE woman said. "Just because *you* wouldn't use it. It's not too terrible. It's been used. We used it. Eisenhower threatened to drop one on the Chinese in Korea. Just a little one. He was going to lend one to the French in Indochina. Don't tell me it's inconceivable."

"These missiles are a danger to this country," the ADA man in tweed jacket and striped tie said. "But after all they are equivalent to our own missiles in bases in England and Turkey. There has to be a general summit-level discussion on the reduction of these forces around the world. Sudden precipitate action . . ."

But Max had stood up in the audience, his long S shape, and started to speak. "Well those weapons may not represent a new danger to us," he said, "but we sure are a danger to Cuba. And this government would prefer Cuba to be defenseless. The Russians are lending a hand to the little kid who's just about to get beat up . . ."

There were shouts of *No, no* and protests; Max slid his big hands into his pockets and went on. "Kennedy says we've got no plans to invade Cuba at the present time. *At the present time.* Well, swell. Must make them feel confident down there." More protests, but Max didn't raise his voice. "Kennedy's risking the end of civilization to get another whack in at Castro. Do we go along? Sixty-four-dollar question."

Splits and oppositions appeared among the groups, an ill will spreading that Kit could only partly perceive. It was like a family argument where what someone said reminded others of everything that person always said or shouted, so that people began responding angrily at the first words, as though they knew what had to be coming. Saul took over the mike and the Fair Play for Cuba Committee proposed a rationale for a march on Saturday, coordinated with the protest marches the national committee was sponsoring in Washington and at the UN. The theme of the march would be Hands Off Cuba. There was real shouting then, and some people walked out.

"Listen," Jackie said to Kit, leaning close. "I don't think you should get involved with this."

"I am," Kit said. "I'm here."

"I don't think you should participate in this thing tomorrow. It's not anything that's going to do you any good."

"What do you mean? Any good?"

He looked away, at Saul going through a list and asking for volunteers, at the darkened windows, and at his hands. "I just think you ought not to," he said softly. "I can't even promise you'll be safe."

"I'm not," she said. "I'm not safe."

"Kit," Jackie said, but still he didn't look at her. "For once. Listen and believe me."

9.

The next night, as if he knew just where she'd be—though in fact he could not have known—Falin stood in the lamplight outside the music building when Kit came out with Fran and her friends.

Kit had insisted that Fran let her come along with her to the rehearsal. Fran's pickup quintet was doing the *Trout,* but only the first two movements, and not perfect, Fran warned her. Kit could not have borne solitude, though it had always been so easy. She sat on a hard chair while they went through it twice, stopping to work on small moments like craftsmen on a jewel, five oddly assorted, even funny-looking people beautiful in their attention, transformed into what seemed to Kit almost a holy unity. The music filled her as though with water, as though she swam, a trout released, too small to keep: escaped.

He tossed away a cigarette; there was no doubt he had been waiting for her. They knew it too, the boys and the girl with their black cases.

"May I speak to you for a moment?"

"Yes sure," she said.

He began to walk away, and she went beside him, uncertain.

"I may have a journey to go on," he said. "A trip. I cannot tell exactly when return. Perhaps now will be last night I am here for some time. I would like if you come to visit, stay. Stay with me for a time."

"I can't," she said. "I have to be in by eleven. It's almost eleven now."

He lifted his eyes, as though to look at the sky, tell time by the moon, but perhaps only to remember. "Of course," he said. "I had forgotten."

"Where are you going?"

"A short journey. If I am summoned, and if I . . . Well. A plan I did not expect so suddenly to, to." He lifted something vague with his hand. He might have meant *hatch* or *come to fruition* or *ripen*. He looked at the watch on his wrist; she didn't remember that he had worn one before. "Well. No time. I should have thought."

"I'm sorry," she said. "I'm so sorry."

He nodded lightly, lifted his hand again, this time to mean *good-bye* or *no matter* or *so long. "Do svidanya,"* he said.

Kit watched him go. Then she looked back to where the others stood, watching and waiting, as still and alert as observers at an argument or a kiss.

"Okay," she said, not loud enough for them to hear. Then she waved and called out to them: "Okay! It's okay!"

She turned, feeling their eyes on her, and ran down to where Falin was opening his car with a key.

"Wait," she said. He looked up to see her. "I want to go."

"Your curfew."

"It doesn't matter," she said. "If the bombs fall, I don't want to be in my dorm room."

"No?"

"I mean I won't be glad I was there. That I kept the rules to the end."

For a long time he stood with his hand on the door. "Perhaps may not be the end," he said.

"Anyway," she said. "Anyway."

. . .

In the dark of the car he put his hands on the wheel but for a time didn't start it. His hands were gloved. He put one over her own clasped cold hands.

"You said you wanted me to stay away from you," she said.

"No," he said, "no you are wrong. I did not want that. Not that of anything."

"You were afraid of me," she said. "Afraid that I'd put you in danger. I didn't know I could. You sent me away, and I guess I understood why, but still."

"Oh my dear," he said. "You could be no danger to me. No. Nothing you could do."

"Well then. Why."

"It was not you who made danger for me," he said. "It was I who was dangerous for you. I wanted you to be not near me, so you would not be . . . caught. Hurt."

She knew it was so: saw him again in his garden, how he turned to her, telling her to go. She knew it was so, that for her sake he had sent her away, though he hadn't wanted to, *not that of anything.* "What danger? Tell me."

"In English," he said, "danger is something not yet come, yes? Something that waits or threatens. Around the corner. Close behind."

"I guess."

"There is no danger then any longer," he said. "What was to come, has come." A passing car's lights stroked his car's interior, his ghost hands, his face, and went away. "Do you know, I thought I had ceased to want things, Kyt. And this I thought was very well. Much to gladden me, nothing to want. But one last thing I wanted. I wanted you to be near. This night."

He took his hand from hers. "But if you cannot," he said.

"I will," she said. "If it's what you want."

His smile, that had never before asked anything of her, anything for himself. For his poems he had asked, but not for himself. In the thundery storm-dark evening he had said *I need you.* And then nothing more.

He started the car. She crossed her hands in her lap and looked ahead. She would ask him nothing more, not where he was going, nor why. The car went out of town and out across the fields to the west, to his house at the end of the road. Every turn of the wheels, every step of her feet toward his door, took her into another world unknown to her, and she could only go on, for the old worlds behind were gone. She would just be with him and be glad, and gladden him if she could.

She thought at first that nothing had changed inside his house. The standard lamp with its flowered shade shone on the brown bearlike sofa, the card table held papers and books. Then a gleam or wink in the corner drew her eye. He had a television.

"Yes," he said, seeing where she looked.

It was a dull bronze color, and set up on a chrome stand: its gray eye closed.

"These," he said, and touched the antennae, "these have name in English. Rabbit's ears. I was told this."

"Yes," she said.

"Did you also know," he said, "that the radiation or broadcast of television waves goes on always, passing through air, through houses, through bodies even?"

"I guess so."

"Yes. I knew but did not think of it till I bought this. Until it was turned on, and revealed them to be here. Then I thought of them, passing always through here, only unknown to me."

"They might make it a law," she said. "To leave it on all the time, so they don't get wasted or lost."

She could tell that for a moment he pondered what she had said, before laughing.

"Oh hey," she said. "This is new too."

It was a phone. A tiny oval phone of the kind she thought belonged only in the pastel bedrooms of teenage girls in movies. "A Princess," she said.

"Yes, is its name," he said. "Look." He lifted the receiver, and its dial lit up, aglow in the corner where it had been installed. "It seems to me a thing found maybe undersea," he said. "Among pearls and treasure. Do you know the name of this color?"

"Um," she said. "I guess it's aqua."

"Yes!" he said, surprised. "Is Latin word for water. So you see." He put the receiver to his ear. "Like shell you listen to. From this might come poems. More than from car radio of Orpheus."

He cradled the receiver with an odd gentleness. Kit felt a dark apprehension suddenly, a certainty of loss.

"Ah," he said, lifting his eyes. "Excuse me. I saw as we came in Miss Petroski's light on. I must speak to her one minute. One minute only." He made a motion with his hands to say she must sit down, and went to the door that separated his rooms from the Petroski house; he knocked, and his small knock was as uniquely his, or uniquely Russian, as the way he washed or held a glass of tea. He seemed to hear a voice, and went in.

Kit sat. When he was gone, though, she stood again, and walked the cold room. A big gas heater, clad in metal made to look like wood, breathed hotly, but still she was cold. On the card table where last summer they worked there were a few papers scattered in the familiar lamplight. The small square letters of his English hand.

> *In this tongue I like poison more than food,*
> *Choose clamor over song, like rain not sun*

It was a poem, or the beginnings of one, words crossed out and other words inserted, the few lines rewritten many times. The accents of the lines were marked with pencil ticks.

> *A storm for which I had no name*
> *Broke all the eggs in Russiaville;*
> *The roofs of Russiaville off came*
> *And flew away like flapping wings*

He was trying to write in English.

In pity and wonder she touched the sheets. It was like watching an athlete who's had a dreadful accident learning to walk again, using all his knowledge and strength to do the simplest things. How long would it take him? You couldn't know, because you couldn't know when you were done. She could never know it of herself, either: she had learned this language at the same time as she had learned to see and hear, and yet she would never know, because you never came to a time when you could say Done. Not until you were shot, like Pushkin. Or like Rimbaud, until you just stopped for good, for ever.

What door, what window was this she felt open within her? God how small it was, how deep.

He came back into the room.

"I have nothing to give you," he said. "No food, no drink."

"I don't want anything."

"Come, sit."

But she had grown shy, afraid of him or for him, and turned away. The great television in the corner like a bored beast: she went to it and pressed the large button that must mean On, and it came to life. A gray western, one she recognized: she didn't remember at first what story it told, only the huge sky, the horsemen.

"Where are you going?" she said, though she had promised herself she wouldn't. "If you go."

"If I go? To the wind's twelve quarters."

"Can't you say?"

"John Gwayne," he said. He pointed to the television. "Do you know?"

"Yes," she said. "I know."

"A big man, always in the right."

"Yes." Once in the summer she had told him what she had heard or read somewhere was a motto of the Texas Rangers: A *little man will always beat a big man, if the little man's in the right and keeps on a-comin'*.

She had begun to shiver, small flutters crossing her breastbone and her shoulders. He put his arm around her.

"What's going to happen," she whispered. "What's going to happen to us."

He said nothing for a time; she felt his breath taken, released. There could be only one thing she meant by what she said.

"Well," he said. "Now is near dawn in Moscow. Nikita Sergeyevich has slept in his office in his clothes; he does not want to be caught in his nightclothes if U.S. has decided on war. He did not sleep well."

Kit turned further into his arms and closed her eyes.

"There is new letter from Dr. Castro in Cuba," Falin said. "He is angry and afraid. From all that he has learned he knows that U.S. will attack Cuba in two, three days. Why does Soviet Union not announce that missiles on the island will be fired at U.S. if Cuba is invaded? So far Nikita Sergeyevich has not even stated that such missiles are present in Cuba. Why not?

"Well. Nikita Sergeyevich will have tea and blinis and think about these things. Cuba cannot be allowed to be destroyed. Politburo thinks if U.S. invades Cuba, Soviet Union should immediately move on West Berlin, but Gensek—I mean Nikita Sergeyevitch, General Secretary— does not see what Berlin has to do with anything."

He bent back his head, looking up, as though looking farther. "By his wristwatch he sees that now it is midnight in America, in Washington. Dawn has not yet reached Ukraine. All West still asleep; because the world is round, and turns its face by hours to the sun. Nikita Sergeyevich, when he thinks of this, remembers always the schoolroom where first he learned of it, and his teacher there, and the smell of the stove, and how hard it was to understand this, and believe it."

"What will he do?" she asked.

He shrugged a slow shrug, shook his head, held out his hand toward the television, as though from it alone could come the future. "Two great ones," he said. "And neither in the right."

"They said it'll be long," Kit said. "Months of hardship and danger. The President said."

He shook his head. "No. Will come quickly now."

She felt again the height of cold air above them, the stratosphere; the rocket's arc through it, *arc-en-ciel*.

"Tell me," he said. "If you could make it stop, then would you?"

"Of course," she said. "Of course I would."

"If to stop it meant that you would yourself not survive?"

She pulled herself away to look at him, to see why he asked. "Well you'd have to," she said. "You couldn't refuse."

"Ah well. You would *have* to. Is not the same as would you. Wouldn't you be afraid, wouldn't the loss be too great to think of?"

"You wouldn't think," she said. She hoped she wouldn't; hoped she would not be given time to think. "It would be like being on a sinking ship, the *Titanic*. You'd have to let the women and children go first. Automatically. You'd have to go down with the ship, if you were the captain."

"You would. But what if no one would know of your sacrifice. If no one knows of my sacrifice, no one could know it was not made. Better to live, no? Better to live than die."

"But everybody dies." She couldn't tell what side he wanted her to take, what he wanted to hear her say.

"Perhaps trust to chance," he said. "It has not yet happened. Perhaps once again it will not. We live in danger but are never destroyed. Perhaps still never." She could see in the silver light of the television that his brow glowed with sweat in the cold room. "I mean, so you might think. You might think, What if my sacrifice is not necessary? What if danger will pass anyway? Then every day that did pass, and the destruction did not come, you would think, Aha: I was right, how foolish I was to think of acting; I need not be hero, and I am still alive here."

"That sounds like hell. Like . . . damnation. Waiting. After your one chance has gone by."

He said nothing for a time. A great restlessness seemed to be in him, in his breathing, a vortex inside his still exterior.

"And if," he said then. "If you loved someone, who must take such action, make such sacrifice. What then? Would you let them go?"

"Wives in war do."

"Not willingly. Not always."

"My mother didn't," Kit said. "She didn't. She begged my father not to go. She had a baby son when he went down to enlist. She stood crying on the doorstep with the baby and calling after him. So she says." Falin arose, as she spoke, from beside her, and stood at the window looking out; had he even heard her? "Anyway, he got stationed in Washington, about six blocks from their apartment."

"Hardest thing," he said, not to her. "Is not suffering. Much harder is to remember what you did to avoid suffering. What you were willing to do. This cannot be erased."

She lowered her eyes. On the television John Wayne brought home the white girl who had been taken by the Indians, brought her home to her mother in the bare bleak house on the desert. And turned away. When she and Ben had watched it years ago she thought he would kill the girl when he found her in her buckskins and feathers. He didn't do that but he couldn't stay there either. He turned away, turned to go, taller than any human, tall enough to walk on in that place, against that sky.

"Kyt." He still faced the window and the dark. "Do you have the translations we made, the poems of this summer?"

"Yes. All of them."

"What do you think, are they poems in English?"

"I don't know. I hope. I think."

"So much undone," he said. "So much that should be done."

"What we did," Kit said. "Working on your poems. It was the hardest thing I've ever done. It was harder than I thought anything could be."

"And yet you did it."

"Yes. It was wonderful. It was . . . it was like water."

He seemed to hear her then clearly, and turned to her. "Now you will write your own poems," he said. "And that will be harder still, and more wonderful still."

On the television their station had run out, and showed only the American flag flying, and the national anthem began, like a burst of cannon. An awful weariness seemed to be filling her up, from her toes and fingertips inward to her heart. He sat again by her on the couch; he touched her throat, where she held her own hand. "What is it?" he asked.

"It hurts," she said. "It hurts a lot. I don't know why."

"Ill?"

"I don't think so. It doesn't feel like that, like a cold. I feel . . . like I've been crying for a long time."

"Perhaps you have."

"I'm so sleepy."

"Yes." He took her hands and lifted her from the couch; she put her arms around him, her cheek on his shoulder, because she was tired of refusing to. She pressed her lips to his throat and the vein that beat along it. She would make him not turn away. But he didn't turn away. After a time he led her to the small room, and she wouldn't lie there alone, or release him at all: she drew him down beside her.

"I should not touch you," he said. "I have no right. You so clean and unsoiled."

No: she held him, took his face in her hands. She wondered if he could really believe it was so, that there was anyone anywhere unsoiled; or if he meant to warn her or ask her. "I'll go with you," she said. "Take me."

"Ah no."

"I will. Anywhere."

"Everywhere is here."

His arms seemed enormous. The heater in the far room boomed softly, igniting. The window in its wooden frame spoke a little note. The gray cat on the rug, indifferent, couldn't keep its eyes open.

"I don't really know anything," she said. "About . . . I never found out."

"There is not anything," he said. "Everything is known."

It wasn't so, that everything was known; she was sure of that. But with him now it was plain what they should do, that they shouldn't refuse anymore. She didn't know anything but there was nothing now she had to guess at or decide about, to stop at or shrink from. She found that out, there, then: that you didn't always have to dare your-self, or make yourself; "yourself" could just be carried along, mar-veling, willing nothing, and who could have guessed that? It was the last thing she would have expected. She laughed, and he asked her why, but she knew she didn't need to answer, that he only asked because lovers do, just to hear her speak.

"You laugh and cry at once," he said

"No," she said, "I don't. No that's silly. No one can. They just say that."

"You do, now."

"Well," she said. "Okay then."

It seemed to her that they spent a very long time there together: not hours but days, years even, the whole course of a long deep love affair: that with him she moved from wonder, and then knowledge, to those astonishing tears and cryings-out without a name that come when everything inside is breached; and then to other things, to plain belonging and necessity, a necessity as profound and permanent and easily slaked as thirst. And then they couldn't do without each other; and that was fearful and awesome, but there was no reversing it, no matter what. The last stars paled, the casement window opened on the cold dawn; they went out, they went on. She got lost, and went on alone; then she was found, and lost, and found again; they went on, they grew old, they died together. That's what it seemed like.

And yet she couldn't actually remember it, long afterward, remembered nothing of what really happened. So it had to be that there was really nothing to remember, because if there were, it cer-tainly couldn't be all forgotten. All she remembered with distinct-ness was that she slept that night in his bed, and that she awoke different. Alone. The gray cat atop her, the steady roar of its purring and the kneading of its paws on the quilt, its little cross-eyed face poised just an inch from her own to smell her sleeping breath. Noth-ing more.

She saw him in the next room on the phone, the Princess, its dial alight in the dark corner. He was dressed, and wearing his overcoat.

She heard him say words in Russian, and she seemed to understand them, but not their import. She heard him say *Da. Da. Da.*

Or she dreamed that, having gone to sleep again. Then he was standing by the bed, looking down on her.

"You slept," he said. He said it as though she had done what she should, as though he were happy for her.

She struggled to stand up. "You're going? Now?"

"I made offer," he said. "Now offer has been accepted." He put his hands in his big pockets. "I had hoped I could bring you back, to University. Was my intention. Now I cannot. I must go."

"No," she said.

"Stay here," he said. "Is not long till morning. Then call your friends. Ask to come and pick you up. Yes?"

"No," she said. "Don't go."

"I must." He smiled, as though to remind her of what she had said, before midnight, before she slept. "If I must I must, is it not so?"

"No. No don't." There was a noise around them, a huge noise like a jet airplane's settling on a runway, and she realized what it was: wind.

"Kyt," he said. He sat by her. "Listen. Tomorrow, later on, they may say they know what became of me, what happened, but they will be wrong. Because an act—any act—may be one thing in one world and something else in another world, a thing that is not like it but has its shape, that rhymes with it. A commonplace thing, accident or loss, it may mean nothing here and everything there . . ."

"There's only one world."

"Yes. Yes there is. Only one." He stood. He had shed the uncertain restlessness that had afflicted him before, and it made her afraid, for him or herself. When he returned to the farther room she got up too, weak as water, pulling on her shoes, and followed him.

"Are you," she said, unable to believe she could guess this, say this aloud, "are you going back?"

"Back," he said. "No. On. I am going on." He took from the table his black case of imitation leather, and filled it with papers, yellow copy paper, typewritten: his poems in Russian. Then he stopped, and lifted his eyes, the lamps of his eyes, to her. "And do you know. Strangest thing of all in this mirrorland. I can only go because you, Kit, my dear, my love, you want me to stay."

Tears sprang to her eyes and she put her hands to her mouth. When he came closer she pressed herself to him, to keep him or stop him. He took her shoulders in his hands so that he could see her face. "I can tell you now. The world, this world, is to go on; it will not end. That is certain now, this day, this morning. No bomb will fall. You will have a life that you must live, a long one it might be. Instead of closing now, it opens, do you see? So you must learn to speak, Kyt. You must find ways to speak."

"I could with you. Without you I can't."

"You can, for you must. Oh my dear love, don't you see. You have to *say*. For them, for him. For my sake too." He held her again, his cheek pressed to hers, and he spoke softly in Russian; she heard her own name, and a diminutive of it, and other words she knew, and then words she didn't know and would never remember.

"I must go."

She released him, having no choice; without haste he picked up his case, and took from his pocket a shiny key on a length of gray twine; he looked at her and seemed to have passed away already, to be seeing her clearly but from a great distance.

At the door he turned, as though there were a thing left to say that he had not yet said. "You will see me soon, Kyt. I promise this."

He went out.

She knew, by now, what it is when someone walks away or goes away saying they'll return, how you can know that they won't, that they are already lost to you even in setting out. She knew it and she couldn't go after him, she couldn't cry out or call him back. The gray cat came around her legs and purred and stroked her in its soft selfish ignorance. She heard the car start, and its lights colored the yard she could see through the windows; the light swayed, diminished; the sound diminished.

She took her coat, went out into the yard. The wind was increasing, an autumn storm come, or passing overhead. The road was entirely dark, only the occluded moon outlining it, and she began to walk along it, and then to run, knowing how far ahead he was, how far behind she was, but running anyway. The tall roadside trees thrashed their limbs and lost their leaves in great cascades.

The main road was dark and empty too. The way east, the way west. She stood, breathing hard. Then down the straight road far away she saw two headlights coming toward the place where she stood. As she watched they seemed to come on with awful, impossible speed, the lights of a huge vehicle, roaring. No, the lights weren't one vehicle but two motorcycles, two that had drifted apart as they came on, fooling her. Still her heart raced. They were unbearably loud. They passed by her, one, then the other, both black, and went on down the straight road.

There was nowhere for her to go, nowhere to follow. She went back toward the house, where only the light in Falin's room was still lit and waiting. She shut the door she had left open. In Falin's bedroom his quilt was thrown back, his shirt on a chair. She took the shirt in her hands and inhaled its odor; she crawled into the bed beneath the quilt. She drew her legs up and held his shirt to her cheek as she had for so long held her white lamb. *Just please don't hurt him, don't hurt him* she prayed, to what powers she didn't know. The wind diminished. She lay unmoving, and after a long time her heart ceased its banging and she knew, astonished, that she would sleep again.

10

All that night a storm moved over the Gulf too, and toward morning Cuba was beneath it: rain and wind and the palms wild and the sea coming ashore to cover the roads and wash away the beaches. Cuban and Soviet officers in the northeastern mountain posts watched it through the knocking windows of their command posts, small shacks with corrugated roofs, and wondered how long their equipment would remain functioning. All the MRBMs on the island were now ready to be fired; they lacked only their nuclear warheads, which were stored away from the missile sites and heavily disguised by *maskirovka*, camouflage, the same word Soviet intelligence used for all misdirection, disinformation, false stories, entrapments. The twenty-four warheads for the R-14 IRBMs remained on the *Aleksandrovsk*, now rocking in the stirred waters of La Isabela harbor. At about ten o'clock the clouds parted; an antiaircraft unit in the mountains above Banes was alerted that a U-2 had been sighted near Guantanamo. It seemed certain that it was taking pictures in preparation for an attack the following day.

The officers at the station had been forbidden to fire on U.S. aircraft without orders from the Soviet commander on the island, but they couldn't reach him; the U-2 would be out of Cuban airspace in just minutes. The officers made their own decision: an SA-2 surface-to-air missile was fired up through the rainy air, found the U-2, and exploded near enough to it to bring it down. The pilot died in the crash.

American plans called for an immediate retaliatory strike on any SAM bases in Cuba that attacked an American aircraft. As soon as the report could be confirmed, the news went to the President. The assumption was that the Kremlin was deliberately intensifying the crisis by ordering an attack on an unarmed U-2.

Great feeble angels, long-winged and slow, all eyes. At almost the same moment, though so far from the sun it was still in the dark of the morning, a U-2 from a SAC base in Alaska strayed into Soviet airspace over the Chukotski Peninsula. Soviet MiGs rose to intercept it, and at the same time, in response to the U-2's call for help, American F-102s armed with nuclear air-to-air missiles scrambled and headed for the Bering Sea. With just a few minutes to go before contact, the U-2 managed to fly out of Soviet airspace: as unintentionally, it seems—as helplessly, as accidentally—as it had wandered in.

No rain fell that night on the University campus, but the leaves of all the trees, yellow elm and hickory, gray-green ash, coppery oak and beech, seemed to have fallen at once in the night: long wind-combed rows of them moving in the still-restless air, dead souls lifted and tossed on gusts.

People were in motion too. Kit crossing the campus from the College Street gate felt them, small eddies or flocks, people coming in from Fraternity Row and from town in numbers, the way they did on class days, hurrying together toward their classes in different buildings; but this wasn't a class day, and they seemed to be all going one way. She went that way too. She'd awakened in the dawn light in Falin's bed, and had not dared or wanted to lift the phone from its cradle. She'd left the empty house and walked in the frost to town, so strangely weak she had to stop now and then to rest, until she came to the All

Night Cafeteria. She sat there with a coffee, thinking of nothing, wondering at the pain in her throat. Was she really sick? Her head felt not light but heavy, made of mud or stone; when she rested it on the cold plastic tabletop and closed her eyes, the waitress shook her awake, and told her not unkindly that she couldn't sleep there, which maybe people did a lot, and she got up and found a quarter to pay with and went up toward the University.

Many people were running, or hurrying as though not to miss something. They were becoming a crowd, rivulets flowing together into a stream and flowing faster. The earth rose up a little there, between the student center and the science building, beyond which lay the central axis of the campus, a broad way starting at the auditorium and lined with the newer buildings. That's where the crowd was going, following the paths or pouring over the grass and through the leaves. Kit came to the top of the rise and saw what it was: the Fair Play for Cuba Committee and the other groups were marching, a little band with signs. Kit could just hear, like a plea repeated, the marchers' voices, and the cries and shouts of the people around them, moving with them and pressing on them, a gauntlet they passed through. There were no more than twenty or thirty of them.

She went down that way, drawn along. There was Saul Greenleaf, in the front, and Rodger in a jacket and tie and his porkpie hat. Max was in back keeping the group together. Black-and-white cars of the University police were pulled up along the route, their lights revolving and their radios emitting staticky communications louder than the protesters' chants. Up on top of the auditorium Kit could see watchers and the tall tripods of cameras with long lenses, men with binoculars. She thought of Milton Bluhdorn. Jackie had said it would do her no good to be here: did he know it would be like this? Photographers scooted along the march route too, and some of them looked like news photographers, and some of them didn't.

She felt a tug at her sleeve, and pulled away, threatened. It was Fran. "Unbelievable," she said in cold scorn. "Can you believe this?"

It seemed that in a short time the furious crowd would fall on the demonstrators and beat them or worse. Kit and Fran went down the slope, hurrying as everyone hurried.

"You can think what you want," Fran said. "You can *say* what you want. But this is ludicrous."

A sign that read *Hands Off Cuba* was torn from someone's hands and ripped to pieces to awful cheering.

"Who *are* these people?" Fran said. "*College students?* They're rednecks."

"Fran."

"Well you hear what they're saying? 'Commies go back to Russia.' I mean come on." She tossed down her cigarette and stepped on it. "Dopes. Know-nothings."

They pushed through the mass of hecklers and yellers that undulated along the march route until they were at the front of the crowd and keeping pace with the marchers. And without ever exactly choosing to, they became marchers, as though sorted from the crowd by a sorter that recognized only two kinds, if you weren't one you were the other. Someone she didn't know linked arms with her. Saul saw her and grinned, amazed, alight, unafraid she thought, or maybe not. A tall athletic guy was bent into his face, speaking curses meant just for him it seemed; on the guy's crewcut head was a novelty straw hat decorated with church keys and a little sign that said *Lets Raise Hell*.

"Where's Jackie?" Kit called, but Saul had to turn away to face his opponent.

It was what Kit had forever most hated and feared, to be pointed at and stared at and mocked. In the Passion story when she was a kid it was this that hurt her most, that the crowds mocked Jesus and spit on him. But she felt none of that now. She could see and assess the crowd around them as though they were etched. Almost all were men, many wearing their fraternity sweatshirts and their varsity jackets, some of them though in blazers and ties, with American-flag pins in their lapels and wolfish grins, not guys who got to be part of a mob very often and seeming to be enjoying it. One guy who bore down on them wore the button that the SANE women had worn, the three white lines on black, but when he came closer to Kit—so close and yelling so loud that she could see the fillings in his teeth—she saw that on his button the white lines were formed into a great swept-wing bomber, and beneath it were small letters that spelled DROP IT.

"Keep the women in the center!" Saul yelled back at his shrinking group. "Keep the women in the center, men on the outside!" The marchers had ceased their chanting, Peace Now and Hands Off Cuba, it was obvious that it just goaded the crowd around them dangerously; but the women who walked with Kit and Fran, arms now more protectively linked than before, started to sing. They sang, amazingly, in Latin: *Dona, dona nobis, dona nobis pacem.*

It was a round: one took up after the other had started, kept on after she ended. Fran laughed aloud, apparently she knew what they were singing, she right away began singing along in a loud hoarse voice perfectly on key, and Kit sang too when after a moment she got the little tune: *Dona, dona nobis, dona nobis pacem, pacem,* the women's voices cycled.

Then through the marchers and the shifting crowd coming and going, Kit saw Falin.

He was just turning from looking elsewhere, and now his look passed over the marchers and the others with interest and something like delight. It seemed he didn't recognize Kit in the mass of them, though she felt the instant of his look toward her like a stab of wonder.

"Then it's okay," she said. "It's okay."

"What's okay?" Fran said.

"It's him," Kit said. "Falin."

He was coming closer to them, it seemed. Kit was about to call out to him when he turned away, looking elsewhere. In a second she couldn't see him anymore. But just before the crowd closed around him she saw—she thought she saw—that his big pale feet were bare.

No. Where had he gone? There was no way to turn back, no way to leave the little group of marchers now, Kit was carried forward by all of it without a choice. She untangled herself from Fran and the women and stood still while the others passed by her, until the rear guard caught up with her and Max came close, his arms wide to keep them moving, like a shepherd.

"We've got to break this up," he said. "Somebody'll get hurt."

"Max."

"Get up and tell Saul and the people in front. We've got to break it up. Go do that."

She went back up along the edge of the marching group, too tightly and defensively bound together now to pass through. When she came to the front she saw that Saul was less certain too than he had been, and that ahead the opposing crowd was coming together in a wall that wouldn't let them pass. "Where's the cops?" she heard him say. "*Now* where's the cops? Free speech, people. Free speech. Land of the free."

In a minute the march would not be a march any longer, it would be a huddle of victims, the ones in the rear were pressing already against the slowing front rank. Almost all their signs were gone. Then, just as their forward progress was about to stop altogether, Saul stepped quickly out ahead and turned to face his group, walking backward like a drum major. With both hands he waved them to the right, off the main way and onto the walks of the campus.

"Okay, *quick!*" he called out. "Keep on, keep together! We're going to end this *at the library!* Everybody hear? Pass that on! At the library steps!" All the while waving them to the right and on. They did go faster too, almost broke into a run, and for the first time Kit felt fear, that they might run, and what might happen to them then. But they didn't, even though the crowd around gave an awful cry of rage and triumph to see that they had given up and were getting away.

But what had happened to him? Kit thought. What had he done, where had he gone?

The library was open. At the steps Saul and Max ushered them all inside, medieval outlaws claiming sanctuary; a few though stayed outside to deal with the crowd—Saul, whose chest was heaving maybe from the unaccustomed exercise, and Max, unperturbed, hands clasped behind his back and even smiling when Kit went by him into the dark silent inside. For a moment she felt it had grown suddenly not dark but black, and her feet lost touch with the floor, as though it melted to liquid; then she felt someone take her arm, and steady her.

"Okay?"

"Yes. Yes. Okay."

How long did they hide there? The librarian came to speak to them more than once, hushing them and telling them, which they knew, that the library was a place of study and work, not conversation and mingling. Someone was crying. Time passed. Above their heads, all around the base of the rotunda, were words printed in gold: *A Good Book Is the Precious Life Blood of a Master Spirit*. The doors kept opening to show the day and admitting more of the demonstrators, and also those who had bones to pick with them, their voices dropping to hissing whispers, until the librarian chased them away too.

Kit sat huddled on the bench by the great doors where you could sit to pull off your galoshes or overshoes, which were not allowed in the halls and stacks.

"Kit," Fran said, studying her. "Are you sick?"

"I don't know."

"How long since you ate?"

"I forget."

Fran nodded. "I do that," she said. "I fainted once in Saks." She sat beside her. "Listen," she said. "What happened. With Falin."

"I saw him," Kit said. "Now, just now, out there. I have to find him. I have to." She bent over, feeling she might fall asleep here, again, on this bench. "My throat hurts so much."

"We'll go eat," Fran said. "Hell with those people."

In the Castle the arguments were continuing; Max came in with an entourage of questioners, not all of them angry, and he sat to talk with them. Saul and Rodger came in too, warily.

"Sit," Fran said. "What do you want?"

"Just a sec," Kit said.

Taking hold of the backs of booths she made her way to the phone in the back, in its little wooden house that had long ago lost its door. She called his office at the liberal arts tower but there was no answer there, the office closed on a Saturday. She called the operator and asked for the number at his house, not expecting to be told it. "Falin," she said, and spelled it, and the operator told her what it was, Orchard 9-5066, not secret at all. She dialed, almost unable to turn the worn dial plate with her finger, why so weak. She listened to the Princess ring. Ben had told her that actually the ring you hear isn't the one that's heard or not heard in the room you call: just an illusion.

After a long time she hung up.

Fran stood by the booth where Saul and Rodger sat. "All those people," she was saying. "It's like they *want* it to go off. Like they're tired of standing on the edge, and they want to jump. But that can't be. It just can't."

"1914," Saul said. "War fever. The workers all joined the armies of their countries. Even though it was in none of their interests. Even though they *knew* it. They just did it. As though they were sleepwalking, or possessed. They weren't even drafted. They *volunteered*. They were called, they went."

"1914 is a date in history," Rodger said. "This isn't gonna be, if it doesn't stop."

"Saul," Kit said. "What happened to Jackie, where is he."

Saul looked up at her and thought a moment. "He's gone," he said. "That's the short answer. He said he had some emergency business. He threw some clothes and things in his car and left early this morning."

For a time she only stared at them, at Saul and Rodger and Fran, thinking she could no longer understand what was said to her. The voices of others came to her loud and resonant like noises made underwater but not seeming to be speech. Where had Jackie gone? Why would he go? "Do you have a car, Saul? I need a ride somewhere."

"Jeez, Kit. I don't. I came in with Rodger."

"Rodger," Kit said. "It isn't far. Just out West North Street. I just can't walk, I can't."

"Kit what are you doing, what are you *doing*," Fran said, clutching her brow.

"I just want to go out and see," Kit said. "I have to see."

"I think you should go to the infirmary," Fran said. "I really think."

"No."

"I'll go there with you."

"Rodger," Kit said.

Rodger regarded her, touching the tips of his long fingers together. "If you don't mind," he said, "I am not ready to go riding a scooter through the west end of town with a white girl on my jumpseat. Arms around my waist. This ain't Greenwich Village, girl."

"What if we waited till after dark," she said.

"Oh," Rodger said. "Oh sure. After dark is good."

She looked at them. She wanted to say that if she could get there, she would just wait alone, wait until she learned something, until she knew something. She saw though that they had ceased to look at her or at one another, that their eyes were drawn to something behind and above her, first Rodger's and then the others', and the sound on the television above the counter was just then turned up, and the hubbub faded. Kit turned to see what they all saw.

A police car, lights revolving, attended on a truck poised on the bank of a river, its big tires planted like feet. From the truck a cable ran, thrumming with effort as it was winched in; and what it drew up from the river, what it had caught with a heavy hook, was a car: a big new convertible. It was pulled by inches up and out of the river, and water poured from it as it rose, from the insides over the doorsills and out from under the crumpled hood.

11.

It must have been near dawn. The little town where that iron bridge arched the river was a couple of hours to the north, on the way, though not the main way, to the capital. Up there the sudden storm had poured a great slew of rain across a narrow band of prairie, flooding streams and washing out dirt roads. The car in the river had only become visible after floodgates downstream were opened at morning and the river's level fell. It might have encountered another vehicle on the bridge, police said tire marks and a scattering of broken glass were visible there where the guardrail was depressed, but nothing was certain. There were plans for a full search of the river, but the authorities said that the rapid flow resulting from the downstream gates being opened could have carried a body very far. Police recovered items from the river that they said might have been discarded by a man trying to swim ashore: an overcoat, an empty briefcase, shoes.

That was all that was said in the Sunday-morning papers that Fran brought to Kit in the student infirmary. There was the picture of the convertible being drawn up out of the river, and the picture of Falin when he arrived in West Berlin the year before. One year, almost two.

There was another picture on the front page of the same paper, and on the front page of a Chicago paper that Fran had also brought. The little group of demonstrators, looking not only few but small, surrounded like damned souls in a Brueghel hell by the contorted crowded faces of their tormentors, yelling or laughing or cursing at them. Most of their signs already gone, except for one that read *Hands Off* and didn't seem to be about Cuba at all. Pro-Cuba March Meets Massive Opposition. Kit in the front, in her leather jacket: her eyes looking away, as though just then catching sight of something, something not part of this conflict at all.

"He's not dead," Kit said. "He isn't. I know it."

"Well then why, where," Fran said. "I mean come on."

The doctor came down the row of beds to where Kit lay. The infirmary was old and small and strangely smelly, the iron beds in an open row. Only one other was occupied, a boy who seemed to be weeping, weeping, face into his pillow.

"How's the throat?" the doctor asked.

"Okay," Kit said. "I guess."

"Doesn't hurt to swallow?"

"It never did. It just hurt."

The doctor put his hands in the pockets of his white coat. "The tests are back. You have mononucleosis. You know what that is?"

"The kissing disease," Kit said. "Mono."

"Well you get it from more than kissing. I mean you can get it in more ways than one. It's just an infectious disease." He bent over her and with warm dry hands felt the underside of her chin, the sides of her throat. "The pain comes from swollen lymph nodes that are producing the white blood cells to fight it off. There's a number of nodes right along here. They don't usually get as swollen as yours, though."

"Is that why she fainted?" Fran asked.

The doctor shrugged, a little shrug, as though he knew no more than anybody. It hadn't been he who had been here when the University police car brought her; only nurses and a student receptionist. She couldn't make them leave her alone, they made her answer questions and show her ID card and then undress and put on a cotton robe, they took blood, they put her into a narrow bed and drew the curtains around it. Sleep, they said, but she said she wouldn't sleep, couldn't sleep, and she started to tremble again as she had before she fell down in the Castle, as though shaking to pieces. She tried to get out of the bed and a nurse held her with a strong hand and another brought a paper cup with a red pill in it, a capsule like a little shiny gout of blood. It was the same pill that the nuns had made her take the first night at Our Lady, when she had not stopped arguing, not stopped shaking. It was like a little death; she knew it, and she took it.

While she slept motionless and dreamless in the University infirmary a message began to be transmitted by cable from General Secretary Khrushchev to the President of the United States. It was broadcast publicly over Moscow Radio at the same time. *The weapons which you describe as "offensive" are in fact grim weapons*, the message said. *Both you and I understand what kind of weapons they are*. It went on to say that in order to give encouragement to all those who long for peace, and to calm the American people, *who, I am certain, want peace as much as the people of the Soviet Union*, the Soviet government had decided to dismantle the weapons that the United States objected to. They would be crated and returned to the Soviet Union. The only condition placed on the offer was that the United States give its solemn pledge not to invade Cuba.

In the Atlantic the Soviet ship *Grozny* stopped and was reported to be standing still. It was afternoon in Moscow, morning in Washington when the message had been assembled and translated. The generals and the Secretaries of State and Defense gathered to study it. The admirals and generals urged caution and the Air Force Chief of Staff demanded that Cuba be invaded anyway, everything was in readiness: but the President overruled them. He ordered that no air reconnaissance missions be flown that day.

An aide to the President said later: *Everyone knew who were the hawks and who were the doves, but today was the doves' day.*

Kit and Fran went out into the Sunday sun. The world was still before them, as it had been the day before and the day before that, which seemed like a kind of miracle: that there should be students walking in groups and in pairs, and at noon the ringing of the University's famous carillon. Fran groaned and held her ears as they walked.

The strangest idea, Kit wanted to say to her. Fran I have the strangest idea, I can't even say it. But not even that much could she say.

What she thought was that maybe he was supposed to disappear. Maybe it was supposed to look as though he had died, but he hadn't, he had gone on. She knew this was possible, that people who were in danger could be made to disappear, or seem to have died, when really they'd been helped to escape, helped to safety. But how could that be? There was no escape; he had already escaped. There was no place left that was safe.

Jackie would be able to tell her, tell her that she was nuts, to calm down. Or maybe not. He had gone too, without a word.

At nightfall a telegram was delivered to her, that had made its way to the campus and to her tower and her room. It was in a yellow envelope with a cellophane window. She took it from the proctor who had signed for it, an object she had never held in her hands before.

"Open it," Fran said.

It was just as in the movies, a paper with typed lines of capital letters stuck on and the dots between phrases that meant *stop*. It was from George and Marion; the picture of Kit in the front row of the demonstrators must have appeared in their paper too.

> THREE QUOTES COME TO MIND ONE MY COUNTRY MAY
> SHE ALWAYS BE RIGHT BUT RIGHT OR WRONG MY COUN-
> TRY TWO I DISAGREE WITH WHAT YOU SAY BUT I WILL
> DEFEND TO THE DEATH YOUR RIGHT TO SAY IT THREE
> IS THIS TRIP NECESSARY LOVE MOM DAD

She slept most of the day and night. In the morning she found in her mailbox a postcard, mailed on Friday, a picture of the carillon on campus. The message said only *I'm sorry. Will write later and explain.*

It was from Jackie. He hadn't signed it but she knew.

The short answer is, he's gone. That's what Saul had said to her when she asked. The short answer. She felt a kind of warning tremor begin deep within her. She thought of the kitchen at East North Street, when Saul and Fred were pretending that Fred was an FBI agent. A joke. But there had to be one, they said: *wherever two or three are gathered together in my name.* And when she had agreed to spy on Falin, Jackie had been there, outside the dean's office, appearing by chance but not by chance. And she had told him everything after that, everything she learned.

She crushed the card into her pocket. The tremor within her had risen to a kind of roar like the roar she felt in her head and breast when she awoke from shocking dreams. She set out across campus. The morning was white with cold.

The dean of students was just arriving at her door as Kit reached it too. She tried to avoid Kit, pretending not to have seen her coming up the steps behind her, but Kit called out to her. "Excuse me. Wait."

"Well?" the dean said.

"I have a question," she said.

For a moment the dean said nothing. Breath came from her red mouth. Then she let Kit through the door and went to the office, Kit following. The secretary's desk was empty, her typewriter shrouded and her lamp off.

"I'm afraid there's nothing I can tell you," the dean said. She sought amid a huge bunch of keys for one that would open her own office door. "Just like you, I'm waiting for news. I'm afraid though that we'll have to prepare ourselves for the worst."

"I was wondering," Kit said, coming into her office behind her uninvited, "if you could find Milton Bluhdorn. He might know something. I think he might know something."

The dean at her desk looked at her as though trying to choose among several responses; Kit could see them come and pass in her features despite her masklike makeup.

"Well I would have no way of contacting him," she said at length. "And why . . . What is it you think he would know?"

For a fearful moment, Kit wondered if she herself knew more than the dean did. "Professor Falin was really afraid of him," she said, which wasn't exactly true. "He was."

"How did Professor Falin know about Mr. Bluhdorn?"

"I told him." The dean seemed to be twisted inside by feelings she wanted not to show; she held herself erect as for a formal photograph, hand on the back of her big chair, but her white fingers pressed deeply into the leather. "You knew I would."

"I know you are a very reckless young lady."

"Why did you let him come here? Mr Bluhdorn. Why did you let him come in here and ask me those things?"

"These aren't matters I can fully explain. Not to you. Mr. Bluhdorn represents our government. There was no reason at all to question his motives or his, his."

"Well can you help me reach him? Please."

"You are not going to see him again. His work here is done." She clasped her hands behind her and lifted her chin, as though trying to grow taller. "I want you to understand me," she said. "Everything that was said in this room between you and me and Mr. Bluhdorn was said in the utmost confidence. You are to say nothing at all about anything that took place here, or anything that was asked of you. That's required, Christa."

"You shouldn't have let him come here," Kit said.

"If you do say anything, anything at all, then what you say will be denied," the dean said. "You can see why that would be necessary. I'm afraid that no one would believe you in any case."

Kit turned away, stricken, and went to the door.

"Where are you going?" the dean asked.

Kit stopped but didn't answer.

"You should know," the dean said, "that the police will be at Professor

Falin's house this morning. They are going to be making a thorough search; they have told me so. I would think they would be there already."

She had left her desk and come close to Kit, who backed away; she took Kit's arm in a red-nailed hand. Kit couldn't look away; she felt her lower lip tremble, as though she were a child caught in the sudden grip of a hostile adult, knowing nothing but fear and baseless guilt. "Now listen to me carefully, Christa. Your years here at the University could be the best years of your life. Don't, don't put them in jeopardy. Do you understand me? I want you to tell me that you understand me."

Kit held still, refusing assent.

"I will tell you something else," she said. "And I mean this in the sincerest way. You should break off with your left-wing friends. They'll do you no good. You can blight your life by whom you associate with. I know this. No matter how smart and capable you are. They'll always have that on you, a connection like that. And when they have need of you they'll use it."

Something had happened to her face, something subtle and terrible. Kit shrank away, extracting herself, in fear and pity.

"You don't understand," the dean said. "And maybe you won't for a long time. But I'll tell you this. I wish that someone had told me what I'm telling you, when I was young. I wish that very much."

Outside Kit stood for a moment on the step. She had lost the power to look back or ahead, Epimetheus and Prometheus, she had strength only to act. She started across campus walking fast until the breath stung in her throat, then slowed until her heart ceased to pound, then ran again. At the campus gate where the cars went in and out she stopped again and leaned on the rough stone pillar. College Street ran down from here to town, down to the square and the courthouse, the Woolworth's and the big hotel. From the drugstore on the corner the Greyhound buses departed. It seemed far away, as though it would recede from her if she tried to reach it.

She did reach it, and at the soda counter asked for a ticket to the capital, the next bus, when would that be? Her fingers trembled as she unfolded crumpled bills from her purse and sought for change to make up the difference. The big freckled woman looked on her with interest, wondering maybe what Kit was running from.

"There. That's right. Right?"

"Yep. Bout nour."

"What? Oh. Yes. Thanks. Okay."

In the drugstore's phone booth were two phone books, a slim battered one for the college town, a fat one for the capital. The Case Columbia Foundation was listed, and its address; she wrote it on her palm with a ballpoint.

She had watched him on that night, speaking on the Princess phone, putting it down. Would he have done that or had she only dreamed it? He'd put on his coat then and picked up his briefcase; and into it had put all the poems in Russian that he had typed on the Undervud. When they found that briefcase it was empty, they said. And once before she had seen him put his papers into that case, his poems, readying himself for a journey to the capital, and she had wondered why.

One hour. Her heart still thudded as though she had not stopped running. She sat on the last stool of the soda fountain and looked out the window; she had spent all her money on the ticket, she could buy nothing.

It was where he had gone, or where he had been going. If it had not been, maybe they would know, they would know something. She would make them tell her what they knew: what had been done to him, what had been planned for him, what had gone wrong.

A front, Max had said; a shell, just a conduit for funds. She could see it, a blank granite building like a bank, closed dark doors, a brass plaque that said nothing but its name. A front. She would have to pierce it. She would have to believe it could be pierced. And then.

And then beyond it lay another front. Beyond those doors. If she had the courage to do this, now, to go as far as she could, she would only reach a point beyond which she couldn't go, beyond which she failed.

Beyond the dean of students and beyond Milton Bluhdorn and beyond the Case Columbia Foundation there were other fronts, for powers that went on without an end. And that's where Falin had gone, where he was able to go, where he had been summoned or had chosen to go. To find them or defy them or to bargain with them. The behind-the-mirror world he had come from was not a place on this earth, and the place to which he had gone, gone back or gone on, it wasn't either. *We have kissed at that frontier* he wrote to her. She would never find him or see him again, he would traverse that distance until he was too small to see any longer or even to remember.

She knew then what world she lived in. As though one of the missiles that had not fallen the day before now fell into her depths and there went off, she understood what world she lived in, what sky she lived beneath. They didn't know it, the colored cars passing and the sham courthouse and the helpless people on the street; Milton Bluhdorn might know it, and Jackie Norden might not, but she knew it, she knew it in her heart's root and could never unknow it. If she cried out in this world her cry would make no echo.

"You okay, miss?"

"Yes. Yes. I'm okay. I."

"Need a glass of water?"

"I've changed my mind," Kit said. "I'm not going." She slid from the stool, pulling her jacket around her.

"Well hold on a second. Hey. Don't go till I give you your money back."

"Oh. Oh right. Thanks."

To defy Power, which seems omnipotent. And if it really was omnipotent, what then? What if it didn't seem to be but was? What kind of being was he, that he could dare to challenge it? He had asked her to let him go and she had, and she felt his leaving as though the vast implosion within her went on and would go on without an end.

It took her a long time to reach Tower 3 again. In the lounge the television was on; and before the single watcher changed the channel, Kit saw again the convertible, the river. Then a scene of divers in black rubber, frogmen, letting themselves down backwards into the opaque waters where he was not.

12

"So the poems were lost," she said to Gavriil Viktorovich Semyonov.

They still walked with her by the river, this Russian river, three or four of them, unwilling to go home; they walked, and she told her story again, it seemed they would never tire of hearing it. She had thought at first, when they came down into the street, that dawn had come while they sat so long in the gold-and-white restaurant; but no, it was that day had never gone: the White Nights of the city on the gulf.

"Lost," he said. "Lost."

"I had only the translations, and there was no one to ask, no one to tell. I hid them. It was silly. I thought I had to."

"You were afraid," said the dark-eyed woman, as though she knew; as though it were simple, obvious. "You could not know. You were very afraid."

"I was."

She hid herself too, for a long time afterwards, one way and another. She ran to hide, from what she had first understood in the drugstore on the square, what she had touched, what had touched her. She ran as though to escape its notice, first from school, dropping out before she graduated and making her way over the country to the coasts, and after that even out of the country for a time. Falin and his disappearance ceased to be news; they said the case remained open but nothing was done, and she didn't dare pursue what they so obviously didn't want pursued: even to think of doing that made her afraid, made her think of running again. All that while the poems she had made with him were locked away, waiting.

It was only when others who were braver than she was stood up to it—to them, to that secret power—gave a name to it, spoke truth to it; only when they came out in their thousands and then tens of thousands singing *Dona nobis pacem*, that she found she could too. And she went to find the work that Falin and she had done together, and think about it, and about the summer days.

"He said there wasn't much time," she said. "He always knew there wasn't much time, and he was right. He knew that those poems would be lost, or taken; that they would be taken away from him."

"Perhaps he did," said Gavriil Viktorovich.

"I was sure it was why he wanted the translations made, when he didn't believe in translation. I thought he needed me, that I was helping him save his poems from being lost. I thought he chose me because I would do it: I would do it as he wanted it done, would only help, and not put myself into what was his. And I didn't mind."

"But was not so?"

"No. What we had done together were not his poems, really, but mine. He knew that."

"Why then?"

"I think that he hoped he could pass on to me something he couldn't keep any longer. He wanted it for me."

"You began then to write again."

"Yes."

"It was what he wanted."

"Yes."

"Not his poems into other poems, then. Himself into . . . into another poet."

"Sort of. Somehow." She stopped; she had not said any of this before. "Can you imagine how strange it is to think that?"

Gavriil Viktorovich clasped his hands behind him, lifted his eyes to his city suspended in the pale light. She had never seen a river so wide that seemed so still. "I can imagine a reason, perhaps, why he would."

"Yes," she said.

"Simply, he loved you."

"Yes. Maybe."

"He was one of that kind, it is easy to think, who to those he loved might give all he had, at once, without thought of gain."

"Yes," she said. "Yes he was. He was one of that kind."

"Sometimes to give away is the only way to keep."

"Yes it is."

"So then it was he who was truly the translator," said Gavriil.

She nodded. The streetlights and the Neva sparkled in her vision and she pressed the cuffs of her shirt to her eyes. "Yes," she said. "All along."

They offered to have Vasili Vasilievich and the black ZIL sedan pick her up the next morning at the Pribaltiyskaya Hotel and take her to the language institute where the conference would begin, but she refused, wanting to make her own way there. And reluctantly Gavriil Viktorovich wrote out the directions for her.

Early then she walked down the wide steps of the hotel and into the morning crowds. The city's smell was distinct; Kit thought every city had its own, one you recognize when you return to it even if you can't remember it when you're away: it's what makes you know it's actual, not a notion or a dream, this smell of yeast and mist and drainpipes, warm stone and the exhalations of open windows, unique and indisputable. She carried with her in her bag a copy of *Life* magazine from 1961, the year Falin left the Soviet Union and came to America. It had occurred to her that here in this country almost no one could know what he looked like, and if she could find it she might bring them the one picture she knew of, the one of him weary and wary in Berlin, smiling, his tie askew and the tiny end of a cigarette in his fingers; and she had found it, this issue amid others in an old bookstore. His lost face.

The subway was different at this hour, herds of people jostling and pushing, the pressure of them at her back creating the sensation of falling headlong down the speeding escalator. By the time she had been packed into a car and the car had moved off with a high whisper, she was no longer sure she was right—the orthography of each stop's name had to be worked out so quickly—and she was nearly carried away from the one she thought she wanted, had to fight her way off.

She came up into a huge empty public space that seemed to have been abandoned, or to have lost its function somehow and become unclaimed, shelter for squatters, a crowd of vendors selling to the people rushing through to the streets beyond. The unventilated air was heavy. Was she in the wrong place? She tried to stop and look for signs. Every vendor with his little blanket or box or cart seemed to be selling the same goods, the same cigarettes and pens and bottles of soap or scent. Today each one was selling the same little toy, a windup girl on a tin bicycle, who went around in circles on the dirty marble floor while her dog ran leaping at her side. A dozen girls, bicycles, dogs. Somewhere someone was singing, a high, piercing cry.

How had they come to this? A family in a pile in a corner, unspeakable blankets drawn around them, mother dead asleep. A bearded man on a plastic sheet, medals on his coat, held a densely lettered sign. *Menia predali*, she thought it said: "I was betrayed." Or was it "devoted"? There was a word, a word Falin had taught her, that meant both. Devoted, betrayed. The crowds went by unseeing, just as the crowds in New York or Mexico City would: as though they passed momentarily through an alternate world that remained invisible to them, only causing their mouths to set and their eyes to fix on some distant goal.

She hadn't known such places could be in this country. She didn't know they could be so abandoned, these people, after having been penned up so long, left without anything of what had once sustained them, without even their terrible abnegation at last: abandoned even by silence.

The singer was a boy, standing on a box and clapping to his singing.

A girl squatted by him, little as a pixie, her hair an astonishing black tangle, bent over a stringed instrument that she beat on. Another boy played an upturned plastic bucket with wooden sticks. Amazing how loud they were, you couldn't pass by them without listening. And Kit saw—she tried to stop, despite the forward press of the crowd, to make sure—that the boy was the same who had taken her hand at the subway the night before, tried to press a rose on her.

Yes the same boy, still in his filthy American shirt, you could see the big blue stars on it banded red and white. The song was one of those radically simple ones that seem not to have been made up but to have always been, she hadn't ever heard it before but knew just what it would do; he moved like a rapper or a pop star to it, and maybe it was a pop song she didn't know. He sang out the last note and jumped from his box to go through the crowd with a paper cup. Far away down the great vault two policemen were coming, Kit saw them but the little band saw them first, the girl calling out to the others to go, go. The drummer gathered his bucket and sticks and followed her, calling after the singer.

"*Nu davaj zhe,*" he said. *Come on.*

But he went on cheerfully working the crowd, tugging at sleeves and lifting his cup and cajoling, people laughed and shook him off or found a coin. He turned toward Kit, caught her eye and read her look, as though he knew her too.

"*Innokenti,*" the girl cried. "*Innokenti, davaj, davaj!*"

He went then, snatching up his box and following, looking back though with a smile even as he vanished, as though to take a bow. His smile. For her alone it seemed: had always seemed.

Then it's okay, she said or thought. As she had in the protest march that October day when she saw him, when he had showed himself to her, just as he had promised he would. It's okay.

For a breath I tarry, nor yet disperse apart.

The crowds pushed on, new crowds from a new train, their heels loud in the marble heights, carrying Kit on. They went out into the day, she and the people on their journeys, dispersing into the harmed city. Buses jam-packed with people, and the earth below them jam-packed too she thought, and the sky above them.

Of course they hadn't been abandoned. They couldn't be. They couldn't be left all alone or there would be neither justice nor order anywhere, not even the hope of it. They couldn't always know that he was near, of course, of course you couldn't know, whatever else you might be sure of. You might not know even if he came close to you, passed right by you, even if he touched you. Probably you wouldn't. And yet you might for a moment think *it's okay*.

She had come to the edge of the wide street, whose name she couldn't find. She looked at her instructions, at the day. She had that unnerving experience that travelers sometimes have, of momentarily forgetting what city this is, what continent. She turned left, then changed her mind and went right. A large black car that had been creeping along the street by her now stopped. Vasili Vasilievich put his head out the window, waved to her, *nu davaj*, and reached around to open the back door for her.

The institute wasn't far, but probably Gavriil Viktorovich was right, she would have not found it, which is what fat-necked Vasili was apparently explaining to her as he took his rights and lefts. Then here it was, another unmodern modern building seeming to be falling apart before having been finished, and he let her out. Going up the stairs just ahead of her were a group from her dinner the night before, and they saw her and came to her. "*Davaj, davaj*," they said, smiling, and took both her arms like schoolgirls, talking rapidly and bringing her within the building, where others she had met turned to greet her.

She was hurried through the crowd of arriving conferees to the wide double doors of an auditorium, which they pushed open to let her through. It was packed, and as she came in people turned in their chairs to see her, people seemed to be telling one another who she was. Could it really be she they had come to see, and why? She wanted to stop, to resist, to run away and hide; she knew she bore nothing for them, nothing but a thirty-year-old magazine: nothing really that she could say, and even that little she couldn't say in their tongue, in his. But Gavriil Viktorovich at the green-draped table on the platform stood up, and lifted his hand to her; and another ancient man arose from his seat as she passed, took her hand, and said, "*Spasibo*. Thank you. Thank you for coming so far."

13

Four days later Christa Malone flew away, from a different city than she had come to: burdened with gifts, books in a language she might now again try to learn to read, honey, photographs in awful Kodachrome and fax numbers and a little wooden doll of Gorbachev, inside him Brezhnev, inside him Stalin, inside him Lenin, inside him nothing. Forgiven for what she had done or not done; nothing to forgive, of course, nothing. And as she ascended, the city was hammered gold and gold enameling, the setting sun glancing off the river and the rainwater in the squares. One swath of strange cloud, all of a piece, stretched like a pelt of crimson lamb's wool over the Gulf of Finland. Near it hung a burnished sliver of moon, like a wedding ring worn so long it was almost worn through, like her own. The Aeroflot turned away to the west, and as it went, it lifted the sun back up over the horizon, as though making its way back into the day before, beating into the past.

. . .

"We came very close, you know," Kit's father told her. "We came within minutes—some people say minutes. Of course we weren't told that then, how close it was. You want a drink?"

"No, thanks, Dad."

She had made her return ticket for Washington, D.C., so she could visit him; she did it whenever she could, traveling down by train from conferences in New York, driving up from home during school vacations. He wouldn't move from the old apartment.

"How we avoided it is a mystery to me. Let me tell you something. There was a Russian colonel, Oleg Penkovsky, who was a high-level American spy in Moscow, and at the tensest moment of this thing he got arrested. The Americans had given him telephone codes to be used only in the greatest emergency. One code would mean that he'd been arrested; the other code meant that a Russian attack on the U.S. was about to happen. Apparently Penkovsky used the wrong code. So the CIA had this warning of a Soviet attack. And what did they do? They didn't do anything. They thought it was a mistake, apparently. Anyway they ignored it; they didn't even tell the President."

On the windowsill he had arranged all the little Russian leaders she'd brought him, in order by size, little to big, past to present.

"Intelligence services are famous for ignoring the wrong information," he said. "It's a signal-to-noise ratio problem: too much coming in through the ether. Stalin ignored warnings that Hitler was going to attack, we missed Pearl Harbor. But this time—this time they made the right guess; this time the coin flipped right side up. No reason I can see."

He sat, carefully, in the big armchair where no one ever sat but him, and crossed his slippered feet. "So what did you learn?" he asked. "Did he have something to do with it? Falin?"

"I didn't learn anything. Nothing. They wanted to learn what *I* know. Which is nothing too."

"Well what do they think happened? What had they been thinking?"

"They think maybe he was killed by the CIA or the FBI."

"Why?"

"They don't know why. I guess they can accept not knowing; they think there are secret reasons for lots of things that can never be known."

He pondered, as though trying to decide if this was true, or made sense, though Kit didn't suppose that was really what he was thinking. Then he said: "And you? Do you think that's what happened?"

"I used to. I used to think it must have been something like that."

"Now?"

"Now," she said: and she thought. She thought of Falin, and the child with his name singing in the naked hall in St. Petersburg. She thought of Gavriil Viktorovich holding Falin's poem, in tears in his little apartment. She thought of Ben, choosing to fight for the right, believing that one power was right, the other wrong. "I think that back then, when he came to this country, there was a struggle going on between the angels of the nations, his and ours; and that in their anger and their fear, those angels came to destroy the world, anyway the parts of it that they were supposed to be watching over—and everything in between too . . ."

"The angels of the nations," George said blankly.

"They should have been keeping us from harm, and maybe that was what they thought they were doing, each in its own way. But the power they had together, the power put in our own hands, was too much, and in the end they . . . they let it go. Mutual assured destruction."

"But," George said.

"But no, of course it didn't happen," Kit said, and she rose up and went to the window, as though to release her thought or her soul that way. "It didn't, it should have but it didn't. Because the lesser angel of one nation interceded. On our behalf. He made an offer; he offered himself."

"The lesser angel," George said. "The *lesser* angel."

She turned to her father, and his face wasn't sarcastic or mocking but only intent and listening; and she thought, How do I dare to tell this, how do I dare imagine it to be so, imagine believing it?

"The lesser angel," she said. "Every nation has one: an angel who is all that the greater angel isn't. Who can weep if the nation's angel can't, or laugh if it never does; who is small and weak and powerless, like us. Except this once. Because the lesser angel could say: Take this as a sop to your anger. And it worked: for just a minute they were distracted, the two big ones, and thought about this, took time to consider it—and they accepted. They took what the lesser angel offered. And in that time the big moment went by. The agreement was reached. The ships stopped. The bombers went home."

"And what was it that was offered?" George asked. "Something mighty nice."

"It didn't have to be much. It wasn't much. It was only the thing most precious to him. What would destroy him to lose. His soul."

"They have souls?"

"His self. His life." A sheaf of papers, yellow American copy paper, the rough uneven lines of Russian words typed on the Undervud. "They couldn't refuse that "

"They couldn't."

"They couldn't. They can't. It's how they are."

He was regarding her with that smile of complicity or amazement with which he had looked on her for decades, for all her life, though it had been a long time since she'd seen it. Love and wonder was what it meant, she knew now: love for her, wonder at her.

But it was true. The disaster we were all implicated in—all of us who should have known better and spoken out, all of us who were foolish and blind and didn't do what we should have done, and who knew it too, and still did nothing, only waited in what we convinced ourselves was helplessness for it to happen, almost as though it had already happened—well it didn't happen. The final logic of this century, this century that believed in logic and history and necessity, the final spasm so long and well prepared: it didn't happen, and now seemed likely never to happen. You couldn't tell, of course, and there were plenty of other things that could and did happen—she thought of Ben—but not *that* one, the worst one. And there ought to be someone to thank, someone to whom to be grateful.

"Well I don't know," her father said. "It doesn't seem like enough. *Their* big angel lost, you know: it was a major defeat." He indicated the row of wooden leaders with his thumb. "Khrushchev did the right thing, but we basically de-pantsed him, cost him his job, which in retrospect was maybe not as smart as we thought. So I mean—wouldn't there have to be something additional paid in return? Something— what's the word here, something more *exacted*? In return for their backing down?"

"Exacted?" she asked. "What, exacted? What kind of thing?" It mattered not at all to George if what they talked of here was real or true; he knew how to make a train of thought come out right whether its terms were ones and zeroes or gods and angels. A kind of poet without poetry: maybe, finally, she had got her talent from him.

"Well," he said. He swirled the ice in his drink, all water now. "For instance. You know what happened a year later. They always connect that with Cuba too. Somehow."

"What happened a year later?" Kit said, and remembered even as she asked. "Oh God," she whispered. "1963."

"Yeah," said George. "Right."

She felt stabbed, as though the story or myth she had articulated had caused it to happen, had right now got him shot through the head in Dallas: the sacrificial goat, the *tragos* of our tragedy. "Oh my God."

"Fair Play for Cuba," George said. "Free Cuba Committee. Castro, anti-Castro. Something somewhere somehow."

It's not so, she thought, and she took hold of a chair's back, feeling she might keel over with strangeness: it's not so, it's only *as though*. It wasn't truth but the economy of metaphor, everything in balance, this side of the mirror with Alice's side, only reversed: Jacqueline cradling his poor head in her bloodstained lap, just a man dying. And yet also, far beyond where we could see, the Gray Gods licking up the same blood from the same bowl. Satisfied: appeased.

"You remember where you were when you heard?" George asked,

not so much because he wanted to know, it seemed, as to change the subject, or its tendency. "You know they say everybody does. Like Pearl Harbor."

"Yes," Kit said. "Sure. I remember." On the straight road north from the University toward that city in whose suburbs she had once lived with George and Marion and Ben. Yes. That day.

There was a little rain and the blacktop was velvety in the soft light. Kit was driving, Fran beside her searching on the radio for something besides Top 40 or preachers. It was so far only a brief sentence, interrupting the broadcast: the motorcade fired on in Dallas, the President hit.

"It's probably really nothing," Kit said. "You know how they get, about every little thing."

"He's dead," Fran said with simple certainty. "He's dead."

They listened, waiting for more, going north. Kit had driven back to school that fall in George and Marion's old Buick station wagon, they had at last got something newer. She had kept it, though she wasn't twenty-one and had to park it at a garage off campus. Fran had a friend—her best friend, she said—who was singing in the chorus of a road-show company of *Camelot* that was appearing in that city. Fran longed to see her, it seemed so close; and Kit had said okay, let's cut and go.

More news, worse. The rain got a little steadier, then seemed to pass.

They went past the junction where a secondary road turned off toward the town where Falin's car had gone off the bridge; after a time they crossed on a wide causeway the same river, grown great. A river to cross.

> *The river of Jordan is muddy and cold*
> *It chills the body*
> *But not the soul*

Kit thought of those lines, and at last began to weep. "Oh my God," she said. "Oh poor man."

All my trials
Soon be over

It was a Joan Baez song, one of the terrible bleak songs she cried out so piercingly, at once wounding and healing. Fran had brought the records back from New York and they listened to them over and over, sometimes when drunk hugging the Webcor like a friend and pressing an ear right to the speaker grille. She longed to hear it now.

Hush little baby don't you cry
You know your mama
Was born to die

He was pronounced dead as evening came quickly on, the darkest time of the year. They passed the city limits, the streets numbered neatly in the hundreds but really just straight roads through the brown cornfields where the crows were arising: you could watch them make for the naked willow grove.

How could this be given to them, how could it, had they deserved it by not knowing that it could be? The farmhouses and garages and flat-roofed split-levels were turning on their lights sadder than darkness.

They came into the city. Kit had laughed, telling Fran she would show her the sights, the high school from which she'd graduated, the church where she was confirmed, the house where she was deflowered. But she found she remembered nothing, it was all black streets and the lights of cars and stores, like everywhere.

They found a phone booth and Fran called the theater where the play was, *Camelot* for God's sake, and after a couple of dimes reached the hotel and her friend. Kit watched from the car as Fran talked, her head lowered and unsmiling, and she almost wept again.

"She can't come out," Fran told her, returning. "Nobody can leave the hotel tonight. Not chorus people anyway. It's a rule."

They sat in the Buick watching the streetlight change.

"I've got to make a call too," Kit said.

She found the number in the phone book after studying all the Eggerts and trying to remember the car dealer's name. Carl. What would he sell now that there weren't going to be any Studebakers? A woman answered after a couple of rings.

"Hi," Kit said. "Is Burke there?"

There was a little pause; it seemed filled with tears too. "Burke doesn't live here anymore," the voice said, hurt or maybe cautious.

"Oh. Well. I'm, I knew him in high school, and well I was passing through."

"No. He's got a place of his own now. Over there on Sunset. With Mary Jo and the baby."

"Oh."

"They don't have a phone yet."

"Oh."

"So."

"Okay. Okay, thanks."

"Well you're very welcome," the voice said, brightening strangely at the last.

"Okay," Fran said when Kit came back. "Okay, I need a drink."

Nowhere in that state in that year could Kit or Fran drink, but they stopped at a liquor store whose bright sign was reflected upside down in the wet pavement, and Fran turned up the collar of her raincoat and lit a Camel. She went in and in a moment came back, cigarette in the corner of her big mouth and her hands in her pockets.

"No luck," Kit guessed.

Fran pulled out a flat clear bottle: a pint of vodka. "First thing I saw," she said. "It helps if you grab something quick." She uncapped it, drank, shuddered in disgust, gave it to Kit.

"I'm sorry about your friend," Kit said.

"Well. I think I like her a lot more than she likes me. You know."

"I know."

"Who was that you called?"

"A guy. The first guy I, you know, made love with."

"Oh yes?"

Kit thought: *Whereof we cannot speak, thereof we must be silent.*

There was nothing to do then but go back along the way they came, and they did that, driving south between fields black and limitless on either side, now and then passing the bottle. All along the road the bars and restaurants were closed, or had filled their changeable signs with new messages:

NO MUSIC TONITE   GOD BLESS HIM

"What should we do?" Kit asked desperately. "There should be something we should do now. We can't just go on, just living, can we?"

Fran shook her head, she didn't know.

"Should we join the Peace Corps?" Kit cried. "Is that it? Is that what we're supposed to think of?" She had taken his hand once, she had, and he had said something to her—yes, he had said Falin's name to her. He had said that poets were the unacknowledged legislators of the world. She had spoken of it in a poem, a poem she had burned with the rest.

Now he was gone too, turned away, lost to her and to everyone. She had lost everything she loved, everything that made her herself, and now she was to lose all that she shared with everyone else as well.

A being such as that couldn't die all in a day and be gone, it would take far longer, wouldn't it? There would be things he would have to do, to tell us. We, the rest of us, can't turn back after we have turned to go, but surely he could, for a time. Oh turn back, she thought, turn back, make this not to have happened all in a day forever.

But if he could turn back, if he were able, then she wouldn't feel this grief, it would be grave and sad but it wouldn't be this riving grief, and it was. It was no different from any grief: for Ben, for the dead child she had seen for only a moment. They couldn't and he couldn't either. And she could speak of none of it, did not dare to call them back because they would not turn, nor would she be able to bear their faces if they did.

Whereof we cannot speak, thereof we must be silent.

She thought: *O my dead. If you return, O my dead.* The road, blurry with rain and tears and drink, turned softly to recross the river.

She would have to learn. It's what she was made to do and was all she was asked to do. She would have to learn as he had done, learn to speak: to learn again, as though for the first time, a tongue: though if she began, she knew she would never be done, not ever.

"Yes," she said to her father. "Yes I remember."

Before she left Washington to go home where her husband and her youngest daughter awaited her, Kit went down to the Mall on the wonderful new pharaonic subway of the city, and walked to the Vietnam War Memorial.

After her mother died and she began coming often to be with George, she used to walk the white city in the afternoons, sometimes for miles, while George drowsed in his armchair. And once she came upon this memorial, finished not long before: came upon it without knowing she would, a secret place, an underworld, passage to the land of the dead. She'd heard a lot about it, and yet she was still surprised by how moving it was, not only in itself but because it suggested that we had come at last to know how to remember war. She saw that people touched the glassy stone where the names seemed to float as in a pool, and touched at the same time the fingers of their own hands, saw their own faces reflected within.

Ben's name wasn't there. George had already told her it wasn't. *He wasn't really Vietnam-era,* he'd said. *Not really.*

Sleepy-warm in the late sun then, as it was now. She had sat there a long time, and she had come back often again. She was then writing— not on paper yet—the poem that would become the title poem of *Ghost Comedies,* and her sitting here and thinking of it would become part of the poem, though she didn't know that then. Then it was mostly about Marion; mostly it was to make Ben smile.

If you return, O my dead, and you will, from your ashes and earth,
Return if you can as the ghosts in ghost comedies do:
Unwounded, unrotted, not limbless or eyeless (though fleshless,
Invisible till you take form, just a drape or a candle-flame fluttering,
A wineglass that rises and empties itself in the air);
Come walking through walls in your nice clothes and your uniforms,
  smiling,
Not to warn or dismay, not with news or reproaches or tears,
But only to visit; play tricks if you want to, make love to me, dance . . .

Christa Malone didn't believe that she had ever been eternity's hostage, captive in time; she had not been among the unacknowledged legislators of the world. She had proffered no laws; she had not in her poems told truth to power, or spoken to the greater angels of the nations, and she would not. She thought that if the time when a poet could carry a nation's soul with him was passing in Russia, it had passed long ago in America.

No, she had only mourned her dead, to lighten her own heart; she had succeeded in that sometimes and sometimes not. But she knew this: when we grieve in our lives, we grieve for just the one person, friend, brother, son; but when we grieve for our own in poems, we grieve for all, for every one. It was all she had done, if she had done anything.

She had wept once for Falin, but she couldn't grieve for him. Because of him she had been given, or given back, everything: her own being, all that she had lost and done and suffered. Through him she had recovered a way to speak; a home in her own heart; maybe even a world to live in, undestroyed. She would never learn what bargain he had made, or what the powers or principalities were that he had made it with; but she knew that Innokenti Isayevich had tricked them in the end. Like the boy in the story, he kept what he had given away.

A slanting light was on the mirror-stone of names. She had been gone a long time, she thought, and there was a lot to do; a book of poems to see through the press, and maybe now another poem to make, one beginning to form itself, too far off as yet to be heard: an elegy too, she thought. And a real poem, perhaps, if she was faithful. She whispered to herself *okay, let's go,* in that motherly or fatherly way we forever speak to ourselves, so that we will do what we should or must. And yet for a while longer she didn't stand and start for home.